I0823331

WRETCH

JEREMY WAGNER

Hardcover ISBN: 9781639511327

eBook ISBN: 9781639511334

Published by Dead Sky Publishing, LLC

Miami Beach, Florida

www.deadskypublishing.com

Cover by Roberto Ferri "Ecate" © 2018

Design & Formatting by Apparatus Revolution, LLC

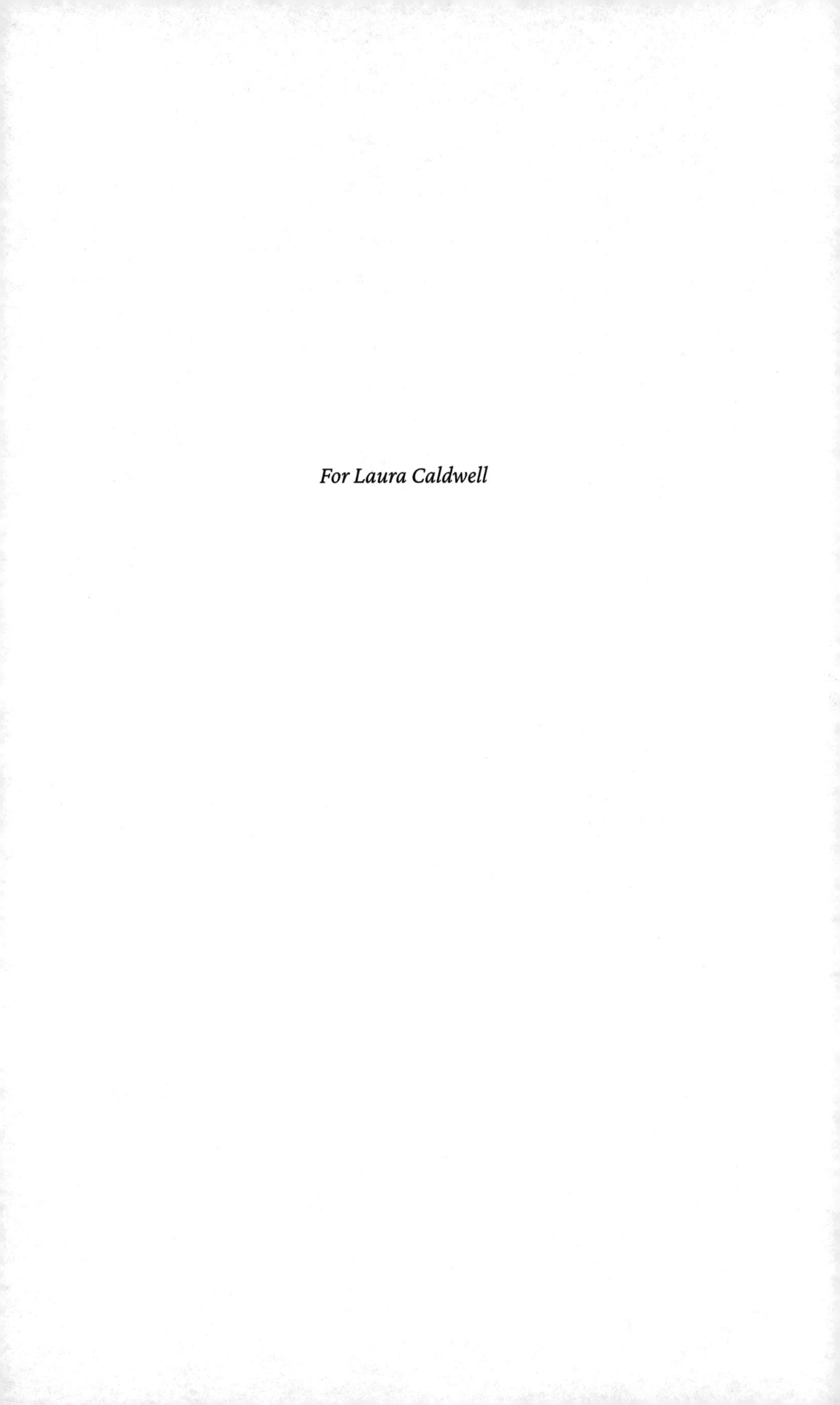

For Laura Caldwell

Lust (aka): amativeness, appetite, ardent, burning, coarse, concupiscence, craving, crude, desire, disorderly, eroticism, fervent, insatiable, itch, lascivious, lecherous, lewd, libertine, libidinousness, longing, lubricious, nymphomania, paphian, passion, prurient, randy, salacious, satyriasis, sexual hunger, thirst, uninhibited, vulgar, yearning, yen.

"Lust is to the other passions what the nervous fluid is to life; it supports them all, lends strength to them all: ambition, cruelty, avarice, revenge, are all founded on lust...

Lust's passion will be served; it demands, it militates, it tyrannizes."

— **Marquis de Sade**

"Sex, drugs, and insanity have always worked for me, but I wouldn't recommend them for everyone."

— **Hunter S. Thompson**

Also by Jeremy Wagner

Fiction

The Armageddon Chord

Rabid Heart

Wretch

Nonfiction

Fireproof: Memoir of a Chef (with Curtis Duffy)

CONTENTS

CHAPTER 1

Fucking Mondays.

Detective Donnie Lynch sat behind the wheel of an unmarked black Dodge Charger Pursuit inching slowly through Chicago traffic. He could put his hidden flashers on, but what for? To get to a crime scene quicker? The dead man would stay put. Still, if he could teleport, he would've been there an hour ago.

He sighed.

Fucking Mondays.

Why was the shittiness of the first day of the week so ineradicable? To Lynch, this was legit fact, not a Monday cliché. The dark patch where burning coffee he'd spilled half an hour ago had fused his khakis to his thigh only provided more evidence to back up that fact. He had a theory: There was something inherently lousy in that unlikable zone where the weekend ended and the work week began for the nine-to-five work force. The ever-worsening congestion—not to mention the roiling impatience of commuters and their bullshit—vexed Lynch every goddamn day, but even more so on the first day of the work week. They honked and flipped each other off in traffic going a steady four miles an hour. Maybe they should just duke it out and walk to work. It would be faster.

And the express lanes?

Another fucking joke—just as slow as the regular freeway.

Lynch believed, like a true Chicagoan, that there were five seasons: the usual four and then Road Construction Season. RCS was in full swing right now with six highway lanes cut down to two for miles stretching from the north and west burbs through the city, rolling on towards Gary, Indiana. It was like this every summer, and Lynch knew it didn't matter where you drove, it was the same everywhere: The I-90/94 Kennedy Expressway...the I-94 Edens split to I-290...every way in and out of the city was logjammed.

"Dickhead!"

The SUV had cut Lynch off with no signal, forcing him to hit the brakes hard with an inch to spare. He laid on his horn then threw his hands in the air. A bumper-sticker on the SUV declared that the driver's kid attended school up in Gurnee. Lynch couldn't fault anyone for working for a living, but commuters from the burbs only added to the gridlock...and his Monday aggravation.

Lynch wondered if any of these agitated, aggressive drivers had ever heard of Metra, the network of commuter trains transporting people into the city. Shit, he'd use the CTA buses or take the El everywhere around the city if he could, but his work and the range he covered made those options impossible.

Serenity now. Breathe.

Lynch tried to adjust his mood. The early morning traffic, the obnoxious heat, thoughts of the murder scene that awaited him all pushed his temperament. The dead guy, he was certain, wasn't a victim of a gang hit. With all the gang busting he'd done over the years in the Chicago Police Department, Lynch knew those perps did most of their shootings at night and slept away the days. That's why the CPD conducted drug and weapon raids in the early morning hours. Most every time, hooligans of every color and brand name were done bangin' and partying by the time the sun rose.

In bed, unawares.

It was a white male in his fifties who'd been knocked off. The guy had pulled over in a seedy neighborhood for some reason. Lynch assumed the man was probably doing something illicit on his way to work—and ended up getting popped. Lynch got the call nearly an hour ago now. That he still wasn't at the scene yet was maddening.

He thought of a line from an Ice T song from back in the day.

"Homicide's my favorite binge..."

He also thought of Sinatra and Chicago being *his* kind of town. Lately, Lynch wasn't so sure he felt the same way Ol' Blue Eyes once did about Chi-Town—or it being his kind of *raz-ma-taz.*

As he finally exited the highway, Lynch noted a crude wooden cross with *Leticia* painted on the crossbeam, tilted amongst vial-and-baggie-covered dirt near a street corner. He'd seen many memorials like this throughout the city. This particular makeshift memorial was for a fourteen-year-old girl caught in the crossfire of some turf beef that Lynch remembered happened just as summer began.

Leticia Guiterrez.

He recalled the name as he drove on. The shooting, like most others, was all over the news locally and nationwide. This only added napalm to Chicago's bad rep as a "killing field," a phrase that some politicians were fond of saying and exploiting along with the press. The haters wanted to scold Chicago for being naughtier than other cities. Lynch figured it was because they weren't fond of the mayor, and a great way to kick the city in the crotch was to say the mayor and CPD were not in control.

One thing he *did* know was that Chicago was his home—he fucking loved it. In his mind, there wasn't a more beautiful town, and despite the infuriating heat this season, summer in Chicago was Lynch's favorite time of the year to be in the city. And the violence? Sure, that black mark was stamped on the Windy City before Capone ever made headlines—but Lynch knew there was more violence per capita in other cities across the country...but no one seemed to address that.

Still, Lynch couldn't deny the shootings, the smash-and-grabs, and the Chicago gangs were more numerous than ever. Ethnic gangs and organized crime was always a constant thorn in the side of the CPD. He shook his head at the thought. More often than not, the innocent were denied justice, many died, and thugs got away. The robbers robbed and the shooters just pointed and pulled the trigger without a care in the world.

Lynch deliberately turned his mind to something only slightly less depressing: The Cubs.

Same shit as last season...

Lynch believed—as did many of his fellow Cubs fans—that the team was still cursed. Sure, they'd won the World Series in 2016 after 108 years, but Lynch figured they were back on track to keep losing for another century. Still, he loved them for some crazy reason, even though he was the only one in his family who wasn't a White Sox fan. Some of his relatives considered that a betrayal. The Lynch clan had planted roots on the South Side in the nineteenth century along with so many other Irish-Americans, so the South Side, and anything connected to it, was held with a kind of reverence.

The Cubs made him think of Sandy...when he'd first met her outside of Wrigley Field a million years ago.

Lynch frowned.

Thoughts of his ex-wife often sneaked into his mind during quiet, solitary moments like this. He gave up everything in the divorce six months ago. Gave it all up with a huge smile, too. Why not? He didn't care about *things*. Sandy owned all that shit after the divorce, including his heart.

Lynch had failed Sandy. Through his many fuck-ups, she had held on fiercely. He'd had more than one opportunity to rescue their marriage. Truth was, he'd simply let it die. Why would any man do that? It wasn't even due to gambling, drinks, drugs, pussy or any other of the typical traps of the cop life.

Lynch was fully aware of how things began to go wrong. It was when that incessant fatigue and weakness first slithered into his life. Even then he'd known the lethargy wasn't work-related. His body had started to feel used up, robbed of energy. Then his libido dropped dramatically and that had worried him. Lynch had always been a horn-dog for Sandy—his lust and love for her was unshakeable—yet something he couldn't explain had deprived him of his healthy passion and sexual desire. The newly sluggish disposition had disturbed him.

Sandy, she sure wanted to know what was happening to him. She had cared. She had loved him so much, didn't she?

"Donnie? Where'd my lover-boy hubby go? Wanna talk to me? Is there a problem with us?"

Lynch heard her voice in his head, and a weight sat on his chest.

Problem? He had told her it was nothing of the sort. The problem—aside from the fatigue and weakness and decline of the hots—was a new, dull and constant ache he felt in his groin. One of Lynch's testicles had shrunk while the other one had enlarged. Sandy gently stroked his balls and discovered a lump. Shortly thereafter, a doctor explained that the mismatch was caused by a tumor in his left testicle, which redirected his blood supply.

The doctor referred Lynch to a urologist who performed an ultrasound and biopsy. The diagnosis: *TC*—testicular cancer. Within days, he was scheduled for surgery.

"Y'know, one of my favorite Bears players back in the late sixties was Brian Piccolo; he was the running back for four years." Lynch's father spoke gravely when he heard the news. "Poor bastard died young because of that shit. A 'germ cell testicular cancer'—I remember that. Yup. They made a movie about him. Poor bastard. Good thing ya caught this shit now and not later, Donnie."

True that. He'd almost certainly survive.

I'd give my left nut to live...

And he sure had.

The doctor's plan: the removal of his left testicle. An *orchiectomy*. Lynch cringed at the thought. Better than a bi-lateral orchiectomy, right? That would have taken away *both* testicles—Lynch cringed again as he imagined *that* scenario.

He had thought that he'd be less of a man. Some kind of eunuch. The doctor assured Lynch the orchiectomy wouldn't affect him in any way other than minor postoperative recovery. For testosterone replacement, he'd need to apply Androgel once a day.

The doctor had also explained that after an orchiectomy, he could still have a normal sex life. Most men were able to father children with one remaining testicle. As a precaution, however, the doctor recommended Lynch and Sandy consider banking his sperm. As it turned out, they didn't discuss anything after the diagnosis. Though he and Sandy had often talked about starting a family before they grew too old, Lynch suddenly didn't want kids. Just two years ago they were excitedly planning when they would try to get pregnant. Then the surgery tainted his every thought. Lynch wasn't sure he ever wanted to have sex again.

He remembered how his doctor was almost cheerful when mentioning that they never cut into the scrotal sac during the orchiectomy. Once they'd made the incision, the surgeon simply pushed the testicle up through the pelvic region. A quick snip here, an easy stitch there, and they'd wrap up before he could say, *Go Cubs!*

Such details provided no comfort.

After the operation, Lynch felt pain from the incision. He wore sweatpants for two weeks. He'd lie in bed for days with no energy. Sandy begged him to get up and get his circulation going, but he felt too languid and irritable to move. He began feeling sorry for himself. Sandy told him that if he just got off his ass, maybe tried working out or doing anything to simply adopt a positive attitude, it would make a huge difference in his recovery time.

Get happy!

He didn't listen. Lynch had thought that being a man with only one ball was the end of the world. He also knew it was so much bullshit, yet he still allowed himself to use it as an excuse to wallow in misery. He felt like punching something as he thought of it because his confidence and healthy attitude were strong as ever.

Goddamn, I acted like a baby...I'm a better man now...

Lynch had fallen into a deep, ruminative depression during this time. Insomnia made it worse. He'd sat up for hours watching Sandy sleep, jealous of her peace of mind.

Now he tormented himself as he replayed the bad times in his mind while he drove.

Poor fucking me. What an asshole I was. Sandy, I'm sorry...

After chemo, Lynch returned to work full time. He went from feeling irritable to acting downright difficult. To avoid the constant battles with Sandy, he just worked non-stop, drinking along the way, purposely avoiding home—and the increasing problems that he created. He blamed his marriage troubles on his post-op trauma. It was a convenient and weak excuse.

At Sandy's insistence, Lynch saw a therapist. He was prescribed anti-depressants but couldn't deal with the seesaw of über-highs and terrible, frightening lows. The doctor switched his medications. He was also popping pills with alcohol, which made things worse. He wanted off his prescriptions altogether. His problems weren't going away; his depression wasn't improving. Against everything Lynch knew about the need to wean slowly off medications, he decided to go cold turkey. All at once.

Reckless?

Lynch guessed that was one way to look at it.

I was out of my fucking mind.

After two days without medication, Lynch wanted to jump in front of a train. He couldn't function at all. So, he returned to the Effexor he'd first been prescribed and then switched to Celexa. From there, he gradually weaned himself from all anti-depressants without issue. By this point, however, his marriage had suffered irrevocable damage. He and Sandy hadn't shared a bed for weeks. He knew full well their troubles were a direct result of his shitty, contentious attitude. Yet even as he tried to do better, he also surrendered to some self-destructive flaw that compelled him to lash out at Sandy.

Embarrassment at being a complete jagoff to her exacerbated his insecurity around her...and he withdrew even further.

I could've done better.

Lynch *was* better than that. He knew it and over the following year, he proved it. He had stopped smoking and drinking. Went to therapy once a week. His oncologist pronounced him healthy and cancer-free. But it was too late. Sandy had already kicked him out and filed for divorce.

Now—free of prescriptions, a testicle, and a wife—Lynch had only recently began *feeling*. He no longer sought personal therapy. Lynch accepted his place without depression, regarding himself as a survivor, not a victim.

But he was still in love with Sandy. That wouldn't change anytime soon—if ever.

He was forty years young, six feet tall. Kept himself clean-shaven. Slim build but he didn't care for his slackening midriff. Or, for that matter, the faint crow's feet around his green eyes. He thought his hair still had style, though, even if it was a little thin on top and some gray was coming in at the temples. The daily on-the-job horrors whitened some cops' hair or made them lose it all.

As much as he missed the home he'd shared with Sandy, he did like his current digs. The tiny brownstone garden apartment was comfortable enough on those rare occasions he found himself there: With the rising number of daily homicides across the city, Lynch became busier and busier as the summer drew on. The August heat scorching the city seemed to barf up the worst possible losers and monsters society had devoured.

"Horrors." Lynch whispered to himself as his car crept along almost imperceptibly. "This city is full of 'em..."

He tried to focus on something more positive. Unfortunately, on top of his own Monday morning blues, Lynch was concerned about a close friend fighting his own battle with motherfucking cancer—and losing. Someone who wasn't as lucky as he'd been.

Goddamnit, Earl...

A lonesome cloud had hovered over Lynch's workdays since he'd been forced to fly solo on the job without his partner, Earl Tipton. Every morning for ten years, he'd picked Earl up in their unmarked Dodge Charger Pursuit, priming their day with strong coffee and filling their hours in the car with discussions of current cases, cop gossip, and praise or complaints for the Cubs or Bears—depending on the time of year and the prowess of the team.

Eight weeks ago, those days came to a screeching halt when Earl learned he had Stage 4 lung cancer. He'd started chemotherapy and experimental anti-cancer drugs. Doctors had considered taking one of his lungs out, but it was too late.

So far, no new partner. Lynch didn't want one. He couldn't bear the thought of his friend at St. Cornelius Hospital, surrounded by hospice caregivers. Earl had always been so strong, so full of spirit and personality. Yet he seemed to go down the tubes fast once the doctors told him that his cancer was terminal. Complications from treatments aimed at prolonging his life weren't helping.

Jesus, the guilt was overwhelming. Why did *he* survive cancer, but not Earl? His friend had a wife and three kids. And it was Earl who'd been there for Lynch—a true *rock*; supportive and tough, getting Lynch through all his cancer scares, depression, and marital collapse. Now Earl was the frightened one, sick with metastasis and riddled with tumors, speedily checking out, no matter how much prayer and support Lynch gave him.

Cancer's a bitch. And life's the biggest bitch of them all.

Two decades older than Lynch, Earl had been a sort of father figure. He'd mentored him, taught him investigative techniques, shared his knowledge of violent crimes, homicides, psychopaths, lust killers, and narcotics. He showed Lynch what it meant to not just clock in as a cop but to be a true detective.

Earl was only sixty—"the new twenty-five" as he had often joked to Lynch. Years ago, the CPD had put a deal in place that allowed cops to retire with some premium health benefits at age fifty-five, rather than sixty. The city was saving money with the deal, and it would pave the way for a new wave of younger officers. But Earl couldn't be lured into early retirement. He loved his job.

Then cancer arrived as an unwanted guest who wouldn't leave, coming in with its own agenda to throw all of Earl's pretty plans in the existential dumpster.

The weekend had broiled the Second City with forty-eight hours of insane heat and today was no different. Lynch tried to ignore it. That was easier said than done as the morning sun climbed and radiated down hard on the city. The Chicagoland forecast had told him it would reach 100 degrees today. He drove down the side streets with the AC cranked. The perpetually frigid waters of Lake Michigan, several blocks east, offered no relief to the air temperature, either.

Cooler by the lake, they say. My ass.

He arrived at the scene, and suffocating heat mauled him the second he got out of the car. How was it possible to be this hot so early? The fresh coffee stains on his khakis continued to acerbate his discomfort and his crummy temperament. He rolled the sleeves of his gray dress shirt up to his elbows and removed his tie. He put on a bulletproof vest—a CPD requirement—the weight of it adding another level of aggravation.

It's a cruel summer.

Hadn't he heard some old eighties' song by that name?

This summer had turned into such a malicious hellion—both the soaring temps and hoodlums confirmed this for Lynch. An average of a hundred people in Chicago were shot since this season started, half of them killed every month since June. The added bonus of the high number of heat-related deaths turned dog days into rabid, tameless days. Lynch figured that before summer finally gave way to fall, the city's countless gangbangers would shoot and kill another three-hundred people, and the heat would probably kill another couple dozen old-timers.

It's more like a sadistic summer.

Lynch approached a late-model Cadillac cordoned off with police tape. Cops and EMTs buzzed around it. A gaggle of locals, including some who were clearly sex workers, stood and gawked nearby. A couple of CPD officers spoke to the onlookers and took notes on their police pads. Lynch flashed his badge to the one guarding the perimeter, gave his name, and bent under the tape to poke his head in the driver's-side window. A balding man with graying hair sat inside, chin on his chest, eyes closed. You'd be forgiven for assuming he was taking a nap if it wasn't for the nickel-sized hole in his left temple.

Blood spatter peppered the man's face and business suit. His pants and boxers were wrapped around his ankles. The head of his flaccid penis peeked out from a gray bush beneath a fold of belly fat—a hairless mole-rat without the teeth.

Lynch turned from the dead man to the tall Hispanic cop standing next to him.

"What's the low-down?"

"This john, he pulled over to get a blowjob on his commute. Got shot in the *cabeza*." The officer shrugged his shoulders. "We're trying to find the whore who was sucking him off. Went running. Somewhere."

"What's the story there?" Lynch jutted his chin towards a young white CPD officer across the way who was looking agitated as he interviewed a tall, Black individual with big, pie-plate eyes and blonde hair that Lynch thought was a little too good to be real. The pink negligee with matching slippers was a nice touch, though. Lynch wished he was wearing something as thin and light in this damned heat.

The cop shrugged. "My boy, Ritchie. He's gettin' somethin' outta that *joto* there. He ran the ID. That tranny may've been a witness—but isn't giving anything up. Got a real 'tude."

Joto. Tranny.

These were words Lynch had heard for years...identifiers that people used to drop with ease, cops and civilians alike. In recent years, however, these terms weren't considered benign slang, they were understood to be downright derogatory, including as far as the CPD was concerned. A new age of respect and sensitivity in today's police organizations had arrived.

Lynch was on board. He got it, adhered to it, and not just because it was compliance. He sincerely believed respect for anyone's flavor was due—as long as it didn't hurt anyone.

You do you and I'll do me.

But Jesus H. Christ, Lynch figured it was going to take a miracle to get most of the CPD to adapt and learn new people-skills after nearly two centuries of being crass as fuck.

Lynch approached Ritchie, the young CPD officer and the interviewee on the sidewalk. "Morning. Who we got here?"

"Hey, detective." The officer nodded. "What we got here is

someone who's making my job hard. Right? This is Timmy 'Astroglide' Rodgers. He was—"

"That's *she*, goddammit. Identify me as I say." Timmy's register crept up as she glared at Lynch and the officer.

The officer looked into Lynch's eyes and sneered. "*She, he* ... my preferred pronoun is *street-trash*. Right, detective?"

So much for training.

Lynch raised his eyebrows. He pulled the officer to the side, out of earshot. "Let's not go there, okay? There's already enough homophobia and racism on the job spewed out from perps. We're classier than that. Colleagues...all of us...we can do better."

The officer looked at Lynch as if he'd just beamed down from Mars. "No offense, but you sound like you're runnin' for mayor with that shit. You should hear what these scumbags call us."

"Think I don't know? Look, a great skill of being a cop is to let the hate slide off you and just roll with the times. The CPD motto, 'We Serve and Protect?' That's a *thing*. You gotta deal with all types, the good, the bad, the undefined. Keep an open mind and respect others—you might get back a lot more cooperation than you expect."

The officer again looked at Lynch like he was an alien. "We're on the fucking street here with hookers and a murder. And this fucker hasn't been polite since I asked *her* to talk to me. Respect or not, the street dictates how I deal with those I meet."

"I feel ya. I've been out here my entire career. The street doesn't always care about feelings or delicate minds. But *try*." Lynch looked over his shoulder at Astroglide and then back to the officer. "I might sound like some old man, but I know the street like you'll never fucking know. And as for running for mayor, you couldn't pay me enough to oversee this city. Now, let's get back to it."

The officer sighed and handed Lynch Astroglide's ID. "I ran that. Waiting on a confirmation. Timmy ... *Astroglide* here claims to have been innocently walking down the street when Mister Suburb pulled up to get sucked off and shot."

"Detective, you can check me out and you'll find I'm clean as a whistle," Astroglide frowned and appraised Lynch. "Them impromptu social calls by my parole officer keeps me comin' out clean."

"So, you have a record, then?" Lynch looked over the ID and then stared hard at Astroglide. "What you get pinched for?"

Astroglide placed a cigarette between her painted lips. "Shit...you got nothin' better to do than harass me, narc-ass? I'm just out here taking a summer walk 'n' you cops gotta torment me. Now, if you don't mind, I need to get back to my crib as I'm missing my beauty sleep. Pig."

Lynch thought about the quid pro quo, all of his pushing respect and professionalism. He suddenly felt old and irritable. He looked Astroglide up and down.

"Beauty sleep? Better lay yourself down for half a century."

Astroglide scowled.

"Lose the fucking cig and talk."

Astroglide crushed the smoke under a high heel then tightened the negligee on her tall, skinny body. "What you want?"

"I want you to quit fuckin' around and answer questions. I'll keep you here all day and we can bake together until you give me something."

Astroglide rolled her eyes. "I still have a rod and a pair of big balls down there, y'know. So quit bustin' 'em and get to it! Asshole."

"Watch it." Lynch raised a finger. "When did you get here? What'd you see? A guy's dead here. Shot in the head."

"Dee-tec-tive." Astroglide threw her arms up. "I's told this cop a million times, and I'm telling you the same: I didn't see nothin'. Shit. I was out for a walk, heard a gunshot and some screams. Next thing I know, the po-po is all over the place."

Lynch shifted around, trying to loosen up his bulletproof vest as he considered Astroglide's answers. Her song-and-dance and bad attitude all grated on him.

So much for letting shit roll off my shoulders...

He studied her body language and tone. There was a lie in it all. He knew it—could see, hear it, almost *taste* it. Lynch's sixth sense wasn't magic, but he had a bullshit detector born of experience. He suspected

Astroglide had seen what went down here, maybe even knew whoever it was that shot the john.

The sun suddenly grew brighter. Lynch squinted as the sweat rolled down the back of his neck. “You’re really going to try to pitch me fiction, Astroglide? We both know you were out here hustlin’. If you don’t give me something to chew on, I’ll turn on you. And I promise to pinch you for somethin’. No one’s gonna be nicer than me right now. So, I suggest you rewind and start over before I learn the truth later and get you caged.”

“That’s not right, man. Can’t pin nothin’ on me. I’ve cooperated. Given everything he fuckin’ asked. I ain’t hidin’ shit.”

“Your nose is growing. You know we’re going to pull surveillance footage from all the cameras on this street. That’s called, *evidence*.”

“Narc-pig.”

Lynch was finished trying to take the high road and improve himself today. He was keen to get off the hot street...tired of sharing oxygen with slippery, disrespectful trash like this.

“You wanna make things difficult? *I’ll* make things difficult. I’ll take your ass down and get what I want. Understand me, bitch?”

Astroglide put her hand to her mouth, her long, painted nails covering her nose. “You’ll be in deep shit with my lawyer, muthafucka.”

Lynch gave her a deadpan stare. He was used to empty threats like this.

The young white cop piped up. “Just heard back on the ID. This one here did all kinds of shit, Detective. One hell of an extensive track-record. Drug dealing, possession, statutory rape.”

“Astro, you’ve led a life of crime.” Lynch half-smiled. “And you’re gonna just fuck up here and make my job easier.”

Astroglide shook an index finger in his face. “Many cases dismissed, chump.”

Lynch swatted Astroglide’s finger away.

“I’m being *nice* and asking for some cooperation.”

Astroglide crossed her arms. Lynch, feeling the sweat pool under his shirt and bulletproof vest, started to get light-headed.

"You gonna cooperate or what?"

Astroglide stamped her foot. "Yo, you can't get blood out of a muthafuckin' rock!"

Lynch turned to the younger cop. "Take him in."

"*Her!* I identify as *her!*" Astroglide put her hands on her hips. "And you can't take me in! For what?"

Lynch glared at Astroglide. "We have a dead man here, so pardon me if I don't give a fuck about forgetting the proper pronouns." He flicked his eyes to Astroglide's crotch and then back to her face. "Said you still got your cock and balls, right?"

Two balls. The world was so fucking unfair.

"So?"

"Then you're still a *he* as far's *my* identifying goes."

Astroglide paused, face crumpling. The younger cop raised his eyebrows and grinned and Lynch thought that was shitty. He frowned. Sure, Astroglide was an asshole, but Lynch knew he had all the power in this situation and losing his temper and punching down wasn't going to improve either his rotten mood or Astroglide's cooperation. He looked over at the younger officer.

"Any warrants?"

"None." The officer looked pissed, like he wanted to bust Astroglide —or anyone—for something, anything. Lynch would've liked that, but he knew he needed to take a step back.

"You're right about the pronouns." Lynch sighed as he looked at Astroglide. "I apologize; it's already too hot out here and nobody, least of all that guy in the car, is having a good day."

The officer's eyebrows shot up, going from looking pissed off to confused.

Lynch wiped his brow. "So, to make up for the pronoun *faux pas*, and because there aren't any warrants out on you, I'm gonna do you a solid. You can go home—we won't be taking you in this morning."

Astroglide huffed, and the officer rolled his eyes.

"But..." Lynch continued. "Here's the deal. I *will* be coming for you soon enough. I'll dig through the statements these cops got, go through surveillance footage...I guarantee I'll find something that shows you were here when this guy got clipped. And if you already know who did it? You're fucked. No games here."

Lynch stared at Astroglide as he took her ID from the younger cop. He took a photo of the ID with his phone. After some resistance, Astroglide gave Lynch her mobile number and he confirmed it by texting her on the spot.

"So, Astro..." Lynch tucked his phone away. "I'll give you 'til Wednesday to get right with me—that's less than forty-eight hours to give me names, descriptions. The shooter, the prostitute, one person or two? Otherwise, count on seeing me in person by Hump Day."

Lynch handed Astroglide his business card, which she looked at with disgust. "You have my card and number. I have your digits and your address now. Call me soon, day or night. Don't make me come chasing you down to bring you in."

"Don't hold your breath for my call, pig." Astroglide laughed and then tripped on her high heels and fell hard on to the sidewalk. "Muthafuckin' fuuuuuck!"

Lynch bit his tongue and tried to help Astroglide up, but she kicked at him and yelled more obscenities. He put his hands in the air and walked to the victim's car to collect evidence and more statements.

His pants were damp.

Fucking Mondays.

CHAPTER 2

Derek Hoffman sat on a weight bench in Dave's Gym, breathing heavily as sweat flowed freely from his muscled flesh.

Working out was one of his many addictions and he'd pushed himself to the limit today.

He recalled years ago, when he was a teenager, a therapist had urged him to lift weights to curb stress and push the release of those "happy chemicals," his therapist called endorphins. So, he took the advice and found that he loved pumping iron. Yet even though a brutal workout provided a painkilling sensation, it never improved his mood —it never, ever, masked the mental pain spiderwebbed throughout his brain or killed the recurring memory-horrors inside his mind. No matter how hard he hit the gym, he was never freed from the harrowing things that haunted and angered him.

Derek Hoffman knew he was mean and nasty 24/7. He was good with that. He didn't care to be nice...the world hadn't been nice to him since he was puked up into it, so he'd give what he got.

He channeled his abundance of anger and aggression into his workouts, which contributed to his monstrous physical development. The rage he tapped to declare war on the weights and machines during intense sets gave him results far beyond musculature and brawn. At age twenty-nine, he possessed a physique that triggered fear and awe at once in everyone he encountered.

At the end of each set, Derek posed in front of the gym mirrors, enthralled by the juggernaut reflected there. He stood six-foot-nine and last time he checked, he weighed 330 pounds.

Weight training was his religion. He built himself with the goal of becoming humongous; to dwarf any of the pussies in the gym—or the world. No muscle on his body was overlooked. Each contractile fiber was ripped and exaggerated. His flesh, tan and shaved clean from the neck down to his ankles, bulged with vein-laden muscles.

His shaved skin made his glistening tattoos pop. Tribal and skull ink covered his body, starting at his right temple and running down his face and neck to both arms, across his chest, and down his legs. Derek stroked his goatee, dyed blood-red, and pushed his fingers through his spiky blonde hair.

As he regarded himself in the mirror, Derek's bright blue eyes approved every inch of his appearance. He looked around the gym and glared at everyone nearby, thinking they should all admire him.

When would they ever see such a magnificent beast? They were all beneath him, weren't they? Yes, people were shit as far as Derek was concerned and he wished he could work out alone. He avoided interacting with anyone. He just wanted to work out and live a solitary life—but life, and people, got in his way. He often wondered how high the body count would be if he didn't work out.

I'm perfect...

Well, he thought, he was *almost* perfect, if not for the fucking scars zigzagging across his cheeks and lips. He didn't care for those ugly reminders, which came courtesy of a box-cutter his face had met during a fight with three Russians outside some dive on the edge of the city. His jaw and his fists clenched at the memory. He'd nearly killed them all. One suffered permanent brain damage, one would never walk again, and, when Derek was done, the third was left with 157 of 206 bones broken.

Ha! I got off on self-defense...

Though his workouts were centered on personal development rather than competitive body-sculpture, those muscleheads in the bodybuilding mags had nothing on him. He worked to achieve nothing less than pure, brute hypermasculinity. He'd pushed the envelope of the physical form even further when he discovered how to augment his body through chemistry. Dietary supplements and protein powders made to enhance his gains simply weren't enough, so Derek instead turned to anabolic steroids. The synthetic mix of testosterone and hormones forced his body to increase muscle tissue production. He'd been cycling, pyramiding, and stacking them hardcore for years. It all provided the most direct route to his enhancement.

He used everything.

Oral. Injectable. Synthetic.

Roids, gear, juice, stackers, gym candy, Arnolds, pumpers, weight gainers—give it a fucking name, Derek didn't care, as long as they built him.

Anadrol, Dianabol, and Deca-Durabolin—all illegal in the USA. Big deal. He was aware that *everything* he snorted, smoked, or injected was illegal.

Aggressive behavior, violence, and fighting were just a part of his daily routine. Exploding on someone every day seemed normal, expected. Much like lifting weights or scarfing down a protein bar.

Derek didn't care about the reported detriments to his health. He was part man, part chemistry experiment—and he also didn't care that one-thousand-plus milligrams of potent steroids intensified his already volatile aggression.

Roid-rage was a legit fact...he'd known that since he first planted a needle into his right ass cheek.

So be it.

All that constant transformation, however, couldn't banish the demons that lurked in his brain. Those he could never purge. Tormenting memories came to him uninvited and unwanted, making him boil over with fury as he worked out. Consumed with hate, he threw himself into another set of heavier weights to avoid facing any weakness in himself.

He knew, underneath the layers of rage, that he wasn't born this way—evil, wicked, mean, nasty—but, rather, he'd been *molded* to be this way.

As an adult, Derek understood that he could credit Dad Hoffman for the damage that bred and then ingrained his violent tendencies, his constant anger, his development into a particularly dangerous specimen. He stood as living proof that his father had wrecked his life. Derek Hoffman Sr., an alcoholic with a heavy hand, had beaten and humiliated Derek Jr. all through his turbulent, stolen childhood.

His father, the worst person he'd ever known, once forced him to wear diapers under his Wrangler jeans to grade school because he had dribbled piss on the toilet seat. Images of his father destroying his toys out of spite popped up in his head...as did the horror of seeing his beloved puppy—Blinkers—kicked to death beneath his father's steel-toed boots.

Mother.

Melinda Hoffman. She lived alone and worked at Slappy's Tavern, the dive near her house where she slung bar food and drinks to shitheads. Other than that, she wasn't the social type. She'd kept herself as isolated as possible for years now.

Useless cunt.

Her purpose had been to feed and dress him when he was a child, but that was where her maternal responsibilities stopped. She never nurtured or loved or protected him. She never intervened when his father unloaded on him.

I wasn't worth it. Right, Mom?

For some reason, his father never raised a hand to Derek's younger brother, Sid. The way he saw it, Sid was meant to be golden while Derek was hated at birth, brought into the world only to be his father's whipping boy. Why was made to endure constant neglect, cruelty, and disgust? He often thought he deserved it...maybe it was a first-born thing.

Dad Hoffman left the house one day after Derek turned twelve and never returned. But Derek hadn't forgotten him. He thought of him every day, always recalling the damage that fuckface had done to him.

Why couldn't he have had a father who loved him? Or at least had one who'd just been hands-off, like Mom? Mixed feelings of shame and anger and denied love wormed through his heart and mind nearly every waking day. And the unpleasant emotions were more often than not paired with terrifying flashbacks.

Thinking of his father now, Derek attacked the bench-press like it was a mortal enemy.

"C'mon, c'mon! One more, Macho Man."

A round-faced, Black dude wearing a gray Dave's Gym sweat suit suddenly stood over him. Jimmy the Gym Rat, one of those fake and happy personal trainer fucks. He always interrupted Derek's routine with his positive, motivational-quote-dropping bullshit. "Be a voice, not an echo," he'd say. Or "Start each day with a grateful heart." Corny shit that irked Derek. On this early Monday morning, he wasn't in the mood for any of it.

He'd never be in the fucking mood.

Dave's Gym hummed with activity. Weak-ass electro-pop blasted through the speakers. Derek tuned out his surroundings and tackled his fourth set of eight reps. He exhaled and benched six hundred pounds. He took on the weight in his extended arms and hands and loved it. What a feeling. He inhaled deep, allowing the bar to come down to his chest with slow and deliberate form. Then he exhaled hard, an agitated Brahma bull pushing the bar, taking time to let his muscles contract to their fullest potential.

This was six hundred pounds?

This was nothing.

Derek knew he could bench more. He could do it on the tip of his nose if he wanted to.

Reps finished, Derek racked the bar. He glared at the man trying to spot him. "I don't need you, Jimmy. Like I tell you every fucking day: I got this all by my lonesome."

"Just doin' my job, keeping gym members safe." Jimmy smiled. "Damn, you always make this look like kid stuff."

Fucking moron. Go away!

Derek rose off the bench and stood up. His temples throbbed in time with the obnoxious tunes he detested pumping through the speakers. Jimmy's choice of music never failed to annoy the shit out of him.

Though Jimmy was well-built, Derek towered over him. It took all of Derek's willpower to keep from using this joke of a personal trainer for a toothpick.

He stretched, feeling his hormone-packed muscles hungering for more torture. Every sinew was famished and his brain needed distraction.

Wiping sweat from his face, Derek looked over at Jimmy. "*Kid stuff*? Sure. It *is* kid stuff to me, all right. But impossible to a bitch trainer like you."

Jimmy gave a nervous chuckle. "C'mon, now. We're cool. Train your mind to see the good in any situation, right? Muscles ain't everything."

"Pfft ... whatever. At the end of the day, it's all about balls and kicking ass."

"The gospel of Mr. Hoffman, huh?"

"You know it."

Derek turned away, contracted and bent his muscles in a floor-to-ceiling mirror, the fabric of his black sweat-shorts and white tank top stretched to the breaking point.

"What's that? A WWE victory pose?" Jimmy stepped into Derek's personal space again.

"Just showing you all what real meat is."

"The vanity don't stop, huh?"

"Vanity? It's not bragging if it's true." Derek flexed his biceps into basketballs. "Don't hate me 'cause I'm beautiful."

Jimmy shook his head. Someone in the gym laughed out loud. Derek spun to locate the suicidal moron who dared to diss him. The other gym fucks were doing free-weight exercises and cardio. Twelve regulars were in the house this Monday morning with more trickling in.

Give me a reason to crack a skull...

Derek relished being the alpha-male bully here, but his reputation was perceived as a blight on Dave's Gym. Every member of the staff had complained to the owner about him at some point. Despite the gripes, the owner, Dave Lucas, kept Derek's membership intact and free-of-charge for life—all because Derek had saved Dave's ass one night, intervening when a young thug attempted to carjack him after closing time. Derek happened to be in the parking lot, his truck parked next to Dave's Buick, when the gunman stepped up to old Dave. He leapt from his truck and tackled the hooligan, beating him within an inch of his life.

The would-be carjacker was in the hospital for two months.

Derek scanned the weight room. The closest people were a man and a woman working out together on an incline bench.

"Somethin' fucking funny?" Derek watched their reaction for a tell.

"Be cool, man." Jimmy opened his arms and palms.

Derek ignored him.

The couple appeared startled and scared and shook their heads a little too fast, avoiding his gaze.

"Didn't think so." Derek grinned. He'd love to backhand this fucker and tear her boyfriend's throat out with his teeth. It would be such fun.

Give me a reason.

"C'mon, bro. No one wants trouble." Jimmy managed a nervous smile.

"Yeah...well, maybe I do." Derek turned away and pulled a pair of one-hundred-pound dumbbells from a rack. He handled the weights with ease, pumping them up and down as he approached a flat bench to begin sets of flies.

"Annoying prick." Derek eyed Jimmy, who hovered nearby. He figured Jimmy must have zero clients since he'd done nothing but bother him.

Derek sat on the bench. As he stared straight ahead into a mirror, he caught the reflection of a man entering the weight room. A spark of recognition and rage flooded his mind.

"Motherfucker..." Derek blinked twice, making sure it was really him.

Santiago. FUCKING SANTIAGO?

The tall man strolled in wearing an Adidas running jacket with matching synthetic pants. The silver hoops in his ears shone as brightly as his overconfident smile. He high-fived a couple staffers.

Santiago was a personal trainer who'd fucked Derek's ex-girlfriend, Melissa, some four months ago while she and Derek were still together.

Melissa had been the only woman in Derek's life to stick around for more than a weekend. She'd been the closest thing to a girlfriend he'd ever had. Most girls in his life had been either drunken one-night stands or women he'd taken on ungraceful dates who ran for the hills within minutes of experiencing his ugly moods.

For his part, Derek had never thought it wrong if he roughed up and cheated on Melissa. He fucked anything with a pulse, without conscience. In Derek's world, however, double standards were a way of life. When he found out Melissa had cheated on him, he threw her across the living room and punched holes in the walls. When she tried to fight back, she earned a black eye for her bravery.

Derek immediately thought of how Santiago used to work at Dave's Gym. But once he'd stuck his dick where it didn't belong and Derek found out? Well, Santiago had quickly found new employment in the suburbs to escape certain disfigurement.

Hence Derek's current double-take.

He must be suicidal.

Why else would this fucker enter Derek's world after what he'd done?

"You're dead!" Derek jumped to his feet and threw the dumbbells at the wall, two-hundred pounds of airborne metal shattering the mirrors as he lunged for Santiago.

Everyone in the gym scattered for cover while Derek effortlessly knocked over weight racks and kicked benches out of his way. It was as if someone opened a gate and let loose the Greek god Alcyoneus.

"Derek! Don't do it." Jimmy stepped in front of Derek.

Big mistake.

The roids Derek had pumped into himself for breakfast heightened his hunger for blood. He picked Jimmy up off the ground and tossed him to the side like a child.

Derek looked into Santiago's bewildered, fearful eyes, wanting to tear them out.

"I'm gonna rip your Puerto Rican face off and wipe Melissa's cunt with it!"

"I'd cool it if I were you, man." Santiago backed away from Derek in the now-vacant weight room. "And don't forget, Melissa and I have a restraining order against you, bro. You better leave here. Like, *go!* And don't come back. Cops'll lock your ass up."

Derek paused. The restraining order...the charges against him for Melissa's black eye...the fines...the days in jail...his ex moving out during his lockup—all this came rushing back to him.

It didn't calm him, though.

No.

It made him *angrier.*

He brandished a five-foot-long weight bar from a nearby bench like a javelin with Santiago as his big bullseye.

"Run, motherfucker."

Santiago turned and bolted toward an exit. Derek hurled the weight bar through the air fast and hard. The end of the thirty-five-pound bar blasted Santiago in the small of his back. He released an anguished cry and crashed down into a weight machine.

"I'm gonna break you into pieces and fuck the remains!" Derek flipped Santiago over on his back, grabbed him by the throat. He began beating the asshole senseless with a hefty fist. Derek's voice boomed through the weight room as he capped off each blow with a thundering, *"Fucker!"*

"Goddamn it, Derek! Stop!" Jimmy jumped on Derek's back, struggling to control him.

Derek's fury wouldn't allow anyone or anything to stop him. As he pummeled Santiago, Derek whipped his head backwards into Jimmy's face. A sickening crunch, a muffled cry, and Jimmy fell away from him. Derek paused and looked down at the red, gooey mess that a few short minutes ago had been Santiago's face. Bloody bubbles formed around his devastated mouth as he mumbled incoherent pleas.

"Pretty boy's hurtin' now, huh?"

Derek felt vivified with every punch. He wanted to wipe away all those handsome features that his ex held so dear. He'd always made it a point to destroy an enemy's face—as countless assault charges over the years would attest.

Scanning the floor, Derek's eyes settled upon a forty-five-pound plate. He raised the plate easily with one hand, cocking his Herculean arm back as he squatted over Santiago's chest. For the briefest of moments, he flashed back to his troubled youth and the Bradley Davis School for Delinquent Boys and Young Men, remembering when he'd first used weight plates to demolish someone's head.

Juvie...

Derek grinned. "Here's something to make ya way ugly."

As Derek began to swing his arm down to bury the weight in Santiago's face, numerous hands grabbed his arms and legs and pulled him away.

"Get off me, you fucks!" Derek roared as the plate fell to the side. He'd fucking beat all these bitch bastards. He was on fire. So pissed off and hostile, he kicked and nailed his antagonists in the face, crotch—anywhere he could and with everything he had. More people piled on him and pinned him to the floor. It took seven men to bring him down. And even that mass of muscleheads could barely restrain him.

"Call the cops!" Jimmy was yelling in a nasal-crushed wheeze. Blood rained from his broken nose.

Good.

Derek grinned.

Jimmy shook a finger at him. "You...you...did it this time, asshole."

Police cars, a police van, and an ambulance soon arrived. Derek cursed and fought as his pumped-up arms and legs were shackled. Cops used four Tasers on him, and he still kept going. Six policemen took him away, straining to carry his huge, resisting body out of the gym. With some help from the EMTs, the cops got him into a CPD wagon and drove off.

On the way to the police station, Derek's adrenaline began to dissipate. No fun in this now. He knew what to expect: jail, court, lawyers. It would all cost him time and money he didn't have. Today's story was no different from all the others since childhood—he knew he had knee-jerk rage, poor judgment, and never thought about the consequences of his actions until afterwards.

Who cares?

As he rolled into jail, he didn't feel any remorse or regret. He'd always taken a kind of pride in failing to do so. He often repeated his offenses out of spite for the system, even after being severely punished. Derek operated in an instinctive, thrill-seeking fashion; doing whatever seemed easiest and provided instant gratification in the moment. Drugs, sex, and violence fueled him. He excelled at violence.

His mind rolled back to the good old days, after his father was gone, when he had begun to get into trouble. Truancy. Fighting. Vandalism. Other forms of antisocial behavior. As he grew older, his transgressions worsened. At age twelve he almost killed his seventy-year-old neighbor with a crowbar.

The old man had told Derek not to cut across his yard.

Derek didn't like being told what to do.

The more things change...

As a result of attacking the old neighbor, Derek found himself on a bus to the Bradley Davis School for Delinquent Boys and Young Men just outside Salt Lake City, Utah. He imagined that his mother was relieved to see him hauled off that far away. In juvie, things didn't get any better. He got into fights; older boys beat him up, a gang of bigger miscreants held him down on numerous occasions.

Those motherfuckers.

They did things Derek wished he could erase from his memories.

The Rough Riders...

Now the bad memories surfaced again as he sat shackled in the back of the rocking CPD wagon.

Derek thought of when he returned home at sixteen, his mother seemed more loving, but he wanted no part of her affection—sincere or not. It was too late. His heart didn't accommodate love. He was the ultimate Grinch. He put all of his trust in hate, raging more than ever at the world.

As Derek's behavior deteriorated, he began accruing a long police record. At one point he'd been ordered to see a psychiatrist, which was a waste of time. Self-help platitudes meant nothing. He loathed his shrink. The one suggestion he took to his empty heart was to keep working out as he'd done in juvie, to try turning rage and hate into something else.

Derek drifted back to how he got here...how what started as a routine at the local YMCA and morphed from dynamite into an atomic bomb—appropriate, considering Derek viewed his life as a war zone. His days were often filled with insults and threats that demanded immediate, forceful responses. Family, acquaintances, strangers... *anyone* could set off hair-trigger fits of anger, the intensity always far out of proportion to the provocation.

Stressful situations also triggered traumatic flashbacks, igniting panic and rage which snowballed until Derek his aggression on people, animals, and property. A judge once told him that his predatory attitude would land him in prison for life—or in the electric chair.

Maybe the judge was right. Here he was on his way...

Who fucking cares? Who fucking cares?! I *sure as fuck don't fucking care!*

Derek inhaled, relaxed, and looked down at his cuffed wrists as the police rolled toward the station.

Fuck 'em all.

Man, he absolutely hated people. He fucking hated life in general.

Sooner or later, he'd make everyone pay.

CHAPTER 3

Tico "The Meat Grinder" Tortellio sat in the back of a black Lincoln MKZ that had just picked him up from his Chicagoland mansion. Next to his driver, Mickey, sat one of two enforcers—Grotto—while the second hard man, Sammy, kicked it in the back with Tico.

"Turn up the AC fan, Mickey." Tico tapped the back of the driver's seat. "It's a broilin' cunt of a day out there."

Mickey nodded and soon the car was chilled to his liking.

Tico took up most of the back seat due to his size. He stood six-foot-four, with huge arms and hands, and he was fat around the middle from a diet heavy on pasta and red meat. His sons, who were fond of nicknames and obscure pop-culture references, liked to joke that their dad was "Brian Dennehy huge."

"This Lincoln smells like heaven, don't it, guys?" Tico grinned, taking in that new car smell he loved so much as Sammy and Grotto nodded. "Mickey picked it up for me yesterday. It was free, of course, since a particular Lincoln dealer is into us for fifty large."

"A new whip always feels special," Grotto offered from the front seat. "And this one's a beautiful ride."

"Seeing as that cocksucker will probably never pay off the loan, not to mention the vig," Tico said, "it's gonna be free fucking cars for the foreseeable future."

He sank into the seat, admiring the interior leather. And what a name: *Cappuccino*. Oh yeah, he liked that. Speaking of which, he wished he had a cappuccino right now. Maybe he'd get one once he arrived at his destination in Chicago's Little Italy. His thick and sweaty head throbbed. Caffeine might help, but he wasn't so sure.

One thing he *was* sure of was that he could firmly place the blame for the ache in his dome on his twin sons, Liuni and Vito. It was their fault he was rolling into his old neighborhood on a scorching summer afternoon when he'd rather be cooling off with a Sicilian Spritz in the pool at his estate on Lake Michigan.

His sons. He'd had high hopes for the strapping young lads. He wanted to believe in them. But they were such a pain in the ass. They still had to walk a long road before earning his respect. But he loved them. He felt as if the twins—now twenty-two years old—had just come into the world. Liuni was born first, little Vito came a minute later. Tico had considered naming Vito, *Rico*—to rhyme with Tico, his own name—but the correlation with the federal Racketeer Influenced and Corrupt Organizations Act (RICO) was too fucked up, even for his sick sense of humor.

Tico was thinking about his day—and about how his boys were ruining it.

Why, why, why the fuck do I gotta personally spell out everything to them? Forcing me to dirty my hands...

Tico was sixty-four. He'd done his street time and now ruled from the throne. He was the goddamned *Boss* and shouldn't be running around to straighten out this bullshit. Unfortunately, he had to, didn't he? He had to look after his boys—and uncoil the knot that their asses were in. They'd let family business shit slide badly. Now dear old dad was having to step in to remind everyone that this was *his* ship—a ship to be run, as Tico thought, *tighter than Mother Cabrini's figa*.

Impressions and rep and balls were everything, were they not?

Tico had made it his mission today to personally admonish the troops that this Tortellio thing of theirs wasn't a half-assed shits-n-giggles gang. It was the most relevant and lethal organization. A nearly century-old institution of formidable power built on domination, influence, fear, and an ocean of blood. A long-standing part of the Chicago Outfit, the Tortellio family had gradually seized a monopoly on organized crime in Chicago over decades to become all-powerful. His family was the largest criminal syndicate in the Midwest and beyond—and the most violent.

It was Tico's father, Carmine Tortellio, who had facilitated the influence of the Outfit to every region of the country and, by sheer ruthlessness, Tico maintained that hold, hadn't he? Yeah, despite all the new gangs and other ethnic mobs who'd moved in over the decades, Tico knew he was King Shit of Turd Mountain.

Let 'em fucking try me.

People thought the Chicago Outfit was dead...they thought the Mob of yesteryear—all the control in New York, Montreal, Vegas, Miami, and Los Angeles—was dead.

Good.

Tico was happy with that perception.

What was that saying he'd heard before?

The greatest trick the Devil ever pulled was convincing the world he didn't exist...

Oh yeah...

Optics being what they are in the press and in culture, it was the street gangs and cartels who stole the headlines and attention. For Tico and his underworld colleagues, this was a blessing. The idea that Italian and Sicilian syndicates were obsolete took the heat off the Tortellio family. As long as Tico and his organization remained discreet and out of the limelight, they would continue to thrive.

Tico possessed more power than ever, and what the public failed to see was that Tico pulled the strings on all of the gangs in the city. All vice and drugs that moved, only moved because Tico made it so.

Gangs? Fuck the gangs.

They didn't exist without Tico's blessing.

He was stronger than all of them.

Dominant...better fuckin' believe it.

Tico was confident in that, yet he had concerns for the future. What would happen to that dominance when he grew too old or passed away? Tico hated to think about it; hated to think of handing the actual reins to his boys, who didn't have a fucking clue what this whole thing meant.

His boys. The twins. They were such smart-asses. Not feared or respected.

Wise guys? Wise-ass guys is more like it.

"Mamas, don't let your babies grow up to be gangsters." Tico chuckled to himself. The other men in the car didn't seem to get it.

Tico looked out the window and wondered, *how the fuck had he allowed the twins to become so sloppy?* He expected them to be vicious and sharp, as he had raised them. To his disappointment, they tripped over their own dicks on a regular basis. It was an embarrassment. Things were getting botched in those vital areas they were responsible for overseeing...which, to Tico's vexation, was expansive.

His progeny had great responsibility and yet their actions sent the wrong message. It wasn't just unacceptable; it was a disgrace.

È una vergogna!

Tico had a mental laundry list of the twins' indiscretions. For starters, they'd allowed the Tortellio social club to become sullied. They'd been too busy partying and showing off; they just stopped managing it, and those under them were getting lazy and undisciplined. It had been whispered in his ear that his sons had failed to take care of a couple of major money drops last week. That was far beyond some *disgrazia*. How the fuck were these irresponsible kids his flesh and blood?

This was how cracks formed in a crime family. Tico didn't tolerate cracks.

"I know you guys got kids." Tico nodded to his men. "Let me tell ya, all that sparing the rod and spoiling the child is horseshit. They take advantage. Cocksuckers."

Yeah...

Tico would send his own personal message to correct this shit. He knew if he didn't step in and show his face...well, then, all the underlings in the family's army might start thinking the Tortellio empire was up for grabs.

That threat to his rep offended Tico's honor. He wouldn't let that slide.

Those assumptions could turn into a malignant infection and leach into the heads of Tico's enemies. Then they'd sure as hell try to make a move.

Tico would never allow himself to be thought of as weak.

No fucking way.

To that end, he *had* to do business today, in person, to remind everyone who he was and to drive home what the name "Tortellio" meant to the world. He was on his way to the Tortellio club to make a rare appearance. He'd fix things and make sure everyone inside and outside his circle were absolutely clear that the Tortellios were stronger than ever—and unconquerable.

He recalled a saying his Sicilian grandmother, Finuzza Tortellio, was fond of blurting out to her kin: *Se nun si' Re, nun fari liggi nova—if you're not the king, don't make new laws.*

I am *the king now. And I'm making a few new laws today, starting with dirtying my hands as Boss.*

Tico rubbed his eyes. "Who do I gotta choke out for a fucking cappuccino?"

The car turned on to Taylor Street. Tico had always been a Taylor Street guy—just like his father before him, though Carmine first landed in The Patch in Chicago's West Town. Italian immigrants had been pulling out of the Little Sicily/Little Hell area on Chicago's North Side for The Patch further west, and then down to Little Italy on the near South Side where Tico was raised. Under his father and through his *capo* days, Tico had elevated himself to a man of power, importance, and respect. Nonetheless, he never forgot where he came from. He was loyal to this community.

Some connected associates once asked him why he didn't just take it easy and move his operation closer to his North Shore home, like Sam Giancana had done when he set up meetings in Forest Park after moving out to Oak Park, or how some of the other Outfit veterans had shifted everything up to North Barrington. To this, Tico had said, "Giancana was an old cunt. I might be up on the North Shore, but you'll never see me abandon Taylor Street for fuckin' Forest Park."

As part of his devotion to where he grew up, Tico offered a safe, mob-controlled neighborhood and protection to residents and businesses. He instructed his *capos* to aid anyone coming through the door seeking help with even minor problems. He placed a stipulation on assistance, however: Those in need must be Italian, and from the neighborhood.

In return for Tico's benevolence and care, these neighbors always kept eyes open for strangers, odd vehicles, and policemen anywhere nearby, which provided the Tortellio club with an excellent security system.

Generous over the years, Tico would spare time for the old man on the sidewalk who wanted to bend his ear or the young child passing by who got a pocketful of change from his large, murderous hand. He paid for a park and a small baseball field, and gave money to restore and maintain an old, community Catholic church down the street.

Residents in this old neighborhood worshipped him, praised him. Tico found irony and amusement in all this kowtowing and popularity as a hometown hero. He knew they all understood he made his bread and butter off murder, extortion, gambling, drugs, money-laundering, pornography, juice loans, and other forbidden ventures.

Tico straightened in his seat as the club drew near.

"There it is. Finally."

Tico had bought the building in 1989 when it had been a failing grocery store. He'd had it gutted and remodeled, replacing windows with brick to keep the prying eyes of any undercover surveillance fucks guessing. An Italian flag hung over the doorway and a sign on the front door read: MEMBERS ONLY.

A great deal of business happened at the Tortellio private club; and it had to be swept for bugs constantly, and the street perpetually surveilled for strange vans or cars.

On any given day, a cavalcade of men came through the door, bringing *capos* money from the many illicit avenues of Tortellio business. Others brought information on new scores, political and commercial activities, law enforcement intel. An infrequent few came over—by invitation only—to solicit themselves as potential Tortellio associates.

Tico used intermediaries and stayed away from participation in specific business interactions. If he had to do anything personally, he preferred to do business old-school-style, in person, with only one or two guys at carefully selected restaurants. He had put his trust into his sons and a few other *capos*, who ran things from inside the nondescript Tortellio club building.

Trust...

On this day, Tico's trust was dwindling. Some of the younger subordinates needed to be checked, slapped in line, and reminded to stick to business. He must impress on those under him—especially his sons—that there was never room to fail the Boss.

Tico had promoted the twins on New Year's Day. They'd inherited epic responsibility. The twins had been *made,* for fuck's sake. Their hands had gotten dirty through Tico's guidance. They were now a pair of underbosses with Tico's blessing. But did they appreciate the esteem and reverence such a position commanded?

Fuck no.

His boys yapped orders at everyone on their watch just to hear themselves be loud. Tico watched with frustrated anger as they acted more like movie versions of made men rather than what they were raised to be.

As he thought of all this, Tico envisioned the scene from *The Godfather* in his head, the one where Don Vito slaps a wishy-washy Johnny Fontaine and roars, *"You can act like a man! What's the matter with you? Is this how you've turned out? A Hollywood finocchio who cries like a woman?"*

Tico chewed on the sad fact that he'd done as much to the twins once before; the slapping, the yelling, the asking them if they were men or fucking bitches hiding under their mother's skirt.

It all got him nowhere.

As of late, Tico had learned that the boys rarely checked into the club anymore. Dropping in here was a duty Tico expected them to do *daily*, but apparently, daylight wasn't their friend. He was well aware they liked to party. He'd seen the evidence; powder on their nostrils, jabber-jawing, too hung over and useless to get up and take charge.

Tico didn't see a problem with selling drugs—it was a massive driver of the family's illicit wealth—but he definitely had a problem with his sons *doing* them.

Tico's daughter Annabella—the twins' older sister—had told him the boys were posting things they shouldn't on their social media accounts. She was worried that their indiscretion could bite her beloved dad on his ass. Annabella was right to worry, and he loved her for her concern.

Tico avoided social media. He didn't want it, didn't like it. He abhorred the idea of sharing anything personal with strangers, so why would he share photos and videos of his private life to the entire world? Nonetheless, when Annabella gave him a heads up about his sons carelessly uploading sensitive content for public display, he looked into it—and then he flipped out.

The thought of it now reawakened his ire.

These two dumbfucks!

Tico had perused countless images and video clips on TikTok—whatever that was—and Instagram of the twins showing off their guns and their cars, flaunting piles of cash, and throwing up memes of *Scarface*, *Goodfellas*, *The Sopranos*, and *The Godfather* onto their feeds.

From Tico's point of view, this was all chum in the water that could attract maneaters of the worst kind: the FBI, the IRS, and every other Federal Prosecutor who would love to swallow the Tortellio family whole.

On top of all this, the twins always added their *location* to their posts, letting their 100k-plus followers know where these indiscretions were happening.

Stupido. Idioti!

How many times had Tico told his sons that the fucking Feds monitored social media? When he saw their pages, he went King Kong-level ape shit and threatened filicide if they didn't start keeping a low profile. They sure whined about that, didn't they? They tried defending the importance of their personal accounts. He thought of the ridiculous fucking thing they had told him as they explained their social posts... they were *influencers.*

What the fuck is an influencer? They're fuckin' Tortellio's. THAT is influence enough!

Whenever he was around them, they were checking their pages or text messaging their asshole pals and downloading ear-torturing shit off that goddamn Spotify. They didn't listen to him. They did what they wanted and neglected to keep the troops in line and do business discreetly.

Up until this new era of the twins, the business and the club had been run tighter than the Pentagon. Tico loved the job his sons' predecessor—the former underboss, Anthony Ferriola—had done. A stand-up guy who'd been with Tico for more than twenty-five years, Tony was tough as an anvil—until he sucked off a twelve-gauge in the parking lot of an abandoned shopping center in Bensenville shortly after he'd been released on bond for an indictment. Tony took his own way out rather than testify against the family.

No, Tico realized...unfortunately, the Millennials and the Generation Zs would never appreciate the most important family values.

I wish they still made 'em like you, Tony.

Mickey eased up to the curb slowly and parked in front of the club. Tico fingered the Rolex on his husky, hairy wrist as he prepared to go in. Typically, he made his visits known days in advance. His check-ins received special attention from residents living near the club. Longtime neighbors would clean the sidewalks around and near the building, put out flowers, and offer every courtesy to the main man of the Tortellio regime.

Today, however, Tico made his arrival unexpected.

Three men were sitting together at a small table under the shade of a tree in front of the club. Their suit coats hung on the back of their chairs, collars and ties loosened. They smoked cigars, drank wine, and laughed it up without a care in the world, oblivious to the Lincoln that had just parked right in front of the club.

"These are Tortellio soldiers?" Tico shook his head as he stared at the men outside from the backseat of the car. "Cocksuckers."

"Okay, fellas. Time for me to amend things and make sure everyone gets the fucking memo."

Grotto and Sammy exited the car as Mickey stepped out and opened the door for Tico.

"Jesus, Mary, fuckin' Christ. How hot's it gonna get?" Tico squinted as bright sun hit his face. He instantly began to sweat. "Mickey, leave the Lincoln running...keep the air conditioning blasting. Come with me into the club."

"Just leave it runnin', Boss?" Mickey looked uncertain.

"Do as I say." Tico looked around. "You know that no one in this neighborhood is insane enough to try and carjack the Meat Grinder's wheels. *Capisce?*"

Tico turned his gaze to the soldiers out front. He gave them a vicious grin. The men's faces twisted and their cigars dropped from their slack-jawed mouths. They jumped up from the table as if electric cattle prods had been jammed up their asses and stood, straightening themselves, looking nervous as they waited for the Boss to say something.

"It's gonna be hotter than a whore with syphilis today." Tico walked toward the front door, while the three soldiers, with ass-kissing smiles, fell over each other to help him inside. Tico turned to them. "You fellas know Capone had syphilis? True story. My father said Capone suffered from syphilis, gonorrhea, and cocaine addiction in his final years. Anyway, I'm wastin' history and trivia on all you assholes. Just stay by the curb and keep an eye on the car, why don't you?"

Tico walked into the club, enforcers flanking him. Framed pictures of old friends and prints of bygone wine and olive oil companies hung on white walls. A few tables and chairs took up a little space in the modest interior of the front room. There was a back room, a kind of break room with a kitchenette, and beyond that the club's office, which Tico's sons shared with capos for quieter business.

But it wasn't quiet today. A hip-hop bass line thumped through the office door as Tico strode up to the two soldiers stationed outside.

"What the fuck's goin' on around here?" He fixed his gaze on the sharp-dressed, supple-framed soldier to his right. The man hesitated and looked at the other soldier. "The fuck you lookin' at him for? I'm talking to you, *finocchio.*"

The soldier gulped as if he were swallowing an invisible cue ball. "Boss...Boss Tortellio. We're, uh, just watchin' the club and screening visitors. Like always."

Tico stared them down. He put the fear of God into everyone that way. His steel-gray, emotionless eyes and the patented death-scowl on his pockmarked face could reduce tough guys to tears. And he was big. At sixty-four, he could beat the dogshit out of the sturdiest men half his age.

"Y'know, used to be when I come here, I could count on hearing some Sinatra, some Dean Martin. Always Louis Prima. What the fuck is this rap shit coming out of the *capo's* office?"

Silence, huh?

The men looked down at their feet and Tico thought that real men never looked down—or looked scared, for that matter—but these two sure did.

Millennials and Gen Zs. A generation of gutless wonders.

"What d'ya think I'm gonna find when I go through that door? Somethin' bad? Somethin' fuckin' wrong?"

Tico pushed the soldiers aside and tried the door. It was locked. Anger welled up in his chest. He motioned to Grotto and Sammy. "Put your heels to this fucking door."

In an instant, the enforcers kicked the office door open.

Inside, music blasted from a large Bluetooth speaker stationed on an old desk in the middle of the room. Behind the desk sat Sonny DiSanto, a Tortellio captain who always had a knack for rubbing Tico the wrong way. Small in brains, common sense, and genetics as far as Tico saw.

Sonny was big and round in body—Tico chalked this up to Sonny's wife's cooking and his love for stuffing Italian beef sandwiches into his chubby face every day. He was running his fat, ring-covered fingers up and down the nude body of a hussy with fake tits and cocoa-colored skin and hair. The music was so loud, his glistening face so fixated on the girl, that Sonny didn't hear Tico bust in.

The ample-bodied babe gyrated her plump ass into Sonny's spare tire while he groped away with a bawdy grin. But when the man's eyes locked with Tico's, all amusement disappeared from his face. The words he uttered were lost beneath the music, but Tico read his lips: *Holy shit!*

Tico strode up to the desk, snatched up the speaker and slammed it into the wall, smashing it to pieces and killing the tune. "Get this whore outta here."

Sammy and Grotto grabbed the naked woman and carried her out of the office.

Tico turned to look at Sonny as his two enforcers handed the woman over to the guards and then stationed themselves inside the door.

"Y'know," he said, "I like my club. I've discussed endless hours of family business here. And it used to be a respectable place."

Sonny jumped up and opened his mouth to speak, but Tico raised the palm of his hand to Sonny's face.

The *capo* shut up.

"Mind if I sit?" Tico softened his voice. Sonny shook his head and stood up as Tico pushed away the chair and sat on a corner of the desk. He looked into Sonny's nervous face. "Does your wife know what you get into here?"

Sonny shook his head. He cleared his throat and his voice cracked. "No, she doesn't, Mr. Tortellio. Hey, listen, this was just—"

"Shut your fat fucking hole. You call me *Boss*." Tico saw the fear grow on Sonny's face. He glared at Sonny and hoped the *capo*'s innards were churning, threatening to bust at any moment. "Where's Liuni and Vito at?"

"Dunno." Sonny's brow was dotted with perspiration. He fiddled with a gold crucifix on a chain that choked his neck and started jabbering like a stoolie under the gun. "They told me they had odds and ends t'do. I think maybe they're checking on some containers, then grabbing some grub. Maybe at Gibson's or somewhere. They'll be back later ... or somethin'."

Or somethin'...I bet.

Tico looked at Sonny with disgust, wondering if *capos* with spines still existed anywhere. He hadn't even begun to bust Sonny's balls, but the *capo* already seemed nervous enough to give up his own mother.

"My boys know what you get into here? They know anything about this private show you were givin' yourself today?" Tico straightened as he sat on the edge of the desk, keeping his eyes locked onto Sonny's own, pinning him where he stood.

Sonny opened his mouth and it sounded like he said, "Yeah."

Tico figured Sonny's tongue worked quicker than his brain. Sonny blurted more words in swift succession.

"I mean, *no!* No way, Boss Tortellio. They didn't know I was fuckin' around like this."

Tico didn't speak. He gazed at Sonny, a wolf eyeing a wounded deer. The *capo* sheepishly shrugged his shoulders.

"I'm real sorry, Boss. Just havin' a little fun with the girl." Sonny held out his palms. "Forgive me, Boss."

"Sit your fat ass down."

Sonny nodded and sat down in his chair.

Tico looked down at him. "Y'know who owns this building?"

Sonny looked away for a moment then back at Tico. He shrugged his shoulders again. "Uh, you?"

"That's right, genius. And y'know what you're supposed to be doin' in my place?"

"Takin' care of business."

"You know it. My twins were right on the money when they promoted you. You're a real smart guy."

Tico looked the desk over as Sonny looked down at the floor. The desk was bare except for a couple of magazines, Sonny's iPhone, and an empty espresso cup. Tico still wanted coffee.

He looked over his shoulder and nodded at the stainless steel La Marzocco espresso machine sitting on a small table in a corner, surrounded by ceramic mugs and espresso cups and saucers. "Hey. Nice machine there. Digital readout and everything. Fancy."

"Yeah. Hey, Boss Tortellio ... y'know, we got a bunch of those off some truck. Want one? It's, uh, totally programmable. Makes great lattes 'n' shit."

Tico smiled. "Bet your ass it does. I've been dyin' for a cappuccino. Y'mind if I make one?"

Sonny relaxed his posture. "Uh, go ahead. Whatever you want."

Tico swaggered over to the machine and made a cappuccino. It took a minute as he added six extra shots of hot espresso and boiling, frothed milk. He picked up the steaming white mug and raised it to Sonny as he strolled towards him.

"Salud."

"*Salud*, Boss." Sonny smiled and folded his hands on his gut.

Tico took one sip and then whipped the contents of his mug at Sonny. Sonny shrieked as the scalding contents hit him in the face and eyes. Tico reached over the desk, drew his arm back, and smashed the ceramic mug down on Sonny's head. It shattered to pieces. A triangular shard stuck out of Sonny's balding scalp. Blood spurted and flowed down the sides of Sonny's round face.

"How d'ya like that?"

Sonny blubbered and fell out of his chair into a heap on the floor. Tico walked around the desk, grabbing Sonny's iPhone off it. He dropped to one knee next to Sonny and beat the *capo* with his own phone.

"A fucking *captain?* This is how you act?!" Tico cracked the iPhone over Sonny's head multiple times until it broke apart on Sonny's skull. "This is a place of business. *My* fuckin' place. Do your goddamn job and keep your pecker in your fuckin' pants!"

Tico hit Sonny one last time before standing up and dropping the remains of the iPhone. He smoothed his hair with his hands. Sonny whimpered and curled into a ball on the floor, crying and holding his bloody and already blistering head and face.

"You're a fat pussy, y'know that?" Tico turned to the corner table, picked up the espresso machine, and heaved it onto the floor. The machine crashed, crumpled and split, vomiting espresso beans, water, and steam. "Grow a pair of balls, be a man, and do your fuckin' job! I see or hear about you doin' shit on my time other than business, I'll come back here and gut ya myself."

Sonny didn't respond. He stayed on the floor, holding himself.

"Let's go." Tico waved his enforcers on and exited the office.

Outside, Tico paused and jabbed a finger at a pair of soldiers. "Clean up that sorry piece of shit in there and get a new door. And for *all* of you fucks, I'm back on the street to kick all of your asses in line! *Capisce?*"

The soldiers, a shade paler than when Tico had walked in, kept their mouths shut and nodded.

Tico got into the Lincoln with his men and headed toward home. He planned on having a sit-down with his boys immediately. If they didn't answer their fucking phones, he'd hunt their asses down and throw them in the trunk.

It was time for him to begin leading by example. Yeah...he'd get some shit under his nails. Tico sighed. He unconsciously wound his Rolex and cracked his knuckles as he thought of ideas. Tomorrow he'd force the boys to hit the streets with him. He'd keep an eye on them the whole goddamn day.

Tico had personally supervised them back when they made their bones, each of them whacking a pair of low-level contracts. The memory was disheartening, though. The importance of the experience had apparently been lost on them. They only seemed to care about the bragging rights and underworld glory of being made.

My fault.

Tico blamed himself for their lack of discipline...their incompetence...their indifference to the family business. This was his burden. His failure—and he'd never been a man who allowed himself to fail. He refused to live another day with any more blunders from his own blood. They were twenty-two years old, for fuck's sake. Failure stopped *today*. Class began *now*. He'd teach his offspring that balls and muscle were required to run this organization. A heavy hand was needed to hammer his wisdom into them. It was time for his pampered twins to get down and dirty.

Sitting in the air-conditioned car, Tico felt the sweat from his exertion lift off his skin, and he basked in the continued adrenaline rush from burning and cracking Sonny's head.

I feel fucking great.

The Boss beating up a captain? Sure, he knew it would raise many an eyebrow. An incident like this, unheard of in their secret circles, sometimes sent bad messages. But good or bad, sending a message was the point, period.

Fuck 'em!

"Y'know fellas, you can take the Taylor Street boy out of Little Italy, but you can't take Little Italy out of the Taylor Street boy. No way."

Grotto and Sammy smiled, seeming to like Tico's maxim.

Mickey nodded as he drove and said, "Amen to that, Boss."

Maybe tuning up Sonny had relaxed Tico's usually tight-lipped enforcers. No matter what, Tico figured they knew they could be next if they got derailed on his watch.

He smiled, replaying Sonny's beating over and over, acknowledging his predisposition for sadism. It was part of his nature, running as deep as his Sicilian DNA. He'd used it as a tool for decades. It was helpful and actually enjoyable when employed on those who disrespected or tried to harm his business or his family—the latter being the chink in his armor. His dark, callous heart retained only enough love for his kids and, of course, his wife, Valentina.

Maybe I should get outta the house more often to do these things.

Yeah, he'd like that.

Tico's thoughts turned from Sonny to the espresso machine he'd smashed. Licking his wide lips, he tapped Mickey's shoulder. "Hit the next Starbucks you see. I still need a fucking cappuccino."

CHAPTER 4

The sun hung low in the evening sky as Lynch pulled a stool up to a high-top table at the Goat Horns bar. He glanced at a wall of TVs. A Cubs game was on. A local news piece cut in during commercials with nothing good to report. A bank robbed on the North Side—an officer shot and the two thieves blown away.

The news also reported the homicide that Lynch had worked first thing in the morning. The victim was fifty-two-year-old George Pallis—a married father of three who ran a law firm downtown. Investigators were still searching for a suspect. The newscaster mentioned that this murder had catapulted Chicago shooting deaths to a new, all-time high. August already had the most homicides of any month in more than twenty-five years.

The police superintendent showed his face for the TV cameras and said the same old shit about how many illegal gun seizures they'd made. He blamed the endless supply of firearms and lenient sentencing laws for much of the gun violence. Said he would push hard for state lawmakers to craft legislation calling for stringent sentences for repeat gun offenders.

Yeah, right. Nothing's changed in nearly three lousy decades.

And George Pallis? Whacked while his pipe was getting polished. Married with children and a lawyer, too.

Gee, what a surprise.

Lynch shook his head. After questioning Astroglide, he'd poked around and gathered more facts from bystanders. The prostitute who'd been in the car with the victim was still MIA. He would focus on Astroglide. If he didn't hear from that slippery fuck by Wednesday, he'd be making a personal visit to his house.

Her house. Right...

Sensitivity was one thing, but Lynch wasn't so sure he'd be handling Astroglide with kid gloves if she'd in fact witnessed the murder of George Pallis and wasn't coming clean.

A brief weather report mentioned it had hit a record 102 degrees today with five heat-related deaths. It promised to be hotter tomorrow.

"Saw that coming," Lynch said under his breath.

"Mind if I join you, Donnie?" A female voice spoke behind Lynch. It was Nikki, one of the twenty-something regulars who frequented Goat Horns. She wasn't hard on his eyes. A tall, slim brunette, she almost made him forget Sandy. He was surprised Nikki was single. They'd flirted before but it went nowhere further. Lynch liked her...smart, cool, maybe a bit younger than he'd consider hooking up with, but she sure had appeal—and damn, it was nice to get attention.

I've always *been a man. I got my groove back...*

"Please. Sit." Lynch appraised Nikki as she sat down. "You watch the game?"

"I actually don't like baseball. I'm all about hockey."

"Go Hawks."

Nikki rolled her eyes. "Freakin' sucked this year."

"My Cubbies aren't doin' too good, either." Lynch motioned to a server, then turned to Nikki. "Can I get you something?"

"Sure. Captain and Coke."

"Captain and Coke and I'll have a Sprite." He watched the server walk away. "Y'know, I prefer 7-Up, but no one has it at bars or restaurants. It's like a damn conspiracy or something."

Nikki smiled. *Damn.* Lynch thought she had nice eyes.

"So, you don't drink, huh? Guess I never noticed when I saw you in here."

"I quit awhile back."

"I'm not the nosy type. I'm sure you've got reasons. It doesn't bother you if I have a cocktail?"

"No. People drink around me all the time. No triggers for me. Doesn't faze me." Thoughts of Sandy resurfaced. He pushed her out of his mind. "I'm on a health kick."

Nikki gave him a sly smile. "What *could* someone do around you that you can't resist?"

Here we go...

Lynch smiled and tried to think of a witty comeback to Nikki's flirting but couldn't stop thinking of Sandy.

Miss you, damn it.

Nikki giggled. "I'll give you time to think of something."

The server brought the drinks, and Lynch gave her a ten. "Cheers." Lynch tipped his glass and clinked it with Nikki's.

"Cheers." Nikki put the small straw between her pink lips and drew a long sip, keeping her eyes on Lynch's. She swallowed. "Yummy."

Maybe I won't be going home alone.

He considered the lone ball swinging between his legs and the testosterone gel he smeared on his chest before work. He wondered if they'd hold up to a decent performance in bed. The idea of it all turned him off. He shifted away from Nikki's hypnotic gaze and looked to the wall of TVs broadcasting the Cubs game. He wanted to focus his attention on something else.

"Aw, shit! These guys could fuck up a wet dream."

"Wow." Nikki held up a hand. "Sounds serious."

Lynch did a double take at the score. He always let the games get to him. He shook his head and laughed. "Sorry. You know...fans. You get it."

"I do, Donnie." Nikki smiled and put her hand out. With a light touch, she traced the veins in Lynch's right hand.

A slight rush hit Lynch from Nikki's touch. A lot of time had passed since he'd been with a woman. Though he met women,

Lynch never pursued them. The vibe was never right. Sure, some of them looked damn good, but he didn't have any game. Hell, he didn't *want* game. He'd hung up the pick-up lines and whatever Lynch charm he'd had long ago. And despite having his libido back, Lynch sometimes had to get his head around having one testicle. The doctor said a woman wouldn't notice a goddamn thing either. He knew it was psychological. He wouldn't allow an orchiectomy to change him.

I'm strong and resolute...and it feels fucking great.

Lynch knew his reasons for steering clear of dating or getting laid were just bullshit excuses. He couldn't fool himself, knowing it all came down to Sandy. His ex-wife was all he wanted. He thought of her day in and day out.

Can't get over you, babe.

Lynch again tried to push Sandy into the back of his mind.

Too busy working my ass off anyway ... forget about getting my dick wet.

Lynch kept telling himself he didn't need sex.

His body told him otherwise. He got turned on if it rained hard—and he was far beyond grateful for that.

He didn't want to start getting bummed out in the company of this sweet girl. He looked at Nikki and...damn, she sure looked hot. Maybe they could just chat and hang out. No harm there.

Don't be a fucking buzzkill...

Before he could ask Nikki about her evening plans, she said, "Excuse me, Donnie. Gotta use the ladies' room."

"Of course." Lynch watched her back-end wiggle across the busy bar.

He wondered what it might be like to make love to another woman. Sandy was his last and it felt as if it had happened back in the Miocene era. Since his divorce, he'd gotten away from his bad habits and self-destructive behavior. He poured himself into work. On the job, he had no mental or emotional obstacles.

Was that all there was now? Work and sleep?

His old man had been a workaholic, doing some shady shit with mobbed-up hard guys, but at least he'd stayed married and actually had a love life. The old man had made time to be home with his wife and kid when he could. Lynch faced a sudden void at that realization.

Sipping on his Sprite, he looked toward the restrooms. He saw Nikki smiling and talking to a bouncer in a black Goat Horns T-shirt. Then she frowned, shaking her head as the bouncer nodded and pointed toward Lynch.

What the hell's that about?

His cop sense told him there was something uncool about the conversation. When Nikki approached the table with a suspicious expression, he acted nonchalant.

"Another round?"

"No thanks." Nikki averted his gaze and looked down at the table. "I gotta run, Donnie. Sorry."

"What's the rush?" Lynch studied her, trying to figure out the deal.

"Just gotta do some stuff."

"Hey." Her green eyes, perky minutes ago, were now cautious. The bouncer grinned at Lynch. *Looks familiar somehow.* He turned back to Nikki. "That guy say somethin' to you?"

Nikki hesitated. "Yeah."

"What?"

Nikki swallowed. "That's Leroy. A bouncer here—if you didn't know. He says you're a cop. An 'asshole pig' was how he put it. Is that true?"

Lynch frowned. He looked over at Leroy, who continued grinning and eyeballing him. He knew the face. He'd seen it somewhere before.

"I'm a detective. Before that I was a regular Chicago cop. Is that a deal-breaker or somethin'?"

"In my world it is." Nikki pursed her lips. "Leroy's a friend, okay? I dig you, Donnie. But I'm afraid I just don't do cops. I've got my reasons. Sorry."

"Right."

Nikki flipped her long hair back and walked out the front door.

Doesn't fucking matter. I'm staying celibate for eternity.

Lynch looked at Leroy from across the bar. He remembered it then. He'd busted Leroy a couple years ago during a rave at an old warehouse in the city where three teenagers died from poisoned meth. Leroy was the grand architect, promoter, and dealer for the whole show. He was nailed on drug charges and wrongful death or something. Those were Leroy's first offenses. Bastard got probation and was let go.

Now he's a bouncer. And a great cockblocker...

Lynch got up from the table. He left three singles and gave Leroy one last glare. Leroy kept grinning. Lynch flipped him off and walked out into the cruel heat of the evening.

CHAPTER 5

It was nearly eight o'clock on Tuesday night, but still remarkably light outside, when Sid Hoffman left the Peithos Labs at St. Cornelius Hospital. The heat and humidity sucker-punched him. Within seconds, his black dress pants and pressed white shirt felt like plastic-wrap on his flesh. He had worked a thirteen-hour shift and was beyond exhausted.

Sid was Clinical Research Coordinator (CRC) for Peithos Labs. He recruited test patients, worked the research floor, prepared case report forms, and managed all the data in each clinical study program. He worked alongside a team consisting of doctors, health professionals, and a few researchers specializing in data science and statistical analysis. He had just finished a trial whose participants had been sequestered for three weeks while the lab tested a new AIDS vaccine on them. Now that they were done, the participants were paid and released. Sid signed them all out. Tired as he was, he wouldn't have a break. The next study was beginning tomorrow for a new erectile dysfunction and arousal drug they called LIBIDONAL.

Ten years ago, Peithos Labs had successfully created Sun Fun 69—AKA the "female Viagra"—to aid women with low sexual desire. Sun Fun 69 was a melanocortin-based med that was originally tested as a sunless tanning agent but research trials also revealed a statistically significant increase in sexual desire for female faux-sun-seekers: It was an unexpected win for Peithos Labs which, once the Food and Drug Administration approved the drug for sale and use in the United States, helped its stock reach new heights. Now licensed in other countries, it had blown up huge worldwide.

Turning from the Female Sexual Function Index (FSFI) to the potentially huge male-enhancement/sexual dysfunction market, Peithos Labs was ready to begin testing what they believed would be their next major triumph.

Libidonal was a red, oval-shaped pill with numerous benefits. It would increase and enhance sexual desire, promote stronger erections, and provide more energy. It was to be a one-stop-shop potency pill for men. Sid thought it might be the closest thing to an actual aphrodisiac to be approved by the FDA. He knew this wasn't some snake-oil shit like ginseng root, powdered rhinoceros horn, or Spanish fly—this was real.

With only a few solid treatments for men's sexual disorders on the market, they saw an opportunity to give male patients a new option. Researchers initially considered making Libidonal an injection into subcutaneous tissue or even a nasal spray, but determined a pill would be easier to market and more appealing to the consumer.

Now in Phase 1 clinical trials, Libidonal would hopefully soon move on to Phases 2-4. Once it received final FDA approval, Libidonal could very well change the world.

First, however, it had to be tested. While drugs produced from the worlds of pharmacology, pharmacokinetics, and chemistry could create positive effects and benefits, Sid knew they could also wreak havoc with hormones, emotional/mental health, and physical health conditions. Sid's role was to provide Peithos with perfect candidates to study and manage the data to make the company's new miracle drug a success.

Sid slung a book bag full of research papers over his shoulder as he walked, looking forward to dinner and wine with his fiancée, Gloria, in their Lincoln Park condo. He crossed the parking lot toward his shiny new black BMW roadster and felt a sudden knot of unease in his chest at the sight of his older brother, Derek, whom he hadn't seen in months.

Derek leaned against the car, dressed in baggy track pants, a white muscle shirt, gym shoes, and black sunglasses, looking like some towering orc. He was also disheveled, with stubble creeping across his razor-scarred face, and unwashed hair. Derek stood straight as Sid approached and greeted him with a wary smile.

"What's up, bro?" Sid set the book bag down next to the car and awkwardly fist-bumped Derek, pretending to be happy to see him. His brother looked larger and meaner than ever.

What's he doing here?

"Same bullshit as always. Got into a scrape at the gym yesterday. Bad news there."

"Yeah, heard about that." Sid wasn't surprised to learn about Derek's new troubles. Trouble had been a staple of Derek's life since childhood.

"Who told you? Mom?"

"Yeah, I call her every day." Sid remembered how upset their mother was about Derek being locked up again. "She said she bailed you out. Didn't say why."

"Had to get the fuck outta jail, Momma's boy."

"What did you do this time?" Sid really didn't want to know.

"I saw the punk who was fucking Melissa behind my back. I ran into him at the gym and showed him I'm not a fuckin' cuck."

Sid was startled at the size of his older brother—Derek had somehow gotten *bigger* since Sid saw him last. He knew his brother was always a giant, but what the fuck did he do to take on more mass? Sid wondered what part of their lineage made Derek so huge because their folks hadn't been anywhere near six feet tall. At twenty-six, Sid was five-foot-five and a slim 150 pounds, with a clean baby face and a healthy head of hair. He was happy to have nothing in common with his sibling, grateful he bore almost no resemblance to the monstrosity standing next to him. The only thing they had in common was their last name and their bright blue eyes.

Someone once joked that Sid and Derek were a lot like Danny DeVito and Arnold Schwarzenegger in *Twins*. Sid had laughed at that at the time, but he'd always wondered how he and Derek were built so differently in body and mind. How had they come from the same parents?

Twins. It had struck Sid as funny, but he wasn't laughing now. He couldn't keep his eyes off of Derek's massive arms, packed with ropy veins and distorted musculature packed into 300 and some pounds of tanned malice.

Sid figured Derek could smash his little roadster into a soda can. He blinked and thought of Derek's recent assault. "Um, is the other guy still alive?"

"Yeah. He'll live, but I managed to pulverize his cheekbones and break his jaw. His eyes are swollen shut...shattered his eye-sockets, I was told. He won't be looking at anyone wrong for a while. Ain't gonna be fucking other guys' old ladies, either." Derek slowly stretched his arms as if he were telling Sid about something trivial, like mowing the lawn.

"Charges?"

"The usual. Battery, disorderly this and that. They said I violated the terms of my restraining order, even though that little cocksucker walked right into my world. Right into my line of fire. That ain't fucking fair."

Sid grimaced at the thought of anyone suffering a blow from Derek's fists. He sighed. "Next time, try giving me a call. I'll come get you out so Ma doesn't have to do anything."

"Didn't wanna bug ya."

"Hey, I'm your kid brother. I'll help you out if I can." Sid tried to sound sincere, hoping to keep his brother's mood on an even keel. He'd never known Derek to be anything other than scary—in temperament as well as size.

"Glad to hear that." Derek grinned and slapped Sid's shoulder with a heavy hand. "Just so happens that's what I'm here for ... *help*."

Sid frowned and rubbed the sting out of his shoulder from Derek's bear-paw. "What can I do?"

"First off, I need a ride back to my apartment." Derek walked around to the roadster's passenger-side door. "I'll tell you what I need on the way."

Sid's heart dropped. He didn't want to drive all the way down to the rough neighborhood where Derek lived. And Sid knew that with the interminable traffic, it would be a two-hour round trip. Gloria expected him home on time. Sid wanted to go home, do dinner, and maybe get frisky with his fiancée afterward. Hanging with Derek required too much babysitting and always came with a hefty price. Sid could only tolerate him in small doses, and he'd made it a point to keep their visits together few and far between.

"Where's your truck?" Sid looked around the parking lot.

"The fucking transmission shit the bed last Friday. Had to take the El up here. Took for-fucking-ever." Derek tried opening the locked passenger door. He towered over the roadster and pushed the body of the car and it rocked like a cradle. "You gonna give me a ride or not, asshole?"

It alarmed Sid to think Derek had expended the time and energy to grab a couple trains to travel across the city just to meet him at work. Derek's scowl—the same one he'd had since they were kids—spoke volumes. Sid knew it meant his irritability was escalating. Soon someone or something would get beaten.

"Yeah, chill. Gimme a chance to open the door."

"Dude, this is like riding in a fuckin' go-kart." Derek grunted as he squeezed and shoehorned his legs and body into the confines of the roadster, his bulk way too big for a car this size. He was bent over and scrunched up between the seat and dashboard. "This fuckin' blows. But I'm sure this ride is comfortable for your short ass."

Sid hated it whenever Derek tried to make him feel inferior.

"So, what's on your mind?"

"I'm hurtin' for cash." Derek's large fingers clumsily played with the AC and the satellite radio, stopping here and there on rock and metal stations. "I haven't worked in months. Can't pay Mom back for bailing me out. I'm gonna get evicted soon and now I've got court, lawyers, and all the other bullshit I always have. I can't afford any of it."

Need your daily drugs, too. Right, brah?

Although he didn't see his brother often, he was intimately familiar with the man: jobless troublemaker. Abuser of narcotics and steroids. Attacker of men and women. Always insisting he was owed something and everyone had to throw him a life-preserver. Sid was sick at the thought of their mother helping this delinquent. In her sixties, she struggled just to keep the electricity on. Sid thought of his mother's two-bedroom ranch on a slab in the city's armpit. It was bad down there. He wished she'd leave, but she wouldn't. She always did things he didn't understand—like endlessly helping Derek out when it was clear her firstborn didn't care for her and blamed her for his woes.

A mother's love is blind. Unconditional, I guess...

"What do you want me to do?" Sid fought traffic and prayed he could get Derek out of the car soon.

"I'm gonna need three grand at least for a retainer. More to keep the fuckin' lights on. Figured you'd help."

Sid chose his words carefully, not wanting to push Derek's buttons. "I'm all for helping you within reason, but...a few grand? What makes you think I have that kind of cash to give out?"

Derek turned down the riffage of some thrash band on the radio and glared at Sid. "You're the smart one. You got your degree, got the good job, blah blah blah."

Derek's rank breath hit Sid's nostrils. Clearly, he hadn't brushed his teeth in a while.

Sid flushed. He'd worked hard in his undergraduate studies of biochemistry, cellular and molecular biology, pharmacology and neuroscience, and even harder to earn his master's degree in clinical research.

"Listen, I might have a degree, but I'm *still* paying for school out of my own pocket. I only finished two years ago. You seem to forget that."

"Fuck school. You got enough bread to get yourself a condo and this fancy car. Right?"

Sid sighed. "I have a mortgage and a car payment, and I'm spread thin everywhere. I'm asset-rich and cash-poor."

"I'm sure you aren't a tight-wad with that pretty little wife of yours."

Sid's anger and heart jumped. He hated when Derek mentioned Gloria. "We're not married yet. Our wedding's this fall, and we're paying for everything ourselves. Her family doesn't have a pot to piss in, so no help there. Another perfect example of why I can't help you."

"You're a thankless little prick, aren't ya?" Derek was starting to snarl. "You forget all the times I bailed *you* out?"

"I guess?" Sid couldn't recall the last time Derek had done anything nice for him.

"Yeah, right. Like the time you decided to take off with the neighbor's car? You totaled it when you hit that telephone pole, but I covered for you. Everyone thought I did it anyway. No one believed that sweet, innocent, little Sid would do a fuckin' thing like that."

"Christ, that was years ago. I was a teenager." He was lucky he hadn't killed himself.

"So, what? I still lied for you and said you were out with me somewhere else at the time. That ain't the only time I done it. I bailed you out of other jams ... underage drinking, shoplifting once. Shame on the honor boy."

This is the best he's got?

"You're talking about kid stuff, Derek. Not that I don't appreciate my big bro helping me back then, 'cause I do. But it's ancient history."

"Well, how about some current-fucking-events?"

"Like what?"

"Like Gloria."

Sid's mouth dried. He knew where Derek was taking the conversation. His sphincter tightened. "Don't even go there ..."

"Oooh, sore spot, huh?" Derek frowned. "That's right. I took care of you that night when ya picked up that slut from the bar. I watched you bang the shit out of her on my living room floor—"

"Enough!"

His last night out with Derek. *Fuck me.* It had happened several months ago, and it pained Sid to think of it. Derek had called him out of nowhere and lured him out of his house for a night of bar-hopping around the city.

Big mistake.

Derek had picked Sid up in his truck—much to Gloria's annoyance—promising to have him back before he turned into a pumpkin. Sid hadn't wanted to deal with Derek's unpredictable and explosive behavior, but eventually changed his mind, thinking he'd try again to bond with him. Finally, he convinced Gloria it would be all right and then he was out the door.

The night started with a bang as Sid watched Derek beat up a pair of loudmouths at the first bar they hit. The guys were cocky hipster types, full of themselves and full of liquid courage. They'd been rude to the staff and clientele and bumped into Derek and spilled his drink. Derek demanded an apology, but when the hipsters told him to go fuck himself, Derek laid them out cold. People in the bar applauded—along with the bartender, who also politely asked the Hoffman's to leave.

Sid didn't remember much after that. He only had a couple of beers at the next bar before getting completely annihilated. He didn't know which way was up or down.

How'd he get so smashed? He knew Derek abused a variety of narcotics, stimulants, and powerful steroids. It wasn't a secret. Big brother bragged about all the shit he took and usually offered Sid a bump of blow, sometimes Oxy and Vicodin, or even DBol pills, which would do jack shit for his physique or recreational pleasure.

Sid couldn't deny that his brother was unselfish with illegal drugs. Whatever he had, he was ready to share—and share he did...in a most terrible way, as Sid went on a hell-ride, later realizing that Derek intentionally put something in his drink to fuck him up that night.

After years of hard work, Sid had built a solid career in the science of pharmacology. He was an expert on all medications and drugs, contemporary or obsolete, and he used that expertise in his work for the Peithos Labs. His older brother, on the other hand, was a foolhardy pro at abusing every possible drug that could stimulate, tranquilize, and/or build him up.

Sid knew the two most common date-rape club drugs were flunitrazepam and Rohypnol—generally called "roofies." There was also gamma hydroxybutyric acid, the hypnotic depressant known as GHB which Derek was fond of. Sid knew some of the street names: Liquid X, Easy Lay, Georgia Home Boy, Scoop, Fantasy, and Somatomax. Grievous Bodily Harm was another nickname which Sid thought was fitting since that's what Derek did to others while on or off the drug.

GHB happened to be a favorite choice of body builders, guys like Derek, because of its alleged muscle-building and fat-burning features. And the blackout Sid experienced that night fit the bill for its effects: forgetfulness, drowsiness, slowed down heartbeat and breathing, and then a coma that could last one or two hours—and then eight hours to recover after it all.

When Sid thought back to it now, it was the same unclear shit in his head: he retained a vague memory of talking to a woman at some bar, then flashes of Derek driving them home, flashes of the woman without clothes, vague memories of sex and then...

Blacked out.

It all made Sid fucking sick with shame and terror. He remembered the clearer stuff, waking the next morning to find himself naked on Derek's debris-covered living room floor. His head pounded, his penis ached, and the smell of sex wafted up from his undercarriage. Sid scrolled through dozens of missed phone calls, voicemails and texts from Gloria. It gave him anxiety. He knew how irate she could get when her trigger was pulled—and it had been pulled *hard.*

He thought his world was about to end.

Sid got cleaned up while Derek sent the woman on her way. Sid came out of the bathroom, his head pounding, and called Derek out for causing his spiral into the black. Of course Derek denied the accusations and threatened to beat Sid up for tearing into him. Sid backed off but he knew his brother had intentionally damaged him.

Derek drove Sid back to his condo, pulling over a couple of times so Sid could vomit. He had been horribly hungover, sick from guilt—and from the fear of Gloria's wrath. Derek laughed and told him not to worry. Easy for him to say. Sid had invested all his love and commitment into Gloria. She was the woman of his dreams and he couldn't even fathom ever cheating or doing her wrong.

I fucked up sooooo bad...

Gloria had gone Defcon One on him when he and Derek walked through the door of the condo like an odd couple off the street. Sid immediately threw in the towel, giving up as Gloria went off. She couldn't be reasoned with.

Then Derek saved the day, didn't he? He'd actually surprised Sid with his talent for lying. The story Derek fabricated, and the sincere tone that went with it, made Sid think that in another life, his brother could've been a great actor.

As Sid watched it all unfold in sick fear, Derek explained how they had been celebrating Sid's engagement a little too much. He claimed they got carried away and Sid blacked out. They caught a cab at two in the morning and went back to Derek's apartment so he could care for Little Sid. Derek blamed the whole night on himself, saying he'd forced round after round on Sid. Then, with uncharacteristic sincerity, he apologized for getting Sid wasted and asked Gloria for forgiveness.

One thing Sid had learned over the years was that Derek had total disregard for the truth. His lies came with ease and remarkable poise. Sid guessed this pseudo-goodwill was easy to pull off since his brother possessed only the shallowest emotions. Derek lacked love, empathy, remorse, and guilt. His strengths and skills lay within his roles as a liar, cheater, and sociopath.

Although Derek was a master of deceit, Sid knew Gloria was an ace at detecting bullshit. He watched her digest Derek's every word and expression—and the anxiety of it all almost made Sid vomit all over again. After a few minutes of silence, Gloria was swayed. She held Sid tight and called him a full-blown asshole for worrying her so. She told him he wasn't allowed to go out again—and he definitely wasn't allowed to have a bachelor party. She also gave Derek the third degree—but when his story didn't change, she paused and thanked him for Sid's safe return. There were even a few hugs before Derek said goodbye.

That was the last time Sid saw Derek—until today.

Now here they were, driving, with Derek threatening extortion.

"Why are you bringing this shit up?" Sid focused on the road. Rush hour traffic was getting worse and added to his increasing stress.

"Well, I figured if I keep your secret, then maybe you'll compensate me for it."

Sid wanted to scream and struggled to find words. "It's your fault I got into that mess that night! I know you drugged me, Derek. Don't fucking deny it!"

Derek shrugged. "I guess you got me, fucker. Y'see, I think ahead, little bro. I planned it all that night. Hell, yeah. Figured I'd call in my chips when I'd needed them. You always thought you were so fucking smart with your degree and fancy job. Looks like I out-brained you on this one."

Sid's insides dried up. He licked his lips but had no spit. His voice rasped. "Why? Why? I've never been bad to you, ever. What're you trying to do? Blackmail me? Ruin me? I'dve helped you without doing it this way, man."

"My way is the *only* way." Derek smiled. "Hey, I'm a desperate man. I figured I could either rob a bank or get some cash from my kid brother. You're way easier. I had you set up as my investment."

"So basically, you're gonna tell Gloria that I intentionally fucked some chick you paid for, even though you drugged me? And you'll do that unless I cough up some cash immediately?"

Derek frowned. "Somethin' like that."

"Fuck you. I should throw your ass out of the car. Piece of shit."

Derek's left arm shot out and Sid's head bounced off the drivers-side window. Derek had his hand wrapped around Sid's throat like an anaconda. His thumb and middle finger almost clamped together at the back of Sid's neck. Sid struggled to keep the car on the road while Derek squeezed his windpipe and jugular.

"Little fuckhead, I ain't playin' a game here." Derek spoke through his clenched teeth and sprayed Sid's cheek with foul-smelling spittle. He squeezed Sid's throat harder. "I need money. You either help me or I'm gonna shit all over your wedding plans."

Sid thought he might pass out. The expressway and the traffic and buildings began dissipating, like streams of melting ink. The roadster swerved and almost hit another car. He fought for air and tried to speak. “Kay ... ugggh ... kay.”

Derek released Sid’s throat and sat back in his seat. “I’ll take that as a *yes*.”

Sid nodded. Fear and hate bubbled inside him. He gasped. “I’ll try to help you, but I can’t give you cash that I don’t have.”

“Better start using your big brain.”

Sid drove and brainstormed, terrified to think what Derek would do to him and even more terrified at the thought of what Derek would say to Gloria. He cut around cars, his brain spinning with crazy strategies as fear and panic ate away at him. There was no way he could touch any cash or assets that he and Gloria shared without her noticing. And even if he managed to pay Derek somehow, that asshole could and likely would come back and blackmail him for more cash again later. But Sid would worry about that later. For now, he just wanted to placate the prick and get through this horrible fucking ordeal.

An idea came to Sid, a farfetched scheme for sure, but it might just work. It could also destroy his career if things went wrong but Sid didn’t have a lot of options.

He allowed a truck to pass him, shifting over into the right lane. “I have an idea. And you’ll walk away with five grand. Five grand, man... that’s two grand more than you wanted to bleed me for. But you have to do it my way.”

Derek turned in his seat and Sid involuntarily flinched. Derek laughed. “Why you so jumpy? I ain’t gonna hit you. Keep talkin’.”

“Peithos Labs, where I work in the Clinical Pharmacology Research Unit? They’re starting a new clinical study program tomorrow. The screening dates have already come and gone, but I think I can get you in there. You’ll collect five large when it’s over.”

“When’s it over?”

“You have to stay in there for two weeks.” Sid knew Derek would hate being locked down.

“Fuck that. I can’t be cooped up in a fuckin’ lab for two weeks straight,” Derek rolled down his window and spit. He kept the window down with his massive right arm holding on to the roof like some kind of ape in a clown car. "I need cash quick. I've got shit to take care of. You gotta think of somethin' else."

Sid wondered what other options he had. Zero, he knew. No way he could tap the joint savings or checking accounts. It would get Gloria's immediate attention, and she'd ask too many questions. He just wanted to pacify Derek.

"Listen ..." Sid turned onto Derek's street and parked in front of his apartment. "All you have to do is show up, take some pills, and be a bum for the duration. If I can pull some strings to get you out of there quicker, I will. I need time with that. You'd still have to return on the last day to sign a release form and collect your check. Easy."

Derek scratched his head, seeming to ponder the proposition. "What about paperwork and piss or blood tests?"

Sid knew it was too late in the game to get Derek in legitimately. It didn't matter anyway because Derek wouldn't pass the normal inclusion and selection criteria. His age was fine, but his blood, urine, and whole system likely pumped steroids, narcotics, and other foreign dross.

"I'll...uh, weave your info into the original survey and screening pile. Then I'll substitute your samples with my own, take care of the necessary forms and get you on the roster. No one will be the wiser. I'll vet that you were accepted since Day One and maybe your paperwork just got lost in the shuffle somewhere. There are over fifty subjects participating, plus I'm supervising the study." Sid shrugged, his confidence building. "If I can sneak you out, you'll still be on board. Kinda like a ghost-payroll."

He glanced over at his brute of a brother and all his confidence in the plan disappeared. "It'll be hard though because you're so ... unique-looking. Hopefully no one will catch on to it."

Derek grumbled something. "Guess, I'll do it. Not like I've got tons of fuckin' options."

Sid didn't reply as he pulled up to the curb outside Derek's place. He was loathing every minute of the conversation. He became more distressed as he thought of all he'd have to do to get Derek into Peithos with the next study group starting first thing in the morning. He'd have to turn around now, go straight back to the Peithos floor at St. Cornelius, and start dummying-up blood and urine samples, and numerous forms. He'd be there all goddamned night for sure. And he'd have to call Gloria.

Fuck!

With some cursing, Derek squeezed out of the car and peered at Sid through the open window. "So, what time do I need to be there? And where the fuck do I go?"

"Meet me back at St. Cornelius. Go to the lobby and grab an elevator to the second floor. That's where Peithos Labs is located. Be there at six-thirty in the morning."

"Six-thirty? In the morning? You gotta be fucking kidding."

"Afraid so. You have to be there for rollcall and your hospital gown. And you're comin' up north. That's not just a stroll up the block."

"Any chicks there?" Derek winked.

"Chicks? Gimme a break. There's only men in the program."

Derek frowned.

"Don't forget to pack toiletries and anything else you might need." Sid paused. "No illegal drugs, Derek. If you get busted, I won't be able to help you."

"Yeah, yeah. Whatever. I'll be there. You better work on gettin' me outta there in a day or so."

Sid nodded. "Sure. I gotta run."

"See ya tomorrow, fucko." Derek slapped the roof of the car and it sounded like a gunshot. He began walking away and then whipped around. He came back and leaned his head inside the passenger-side window. "What exactly am I supposed to be doin' in this study thing?"

Sid knew anything pharmaceutical would be of interest to Derek. Drugs could motivate him more than money. "The study program is for a new drug Peithos Labs is developing called Libidonal."

"Libid-a-what?"

"Libidonal. It's basically our branded version of Viagra, but in a red pill instead of blue." Sid assumed that Derek had popped Viagra before. What hadn't he taken? "These two pills—Libidonal and Viagra—

remind me of *The Matrix*, know what I mean? When Lawrence Fishburne asks Keanu Reeves if he'll take the blue pill or the red pill?"

"*The Matrix*? What're you fuckin' talkin' about?"

Sid blinked. "It's a movie. It was really popular."

"A movie?"

"Yeah."

"I don't watch movies unless it's horror, man."

Sure. Or porn, right?

"Or fuckin' porn." Derek said this with some intensity as if he'd just read Sid's mind. "Red and blue make me think of cop cars lights. Fuck that shit."

Sid always thought Derek was in his own world, but now he realized more than ever that his brother was completely out of touch. Sex, drugs, and insanity were what revved Derek's engine.

"The thing here is, we want our branded red pills to be a huge homerun." Sid didn't expect Derek to care. "Peithos is stepping up to help men with erectile dysfunction...ED. It's a big deal for men who struggle with it."

"Not this guy."

"Lucky you." Sid shook his head and wished that he could wake from this bad dream. "Anyway, if all goes well with the results from this program you're participating in, the FDA will approve Libidonal and Peithos will give Cialis, Levitra, and Pfizer a run for their money."

"A hard-on pill?" Derek grinned. "A drug for my cock? Sign me the fuck up."

Sid sighed.

Derek stood up from the window and yawned. "Y'know, my roids actually increase my sex drive. Sometimes I get unexpected hard-ons."

TMI. Jesus fucking Christ...

"We won't be marketing illegal steroids as sex-drugs."

"Yeah, right. Well, I know all about sex-drugs and shit." Derek sounded happy. "I've mixed Ecstasy and Viagra together and sold it at nightclubs. They call it Sextasy or Trail-Mix. Chem-sex, brother. Taking that shit to increase the rush is what it's *all* about."

"Oh, I know what it's all about; methamphetamine, mephedrone, your GHB and GBL and alkyl nitrites—poppers. It all makes for elevating high-risk sexual activities under the influence. Dangerous on lots of levels."

Derek shrugged and laughed. "Tell it to someone who gives a fuck. Sex, drugs, and rock 'n' roll. Now *that's* up my alley."

Derek turned and walked away. Sid stayed in his car until Derek disappeared inside his apartment building. Then he pulled away and drove back to Peithos Labs.

He began to cry.

CHAPTER 6

Lynch's mood spiraled downward. He was on Shit Day #2 and heading for Shit Day #3 tomorrow if things didn't change for the better. Feeling grim was getting really old.

He'd received a morning phone call from Earl Tipton's wife, Angela, telling him that his old partner's health had taken another nasty turn. Tumors had spread throughout his brain and time was short. Earl had instructed his wife to tell Lynch to get his ass over there. Lynch said he'd visit Earl in the morning for sure.

For now, he was ready to call it a day. He'd done a lot of ugly work since he'd clocked in.

This job is always ugly...

He figured this was true every week, but today had delivered a constant theme: body parts. An upper torso turned up in a dumpster early in the morning before the bottom-half was discovered in a trash can a block away. Later, a woman chopped her husband's fingers off with an electric bread knife and then sliced his throat because he'd hidden her Amazon delivery of Sephora beauty products. Then, in the afternoon, some kids fishing at the Humboldt Park lagoon turned up a head, hands, and a foot—all wrapped in a burlap bag. One of the kids told Lynch the amputated pieces looked "wicked-cool."

The hotter it gets, the worse it gets...

Lynch decided to make a pitstop before going home. After dealing with the vicious heat and the hellacious details of dismemberment, he wanted something better than a microwave burrito. Stopping at Irene's Bistro, a favorite restaurant he hadn't been to lately, would be leagues better than Goat Horns.

Fuck that dive...

He dug Irene's. It was a cool place—bustling with a great vibe and a menu more original than most. Lynch loved the potato leek potage and the grilled hanger steak with a dry garlic rub. The thought of them made his gut rumble. He walked in and made small talk with the hostess, who asked him to wait while she checked to see if there was a small table available. As he stood scanning the room he was shocked to see...

Sandy?

What the hell was she doing here? Irene's was a bit off the beaten path and nowhere near her house.

Shit...my old house...

Sandy was deep in conversation and smiles with a younger-looking man in a nice suit. She threw her head back as she sipped a glass of red wine that Lynch suspected was probably her favorite, pinot noir. Her infectious laugh filled the restaurant.

Goddamn, she looks amazing.

Lynch's stomach tightened at the sight of her. She didn't notice his arrival and before the hostess could seat him, he rushed out of the restaurant.

Driving home, loneliness engulfed him. No way he'd ever enjoy Irene's Bistro again.

What was it about this week that just had it in for him? And it was only Tuesday.

Lynch's heart twisted. He remembered times when he'd put his hand up under her skirt as they sat next to each other in booths at their favorite restaurants. Visions of Sandy taking his hand and then sliding it under her panties with a naughty smile killed him.

Now some young stud would be finger-banging her...

He paused and wondered how many times he was going to beat himself up.

Fucking get over it already. You're already in a much better place.

What could he say? Sobriety made Lynch man up, and it made him feel regret. He felt like some cliché, an oh-woe-is-me douchebag. But he couldn't change how he felt, right?

He wished he had tried harder to make things work when he had the chance. Like most cops, Lynch didn't want to discuss the job at home, but he realized he could've discussed his *feelings*. He could have talked more and welcomed marriage counseling rather than just worrying about his own therapy. All Sandy asked for was for him to try to show he cared. He deserved the pain, knowing he had taken his wife for granted. He owned it and knew he couldn't have been more selfish.

Is it too late to say I'm sorry?

Lynch parked a block away from his garden apartment. He walked in and turned on a light. The place felt hot and muggy.

"Home, sweet home." Lynch whispered to himself as he locked the door behind him. Lynch swatted the air conditioner unit in the window with his palm and it kicked back on. He looked forward to getting in bed.

On days like this, he remembered Jack Daniels and pills making the horrific seem wonderful.

Fuck that.

He was grateful to be sober. He'd found sobriety steeled him even more for all of the atrocities he dealt with on the job. He possessed new clarity and appreciation for everything.

His mouth was suddenly dry. He went to the kitchen and poured a tall glass of water and sat down at the table to drink it. He relaxed and placed his wallet, mobile phone, and his holstered S&W .40 sidearm in front of him. He looked through bills and tossed junk mail, then picked up his phone and checked voicemail. There was a brief message from his parents in Peoria. He needed to get back to them soon. He hadn't spoken to them in two weeks.

Lynch was about to check some emails on his phone when it vibrated in his hand. Astroglide's number appeared on the caller-ID.

This day's full of surprises...

"Detective Lynch." He tossed his tie and unbuttoned his collar. Even with air conditioning blasting away, the humidity in the living room was still thick as it settled on him. He was so done with this nasty and sticky day.

"Yo. Gots'ta make this quick. I think I can link you up with that hooker. The one that was in the car? Gettin' a name 'n' shit. Rumors on the street about the shooter. Maybe get that for you 'cause I'm the shit."

Could Astroglide's voice annoy him more? The arrogant, high-pitched tone cut Lynch's patience to pieces. But she had his attention.

"Glad to hear. Guess you *can* get blood out of a muthafuckin' rock. Give me what you got."

"What you think? I'm stupid? Oh, I ain't gonna give you names over the phone." Astroglide's voice quieted. "I'll tell you in person, by my crib. No shit over the phone. Not no code, either."

Lynch's patience began to wane. "What's the difference? You're talking to me now. This isn't a game, Astro. Just give me the info. Come down to the station then. We can talk there."

"No way I'm goin' into a pig station. Word. I want a guarantee on gettin' nothing more than a fuckin' hand-slap. Ya feel me?" Astroglide sounded paranoid. "An' you gonna owe me one after I give you somethin'."

"We'll see." Lynch detected a funk rising up from his armpits and realized a shower might help both that and his exhaustion, which Astroglide was making worse. The day had burned him out. Would it ever end? "You gotta trust me."

"I don't trust pigs."

Lynch was tired of playing chess with street trash. "Well dickhead, you don't have a choice."

Earl's wise words popped into his head.

Sometimes we win, sometimes they win.

Lynch wanted Astroglide's info so he could close up this homicide and move onto whatever new disaster of human wreckage awaited him.

Gee, I can hardly fucking wait.

He suddenly felt a sensation in his gut, something that told him Astroglide was wasting his energy.

"Give me names. Or it's lockup time."

"'S all good. Meet me in the alley by my joint in the morning. You got the address."

"Can't, not early. I've got other work first in the morning." Nothing would divert him from his promise to see Earl. His temples throbbed, thinking about Earl and the backlog of paperwork waiting for him. "I'll be there sometime in the afternoon. Say around one-thirty."

"Sure. I be there."

"And hey, *Timmy*, just remember this—don't try and fuck me."

Astroglide was silent for a moment. "I hates it when anyone call me by my dead name, pig."

"Yeah? Well, you call me *pig and narc.* Really? What age are you living in?" Lynch was hot and played out. His tone grew testy. "One-thirty tomorrow. Be punctual and deliver."

"What da fuck's *punctual* mean?"

Why me?

Lynch squeezed his eyes shut. "Just be there and on time. 'Kay?"

"What I say? I'll fuckin' be there." Astroglide hung up.

Lynch walked back to the kitchen. His feet felt heavy and he was dragging ass. The humidity had ebbed in the apartment but sweat still sucked onto him. He wanted to scrub down in a long, cool shower—and scour his mind of the last two days. Fuck, he wanted to whitewash the last ten *years.*

It can't get any worse, right? Ugh. It's only Tuesday.

Lynch stripped down and kicked his moist clothes into a pile. He stepped into the small shower stall and welcomed the cold water running over his exhausted body. He regained some of his equilibrium as he relaxed and cooled.

You signed up for this, dude. To serve and protect, right?

Yeah, he knew that. He had to stomach and weather all the misery this wonderful bitch of a city poured onto him. Tomorrow morning's shower would be an opportunity to mentally prepare himself as he always did for all the horrors that might float his way on this August heatwave. But tonight, as he scrubbed and cooled down, his only job was to clear his mind enough to get some sleep.

CHAPTER 7

Annabella Tortellio watched the valet pull up with her Mercedes GT in front of the dance club. She couldn't believe how hot it still was outside, this many hours after the sun went down. Her white Capri pants, pink halter, and black heels were all skimpy, but not enough to keep her cool this steamy night. She tipped the valet a twenty and got behind the wheel. Her best friend Janet got into the passenger's seat.

"Let's go to the St. Regis. There's a cute bartender who works the bar there." Janet played with her red hair as she touched up her makeup in the visor mirror.

"I don't know, Jan. It's nearly one. I gotta get up in like five hours for work."

Annabella wasn't in the mood to party anymore. As she drove east toward the lake, her eyelids grew heavy and she yawned. She longed for her city loft and huge bed.

Put a fork in me already...

She had worked all day yesterday and the day before that—and still had gone out and partied both nights. She dreaded the thought of her alarm clock.

But Annabella prided herself on responsibility and running her business like a champ.

"Anna, you're the boss. Like your dad. Go in late. I mean, who's gonna say shit to Tico's daughter for rolling in whenever you want?"

Annabella frowned and sighed. "You know I don't want people scared of me 'cause of my dad. I'm my own woman here, okay?"

Janet laughed. "You can be your own woman, but you can't choose your parents. No way."

"Truth."

Annabella thought of her father and how lucky she was that he really did dote on her. She was his only daughter, and an exact replica of his true love—Mom—at the same age. She was twenty-five years old, curvy, with a tumble of black, curly hair, big brown eyes, and full lips. Her father liked to call her "Angel Face." Her mother often said Anabella's Sicilian genes were what made her so beautiful. Annabella always rolled her eyes at that.

Her father would drop Sicilian proverbs on Annabella that his Grandma Tortellio, Finuzza, had affectionately pushed on him. He'd first speak to them in Italian, but to this day she couldn't understand the language. So, he'd repeat them in English. One of the most common ones was, "A woman who is young and beautiful is never poor." Then he'd kiss the top of her head.

Annabella adored the man she and her brothers affectionately called Pop. Warm-hearted and loving, he was a devoted family man who always took the time to talk with her about all things good and bad in her world. Even though Google had archived hundreds of pages detailing the life of the ruthless, brutal, and iron-fisted Outfit chairman the press and police referred to as the "Meat Grinder," and that Amazon displayed a number of unauthorized biographies on him, Tico Tortellio was first and foremost her father, and she loved him unconditionally.

Love him with all my heart ...

Though it hurt her to see him portrayed in the press as a fucking psychopath.

She and her dad spoke openly about the things she'd read. Pop didn't deny anything, but he didn't exactly own up to much, either. He had once told her that the nickname "Meat Grinder" was just a mean joke some scumbag journalist had tagged him with.

Pop gave Annabella her own nail salon to manage. She already had the business degree, now she had an actual business. She always did her books...*by the book.* Her younger brothers, however, had always been too eager to become mobsters. She worried about the twins, those immature delinquents who saw themselves as social-media celebrities, riding the coattails of their infamous father, flaunting things in an ostentatious manner that would've gotten people in Cosa Nostra whacked in the old days. Groomed for years to run the unclean aspects of the family business under Pop's eye, they were successors to the Tortellio throne, heirs to the Outfit's next century.

God help them when they're adrift at sea without Pop. The shit they're getting in...

Annabella kept herself apart from incriminating specifics, preferring not to know anything of the rumored racketeering, money-laundering, guns, drugs, murders, and other noxious activities happening under her father's thumb. On some level, she knew they were all three bastards, but she played naïve because she wanted Pop and her brothers to remain—in her mind, anyway—the sweet men she'd always known them to be.

"If you want, I can drop you off at the St. Regis and you can take an Uber home."

"Maybe I won't have to take an Uber if that hot bartender puts me in his pocket for the night." Janet winked.

"I hope you have the best sex of your life, and I also hope you know I'm kinda jealous."

They laughed at that as Annabella drove away from the club and toward the St. Regis on the lakefront. She stopped at a red light and yawned. Damn she was tired. The sooner she got in her own bed, the better. The light turned green and she accelerated around a cab and drove toward the intersection. She was almost through when she caught oncoming large, bright headlights out of the corner of her right eye. Janet's scream cut off as Annabella's ears filled with the sudden roar of colliding metal and smashed glass. Horns blared as her car crumpled and bounced up into the air.

The airbag deployed and smashed into Annabella's face. Her seatbelt held while the car flew up and rolled. Pressure built up as pain began to course through her. The car flipped twice more before another collision wracked and crushed Annabella's body. The car bounced into an upside-down spin before coming to rest.

Annabella's head rang with noise, a ringing. Her nose still worked, she realized; with her face buried in Janet's scalp, she could smell her shampooed hair.

Janet? Janet?

Annabella tried to speak, but her lips refused to form her words. She tasted blood and it ran down her throat. She tried to see, but blood drowned her eyes. The noise in her head quieted, her eyes fluttered, and into the black she went.

CHAPTER 8

Derek Hoffman reclined on a beat-up couch in his apartment. He had just cycled, ingesting an oral anabolic steroid with a Muscle Milk chaser, then followed that with subcutaneous and intramuscular injections into his muscle-dominant regions—buttocks, lower arms, and abdomen.

He had a lot on his mind, thanks to the Ketamine rails he'd just snorted off his mobile phone. K was good like that—but Derek didn't always enjoy inward reflections.

Sid had better come through and help him get out of this.

Or else, little bitch brother is gonna get his.

Derek was never, ever going back to being incarcerated.

He'd spent four lost years—ages twelve to sixteen—at the Bradley Davis School for Delinquent Boys and Young Men.

Derek could see himself there, as if he were in that shitty place right now. Maybe it was the K taking him there, maybe it was just the way his mind worked. Demons haunted him, he knew too well. Drugs could only keep painful flashbacks at bay for so long. Sometimes, like now, they made them flood in...

Located in a remote area fifty miles from Salt Lake City, the Bradley Davis School for Delinquent Boys and Young Men was supposed to have more room and a better system than the crowded juvie centers in Cook County or Southern Illinois.

The school overflowed with kids from ten to eighteen. Utah had mountains and lots of space, that was for sure. Bradley Davis had boys and teens in residence who'd done everything from robberies and assault to rape and attempted murder. Run by middle-aged former military or corrections men, the staff were sadistic and devoid of sympathy, patience, and any legit teaching skills. And Mr. Tobias—the lethal, forty-something, ebony-skinned gym teacher, brought a new definition of cruelty to Derek's world.

Tobias was a former Golden Gloves boxer, Army grunt, and—in his younger Tupelo, Mississippi days—a felon. He punished Derek and the other boys with brutal workouts, trying to break them, using his drill-sergeant-like work ethic and terrifying demeanor to scare the boys straight.

But he wasn't the scariest thing at Bradley Davis.

Not by a long shot.

Above anything, the boys feared a small gang of four seventeen-and-eighteen-year-old boys known as The Rough Riders: Tommy Slint, Chad Dawes, John-John Pineda, and the leader of the bunch, Colin Miller.

The Rough Riders all came from the same town somewhere in Idaho. Sent to Bradley Davis for the gang-rape of a young woman, they entered the school as a pack of predators, stayed thick and tough, and soon took over the adolescent world inside the institution.

The Rough Riders played football and wrestled under the coaching of Tobias. They shaved their heads, lifted weights, ate whatever they wanted, and were taller, stronger, and meaner than everyone.

Derek, who hadn't yet achieved his full height, arrived at Bradley Davis with a busload of other fresh-blood boys. The newbies were dispersed among the ranks of the strong or weak of the school hierarchy.

"You'll learn the pecking order fast, brah," some veteran teen had told Derek the day he arrived. "The Rough Riders don't fuck with any of the big, strong, or just plain crazy dudes in here." The teen had looked Derek up and down and smirked. "But the weak kids...they're a prime target. The Rough Riders'll steal from you...and you'll hope that's all—if you're lucky."

Lucky? Derek thought about how his life hadn't been lucky at all then or now. Myriad violations awaited him.

Back then, Derek was tough, but he was a wiry, skinny kid. He had a short and violent fuse and despite attacking his seventy-year-old neighbor, he wasn't exactly a fighter. Within weeks, The Rough Riders had singled him out. They stole his personal items, blackened his eyes, bloodied his nose, dealt him various poundings. Derek didn't just roll over, though, he fought back with a new viciousness. He'd landed some punches and headbutts, but with the four-to-one odds, The Rough Riders were always too much.

None of the staff did anything to help Derek—or, for that matter, any other boys. It seemed the gang of four ruled with free rein.

One day, Derek and a dozen other boys spent their gym class being kicked around and driven into the dirt, boot-camp-style, by Mr. Tobias, who'd made them do hundreds of pushups, and half a dozen track laps outside in the blistering peak of summer. Afterwards, everyone fled to the showers but once they got there, everyone took their time winding down, hanging out in the locker room smoking, chewing tobacco, telling crude jokes, looking at the porn-laden contraband in girly mags, and hurling homophobic insults at one another.

But when The Rough Riders entered the locker room, everyone paused. Each one of the gang glowered at the other boys as they stripped and stood naked under the showerheads in the steaming, tiled room, scrubbing and joking among themselves. None of the other guys went near them. Some walked out while others, Derek included, waited with caution at the far end of the locker room for The Rough Riders to finish up.

The Rough Riders finally completed their showers and got dressed, slapping around a few boys before making their exit. Derek hung out alone as his remaining juvie mates jumped in, jumped out, and left; then he peeled off his sweat-soaked gym clothes and grabbed a towel. Sweaty, filthy, and tired, Derek was relieved to finally have the showers to himself.

Hot water blasted him. Steam rose and curled off his pale flesh as his head hung down in relaxation. But when he looked up, he was alarmed to see the bald heads and necks of The Rough Riders surrounding him. They were all glaring at him, looking as if they'd just been pulled from a boiling pot of water.

And they were all naked.

"We wanted to make sure you washed behind your ears." Colin Miller folded his large arms, as did the other three, all mimicking Colin's every move.

Derek grabbed a bar of soap and tensed.

The first blow hit him in the back of the head. There was a bright flash behind his eyes. His face slammed into the tiled wall, and he dropped to his knees as the spray diluted the blood running down his face and chest.

Derek could hear The Rough Riders laughing as he doubled over and writhed in pain. He immediately regretted not having taken a shower with the other kids or just left the locker room without cleaning up.

As Derek hunched over on all fours, Tommy Slint and Chad Dawes kicked him in the ribs with the balls of their feet until he collapsed, choking, on the shower room floor.

"Let's piss on 'im," John-John Pineda said.

"Great idea." Colin aimed his penis at Derek. The others did the same. Colin looked down at Derek and said, "One ... two ... three!"

Derek could smell the asparagus streams of urine cascading over him from all directions as he thrashed on the floor, clamping his jaw shut, struggling to hold his breath. Every second of the ordeal was a year to him. Then mercifully, they were finished.

"Get up, maggot." Colin yanked Derek up by his hair and pushed him under the scalding shower. "Clean that piss off, ya nasty fag."

Derek couldn't get the smell out of his nostrils. He wanted The Rough Riders dead; the same way he wanted Dad Hoffman dead.

"What should we do with this piece of meat?" Colin reached under the shower spray and clutched a fistful of Derek's hair.

"I got an idea." John-John said, as Derek wrenched his head around to see him lathering up his inflating penis with a soapy hand.

The Rough Riders grabbed Derek's arms and legs and lifted him off the shower room floor. He kicked and twisted, managing to shove a knee into Tommy's forehead and an elbow into John-John's neck, but The Rough Riders held him tighter while Colin yelled orders for the other three to force Derek down on his stomach.

"We gonna break this bitch in, right?" Colin voice rose up in pitch and he leaned over and grinned in Derek's face.

Derek screamed obscenities, but the more he fought, the wilder they became, snarling and shoving him down, stretching his legs open.

"Hey!"

Everyone froze. There stood Mr. Tobias at the entrance to the showers in his stained running clothes, whistle around his neck, scowling.

Derek blinked water away as he looked up over his shoulder and stared hard at Mr. Tobias, whose dark eyes moved over the group.

Good...good.

"Help me, please." Derek locked eyes with Mr. Tobias as The Rough Riders clutched him even more tightly. Surely, he would comprehend the situation—a gang of teenagers with a naked twelve-year-old.

Mr. Tobias gazed back at Derek and crossed his arms while The Rough Riders eyed him sideways. Then, Tobias looked past Derek and addressed The Rough Riders. "Don't forget to shut off the water and all the lights down here...once you're done playin' with your friend."

Derek screamed in protest as Mr. Tobias strolled away. He fought hard, clenching and tightening, trying in vain to deny access to his body. But they beat him into submission, forcing their way into him, taking turns, poking and penetrating with savage malice. They spat on Derek's back and then high-fived each other as they finished.

Then they left him, twisted in pain and disgrace on the floor of the shower room, his body battered and polluted by their assault, having killed every last microscopic bit of anything good remaining in Derek's spirit.

For months, Derek endured The Rough Riders' physical and sexual abuse. Though he tried ditching Phys Ed, Mr. Tobias always found him and kicked his ass back to gym. He never used the showers when The Rough Riders were around but they found ways to corner him.

So, since he couldn't avoid his gym class and he couldn't avoid The Rough Riders, Derek began a serious weightlifting program to make himself as intimidating as possible. By the time he turned thirteen, he promised himself he'd never take shit from anyone again and turned his focus into becoming badass *numero uno*—the ultimate attacker, because in his world, you were either a predator or a victim—and, as such, he quietly developed the strictest workout regimen in Mr. Tobias's class.

Right before he'd turned nineteen, Colin Miller completed his juvie sentence and was released, taking with him a high school diploma. John-John took over, but his rule only lasted a couple of months, until he, too, received his walking papers.

Suddenly, Tommy and Chad, who had believed their reign in juvie would last forever, were on their own. Without the alpha males of their pack, they couldn't enforce anything, and bigger boys began ganging up and beating on them. Derek kept an eye on them as he concentrated on building his strength, awaiting his opportunity for revenge.

It came late one night as the boys slept. Derek snuck out of his room and slipped through the dark hallway. Dodging the night monitor patrolling the school, he crept into Tommy and Chad's room carrying a laundry bag filled with five-pound weight plates he'd stolen from the gym.

Derek found it odd that they were sharing a single bed, nestled under a blanket, but it actually made things that much easier. He stood over them, staring down, and thought of the words that Colin Miller had said the first time.

We gonna break this bitch in, huh?

Miller's words tumbled in Derek's head, and he shook with rage.

My turn.

Derek whirled the bag over his head like a ceiling fan and smashed it down, slamming the pair unconscious with a fast, concussion-carrying blow that destroyed both their faces at once. He followed the first hit with two more and then tiptoed out. He dropped the bloody, weight-filled bag down a laundry chute and quietly retired to his own room.

The next day the two boys failed to appear at roll call. Correction guards found them with their faces crushed and their beds soaked with blood. An ambulance raced them to the hospital.

The staff soon discovered the laundry bag and the weights. They turned the entire school upside down and questioned everybody about the assault. As Derek was the primary suspect, he was grilled hard, but he denied doing anything, he didn't have a scratch on him and there was zero evidence he'd done it. None of the other boys suggested or admitted seeing anything; they were all delighted with this turn of events. All the boys knew Derek had done it. He became revered and feared. Derek had begun to display predatory traits, and his fellow inmates didn't want to risk him turning his temper in their direction—so they all left him alone best they could.

Tommy and Chad never returned to the Bradley Davis School for Delinquent Boys and Young Men. From what Derek was told, all the surgery in the world was unable to save their original features or correct the neurological damage they'd sustained, which had led to a number of physical impairments.

Derek had also fantasized about tracking down Colin and John-John, but he never got his chance. A year after nearly killing Tommy and Chad, he learned that the two were killed while trying to rob a liquor store in their Idaho hometown. He hoped they suffered long and hard before they died.

At sixteen, Derek was released with a stipulation to see a psychiatrist for the first six months post-release. His walking papers indicated good behavior and good grades even though he'd flunked out of all his classes and his days had become filled with occasional fights. He figured the administration wanted to be rid of him.

On the day Derek walked free, he clutched the lousy hundred bucks he'd earned, a backpack, and a bus ticket. But before he left Utah, he planned to take care of one last detail.

The school bus dropped him off at the bus station in a small town a few miles from the campus several hours before his bus to Chicago was scheduled to depart. After waiting in the terminal for half an hour, Derek put his belongings in a locker and walked a few blocks away to a strip mall with a pay phone and called a cab. He told the driver to take him to another gas station a mile from the Bradley Davis School for Delinquent Boys and Young Men, a three-dollar ride. Derek gave the driver forty dollars, asking him to wait and keep the meter running until he returned.

Evening fell as Derek stepped out of the cab. Derek knew the school staff would be busy during turnover to second shift. He walked down the stretch of road between the gas station and the school and stepped in a ditch fifty yards from the entrance, watching the afternoon-shift staff leave the buildings and walk to their cars as the overnight shift employees arrive.

He snapped to attention as he observed a Ford Mustang leaving Bradley Davis. It turned onto the road, driving toward him with its headlights cutting through the faint light. When the car drew close, he jumped up from the ditch, lifted his arms above his head, and hurled a small boulder at the windshield. It exploded and left a gaping black hole on the driver's side. The Mustang swerved violently. The car hit the ditch, its front-end ramming into a bank of hard dirt and gravel and then it flipped up and over, landing on its roof.

Derek looked around; there were no other vehicles in sight. He ran to the crashed car, kneeled down, and peered into the shattered driver's side window. Inside, Mr. Tobias was strapped into his seat, upside-down, moaning and wheezing, with his body contorted and the boulder next to his head on the interior of the caved-in roof. Bits of glass lacerated his face and head and he blinked and blinked again, struggling in vain to clear his vision as his eyes drowned in the blood pouring out of the wounds. His broken arms hung down, useless.

"Help me, please." Tobias pleaded through a mouth full of broken teeth.

Derek gazed upon him, assessing the bones protruding through skin from head to toe; it appeared he'd suffered broken facial, arm, leg, and rib bones.

He savored every second with satisfaction.

Don't forget to shut off the water and all the lights down here once you're done playin' with your friend...

Derek reached in and unhooked Tobias's seat belt. Tobias screamed in pain as he crashed down into the car. Derek stood up without a sound, pulled out a rag from his pocket, and walked to the rear of the Mustang, where he found the gas cap punched into a dented corner-panel. He unscrewed the plastic cap and stuffed the rag down into the gas tank. With a few inches of cloth to spare on the outside, Derek lit the rag and then began jogging the mile back to the gas station.

Derek heard a heavy *whoomph!* as something ignited and then exploded.

He never looked back.

As he neared the gas station Derek slowed his pace, walking confidently to the waiting cab, which soon pulled away in the opposite direction of Tobias's fiery wreck. The driver asked no questions and Derek said nothing.

He caught the bus to Chicago with time to spare.

"I got them. All of 'em. Fuckers."

Derek spoke his words aloud to his empty apartment as he returned to the present.

He snorted more K, hoping it would anesthetize things. It didn't help much.

The fucking present sucked as much as the fucking past.

CHAPTER 9

Lynch had been inside hospitals hundreds of times. He hated them. He figured most people saw them as sparkling-white places of pain and physical repair. For him, hospitals contained the deep red of fresh blood and the gray-brown of a Lake Michigan corpse. Alongside the disinfected, sanitary smells, he knew there lurked the stench of rotting flesh.

As the elevator climbed to the fifth floor, Lynch gave thanks that Earl was in the cancer ward at St. Cornelius. It was considered the leading hospital for...*everything*. Not that they'd be able to save Earl, but they'd do their best to make him as comfortable as possible. This was only a little consolation.

Lynch exited the elevator and walked down a hall bustling with nurses, orderlies, and doctors. He yawned. It made him tired just seeing the energy they all had so early in the morning. He had woken up before the sun, beginning his Wednesday much earlier than usual, but he'd been told that this visiting hour would be the best. Earl would be at his most alert and it wouldn't intrude on his family visiting time. So, Lynch got his ass up in the dark to rise and shine, keeping his promise to spend quality time with his old buddy before going in to the office. He also hit a McDonald's to bring Earl something to fuck up his diet—with love.

He entered the ward and saw the name Tipton, E. written on a small white sign mounted to the side of a door with a mesh-wire window. Lynch stopped but didn't peek in. He paused as his heart pounded and a nervous sweat slicked his palms.

Get a grip for the man.

Earl had been a rock for Lynch when he was spiraling. Now Lynch had to be Earl's rock.

He took a deep breath, mustering all the strength he had for his friend, and walked in. The sun hadn't come up yet but the glow from a streetlight illuminated the room through an uncovered window. A large floral bouquet sat on the windowsill, causing the room to smell like a flowery Band-Aid. Earl was resting, propped up so he could watch the television that was mounted in an upper corner of the room.

Lynch looked at Earl, who no longer resembled the tall, robust man he had worked with every day for over a decade. The trademark handlebar mustache had disappeared from his gaunt, skeletal face and his skin had turned a grayish yellow. Earl must've lost a hundred pounds since being diagnosed. Lynch steeled himself and walked up to the bed, glancing over at the weather report on Earl's TV.

"What's the forecast?"

Earl turned to Lynch. "Same ol' shit. It's gonna be hotter 'n hell again. A new high for the year. For the history books, even."

"No doubt. I'm feeling it hard out there."

Lynch leaned over, gave Earl an awkward hug, and patted him on the shoulder—nothing but bone where firm muscle once reigned.

He's only sixty...

With noticeable effort, Earl pointed the remote and clicked the TV off. "So, how's things in the wonderful world of Chicago crime?"

"Same shit." Lynch pulled up a chair and sat next to Earl's bed. "You know, shootings, body parts, homicidal wives, that stuff. And that history-breaking heat. It's too fucking hot outside...I can't stand it."

"Wish I was with you—heat be damned."

"Me too." Lynch looked away. Earl had been a two-and-a-half-pack-a-day unfiltered Camel man since he was a teenager and now a million coffin nails had come to collect. Lynch gave silent thanks he'd quit smoking—a credit to Sandy's insistence.

"Hope you're not getting bored out there."

"Bored?" Lynch laughed. "You know what it's like. I kicked Monday off with a murder and no solid suspects yet. I've been busier than ever now that ... you know. How you feeling?"

Earl smiled. "Not bad for a dead man."

Lynch frowned. He didn't want to hear it. "We're all praying for you back at the office. Teresa Hernandez told me to give you a kiss. I said I'd just mention it. Ha!"

"Proud of that one. She's turning into an amazing Chief of Detectives." Earl managed a weak smile. "She came by to see me."

"Yeah? Did she tell you tell you she's been expanding our sensitivity training?"

"No. Didn't get the memo from Hernandez, but seeing as she's both gay and on the board at Center on Halsted, she's always up to speed. What's the latest?"

"She says LGBTQ is going to be known as 'LGBTQIA' soon."

"I'm sorry, the *what*? The whole alphabet?"

"LGBTQIA: Lesbian, Gay, Bisexual, Transgender, Queer, Intersex, and Asexual."

"Hey...I welcome positive change even if I can't keep it all straight —no pun intended." Earl smiled. "You 'n' me, we roll with the changes. We don't judge...we've always been, 'you do YOU and I'll do ME', right? Everyone deserves to be happy in this life."

"Amen." Lynch half-smiled. "Anyone else drop by?"

"Oh, other cops I know from around the city and even some from the burbs. Family and friends."

"Glad to hear it." Lynch wasn't sure what to say next. The brief silence made him feel awkward and self-conscious.

Earl broke the spell. "What's in the bag?"

Lynch looked down at the paper bag in his hand. He'd forgotten he'd stopped by McDonald's to pick something up for Earl. "Oh, I got you breakfast. An Egg McMuffin. You know, the old reliable."

Earl smiled and wheezed. "Thanks, pal. Just set it on the side for me if you would. I haven't had an appetite lately. The only thing I hunger for these days is morphine."

"Okay." Lynch placed the bag on the bedside table. "They must feed you something, right?"

"They do. Last thing I recall tasting good was Ensure." Earl waved at the equipment attached to him. "These machines are supposed to help me out, but they don't do shit. The only thing that feels good is morphine and the oxygen tank, but I hate having tubes up my nose."

"Guess you're staying away from the usual four food groups?" Lynch attempted to smile.

Earl mustered a laugh. "Ha! You can't forget those."

"Coffee, hot dogs, bourbon, and cigarettes."

"That's right." Earl smiled and took a shallow breath. "Unfortunately, I don't like coffee anymore. Weird. I do miss beer and dogs at our Cubs games, though."

"Me too." Lynch's heart fractured. "You catching the games? Cubbies aren't doing well at all. This is what we get for our blasphemous ways."

Earl snorted. "Yeah, yeah...I've been watching the games in here. Homeboys breaking our hearts again, as usual. Whatta joke. Good or bad, you and I got a thing for Wrigley we'll never abandon. We don't gotta defend shit to the haters, yeah?"

"Amen."

"Can you believe I still itch for a smoke? Sick, huh?"

"I hear ya. I still want them too. Sometimes I want a beer and a shot and a Vicodin." Lynch shrugged. "It's all about discipline and willpower at this point."

"I'm really glad you got off the pills and booze. I hated seeing you so low, Don. Holding up okay?"

"Yeah, I am. Feelin' back to my old self again. Stronger. Better. You really were there for me when everything fell apart. Thank you." Lynch thought about the losses he'd suffered on his way to sobriety. He sighed. Self-pity was the one thing he still grappled with, but he had it by the throat. But wasn't ready to let go of all of everything that came before. "Thing is, I wish I coulda kept it all together before it cost me Sandy."

"You're a survivor. At least you're not in my shoes, pal."

Earl's words hit him in the gut. Lynch nearly flinched from an odd combination of guilt and relief. He hated seeing Earl this way and was also grateful that he'd caught his own cancer early. He wished he could personally pull the disease out of his old partner.

"Cancer's a scary, heartless bitch." Lynch shook his head. "I'm here minus a testicle *and* a wife. For a long time, I felt like I wanted to bite it."

"Don't ever say that again." A frown crossed Earl's face and he grabbed Lynch's hand. "I got this shit in my lungs, and before you know it, it's in my brain and my bones. I'm in pain you don't want to imagine, but you don't hear me whinin' about it. I'm glad for the life I had. You should be grateful, Donnie. Bad shit happens. But you still got your health. Even after cancer. You're alive. Don't shrug that off. *Ever.*"

Lynch swallowed and nodded, knowing everything Earl said was true. He didn't want to be some asshole playing the victim card in front of a dying friend. "Sorry, Earl. I said I felt like it once. But I'm glad to be here, sober and alive, and I'm especially glad to be here with you. It's just ... I fucked up good. It still hurts knowing that's on me, y'know?"

Earl gave a sympathetic nod. "You miss her."

"Like I miss my left ball."

At that, the old partners began to laugh and kept at it for a good minute with tears coming out of their eyes.

"Personality and courage trump balls—and you got it all, my friend. Laughter's the best medicine, someone said." Earl wiped his eyes. "Feels good."

"It's cathartic, Earl. And I needed that...especially with the way this week has started." Lynch exhaled for what felt like the first time all week. "Anyway, Sandy. Been thinking about her a lot lately. Saw her last night, actually...at that place I told you I liked, Irene's Bistro? She was having a grand fucking time with some guy who looked half her age."

"Ouch." Earl blinked. "This is tough love, pal, but you gotta know Sandy's doin' her thing. Maybe you need to start cutting a new path for yourself and play the field."

"Yeah ... well, I'm not so sure about that, buddy." Lynch sat back and crossed his arms. "Guys like you and my dad managed to stay married all those years while working seven days a week and loving the cop life. How?"

"The secret is finding a woman who tolerates your bullshit." Earl raised his bony right arm under the blanket that covered his lower half. It looked as if a teepee was over Earl's waist. He grinned. "It also helps to be hung like a goddamn mule."

Lynch snorted out laughter all over again. "You fuckin' wish!"

Earl laughed and wheezed. It warmed Lynch to see his old spirit return for a moment. Earl crossed his arms across his lap and his laughter subsided. "Donnie, you're still young and eventually, your heart will be right as rain."

"I wanna see *you* right as rain." Lynch leaned toward Earl's bed.

Earl offered a smile.

"Y'know..." Donnie collected his thoughts. "Aside from wanting a normal marriage, this business of being a cop, it ain't easy. We both know what being a detective means. It seems like even when you're off the job and away from the shield, people judge you. They avoid you if they hear you're a cop. It's not how it used to be. Not everyone was a cop hater the way they are today. It's gotten worse with social media clips of citizens refusing to cooperate at traffic stops, making cops look like a buncha menacing assholes."

Earl shrugged. "There's that, yeah. And it also doesn't help our image when officers shoot unarmed citizens in the back in broad daylight—not to mention at night."

"I know, I know. There isn't anyone in Chicago who's gonna forget about Laquan McDonald."

"Shot sixteen times by one of our own." Earl exhaled long and shook his head. "And most of those shots hit him in the back. You know what that means."

"Of course." Donnie shook his head. "Then there's George Floyd and the fallout from that. A white cop kneeling on a Black man's neck... killing him. That didn't help the image of any cops in this country."

Earl nodded. "Those scumbags should've never been given a badge. To that type, *Serve and Protect* are just words to ignore. When you give someone like that a badge and a gun, the results are beyond horrific. And the way the country looks at our city here...it's a fuckin' shame."

"As much as I hate it, I sometimes understand why they call us *pigs*."

"We've always been called pigs, Don. Insults flung at you, me, all cops out there. And now? Forget about it...it's worse. We're all stereotyped across the board. People don't respect the police." Earl closed his eyes. "Angela give you an update?"

"Yeah. She said things weren't looking too good. The word is they don't expect you to recover."

Lynch thought he was going to lose it, thinking of how Angela had in fact told Lynch that Earl could go at any time now.

"That's true, pal." Earl opened his eyes and gave Lynch a crooked smile. "My watch is gonna wrap up soon."

Lynch blinked a few times and placed his hand on Earl's chest. "How d'ya...like, how you feel about this?"

"I'm good with it, Donnie. I've accepted it and I'm not scared. The only thing breaking my heart is not seeing my kids really come into their own." Earl paused for a moment and shrugged as if contemplating whether or not to cry. His breathing was labored but he smiled at Lynch. "I hope my family will be all right when I'm gone. That's my only concern."

Lynch patted Earl's bony chest. "They'll be so good. I promise. Angela and the kids are strong."

"You got that right."

Another awkward pause then Lynch sat back. "I'm sorry. I gotta get outta here. Assholes to attend to. Good to see you, partner."

"You, too. Come back if you can, okay?"

"Bet your ass I'll try." Lynch stood and kissed Earl on the forehead. He walked to the door and turned. "I'll see if I can bring you good news next time."

"Go Cubs."

Lynch smiled. "Go Cubs."

He waved goodbye.

Lynch made his exit and walked to the elevator, barely able to restrain the hot tears that threatened his vision.

This fucking life ... the hits just keep coming.

CHAPTER 10

His mobile phone's persistent vibration roused Tico from sleep. Eyes closed, he reached out a bear-like hand and picked it up. "Who's this?"

"This is St. Cornelius Hospital calling." A woman's voice, calm and cautious. "Mister Tortellio?"

Hospital?

How'd they get his number? He sat up. He glanced at his alarm clock. It was nearly six on Wednesday morning. "Yeah. What d'ya want?"

"Mr. Tortellio, we couldn't get a number for you until now. There's been an accident involving your daughter, Annabella."

Tico was wide awake now. His heart jacked up. "What happened?"

There was a pause. "There was a car accident. Your daughter Annabella was involved. She's alive. Can you come here?"

Tico whispered, trying to control his voice so he wouldn't wake his wife, Valentina. "Car accident? What happened to my girl? You tell me right fucking now, *WHAT* happened?"

"Sir, I can't—"

"Y'know who the fuck I am? Any idea?" Tico's impatience soared with his heart rate.

"Mr. Tortellio, I understand this call is upsetting. I'm not being vague to hurt you. Please calm yourself and come to the hospital."

Tico took a breath. "Okay, who's the fucker in charge over there?"

Another pause. "Ask for Doctor Weinstein. He's been with your daughter since she was admitted and he's still on duty now."

Tico hung up the phone. He sat on the edge of the bed for a moment, thinking. How in the hell was he going to tell Valentina? Before he could figure that out, his phone vibrated again. He picked up. "Yeah?"

"Dad, it's me, Liuni." He sounded flustered. "You hear about Anna yet?"

The sound of Liuni's voice instantly made Tico's blood pressure rise. He had finally caught up with the twins after his visit to the Tortellio private club the day before. One of Tico's envoys had found them at a Tortellio-owned gentlemen's club on the North Side and tipped Tico off. He and his enforcers had driven straight over and rolled in like a tornado. He'd found the twins in a VIP lounge, coked-out and drunk, with five strippers. It was one in the afternoon.

Tico didn't know what made him angrier; the twins being MIA for days or discovering them at a strip club or seeing them fucked up so early in the day. He didn't take time to break it down. He dragged them out to the sidewalk and beat their asses silly, slapping them around and berating them as his rage erupted. Then, he sent them to his house via Uber and followed them home in the Lincoln. Once there, he hammered it into their heads that he'd be personally taking them around the city to instruct them by example on their Outfit roles. After dinner, when he finally let them loose that night, he made sure they understood that for the foreseeable future, they were under his thumb.

And now this shit...

"The fuckin' hospital just called but didn't say squat. You know somethin'?"

"Yeah. One of the cops at the scene is one of ours. He called my cell and told me Anna was hit by a drunk driver somewhere downtown. It's not good."

Tico's hands flexed. "Hit by a drunk fuckin' driver?"

"Yeah...and the drunk bastard's just fine, too. Anna, she's all messed up, Pop. Her best girlfriend's dead." Liuni paused. His voice cracked as he tried to speak again. "Vito and I are on our way to St. Cornelius. Can you meet us there, Pop?"

"I'll be right there." Tico looked over at his wife and whispered as quietly as possible. "That cop tell you her condition?"

"Like I said, messed up. She won't wake up. It's bad."

Tico closed his eyes and rubbed them with his sausage fingers. "I'll see you there."

He hung up the phone and sucked in a breath, barely restrained himself from punching a bedroom wall. He wished to Christ he was dreaming all this.

Valentina stirred and mumbled something and then sat up and spoke in a sleepy voice. "Who's that on your phone?"

Tico turned and for a moment, he found himself unable to speak, helplessness mixed with rage spiraling him down into depths rivaling the Mariana Trench—which Annabella, of all people, had once explained to him was the deepest and deadliest chasm in the ocean. The numbness crept over him as he clawed to regain a sense of power in his life, a sense of control.

There wasn't anything in the world Tico feared more than harm to his children, unless it was seeing his wife's heart break. He crawled across the mattress and pulled Valentina to him. "C'mere, hon. I've got somethin' to tell ya."

He held his wife close tight and as he told her about the accident. Valentina collapsed, sobbing and struggling with hysteria in his embrace.

Would Annabella be all right? Are these doctors the best? Not even divine intervention will help that drunk prick when I find him.

CHAPTER II

Derek sat in a small room in Peithos Labs at St. Cornelius Hospital. Nine in the morning on Wednesday. This was bullshit, but he needed that green more than ever, didn't he? He hadn't slept one wink last night. No, he'd partied through until daybreak, then just sucked it up and surprised himself by arriving on time at 6:30 in the morning. Still buzzed. Drowsiness was a constant, but he'd deal. Now he was looking around, wanting stimulation, a hard fucking workout...he thought he might need to rub one out somewhere to calm down.

What a bunch of shit. Just wanna get paid...antsy as fuck and want outta here already.

Sid had personally walked him through the check-in process and roll call, had his gym bag stored away in a locker. Derek had signed all the necessary paperwork for the program—every page full of false info—except for his name.

Dressed in a hospital gown, slippers, and a pair of boxers, Derek sat across from Sid, who looked as nervous as an altar boy on a bishop's lap.

"You gotta promise me you're gonna be cool in here." Sid spoke in a hushed voice, dripping paranoia. "I had to get creative to fast-track you into this study group overnight. I substituted my own blood and urine samples in place of yours so you'd come up clear. All the paperwork is taken care of, and thankfully, my colleagues haven't even thought anything of any of it. And I used your real name so you can cash that Peithos check. But we're not related. Understand?"

Derek yawned and folded his arms.

Boring.

"Yes, I fuckin' understand, already, little brother. Shit, you never wanted to be related to me anyhow."

Couldn't Sid shut the fuck up already? His brother's concern didn't mean shit to him. Derek's thoughts shifted to more important things; like how he'd missed his workout ritual. Two days in a row, wasted. The thought infuriated him.

"If you behave and act like a normal participant, you'll walk out with that five grand," Sid told him. "But you absolutely must play along—and play along nicely. My ass is really on the line here."

"You want some cheese to go with that whine?"

Sid frowned and flushed. His tone changed. "This isn't jerk-around time. You want your money, you blackmailing fuck? Then you better do as you're asked and keep cool. If you get booted from this thing, you'll be out of that cash and if someone connects the dots, I will absolutely lose my job. There'll be no other way you'll get this kind of cash from me...no matter what you try and threaten me with."

Derek looked at his brother, knowing he could snap the little bastard's neck so easily. He smiled at the thought of doing just that if Sid said one more word that irked him.

Derek watched Sid take a breath and lock eyes with him. "I need to know what drugs you've been taking up until today."

"None-ya."

"What?"

"None-ya." Derek grinned.

"What's *none-ya*, mean?"

"None-ya fuckin' business." Derek watched Sid's eyes narrow and his mouth compress into an angry line.

Uptight little prick.

"Goddamn it, Derek. It *is* my business! This isn't a game." Sid hit the table with the palm of his hand. "It's really, *really* important to know what drugs you might be on or have recently taken. Y'see, you could damage yourself beyond repair. You'll be taking untested Libidonal pills; that's why you're here, right? No humans have taken it yet."

"Yeah, so?"

"It's not kids' stuff here."

"You're not scaring me."

"Well, if nothing else, do you want your dick to go numb?"

"What are you talking about?"

"This Libidonal—it's the new, next level in E.D., designed to give men even better results than Viagra or any other competitor out there. Used correctly, your blood and brain should amp up and make your genitalia the center of the universe."

Derek tugged on his goatee, imagining his man bits becoming even more important than he already believed them to be.

"Anything else in your system could fuck that up."

"Nothin's gonna make my dick go numb."

"Listen, what other drugs are in your veins is relevant to your heart and your bloodstream and your whole system. Knowing that is relevant to your safety. As much as I don't want to care, I do. I don't want you to leave here in a body-bag, right? So just tell me exactly what you've been doing over the last twenty-four hours so I can advise you on what *not* to do."

Derek sighed. Who was this moralizing, do-gooder asshole? What did Sid expect him to say? Was he supposed to divulge all the fun he'd ingested only to get a lecture on how evil and bad drugs are?

Fuck that.

The last time Derek had seen a doctor, he'd come clean about what he was taking on a daily basis. The doctor had been most concerned about the anabolic steroids and had warned Derek of the consequences of mixing them with recreational drugs. The doc said they aggravated the antisocial and sexual demons in Derek's head. He said *demons,* because Derek had confessed that he had very dark and animalistic thoughts and urges. Upon hearing that, the doc had recommended Derek seek professional treatment for his aggression.

Been there, fucking done that.

Derek had told the doctor that he actually had been to therapy and his former therapist was worthless. He didn't need a doctor—or Sid, for that matter—bothering him with warnings and advice.

Derek returned his thoughts to the present and stared Sid down. "I don't wanna hear some speech."

"Look, I'm not giving you a speech. It's just important that I know, man." Sid looked concerned. "Libidonal's extremely experimental. I'm warning you of the potential it may have to go ballistic in your system if it's taken with a certain pre-existing body chemistry."

Derek looked at Sid. Sure, he figured he could tell him what he'd done. Why not? It didn't matter what Sid thought or had to say. Derek did whatever he wanted, with or without warning labels. And he was doing this fucking program no matter what. The money was all that mattered.

"What have I done lately?" A grocery list of pills, narcotics and everything else he'd pumped into himself ran through his head. "Shit, I don't know. I did some blow last night, drank some ... ummm, took some GHB, my roids, some bio-engineered growth hormone stuff. I don't know ..."

Sid shook his head. "You're a walking, talking, hydrogen-bomb."

"Thanks." Derek smiled. "My kid brother actually gets me now."

"I'm serious. I'll bet your heart is ready to explode and you're not even thirty yet. You've known for years your aggression was off the charts, even before you ever tried playing with chemicals. It's just going to repress your serotonin and make you even more prone to violence."

Derek shrugged. "Hey coach, you're pretty observant. Don't act like you give a shit. And if you're gonna read me the riot act next about my balls shrinking, my liver dying, acne, my hair falling out, and the slope of my Cro-Mag brow, you can skip it. I've heard it all a million times."

"I'm not here to read you the riot act. And I *do* give a shit, dummy. I'm trying to inform you of some potential dangers with the stuff you take *and* the stuff you're about to take. If you're not careful, Libidonal could send you over the edge. Maybe kill you. What sex-drugs have you taken recently?"

Derek thought of his favorites. "Well, there's Ecstasy...if that's considered a sex drug. I mean, it makes me wanna lay some serious pipe on every bitch I see. I take that and some Viagra. Usually, I throw in some Oxy and Vicodin...sometimes with Special K. Oh, yeah, you look shocked."

Sid took a deep breath. "Here's a friendly warning. If you're on anything like Viagra or MDMA—whether it's Ecstasy or Molly—there's likely gonna be serious side effects with Libidonal in the mix. Hopefully, they're dissipating out of your system."

Derek grinned. *Side effects*. He liked the thought of that and didn't care about risk. He looked at it all as a bonus for sex and body sculpting.

"Sex drugs are hot on the street. None of them have killed anyone."

"You know what? Two years ago, when we first tested Libidonal on monkeys, they humped everything nonstop until they died. Major heart attacks and whatnot." Sid picked up a pen and tapped the table-top. "It was reformulated and after more testing, monkeys took it fine, showing promise that it could work on humans. It's since been revised again and now it's deemed safe for human testing. I say that, but just know that this maiden voyage could go anywhere. Being the broken record that I am, I'm telling you one last time, if you have sexual and mood stimulants or any hormone-altering drugs in your system, there could be serious consequences."

"Don't worry about me getting too horny. I won't be fucking anyone since there's nothing but guys on this floor. I'm not gay." Derek frowned at the memory of his days in juvie. The Rough Riders. What they called him, what they did to him. "Fucking sausage-fest 'round here."

Sid looked away and then locked eyes with Derek again. "There's nothing illegal that we didn't catch when we inspected your gym bag?"

Derek laughed and lightly tapped his right leg to feel the Ziploc freezer bag taped to the inside of his right thigh. It was full of Oxy,

Ecstasy, Vicodin, and a vial of anabolic steroids. This variety pack of illegal fun had all come from his dealer, Astroglide, who always seemed to have everything a man could want.

For Derek, this program offered an opportunity to score some side-hustle cash. People liked to party, right? He planned on selling the various pills he'd smuggled in to any takers in the program. The steroids were for his own use. He had to load himself on a regular basis if he wanted to maintain his gain.

A dose a day while the gym's away ...

"Naw, there's nothing in my bag." Derek placed his right hand on his heart. "Honest."

Sid sighed and rose from the table. "I've said my piece then. I'll be supervising the program during the day, so come to me if you need anything. At night, just take the pills they give you, and only talk to the staff if you've got a problem. Other than that, you can spend your free time watching movies, reading, playing games, whatever. Not a bad gig." Sid stood up and looked down at Derek. "Listen, I wanna know that when this is over, you'll never say a word to Gloria. You promise me that."

Derek smiled. "Promise."

"I hope so. You're a real beast, you know that?"

Sid walked around behind Derek and out the door, slamming it behind him. Derek frowned. Was that just a diss from Sid? Derek had his own principles—fucked up as they were—his own pride, and he never allowed anyone to ever insult him without giving them a beat-down. Still, he didn't feel the need to beat his kid brother. After all, he had the dirt on Sid and could always hang it over his head again.

Two Libidonal pills later, Derek sat in a room with the other men in the study—twenty of them, ranging in age from eighteen to fifty-five. This was a voluntary meeting; an in-depth presentation on Libidonal for anyone interested. The subject of sex drew in most of the participants, and Derek thought it might be a cool distraction. Plus, sex was of great interest to him.

Then the doctor began to explain what Libidonal was designed for and what Peithos Labs hoped to do with it, and the info-dump was not only boring Derek beyond measure, it began to make him angry. Derek's attention and temparment were fleeting. His eyelids began to droop.

Derek fixed his sleepy eyes on a large poster of male reproductive organs in cross-section on display at the front of the room. On the wall next to it was a chalkboard with scrawled words:

SIGMUND FREUD
The Energy of the Id

Sex instinct
Creation
Man's most primitive drives
Aphrodite: Greek goddess of sex and beauty
Eros: Greek god of love and procreation

ORIGINS of SEXUALITY
Gods/Goddesses and Contemporary Terminology

Himeros: Greek God of Sexual Desire
Peitho: Greek goddess of persuasion and seduction
Priapus: Greek god of sexual intercourse, genitalia, fertility, and lust

Libido (def): Latin for pleasure and lust
Aphrodisiac (def): Greek (Aphrodite) Food, drink, or drug that stimulates sexual desire

What the fuck was he reading here? Sex Ed and Greek history class? This shit was for nerds with big heads, like his weak-ass brother.

Sid's gotta love sending me back to school just to piss me off...

Derek studied the assholes sitting around him with disdain.

A small Asian man in a white lab coat and glasses entered the room and jabbered away about erectile dysfunction, penile anatomy, the physiology of an erection, the FDA, and better sex through chemistry. Some gibberish about sexual stimulation being both physical and cognitive followed. The human brain was supposedly the most important sex organ of all. Derek was skeptical of everything he heard.

Lab Coat explained that Libidonal would heighten male sexual arousal. Test subjects would find that during tumescence, the veins in the penis might become more prominent with a tightening that could cause retraction of the foreskin and expose the glans penis in uncircumcised men. Other side effects could include pre-ejaculatory fluid emissions, testes swelling/testes ascension, a tensing and thickening of the scrotum, noticeable and continuous sexual arousal, and pupil dilation.

Lab Coat pointed to a cross-section showing what he explained were two *corpora cavernosa* close to the top surface of the penis, and the *corpus spongiosum*, which surrounded the urethra near the bottom surface.

"Erectile tissue, gentlemen," Lab Coat turned to the participants, "which has numerous vascular spaces that all become engorged with blood. A clitoris has these as well. Specific to the penis, when you experience an erection, the *corpora cavernosa* becomes engorged with arterial blood...we call this process *tumescence.* This provides physiological stimuli, the most common being sexual arousal. There's also the *corpus spongiosum* here, that's the lone tubular structure sitting right below the *corpora cavernosa* and it also becomes engorged with blood—but not so much as the *corpora cavernosa...*"

Lab Coat went on for forty minutes.

The constant cock-talk sounded like mush to Derek. He didn't want to be here for sixth grade Sex Ed. It certainly didn't turn him on. He wanted a nap.

After Lab Coat finished talking, the study group was escorted into a casual dining room. Everyone was given a light lunch with a glass of water and two bright-red oval Libidonal pills in a small paper cup. Derek gave a blasé ear to Lab Coat, who explained that most of the pills were the real thing, but some were placebos. After an hour, the men would receive physical checkups on their heart rates, blood pressure, and eyesight.

From what Derek retained, the Libidonal pills were twenty-five milligrams each. The men had received two pills in the morning and these two more pills in the afternoon—and that was it for the day. Daily dosage wasn't to exceed 100 milligrams.

Derek cared nothing about dosage. He didn't plan on taking *any* of these pills. Rather, he was scheming to hoard all of them. He wanted to be the first to get this on the streets. He hoped to sell them to clubbers or swap them with his dealer for a new batch of roids as soon as he finished the study. If this drug was as potent as Sid had hyped it to be, Derek figured even a handful could command serious cash.

Cash...always a stone in his shoe. Roids cost a fortune nowadays and Derek wasn't happy about spending his last three-hundred dollars on six-hundred tabs of Dianabol. All the drugs he used to chemically etch his body, not to mention the recreational drugs, made for an expensive lifestyle.

Derek looked around the lunchroom as he finished up his water and snack. No eyes or security cameras watched him as he stealthily tucked the Libidonal pills in the Ziploc bag taped to his leg, next to the Oxy, Ecstasy and Vicodin he'd brought from home.

He scanned the lunch tables looking for someone who might be interested in purchasing some of his recreational drugs. No one made eye contact with him. He knew he stuck out like an exotic, predatory thing and he thought they all looked like pussies. If he wanted to paint the walls red with them, he knew he could. Instead, however, he corralled his thoughts of violence and focused instead on greed.

His eyes came to rest on a balding, fifty-something man, who smiled and wiggled his fingers at Derek. "Hi, handsome. I'm Henry."

Is this bitch hittin' on me?

Derek flexed his jaw. "Fuck off."

Henry frowned and looked down at his lunch tray.

Derek got up and walked around the Peithos Labs floor, widening his search for potential customers. He peeked into television rooms, game rooms, and patient dorms, but didn't see anyone approachable.

He walked past more rooms, through the lobby, down a side hallway, in search of a bathroom. The bag taped to his leg was rubbing against his crotch and making it itch. His skin was as chafed as his temperament. Everyone and everything began to offend him in some way.

Nearing a men's room, Derek saw a nurse approaching, pushing a stainless-steel cart with a tray full of paper sample cups. As she passed the men's room, a young man in scrubs came out and called her name. The two began to chat. The guy said something in the woman's ear; she giggled. The guy invited her to sit on a nearby bench in the hallway and she left the cart behind and walked away with him.

Derek moved over to the cart with slow, deliberate steps, and when he was sure the couple weren't paying attention, he swiped a fistful of paper cups, then disappeared into the men's room.

The smell of feces filled his nostrils. Derek scanned the restroom, checking. Of the six stalls against one wall, the first was occupied. Beneath the partition, Derek saw a pair of slippers and the bare calves of a study patient who bellyached hard as he worked something out in the stall.

With quick steps, Derek entered the last partition against the wall, furthest from the stranger. Inside the stall, he looked in his hand and smiled. He'd nabbed four sample cups with two Libidonal pills in each. He'd been given two pills earlier to start the program, and he had pocketed them. He now had a grand total of ten bright red pecker drugs.

Astroglide...

That was where the money was. Oxy and Molly were selling at an all-time high on the street. He knew his dealer, Astroglide, would want these pills and he could make him pay top dollar.

Derek flushed the toilet, masking the sound of the plastic drug bag he pulled away from his leg. He put the Libidonal in the bag along with the other drugs, wrapped it all up, and re-taped the bag to his leg.

The occupant of the first stall was continuing his war with the toilet as Derek left the restroom. Cautiously, he looked down the hallway. The nurse and her guy had disappeared with the cart. Derek exhaled and grabbed his thigh, reassured that his plunder was still in place. He walked down the hall, wanting to get back to his room. As he approached the lobby, a commotion ahead got his attention. As he drew closer, he stumbled upon erotic chaos.

What the hell?

A dozen men from the study group were walking around with openly displayed erections. Some were masturbating, unabashed, and some kissed each other, while others filled the lobby with hysterical laughter and anguished cries.

Derek watched nurses, guys in scrubs, and Sid running around trying to calm and restrain the boisterous test subjects. Two men in lab coats rushed past him, yelling at each other.

"Libidonal is adversely affecting this group!"

"You think?! I told you and corporate that this program was premature. The test simians went off the rails just like this before. My reported observations went ignored and everyone announced that their reactions had 'improved.' *You knew!* Corporate knew!"

"Stop blasting me with your self-righteous crap and help me get this under control."

Derek leaned against a wall in the hallway. He watched a participant dry-humping a chair as a voice came over the intercom ordering security to come to the Peithos Labs lobby, stat. Derek bristled with disgust, watching as more men—intoxicated and aroused by the little red aphrodisiacs—poured into the lobby and adjoining hallways.

Night of the Living Hard-Ons...

Derek chuckled as he watched Sid vainly barking orders to the Peithos crew as they tried to corral and control the horny mob.

Someone tapped his shoulder from behind. He whirled around and faced the balding, fifty-something man who'd wiggled his fingers at him in the lunchroom earlier. Aside from a pair of hospital slippers, the man was now naked. He stroked his erect penis while staring into Derek's face.

"I'm Henry."

The man ejaculated. Thick gobs of semen spurted out and hit the front of Derek's gown and his left forearm.

Derek watched the ejaculate pop, feeling the wet warmth spatter his skin. He looked down at the greasy, white splotches. For a moment he closed his eyes, almost blacking out as his body filled with abrupt fury. He was triggered again; images from his traumatic time at the Bradley Davis School for Delinquent Boys and Young Men choked his thoughts. He opened his eyes and clenched his fists.

Then Derek went *postal.*

Derek pummeled the man with fists as hard as granite. Henry fell backwards, his right hand still clutching his penis as his skull crashed hard on the tiled floor.

"Fucking round-mouth fuck!"

Derek bent down and battered Henry's face, wanting to pound his head into jelly, his anger rising still further as the small man bled and came again at the same time.

Derek bellowed, stood straight up and stomped on Henry's body.

A nurse ran up to Derek, ordering him to stop. He ignored her. Surging with rage, he focused on the destruction of the bastard who'd soiled his skin. The nurse grabbed Derek's right arm, attempting to pull him off Henry. Derek yanked her up by her hair, threw her, and slammed her into a hallway wall.

"I'll kill all of you!"

Derek turned back to Henry, but as he raised his foot to strike, six large men dressed in black Peithos Labs security uniforms charged toward him.

As he shifted his stance to fight the security guards, Derek remembered the bag of fun taped to his leg. What if they subdued him and then found it? They'd find all the drugs and turn him over to the real cops, and then he'd be busted even harder for possession on top of that assault.

Motherfuckers!

He'd be damned if he'd let security trap him. He kicked Henry one last time and sped down the hall, on the lookout for an open room or exit door, bulldozing people as he barreled past. Stopping abruptly, he went through a door with a custodian sign on it and locked it behind him. He turned around and saw it was a small janitor's closet featuring a swimsuit calendar and a set of metal shelves stocked with cleaning supplies, a dirty yellow bucket with a mop and some brooms. In the corner stood a utility sink. Here was one way out, he thought. He'd dump the drugs and rinse them down the drain.

Derek went to the sink and turned on the faucets—but not a drop came out. He jiggled the handles.

What?!

Something was broken or disconnected—and his time was up.

"Open this door, asshole!" The security guards rattled the locked knob, pounded on the door.

Inside the claustrophobic confines of the closet with authority closing in, flashbacks rose up in Derek's mind of his dark days at juvie, flashes of his father locking him up in a dark hole...

Derek's heart accelerated as he tore the drug bag off his leg and emptied the contents into his left hand.

Can't flush 'em. Fuck it! Eat 'em...

The guards mumbled something outside the door. Derek heard the sound of jangling keys. One of the guards cursed, trying one wrong key after another.

Hurriedly, Derek stuffed his mouth with Ecstasy tabs, Vicodin and Oxy tablets and ten Libidonal pills. He began chewing and it tasted like pure shit. He tore the top off the vial of steroids and tossed it back like a shot glass. That tasted even worse. His mouth burned as he masticated the pills and liquid together into a paste and choked all down.

Derek tossed the empty plastic bag and the vial into the mop bucket just as the guards unlocked the door and piled on top of him.

CHAPTER 12

Wednesday morning had rolled in too fast for Lynch's liking. He drank coffee in the breakroom at the station and picked up a copy of the *Tribune* someone had left there. His eyes landed on the headline, and boy, it was a doozy.

DAUGHTER OF CHICAGO OUTFIT BOSS IN FATAL CRASH.

Everyone at the station was talking about it.

Lynch read through the article, which described how Annabella Tortellio and her passenger had been hit at high speed by a drunk driver behind the wheel of a Cadillac Escalade. The drunk survived with minor abrasions. Annabella's passenger died at the scene. Annabella herself was in critical condition and comatose at St. Cornelius Hospital.

There's no wrath like a gangster's wrath. The guy who hit Tico's daughter is a dead man.

Lynch tossed the paper onto a table and made his way to his desk. He sipped his coffee, hoping it would keep him going. He hadn't slept well last night. The early morning visit with Earl had taken a lot out of him, too.

If he were to juggle the work of two detectives, Lynch needed all his energy for the day ahead, but Earl's absence made his heart even heavier. And he still had the unsolved murder of lawyer George Pallis from Monday morning on his plate.

Astroglide...ya better step up.

He rubbed his eyes, exhausted and overwhelmed.

"Get with it, man." Lynch whispered to himself and got back on track.

Taking a drink of coffee, Lynch began to tackle the backlog of reports and emails and the disorganized piles of notes scribbled on case tips, paper towels, the back of receipts.

The paperwork offered nothing but heartbreak.

Gang shootings and gang-related homicides, which at this point were happening every other day across the city.

Domestic violence homicides.

Drug-related homicides.

Garden-variety killings all over.

And there weren't enough detectives in the city to cover it all. The CPD was spread thinner than ever.

How the hell did Dad do this for more than thirty years?

Donnie's father—Detective Jake Lynch—and all five of his uncles had been cops. Prone to drinking and gambling, they fought vice on the job and then rolled around in it for recreation. When they got together, his dad would often tip one back and pontificate on what he and his brothers had done during their careers—highs and lows, wins and terrible mistakes. Three of the five had died in the line of duty and the other two drank themselves into Queen of Heaven Cemetery out in Hillside.

His dad, who'd begun his career at age twenty-one, often told him things weren't so different back in the day; that when it came to lowlifes, crime, and the shitty situations in life, nothing ever changed, the perpetrators just had new faces. The loansharking, extortion, prostitution, gambling, political and police corruption—and murder—would always be the bread and butter for the nefarious. And when he'd had too much to drink, his dad would sometimes share such heartwarming insights from his time on the job as, "Chicago is a savage, violent, and merciless city with a sinister past—and an even bloodier future."

Nevertheless, his dad was fond of Chicago and its history. He'd wax poetic about how Chicago had once been the anchor of the country's meat-packing industry, known as the "Hog Butcher to the World," and how the Union Stockyards, down around Halsted and 47th on the South Side, had been a miserable landscape of livestock pens, slaughterhouses, and industrial rendering plants. Then he'd go on about how even though the blood of cattle and pigs didn't run into the Chicago River since they'd closed the last of the stockyards in 1971, he'd still seen plenty of blood in the streets.

Donnie's dad hadn't urged him to pursue a cop career. He didn't dissuade him, either.

"Being a Chicago cop...maybe it wasn't worth it. I dunno...hell, maybe it was," he'd say. "If you don't get killed in the line of duty, I guarantee that when your watch ends, your mind and soul ain't walking away without some scars. I coulda been a security guard or a goddamned lifeguard at the Y, but I was a Chicago cop. And your mother, God rest her soul, didn't approve of any of the shenanigans your uncles and I got up to, but she was proud to have a husband who worked to make this goddamn city a little safer. And hey, at least I got the pension. And now I get to drink warm Old Style and reminisce."

"That's what motivated me," Donnie would say. "Just like you, I wanted to help get the worst guys off the street."

His dad would laugh. "You don't even know. I've seen the heart of hell in the filthiest slums but also in luxury homes on the Gold Coast."

But Donnie thought his father hadn't given him enough credit in that regard. Like his father had done, Lynch toiled in the dark sides of the city, in the stinking alleys, SROs, slums, abandoned properties, suburban homes, and luxurious penthouses, and he'd come to learn that his father was on point with many of the virulent tidbits he'd offered. On any given day, Lynch dealt with pimps, prostitutes, drug-dealers, wife-beaters, pedophiles, and psychopathic maniacs, all of which contributed to a foul metropolis that bred the worst kinds of criminal activity.

And then there were the gangsters—more recently, the Russians and the Asians were developing strongholds alongside the Italians. Like most cops—and, to be fair, most armchair true crime enthusiasts —Donnie was hip to Chicago's mobbed-up past. The Outfit had had a colorful history since the twenties, back when Johnny Torrio and Al Capone became powerful during Prohibition with their bloody gang wars over control of illegal hooch. So much had been written and discussed about all of the classic Outfit rogues—Sam Giancana, Tony Accardo, Anthony Spilotro, Salvatore DeLaurentis, Angelo LaPietra, "Mad Sam" DeStefano, and Carmine Tortellio, whose son Tico was the current Outfit head, and whose daughter was currently fighting for her life at St. Cornelius.

Lynch had worked a few Outfit-related murder cases that brought home the magnitude—and the brutality—of the family's criminal empire, a huge underworld network that generated hundreds of millions of dollars yearly in illicit trade.

Despite these unwholesome realities, Lynch, like his father, loved his city. He loved going to Cubs games at Wrigley Field, taking walks around Millennium Park, getting behind the wheel for an afternoon cruise down Lake Shore Drive. And more than anything, he loved the food and so many of the people. There was a vibe and uniqueness that made the Windy City his kind of town.

He wouldn't trade sweet home Chicago for anything.

After knocking out a considerable amount of his to-do list, Lynch strolled into a media room at the station and sat down to review security footage obtained from businesses and a CPD camera on the street where George Pallis had gotten himself murdered. Lynch took notes as he reviewed clip after clip. In some footage, he saw Astroglide in her pink negligee walking with what appeared to be another prostitute in yellow lingerie and a bright red wig. On other tapes, nothing. Then, in one clip captured by a camera blocks away, Lynch saw what appeared to be Astroglide and her companion walking up to George Pallis' car—but the vehicle and the individuals were too far away and hard to make out.

Still, it was enough for Lynch.

He exited the media room and glanced at his phone; it was nearly 11:30. His planned rendezvous with Astroglide wasn't happening for two more hours, but there was no reason now for him to wait.

You'd better be home, fucker.

Lynch walked out into the late morning heat and got in his car.

CHAPTER 13

"I'll get him out!" As the Peithos security guards wrestled Derek down to the floor and yelled for staff to call the police, Derek watched Sid arrive and flash his program badge at the guards.

"I'll take it from here. I got the responsibility." Sid gave the men a pleading look. "The testing we're doing caused both this man's violent actions and the test subjects' impulsive behavior. I'll get him somewhere safe so you can deal with the others."

The security guards looked at each other and then at Sid and shook their heads.

"Dude," one of them said, "that was a vicious assault. We need to detain him until the police get here. What's his name?"

"Derek's my name, motherfucker." Derek blurted this out as he struggled to get the security guards off of him.

Sid became instantly nauseous as Derek gave up his name to everyone nearby. "No need for the police." Sid spoke smoothly and smiled as if that was going to comfort everyone. "We'll file it as a consequence of the Libidonal testing. Peithos Labs' insurance will cover all the medical expenses for the man who's on his way down to the ER, since the assault happened when everyone was on experimental drugs while enrolled in the research program."

A code red alert sounded for more assistance down the hall.

"Well, it's not like we don't have enough to do," one of the guards said.

Reluctantly, they released Derek and moved on to tackle the others in the study group who were running amok, aroused, and unstable.

Sid grabbed Derek by one of his enormous arms and rushed him to the room he'd been assigned. "You really did it this time. How stupid are you? Huh? You've fucked up beyond my wildest imagination."

Derek shrugged and tore off his hospital gown, and got dressed in the black sweat shorts, yellow tank top and white gym shoes he'd been wearing earlier that morning. "Whatever."

It was true, though. Derek knew he's just kissed the five grand away with the first punch. He knocked that Henry guy senseless, nearly beating him to death. But what was he supposed to do? The perv had jerked spunk all over him. Derek was happy to beat the fucker's ass.

"I still need cash." Derek gripped his gym bag, which was now filled only with toiletries and his wallet.

"You can forget any money from me or anyone else." Sid was all riled up as he rushed Derek down the corridor toward the bank of elevators at the other end of the hall. "Just be thankful you didn't go back to jail today."

Derek seethed with rage and frustration. "Guess you forgot our arrangement, you little maggot. I'm not leaving here empty-handed. I'll destroy you."

"Do what you want. If you call or come near my place, I'll get the cops all over your ass. That'll be it."

Derek clenched his fists and took a step toward Sid. He could see Sid's bravado evaporate as he turned pale and backed away with his hands up. Derek wanted to blast Sid's face but he hesitated at the sight of security guards walking quickly toward them. Also, the feeling of rage was suddenly shifting into a *strange* feeling that swayed his aggression.

Sid punched the elevator button and eyed Derek, concern filling his face. "Did you take anything aside from the Libidonal you were given?"

"I told ya what I took last night. Why do you care?"

Sid shrugged. "You don't look right.

"I'm fuckin' fine."

"Well, at least you don't seem to be experiencing the same side-effects as the other Peithos Labs participants."

"You see *me* jerkin' off on anyone? I'm fine."

Derek said those words, but as he did, he realized he was beginning to feel extremely *odd.*

The elevator doors opened.

Derek jabbed a finger into Sid's chest. "It...it ain't over. Five grand. You'll ... you'll pay up today. I...I'll catch up with you later, motherfucker."

Sid didn't reply. He stared at Derek with a face full of fear and puzzlement.

Then the weirdest feeling took hold of Derek as he stepped into the elevator and pressed the first-floor button. As the elevator descended, Derek shuddered. An intense wave of heat had begun spreading outward from his groin. Every muscle seemed to glow. His lips, tongue, fingers, toes, and penis were electrified. A charging current generated from his crotch and propelling itself through the rest of his body.

"Whoooooaa." Derek moaned. His voice reverberated in the empty elevator. Eyelids fluttering, he backed into a corner, moaning in pleasure as the contact between metal, glass, and his flesh mimicked the caress of a lover. He turned to the mirror and took in his reflection. He was the most beautiful thing ever made. Hot and ripped.

How could anyone resist all this?

Derek put his face closer to the mirror until his nose was inches away from his reflection. He licked his lips.

Kisses ... I want kisses.

He stuck his tongue out to lick the mirror just as the elevator stopped on the first floor with a ding. Derek snapped out of his moment of self-love at the sound as the elevator doors opened. He walked out into a hallway.

What the hell was I doing here?

Derek came to grips with reality and forced himself, for the moment, to focus on the way his mind and body were feeling.

Oh yeah...I'm at the hospital. Sid's labs. Man, I'm fucking highhhh...

Then a riptide pulled him back into a warm, erotic, and hallucinogenic womb.

Derek's body hummed. He felt an urge to tear off all his clothes. A hundred different smells overwhelmed and flooded his nostrils as if he'd been released from an airtight chamber and had entered a world of powerful odors. He reveled in awe at the reek of it all, breathing it in until his lungs burned. Nurses, doctors, and patients passed him in the hall. A fusion of perfume, cologne, hairspray, deodorants, sweat, shit, urine, plastics, rubbing alcohol, and more flooded his nasal passages and almost knocked him over. Down the hall, a janitor swabbed down a section of tile floor, and Derek inhaled a dose of mildew and fresh detergents.

He began walking down the hallway to figure out which floor he was on and find his way out of the hospital. Every step injected a sensual warmth into his legs, each stride was like the slick, hot manipulation of a masseuse's lubricated hands going up and down his thighs, calves, and buttocks.

A new fragrance bombarded him.

Mmmm ... flowers. Flowers.

Derek spied them in a glass vase on the counter of an empty nurses' station. No one noticed as he dropped his gym bag to the floor, snatched the bouquet and walked away with it.

He buried his face in the flowers, breathing in their intoxicating, heady aromas. The petals caressed his face like lips on his cheeks and mouth, tickling and delighting him. Derek licked the flowers and began eating them.

A child holding a young woman's hand turned the corner, laughed and pointed at Derek, her face lit up with joy. "Lookit the giant man eating flowers. Why's the giant eating flowers, Mama?"

Derek stopped; roses, irises, and stems stuffed his bulging cheeks. He studied the mother and child with wonder. The child's laughter was a strange music to his ears.

The expression on the mother's face was one of revulsion. "Keep walking, Cindy." She fixed a wary eye on Derek as she hurried her daughter along.

Derek watched them disappear down the hall. He closed his eyes and picked up the dissipating scents of perfume and stale cigarette smoke from the woman's blouse and hair. He swallowed the masticated floral arrangement and dropped the vase to the floor, where it smashed. He caught his reflection in a window—huge, muscled, hot... he was attracted to his own image again.

He turned the corner, feeling restless and passionate, avid for sensations, wanting to breathe fresh air and get a firm grasp on his surroundings. He stood still for a moment, overwhelmed by the sight of people walking and hurrying through the hall, the voices of young and old, the sounds of clinical chatter, and the pages for surgeons reverberating out from the hospital PA system.

A glowing exit sign at the end of the hall beckoned him. He started walking again but then stopped to watch a group of rowdy men dressed in sharp, black suits and sunglasses spill out of the door from the ICU area and into the main hallway ahead of him, which was filled with nurses, doctors, journalists, and cameramen taking photos and video, turning the crowd into a mosh pit as they yelled, cursed and pushed their way through.

The men appeared to be surrounding an older guy, large and formidable in a shiny gray suit, protecting him from the throng as they shoved their way through. He didn't say a word or break his smooth stride as the men around him ushered him past Derek, who could detect his aftershave riding on a scent of raw anger.

The journalists continued taking pictures and video, much to the irritation of the men in black suits and sunglasses. One of the journalists yelled out, "Tico! Tico Tortellio! How are you handling your daughter's accident? How is she?"

Four CPD policemen in blue uniforms arrived to break up the group. Red flags of unease rose in Derek's brain, and his body flexed in defense as the officers shouted and pushed the journalists back, keeping them at bay while two more escorted the Tortellio group through the lobby and outside.

For a moment the hallway was dead silent. Derek approached the door to the ICU. The air outside the room held displaced odors and the faint traces of something akin to what? Hostility? Derek detected it all like a bloodhound.

He soon discovered new, stronger aromas surrounding him from the ICU. He stood in front of a door, staring at a rectangular plaque with numbers etched into it. He put his ear to the door, closed his eyes, and wonderful vibrations hummed toward him. On the other side of the closed threshold, he detected some sort of sweetness he was compelled to sample.

He opened the door to this strange room and an explosion of scents enveloped him. Bursting with fancy flower arrangements, the room was a fragrant heaven full of smells almost too redolent for him to bear. As he stepped in, the room began to light his body afire and lick him with a gentle and invisible tongue.

A sleeping, black-haired beauty lay on a hospital bed with tubes and electrical wires attached to her bandaged, swollen face. Her legs, both in casts, were suspended in the air, and her arms were crossed over her stomach. Her chest rose and fell with her deep, even breathing. Derek walked forward and bent over her. He detected faint scents of gauze and linen.

Something stirred below his waist, and, looking down, Derek saw his erect penis pressing hard against the fabric of his sweat shorts.

Pitching a tent...

He wanted release.

The room had a large window into the hall through which passersby could observe this beauty like a mermaid in a fish tank. But there were no nurses. No one was here. Just him and this gorgeous, broken creature.

Derek put out a hand, reaching for the young woman in the bed. Before he could touch her, however, a square-headed man in a sleek black suit entered the room. Derek froze, muscles tightening. He held his breath while hunching over the woman, like some pumped-up gargoyle.

Tall and broad-shouldered, the intruder looked and smelled like the other loud men who'd just left. Derek's nostrils flared. The man's face twisted in alarm as he and Derek locked eyes.

"Who da hell ...?"

Derek grinned wide. His facial muscles stretched his lips nearly ear to ear as he inhaled. He could smell the man's perspiration. As he exhaled, a thick string of saliva rolled off his bottom lip.

The man shot a glance down at the protuberance below Derek's waist and looked back up, snarling as he reached underneath his suit jacket. "You fucking—"

Derek jumped. He squeezed the man's throat in the vise grip of his hand. The man gurgled as his arm went limp, dropping an automatic pistol to the floor as Derek's free fist exploded into his temple. Unconscious, the man dropped to the floor.

For a moment, extreme fury pushed back all the sensations of warmth and arousal that had so recently overtaken Derek. He panted like a big cat standing over his prey.

Hitting the man felt so good. He wanted to inflict even more damage. Crush his skull. Break his limbs. Taste his blood. But the rage ebbed as the throbbing between his legs recaptured his full attention.

Derek turned to the woman with renewed interest. They were alone again. She waited for him, unconscious.

Fruit for the taking...

A sudden flash of the long-ago shrink who diagnosed Derek rocked through him. The shrink...what did he say? Derek was incapable of affection or tenderness, emotionally unavailable to any woman unless she enraged him.

On brand, Doc...

This assessment was given by the time Derek was sixteen—attached to his fascination with sadomasochism, radical fetishism, and non-consensual kink that had caused the doctor to raise concerns that it could easily morph into pathological impulses and extreme violence.

What did the shrink call those things? Paraphilias...

Derek, the sex offender. The antisocial psychopath...that's what the shrink warned me I'd become.

He thought of Lab Coat, the sex doc at Peithos Labs and his charts and the chalkboard.

I am be-come-ing...like those Greek gods of sex...

The god of fuck...

Yes. The god of fuck. This title was most appropriate to him, for him, for-fucking-ever.

Derek ripped the sheets away from the woman, who remained still, lost to the world. He grabbed her hospital gown with his huge hands and tugged it free from her body as he devoured her with his gaze. She had a black eye, puffy lips, and lacerations on her face. Bruises and cuts crisscrossed her breasts, arms, and stomach. Her lower abdomen was bandaged with gauze, wrapping her like a mummy, and just below the dressings, a trimmed patch of black pubic hair came into view.

Derek's heart beat faster and harder.

Pulling off his sweat shorts, Derek gingerly climbed over her, careful not to disturb the attached tubes and cables—he was partially sober enough to know they'd set off alarms if yanked out. He spread her suspended legs and crawled between them. He was bigger than the bed. As he mounted her, he looked down. She seemed so much smaller than he was.

Like a little bird.

His breathing sped up. Fire coursed through his veins; his skin and his member came alive with heat. Unable to restrain himself, he forced his way inside her, grabbing a fistful of hair as he moaned and bucked, the hospital bed rocking, the wires, tubes, IV, and monitors jiggling and rattling.

Derek's scrotum became a magma-filled cauldron, swelling, rising, slamming and finally exploding into the woman as he bit down hard into her shoulder, rewarding himself with a mouthful of blood that lit up his tongue.

Delicious. Blood...it tastes like wine.

The woman didn't make a sound.

After he withdrew, he looked down to see his penis still ejaculating fluid onto the woman and across the floor. A red and white substance spilled from him.

Bloodcum?

Whatever it was, Derek didn't feel pain or discomfort. He gripped his erection and closed his eyes. His body numb and warm, he fell in love with himself.

I'm painless. I'm bulletproof...

Intoxicated, Derek rolled off the hospital bed, temples beating like floor toms, senses on overdrive. Everything he viewed, touched, smelled and tasted brought pure pleasure.

Although no longer spurting fluid, his penis remained stiff and throbbing. Derek put on his sweat shorts and stared at the woman he'd debauched, naked with her legs in the air, arms limp, body still hooked up to the machines. The bedsheets were stained with blood from her shoulder bite as well as the red and white semen from Derek's violation. He turned, looking down at the man on the floor who remained as lifeless as the woman.

Part of him wanted to fuck them both, rip them apart ... taste them. His mind suddenly ping-ponged between right and wrong and he wondered what the fuck he'd just done. The introspection fleeted as fast as it had entered his mind.

The hospital room felt stuffy. Derek wanted fresh air and yearned for more stimulation from a new source. Gathering himself, he stepped over the unconscious man and departed the room. He walked down the hall toward the exit sign.

Exit. Exit. Exit is the ticket.

His steps became awkward, his stride encumbered by his erection as he flung the exit door open with a violent bang, entering the blast furnace of the morning.

On his way out, Derek smashed into a man with shiny, sable skin who was leaning on a broom and smoking a cigarette just outside the door.

"Aye, mon. Watch it, huh?" The man sounded pissed off. Derek paid him no mind and clomped down the sidewalk, leaving St. Cornelius behind.

The man, a hospital janitor, later told investigators that he actually ran into Derek Hoffman as he fled the hospital. “Mon was scary big ‘n’ ugly. Never seen such a biggun like dat. Like some big ‘ol Frankenstein with a chubby. Them Peithos Labs boys turned a monster loose on the city, huh?”

CHAPTER 14

Tico sipped a cappuccino at a table on the patio next to the swimming pool overlooking Lake Michigan, his back to the wall. Vito and Liuni sat across from him; Sammy and Grotto sat on either side of him at adjacent tables.

They had brought Tico's wife home to rest. His sweet Valentina. Vito and Liuni, rough around the edges from their night of hard partying, looked as though they could use some rest, too, but Tico was having none of that. It was time, he thought, for his boys to have a history lesson to prime them for the training they were about to encounter.

"You all know about the old Outfit shylock, Mad Sam?"

Tico's sons and Sammy shook their heads, but Grotto nodded.

"Yeah...I know of him." Grotto leaned forward. "He was a loan shark back in the sixties, right?"

Tico nodded, encouraged that someone in his circle had some knowledge of Chicago Outfit history. "That's right, Grotto. Very good."

"If I remember correctly," Grotto said, "The FBI referred to Mad Sam as the worst torture-murderer in the history of Chicago."

"Yeah, Mad Sam was a true hook and torch guy." Tico smiled. "I knew him, and he was an absolute inspiration to me when I was younger."

He glanced over at his hungover sons. Liuni was starting to drift off and Vito was furtively checking his phone. Tico tried to calm himself as his blood pressure rose.

"Am I fuckin' boring you little pricks?"

"No, Pop." Liuni snapped to attention.

Vito set down his phone but kept his hand on it. "Pop...we aren't bored." He stretched. "It's just...this oral history stuff...we've heard all the stories before, and they aren't really relevant now."

Tico slammed his fist on the table. "I don't give a fuck what you think is important and what you don't. You'd rather be one of those... what is it? *Influencers*. You fuckin' tools. You best remember this history and remember where you fuckin' came from. Ya hear me?"

Both boys nodded.

"And don't let me hear you belly-aching for an espresso to keep you awake." Tico tried his best not to have a meltdown. "Now, as I was sayin', Mad Sam DeStefano. He was a man who led by example."

"That he did," said Grotto.

"Now there was this one low-level, three-hundred-pound bully, Action Jackson, who worked for him as a juice loan collector and a leg-breaker. Mad Sam suspected him of being an FBI snitch, so he lured him to this meat-rendering plant down on the South Side to take care of him."

Liuni leaned his elbow on the table and used his hand to prop up his head. "Pop...those plants closed down decades ago. How old is this story?"

Tico backhanded Liuni's elbow out from underneath him and Liuni's jaw kissed the table with a smack. "You're askin' about fuckin' decades? Who cares? I'm tellin' youse how important it is for you to know the world will never respect you unless you show that you're the predator and not the prey."

Liuni pushed himself back up and massaged his chin where it had hit the table. Vito helped him settle back in his chair. Tico stared them down until they'd finished adjusting themselves.

"So, when Mad Sam got his hands on this guy, he hung the rat-fuck from a conveyor belt by planting a meat hook in his asshole."

Vito flinched. "He did not."

Grotto leaned in. "Oh, yes, he *did*. Some others who were there shared the story. Jackson was so heavy, the hook actually *bent*."

Vito frowned, squirming in his seat. Liuni looked up, his complexion waxy.

Tico eyeballed them both, making sure he continued to hold their attention. "Jackson wouldn't admit to squealing so, while he dangled up there with a hook shredding out his asshole, Mad Sam smashed his kneecaps with a hammer. And then when he kept denying it, everyone else got pissed off, too, and started stabbing Jackson with ice picks. And then Mad Sam went after his cock and balls. Zapped him over and over again with a cattle prod."

Liuni wobbled in his chair, a tinge of green creeping up in his complexion. Vito shook his head and frowned, sweat popping up around his hairline. "Did he...like, finally admit it?"

"No. They don't make 'em like they used to. Nowadays, you pussies can't even *hear* about teaching someone a lesson without gagging. Look at you two. *Disgrazia*." Tico shifted in his seat and his tone shifted as well as he took pleasure in telling the story to the room. "But Jackson, even with a meat hook up his ass, he never caved. When Mad Sam would hit him with that prod, his soldiers were throwing water on him to amp up the electrical charge. He screamed so loud you could hear it all over that meat plant, but he never 'fessed up. Three days he hung off that conveyor cable with everyone working him over before he finally died."

"Pop," Liuni said. "I don't feel so good."

Next to Liuni, Vito shook his head, squinting his eyes.

"Show some respect, you two," Tico said. "You're soft as fuck. You're acting like easy targets with no balls. Now listen up. This is important. After he died, Mad Sam threw Jackson into the trunk of a Cadillac, and had someone drive it over to Lower Wacker Drive and just abandon it there. The cops finally discovered the body because of the stench from the rotting corpse. You know what they call that kind of disposal?"

The twins looked at each other, the Outfit trivia lost on them from what Tico could see.

"It's called, *'trunk music'* you idiots." Tico wondered where he'd gone wrong with these two. "That's fuckin' mob-style murder where the victim is tossed in the trunk of a car to rot and stink to high-heaven. Anyway, when the medical examiner showed up, they all saw Jackson riddled with blow-torch burns, a gunshot wound, countless lacerations...his ribs and lungs crushed, his asshole destroyed, and his wrists and feet cut by the ropes that Mad Sam had tied him with."

Vito and Liuni shrugged.

Tico was about to give the twins another earful but paused as Grotto answered his phone. "Is this the call we've been waiting for?"

Grotto nodded. "Yeah, Boss."

Tico stood up. "Boys," he said to the twins, "help Sammy and Grotto get both the cars ready. I'm going upstairs to check on your mother, and then we're heading down to the stockyards ourselves."

The rendering plant was located on a nondescript block on Chicago's South Side in the Back of the Yards, an industrial and residential hood named after the old Union Stock Yards & Transit Co. The Yards, as it was also known, had comprised Chicago's sprawling meatpacking district in Chicago for more than a hundred years. It had been nothing but marsh before a group of railroad companies acquired the land in 1865 and turned it into a centralized processing goliath which employed thousands of working-class European immigrants and later, in the early twentieth century, Black migrants from the American South. The newest inhabitants, after the closings of the processing plants, were mostly Mexican American.

The Tortellio family owned a stretch of factory buildings and ware-houses on a side street with no houses nearby, utilizing them for storing stolen cars, repackaging illicit goods, and other criminal undertakings that required privacy.

The late-morning sun shone high and bright, turning the inside of the defunct factory—with no air conditioners, no fans, no mechanical equipment at all—into a kiln. The building was filled with hundreds of shrink-wrapped pallets of misappropriated property, along with a few dozen luxury cars hiding under grimy tarps. Crematoria on wheels, Tico mused, thanks to the heat of the summer day.

He, his twin sons, and his enforcers, Grotto and Sammy, stood on a plastic-covered floor at the far end of the building, surrounding a bleeding and beaten man tied to an office chair.

The man was thirty-five-year-old stockbroker Charlie Reynolds, who earlier that morning, had been bailed out of jail. A Tortellio-owned cop gave Tico's crew the word that even though Reynolds had two prior DUIs, it was discovered at the station that the breathalyzer results had been compromised at the accident scene. Given that and the slick lawyer he'd hired, who was known for enabling drunk drivers to get back on the streets, Reynolds would probably walk out of this accident with just a few moving violations, while Annabella Tortellio, if she didn't die from her injuries, could remain a vegetable for the rest of her life.

After Reynolds' release, he'd headed home, with Tortellio soldiers tailing his every move. Shortly thereafter, he'd strolled over to a nearby liquor store. That's when they nabbed him. They'd roughed him up a little while tying him to the chair.

Now, everyone looked at Tico, waiting for him to issue his first orders.

Tico paused and took in the eerie quiet before the storm he planned to unleash. His nostrils flared and he inhaled the musty, mildewy scents of the old warehouse—rodents, dust, humidity, urine and gasoline—foul, airborne odors.

It smells like death.

"Hold this." Tico handed his gray Armani suit jacket to Grotto and ran a hand through his thinning hair, feeling the sweat breaking out on his scalp. "That jacket touches the ground, I'll beat your ass."

The enforcer nodded.

Tico narrowed his eyes. The younger man clearly feared him. *Good.* Tico had worked years under his father in order to earn the respect of the men working beneath him...it was sweat equity he earned and never forgot—especially on days like today.

As he rose up in rank, Tico had discovered fear wasn't created by intimidation, but, rather, by example. Today, he would show his sons why his enemies had come to dread him, demonstrating how the urban legends, in this case anyway, were based on fact.

His goddamn sons. Had he and Valentina indulged them too much or was it just the way of the world now? Tico often speculated on where the vine had gone sour with the twins. They were like so many others in the new generation of the Chicago Outfit, or in the New York *Mafioso*—all about fashion trends, luxury cars, fancy houses filled with hot women and drugs of all kinds. Wannabe mob rock stars trying to front like they were Tony Montana or reality TV celebrities or one of *The Sopranos*. But that's all they were—wannabes. He blamed guys like the late Gambino family boss, John Gotti, whose public persona had made Tico sick with disgust. All that flash for the press, who'd called him Dapper Don, and then "The Teflon Don" because it looked like no one could get charges to stick.

Tico figured he sounded like "Old Man Tortellio" whenever he bemoaned these facts. But it *was* fact from his POV. Kids these days didn't make the connections—all that kinda flash led to Gotti's undoing. He *did* get pinched—all that press just made the FBI *determined* to make an example of him—and he'd ended up at that Fed Pen in Marion, Illinois. And *Scarface*—well, Tony Montana ended up strung out and then floating face down in a swimming pool with a shotgun blast in his back, didn't he? Celluloid role models were what these kids were choosing to lead them?

Christ, Tico couldn't wait for his boys to get their shit together. He'd expedite their maturity and *make* them get in line. It was his responsibility for the future of the family.

Tico knew what he was walking into here was a risk. His *consigliere* had long ago advised him to never be anywhere near the scene of his illegal activities or to lower himself to a soldier's status by engaging in physical violence.

Stick your advice up your ass.

The truth was, Tico loved getting his hands filthy. Violence and brutality were his stock-in-trade, and he couldn't just take them out of his system any more than one could pacify a Kodiak bear high on blood. It had been a while and he was amped up, ready to go.

He rolled up his sleeves, revealing a gold Rolex and large, hairy forearms. He put the watch in his pocket and pulled out a set of well-worn brass knuckles, slipping the metal onto his right hand. He had first brandished them as a teenage street thug, breaking countless jaws while working his way up his father's underworld ladder. He hadn't used them in years, but he was enjoying this reunion with them—for both sentimental and sadistic reasons.

Tico paced around Charlie Reynolds, his fury building as he circled this miserable prick.

"Ready for some pain, cocksucker?"

Charlie shook his head and began to cry.

"I'm sorry! Please! I'm so sorry...have mercy!"

"Apologies? Mercy? That shit ain't on the menu today." Tico turned to his men. "Give this fucker a tune-up."

Tico's enforcers began to work Charlie over. To his pleasure, Tico's sons—who hadn't been happy to start their day early after their salacious night out—also stepped up to the piece of shit.

"Liuni, Vito...go ahead, work out your hangovers on this fuck."

Tico watched the twins phone it in as they slowly walked over and beat Charlie with little enthusiasm. Between their poor physical condition and the stifling hot warehouse, Tico thought they were going to puke.

"Okay. That's enough," he said, nodding at the enforcers who ushered Vito and Liuni several steps back. Tico raised his fists and grinned at his sons. "My turn. Watch how it's down. You better get used to inflicting pain. Training's just startin'."

For the next five minutes, Tico bludgeoned Charlie's face and crushed his body. His exhilaration was tempered, however, by the exertion in the extreme heat, which made him feel as if he were boxing in a raging woodstove.

Tico steadied himself. Light-headed and breathing hard, he knew it was time to step back and move on to the next phase. His dress shirt and suit pants were spattered with blood and soaked through with sweat; he was too winded to punch the man any further.

"Christ on a whore." Tico spat and unbuttoned his shirt. "I'm gonna need another set of clothes." He gestured to Grotto. "I gotta fresh Bears t-shirt and running pants in the Lincoln." He took a breath. "Fuck me. I need a portable shower."

Vito leaned forward, wobbling on the toes of his expensive leather shoes. "Can we take five in the Caddy and get some AC?"

Liuni nodded. "Yeah. Please, Pop. I don't feel so good, okay?"0

Tico mimicked the sound of an adult baby. "Oh, boo-hoo. Daddy, I'm hungover. It's too hot. I wanna play on my phone." He wiped his brow. His tone sharpened. "I swear, I'm a cunt hair away from puttin' ya both in the hospital with your sister. I told youse to watch me and learn somethin'."

He pointed to Sammy as he wiped bits of flesh off the brass knuckles with a handkerchief and shoved them in his pocket. "You. Gimme the raincoat."

He removed his soiled shirt and gave it to Sammy, who handed him a large yellow raincoat. Tico kept his undershirt on, along with the gold necklace and crucifix his grandmother had given him for his first communion. He kissed the cross and then dropped it into the sweaty mat of gray hair on his chest.

In this heat, Tico knew the slicker would roast him, but he'd rather broil than take a literal bloodbath. As he zipped up the coat, he walked to the front of his Lincoln, where a long, hard plastic case rested on the hood. The corner of his mouth curled up at the sight of the large *Stihl* logo on the case.

Tico opened the plastic case and pulled out the large chainsaw. Big enough to cut down a large tree, it could do wonders to a man's limbs.

He stood in front of Charlie Reynolds and waved his free arm.

"You know, we're standing right near the epicenter of the Union

Stockyards ... the home of the three big meat-packing companies of yesteryear: Armour. Swift. Morris. Some five-hundred fucking acres full of cattle and hogs that were butchered and processed on a daily basis. You should appreciate the history here. They owned this country. And now they're gone, but I own this city. You know why they call me the Meat Grinder?"

Charlie Reynolds shook his head. He choked up.

"It's a no-brainer. I got the nickname because I've used a meat grinder to render people into fucking hamburger. I'd feed a guy through the top and what came out the other end I'd feed to the strays. I try to keep this type of work quiet...it's nasty and bloody. But I guess when you cut, chop, grind, and press people into ground round...well, that kind of news is gonna get out somewhere. I'm still waiting for OSHA to charge me with somethin'."

Tico laughed at his own wit. His sons and his enforcers stood at attention.

Charlie Reynolds began to sob. "Please," he said. "Tell me how I can make it up to you and your family."

Tico ignored him and kept on talking. "Speaking of meat grinders, there she is." He pointed at a large, industrial-sized, dust-covered machine the size of an Army tank. "That bitch over there was the finest in her class when she came out years back. What a beauty. Stainless steel. She's been mine since she fell off a truck. For years, she never once let me down. I call her *Vivian*. In her prime, she could process almost two tons of frozen meat per hour. That's high-volume, Charlie. Vivian's got a conveyer belt, big-ass hopper, two-speed working worm, and a state-of-the-art hydraulic pressing device to push fuckers like you into the mixers, grinders, and cutters. I even got a built-in mirror at the top so I can watch dickheads like you go up the conveyor and into the hopper, and then down to all those metal teeth to get eaten up. Fucking perfection."

Charlie Reynolds' eyes rolled back in his head.

"Hey! Don't you pass out on me!" Tico slapped him back to reality. "Now...about Vivian. It's a real shame she's down because I'd love to show you how she works. Lucky for you, she's on the fritz and due for major maintenance...so I'm gonna do you another way. You shouldn't drink and drive, cocksucker. Stand aside, guys."

Their faces sober, the two soldiers and the Tortellio twins backed up as Tico prepared to go to work. With one hard pull, the chainsaw fired up and filled the factory with noise and oily exhaust. He saw the twins turn pale. *Couple of pussies. Time to show them what it really means to take care of your own.*

Tico walked toward Charlie Reynolds, smiling, with the chainsaw vibrating in his hands, as his captive stared, screaming incoherent words from his bloody, obliterated mouth.

"Can't hear ya, asshole." Tico's voice grew louder. "You put my little girl in a fucking coma. There's nothing on God's green earth that's gonna save your ass."

Tico pressed the chainsaw's trigger, and it roared for him—just the way he liked. Tico caught his sons' jump at the sound of the chainsaw revving.

Pay attention, goddamn it! You wanna be in charge one day? You got what it takes? This is where we separate the men from the boys...and in some cases, heh-heh, the boys from themselves.

Charlie Reynolds jerked his head back in vain, as if he could steer clear of the menacing chainsaw. Tico's face twisted from a frozen smile into an angry grin. With the controlled movements of an ice sculptor, he leaned over and nipped off one of Charlie's ears and then parted his scalp. As blood spurted back onto the raincoat, Tico saw Liuni sag against Sammy and begin to retch.

He turned back to the object of his rage, slicing divots into his torso. "Like that?" he shout-snarled, his words barely audible beneath the din of the chainsaw—as were Charlie Reynolds' screams.

Tico was about to get creative with the man's legs when his eyes caught Vito answering his iPhone. Tico glowered as he killed the chainsaw. He dropped it to the ground and watched Vito shake his head, his face contorted in shock and confusion as he asked questions and yelled into the phone.

The building filled with smoke and Charlie Reynolds's continued screams.

"Shaddup!" Tico slapped Charlie across the face then wiped the blood from his hands on Charlie's shirt. He kicked the chainsaw and glared at his son. "Vito! You interrupted me? For what?"

Vito slid his phone closed and looked up at Tico, his face flushed with pain. Liuni stood up straight; he, Sammy and Grotto froze in place, their eyes darting between Vito and Tico.

Tico raised his left hand in the air and waved it at Vito. "I swear to Christ if that's one of your fuckin' girlfriends, I'm gonna use this saw on *your* ass."

"It ain't one of my girls, Pop. It's one of our soldiers." Vito's voice caught in his throat. "He's got some bad news."

"What is it?"

"It's Annabella." Vito paused.

"I don't like your tone," Tico said. "Out with it."

Vito swallowed. "Sonny says ... he says she was *raped* in the hospital."

Liuni stomped his foot. "The fuck you say? Rape? There's no rape."

Tico clenched both fists, shaking his head in denial. "You're nuts. She's in a goddamn hospital! You can't get raped in there. 'Sides, Giorgio's guarding her room. Where's that *cazzo*?"

"The rapist bashed him in the head." Vito tugged at his collar. "They say some big bastard came in, dropped Giorgio before he could do anything, and then ... Annabella."

Tico kicked the chainsaw aside and leapt on Vito, lifting his son off the ground and shaking him violently. "Take that back! Annabella wasn't raped! That's your *sister,* you liar!"

Liuni grabbed Tico by the arm. "Pop! Stop! Don't kill the messenger."

Tico dropped Vito. His vision blurred. He saw Annabella, alone, helpless, unable to even cry out.

Raped? How? How in the hell could this have happened?

His mind filled with amplified fury.

If this was true, he wanted her attacker *now*...

He wanted to torture and kill this sick fuck...

He wanted to kill the hospital staff...

He wanted to spit in the face of God for bringing such heartbreak into his life—for destroying the honor of his only daughter. What would her life even be like after this?

"First of all—" Tico swayed for a moment. The heat, the news he just got, it was too much. Then he caught himself and focused on his sons. "Make sure no one gets to your mother before we can tell her about this ourselves." He turned to his soldiers. "I want you to call every single man on our crew and all our *friends* in the police department. I want calls in to every sorry bastard who owes me a favor." Tico's hands trembled with rage. "We're gonna hunt down this cocksucker. Cops can't have him. I want him alive, *capisce?* I'm gonna work on him for fucking *days*."

"What about Giorgio?" Liuni held up his phone. "He's still in the hospital."

"*Terminate* his fucking employment!"

Tico turned back to Charlie Reynolds. This guy...he was to blame for all the misfortune brought down on his baby girl.

The chainsaw screamed along with Charlie Reynolds.

Tico brought the saw down on Charlie's collarbone and cut, bisecting him from his neck down through his buttocks.

A hot spray of blood, bone fragments, and shreds of tissue sprayed Tico's raincoat. He didn't stop until he'd sawed all the way through Charlie Reynolds and the office chair he sat in. In a cloud of two-cycle exhaust, both the man and the furniture collapsed into pieces.

The Meat Grinder was just getting started.

CHAPTER 15

Derek walked aimlessly for miles down the middle of a street that radiated waves of infernal heat. The sun hung high in the sky, and its burning rays became too much for him. He was drenched in sweat—every pore wept. He ducked down sidewalks and alleys, trying to stay in the shade.

The streets were quiet, with most people staying inside their air-conditioned homes or businesses on this day of record-breaking temperatures. The random joggers Derek encountered appeared to be miserable, heading for heat exhaustion or sunstroke. Groups of kids played with garden hoses and splashed in the spray from corner hydrants. The few people who walked by looked at him with startled, repulsed expressions.

I'm the ogre...passing through your barrio...

Derek didn't give much thought to them. When he caught glimpses of himself in the windows he passed, he saw a gorgeous, fiery, crimson god.

His senses were on overload. Everything in his vision popped brilliant, bright, red.

Smells and tastes seemed heightened.

I can taste atoms...

Oh, how he hungered for new sensations.

Derek gave in to the chemical stew saturating his mind, commanding his every move, intoxicating him without dulling his senses or reflexes.

Everything was enhanced.

A sudden thought twinged at the back of his mind. There was someone he'd wanted to see earlier...with urgency. Someone he had intended to—

Astroglide...

If his now spotty, erratic memory served him, Astroglide's crib wasn't too far from where he was right now. Not far by vehicle anyway.

Derek spied a man in a pickup truck idling at a stop sign and yelling in Spanish to someone on his phone. Approaching the truck on the driver's side, Derek yanked the door open and punched the man hard in the forehead. He slumped, lights out. Derek shoved him over into the passenger seat.

Inside, the air-conditioned truck felt frigid, but Derek burned. He stomped on the gas pedal and city blocks flew by; cars screeched and blared horns as he blew through stoplights. *All* the lights looked red. He operated on autopilot—not quite in control yet knowing he was headed for a familiar destination. The motor part of his mind drove the truck and guided it through the city while the drugged part reveled in the *red* coursing within and around him.

Almost fuckin' there...

Pushing the gas pedal into the floor, Derek made a wide turn into an industrial area of warehouses, loading docks, and lots filled with semi-trailers. As the erotic red swallowed him up, he closed his eyes and touched himself. Opening his eyes, he found himself drifting to the left and heading toward a brick wall. He cranked the wheel hard to the right. The tires squealed. He overcorrected. In seconds, the truck smashed through a chain-link fence and crashed into a stack of railroad ties.

Derek bounced off the steering wheel, smashing it with his barrel chest. He felt no pain, merely a wave of exhilarating pleasure as his blood pumped with ferocious intensity.

He *heard* his blood pumping.

Steam billowed from the crumpled hood and Derek saw it as undulating clouds of scarlet. The truck owner, injured and bloody from the crash, began to stir and moan. Derek punched him in the face. The man crumpled where he sat.

Exiting the smoking wreck, Derek pushed out into the heat of the day, instantly sweating again and still hard, until he came to a bleak area filled with abandoned commercial buildings, vacant lots, and drug houses.

Candyland...

He'd driven through here every week for the last four years. It's where he came to get his good stuff. He'd never paid mind to his surroundings as he blasted through these dilapidated neighborhoods in his truck. Now, however, on his feet, the architecture, the cracks in the pavement, the filthy smells brought brand-new stimuli.

A police car ripped past with high-pitched sirens blaring. Derek's insides churned as he flashed with aggression, ready to jump at it. Within seconds, the car vanished. Feeling recharged from the adrenaline in his veins, Derek strode by the corroded factories, climbed over weed-covered railroad tracks, and strode past a lone, industrial nightclub called Megawatz—one of many spots across the city that had blacklisted him for peddling club drugs.

Sex-drugs.

Derek touched himself as he walked. His shorts felt damp from perspiration and intermittent drops of fluid dribbling from his rigid penis.

Finally, he arrived at a post-apocalyptic block devoid of trees, strewn with litter and junked cars. A few run-down houses and apartments huddled together on each side of this street of immolated dreams. Down the block was the apartment he knew so well.

He walked past the tumbledown porch of an uninhabited, but still fortified, drug house where the lost went in and ruined their minds on heroin, fentanyl, bath salts, who knew what the fuck else. Derek encountered a large, grungy dog that jumped up on the porch. It growled at him, the dog stood with its ears flattened, tail tucked between its legs, its muzzle drawn back, revealing a mouth full of sharp teeth. The snarling dog fixed its gaze on him, body tensing as if preparing to maul.

Derek filled with rage. He glared at the dog, wanting to decimate it. He could smell its ferocity and aggression, much like his own.

The dog's scent stirred him into a spinning fervor of belligerence and sexual stimulation. He'd been erect for what seemed like an eternity, but now his member strained further as he envisioned the unpleasant things he could do to the animal. As he touched himself again, his eyes rolled and he imagined a litter of man-pups suckling the bitch-mother.

Derek considered how easy it would be to kill this dog. He could break the bitch's neck with his powerful hands, beat its head in, and then he'd have his way with the carcass.

I'll make it fit...

Derek grinned, muscles flexed, and a warm spurt oozed from him as he approached his prey.

The bitch's body froze up as she caught wind of his scent and then she yelped and bolted off the porch and across the street before Derek could grab her.

He growled in frustration. He wanted to put himself into something warm, to feel flesh around him.

Give me holes. Meat holes.

Why was he here again? Oh yes, he remembered. He'd been here before, too many times to count. Weekly. Years.

Astroglide...

Derek could suddenly feel the flesh he longed for.

A couple of men sitting on the shaded steps of the apartment entrance glanced over at Derek as he approached. Their eyes bulged at the sight of him. They jumped up and fled. Derek watched them run, amused that he'd struck fear in their hearts.

Flattened beer cans, empty wine and malt liquor bottles, coke and heroin and meth baggies, vials, and cigarette butts littered the steps. The building entrance was locked, so he rang the bottom buzzer for apartment number one. Derek massaged the buzzer, thinking of it as a clit. The thought excited him.

Constant buzzing like the moans of some slut...

"Who be ringing me?" A high-pitched voice shouted through the small speaker. "That you, pig?"

Derek didn't reply, too caught up in his foreplay with the intercom.

"Fuckin' kids, out there? Quit pressin' that buzzer. 'S notta toy!"

Derek pressed the button harder and growled.

"A'ight! Gonna kick your asses now."

A moment later, the door banged open and a tall, Black—*woman-man?*—appeared, clad in a pink nightgown and brandishing a baseball bat, cursing and yelling through bright, red-painted lips. When the inhabitant saw Derek, the voice calmed. "Oh's you. Fuckin' Derek."

"Who...?" Derek blinked, confused for a moment as he stared at the uppity character in front of him. Then he realized...

Astroglide!

The dealer he remembered, who insisted that *he* be identified as *she*. She glowed with a red aura that made Derek *want*.

"Asssstrooogliiiide," Derek slurred.

"What y'doin' here today?" Astroglide looked past Derek with a nervous expression. "Y'know you call me first, I call back, and you place an order. Not this social-call crap, fool. I don't got time for you. I gots an appointment soon and—"

"Need stuff." Derek's words felt warm and liquid as they came out, like nectar falling from his mouth. He wasn't sure he could talk.

Astroglide studied Derek's face and scowled. "Boy, you're fucked up, ain't ya? Whatchya on? Acid? Ecstasy? All the above?"

Derek grinned.

Astroglide looked down, her eyes settled on something below Derek's waist and ran the tip of her tongue over her lips. "My, my, someone's happy."

Derek fought a strong urge to attack Astroglide right where she stood. He wanted to bash her, break her, and taste her blood. It took great restraint not to reach out and rip the dealer's face off.

Not here. Bad idea. Wait...

Derek's jaw clenched and muscles popped out in his face as he controlled himself.

"I need stuuuuff."

"A'ight." Astroglide's voice registered unease as she looked over Derek's immense, trembling body. "Get your ass in here and I'll hook you up. We's gotsta hurry, though, cause I'm busy. Got me a meeting soon. I'm short on roids right now, but I gots some other shit. Get what you pay for here."

Meat holes...

Astroglide led Derek into her dark apartment, only a little light filtering through the blinds in the living room and kitchen. A rackety ceiling fan whirled full blast with no effect.

"Stay put while's I get somethin' together." Astroglide set the baseball bat on a kitchen counter.

"Flesh."

Astroglide raised a waxed eyebrow and laughed. "Goddamn, white boy, if you ain't fucked up."

Derek didn't say anything, just sniffed the air, detecting flowery, acetone scents of Astroglide's cheap perfume and the acrylic of her long, enameled nails as she left the room. Inhaling, he looked around, standing in the middle of the living room, waiting to see what treats Astroglide would bring.

A minute later, Astroglide reappeared with a cardboard box in her hands. Inside were plastic bags full of pills and tabs of Ecstasy and what appeared to be a dozen eight-balls of cocaine in little baggies.

"Sit down and check out this shit." Astroglide set the box on a coffee table littered with crumpled fast-food wrappers. She drummed her fingernails on her thigh. "But make it quick. You gotsta go."

Derek walked over to the box and studied the contents before reaching in and pulling out a bag of pills. He tore it open and put a handful in his mouth. They tasted terrible.

"Asshole! You don't just tear into my stash and take shit. That'll be three hundred bucks, fool."

Derek ignored her as he choked it down.

"Yo, dickhead! You *tryin'* to fry your brain?"

Derek ignored her and rummaged through the box. He grabbed a plastic-wrapped eight-ball and pulled it apart. Powder and rocks of cocaine exploded out and covered Derek's sweaty face and chest like chunky flour.

"Ya fuckin' kiddin', bitch?!" Astroglide turned and reached for the baseball bat. "Gonna beat some manners into your head, muscle-fuck."

Derek leapt through the air across the coffee table as rage, fueled by bloodlust, welled up. He grabbed Astroglide from behind, wrapping his gorilla arms around her in a crushing bear-hug. Astroglide screamed as he lifted her into the air and shook her furiously back and forth, like a great white shark with a seal in its jaws.

Blood blew out of her mouth in a thick spray as Derek squeezed harder, crushing her ribs, puncturing her lungs and silencing her scream. Then, with both hands, he grabbed Astroglide's head and smashed it into the kitchen counter.

Astroglide gasped and the cruel sounds of every fracture, every break, every thud from her head as he battered it against the counter was all music to his ears.

Derek dropped Astroglide to the floor and looked at her. Her countenance was rubble. She wheezed in long, harsh breaths, each inhalation and exhalation wet and labored. Derek smelled the blood in the air.

Turning away, he looked at the box of drugs on the coffee table and walked toward it, hoping to discover more treasures. As he approached the table, he noticed his reflection in the mirrored black screen of a large television mounted to the living room wall. He liked the way he looked—muscles bulging, covered with sweat, seeing the world through a Libidonal-red veil.

Derek opened his mouth wide and stuck out his tongue. He waved it like a snake coming out of a hole. Fascinated and engrossed with his own reflection, he didn't hear Astroglide get up, but he caught her motions in the TV screen as she hobbled toward the apartment door.

No...you're mine, little lamb.

Infuriated, he tore the television from the wall. The flatscreen was light in his hands. He whirled around, ripping out the power cord and wall mount with an audible cracking as Astroglide wrapped her fingers around the knob of the apartment's front door.

Derek whirled and struck her with the television, bringing it down with such force that her head, shoulders, and arms crashed straight through the screen and electronics. Blood gushed from her head as she fell to her knees and let loose a low, bleating sound.

Derek lifted Astroglide with ease, holding her up high by her neck before throwing her across the living room. He pounced on her, head-butting and pummeling her until his fists and forearms were covered in blood. He pulverized bones, cartilage, and teeth under a blitzkrieg of heavy blows until he could tell Astroglide was no more. Derek stopped, closed his eyes, and savored the moment. It electrified his senses.

Astroglide's broken body lay sprawled out on the floor. No more movement, no breath, no signs of life. Her once round and feminine face had become a pothole of clabbering goo. Her bottom jaw yawned, crooked, and her body was turned and twisted around, the blood-stained nightgown jacked up to her waist, exposing her buttocks. Derek caught a glimpse of Astroglide's hairless testicles and a penis that resembled the tip of a thumb.

Derek stared, momentarily confused.

He? She? He is she and she is he...

He laughed a low, intoxicated chuckle. His victim looked absurd on the floor in a beaten pile, like some child's discarded doll. His amusement turned to lust as he fixed his eyes on Astroglide's bare ass.

Separating Astroglide from the TV, he picked up the limp body and tossed it over an armrest on the leather sofa. Within seconds, Derek pulled down his sweat shorts and tore off Astroglide's nightgown.

Drunk on the unholy salacity that owned him, Derek gave no thought to right or wrong, morality or depravity, as he embraced the ravenous impulses that begged to be sated.

The god of fuck hath risen...

All that mattered to him now was the touch and taste of anyone or any*thing* that turned him on...and that he could brutalize.

His most primitive instincts had overtaken him.

Fuck. Feed. Kill. Repeat...

As he desecrated Astroglide's lifeless body, Derek thought of the dog, the she-mongrel that had escaped him down the street. The thought of the bitch made him angry, and it also made him hot.

Derek plunged again and again, an unstoppable fuck-machine penetrating Astroglide's corpse.

CHAPTER 16

Tyrell Robinson came out of the malt liquor stupor he'd been immersed in since he'd passed out on the dirty sidewalk just after sunrise. Forty-six years old, he spent most of his days drinking everything from Colt .45 malt liquor and Night Train wine to Listerine and cheap cologne. He lived life by the drop, unhoused, hanging in and around this neglected piece of Chicago wasteland folks called Candyland, eating his meals out of dumpsters.

He sat up on the curb. It was hotter than hell under his ass. *Everything* was hotter than hell today. His polyester pants and T-shirt were dirty and ripped, the tattered clothing making him overheat even more in the terrible sun on this burning, treeless street.

Tyrell wanted shade, alcohol, and maybe a bite to eat. The nearest liquor store was blocks away—but it had trees. He could recline and chill there. He'd buy some booze once he'd bummed enough money.

Tyrell ran filthy fingers through the sweaty, gnarled curls on top of his head. When was the last time he'd bathed? Rain a couple weeks back was the closest he'd come to showering. Sobering up, he smelled-checked his pits and couldn't deny how rank he was. But hygiene and sanitation would always take a backseat to the bottle.

A whining dog across the street grabbed his attention. The untamed bitch was running up and down the rickety steps of a decrepit drug house. It seemed in distress, yelping around the porch.

"Crazy-ass mutt." Tyrell sputtered the words to the street. "Got rabies?"

Maybe too much sun.

Tyrell looked at the apartment building next to the drug house, and fear sparked immediately in his brainpan. A stranger had appeared from nowhere—the biggest and most insane-looking, white mother-fucker he'd ever seen. The monstrosity stood on the top step, gaping at the dog and licking his lips, with his shorts down to his knees, playing with his hard dick.

"Wha' the Jesus...he doin' that?" Tyrell muttered, trying to stand up.

The big boy across the street looked away from the dog and stared at Tyrell with psychopathic intensity while still stroking himself. He took a deep breath and his thickset, upper torso expanded, making him seem even larger. He stuck out his chest and exhaled as he hissed out: "You smell ... stinks...sex good stink."

"An' you crazy!" Tyrell scrabbled down the sidewalk on all fours, sweating harder as extreme heat and extreme unease overtook him, trying to reach something, anything, that he could use to leverage himself upright as the big boy pulled his shorts up and descended the stairs, cock swollen and peeking over the elastic waistband. The nut-job grinned large, his eyes fixed on Tyrell, a thick stream of saliva hanging from his bottom lip as he advanced to the street.

"Aw, hell no." Tyrell watched the freak lumber toward him as he pushed himself up on the crumbling concrete steps of the building behind him. Judging by the aggression in the way he carried his muscle and build—not to mention the menacing bulge in his shorts—Tyrell figured beating and raping were in this fool's mix. Well, no one was doin' that to Tyrell. Fools that tried it in the county lock-up got shanked by Tyrell.

Not happening, boy. No fucking way.

Frantic but unsteady, Tyrell looked around for anything to use as a possible weapon. Nothing. Not a soul in sight, not that it would make a difference. No one in this neighborhood responded to cries for help.

"Come, little lamb." Big Boy let out an intoxicated laugh as he approached, tall and wide, tan, his enormous muscles and ropy veins crisscrossing his tattooed, hulking frame, the swollen meat pipe leading him around like a divining rod. "Derek had a little lamb. Its fleece was ... was black."

Angry white man? Peckerwood? Big boy was all that 'n' more—literally...

He was steps away when Tyrell snapped to his senses, bolting down the sidewalk just as the monster's fingertips grazed the back of his neck. Tyrell screeched at that and doubled his speed.

Half a block down, Tyrell glanced back over his shoulder. The big boy wasn't behind him. Tyrell stopped running and doubled over, his hands on his knees, to catch his breath. His side hurt, like a knife blade had stabbed him. He hadn't run this fast since some cops chased after him last winter.

The heat, alcohol dehydration, and exhaustion were causing his stomach to roil. As he stood up to try to stabilize his gut, around the corner came Big Boy, hands on his crotch, grinning and staring at Tyrell.

"You...crazy...mutha." Tyrell spit and wheezed while the freak continued to come for him, staring intently and fondling himself along the way.

Tyrell jumped into a painful sprint and then disappeared between two dilapidated houses. He promised himself that if he made it out of here, he'd do two things: First, stay away from the bottle—at least for the rest of today—and drink a lot of water. Second, find a nice, cool place to hide.

He slowed as he came to a more populated hood with a patrol car pulling up to a curb down the street. Tyrell wasn't a fan of cops—they'd caused him worlds of grief over the years on the street—yet, maybe he should flag one down before that big boy force-fucked someone...or worse. That fucker scared him more than any pig.

Startled, Tyrell jumped at a sharp sound in the distance. He wasn't sure, but it sounded like an animal, or some crazy animal-person, was howling in the streets behind him.

CHAPTER 17

Lynch left his desk and went to his car. Outside, the late morning heat clung to him from his scalp to his ankles, leaving him drenched and sticky.

"Fuck you, summer." Lynch slid into the Dodge Charger Pursuit, which felt akin to entering a pizza oven. He gasped, rolled down the windows, and cranked the fan on his cold-climate control.

He wanted to get to Astroglide, but he also wanted to grab a bite.

Lynch wondered what Sandy was up to right now.

Wish she was doing lunch with me.

He didn't want to think about her, but how could he keep away thoughts of someone who owned his heart? Though he didn't want to picture her with the guy from Irene's Bistro, he couldn't purge the image from his head. He couldn't get Sandy out of his mind, period—the way one corner of her mouth would begin to curl up before she turned on the full power of her alluring smile; the way her eyes held his attention. She smelled the way an angel should smell.

Fuck it, he'd eat later.

He put on his shades and drove. His parents had loved her like a daughter, too, always saying she was the best thing to happen to Donnie. Why the hell did he let that slip away?

Keep beating yourself up. That'll help...

Driving through traffic, Lynch grabbed his mobile phone. *Should I or shouldn't I?* He wanted to call her, to hear her voice. Maybe spill his guts a little. Not a word had been spoken between them in months, and the last word wasn't good. Times like this made him wish for the courage of Mr. Daniels.

What would Earl say if he knew I wanted to call Sandy? 'Let her go, Donnie, ol' pal?'

Lynch turned a corner and hit the call button to Sandy's number. The line rang and his mouth went dry. A hundred different things he could say went through his head, but no perfect words came to mind. What the hell could he say? What did he *want* to say? Even with the air conditioning on full blast his palms were damp.

After three rings, Sandy's voicemail picked up and Lynch delighted in every word of her greeting.

What to say? What to say?

His nerve evaporated. He hung up.

"Maybe next time. Maybe ... right."

He put the thoughts of Sandy in the back of his mind. He knew she'd pop back up again, though, in images or memories. He could count on it because he sure loved to rehash pain and torture himself, right?

He turned his thoughts to Astroglide, his appointment for the day. He smiled to himself. The job helped him get his mind on to other things. Focusing on work—that's where he wanted his mind to be.

She'd better be there.

Lynch drove slowly. Time was on his side today. Even taking his time, he'd still arrive early. Stay one step ahead. Earl had taught him to do that much. What had he said exactly? Something like, *"Stay one step ahead or the underbelly of this city will take you down in one dark and ugly wave of blood and guts and horror."*

Lynch pulled up into the alley behind Astroglide's place. This was one shitty neighborhood. He called her from his idling car, but no one answered.

"This isn't the way to get on my good side." Lynch figured he should've just gone right to the door. He put the car in drive, cruising around to the front of the building, not caring if Astroglide got upset at his lack of discretion. He muttered, "You're pissing me off, *Timmy*."

There was no sign of life on the filthy, sunbaked street other than what appeared to be some tatted-up, super-huge musclehead in black shorts and a yellow tank top walking off in the distance. Lynch thought the dude looked bigger than any professional wrestler he'd ever seen on TV. The heat waves from the pavement distorted the man's hulking outline as he left Lynch's sight.

How big can a guy get? That's just un-fucking-natural.

Lynch parked in front of Astroglide's building and got out of the car. Putting on his bulletproof vest, he climbed the trash-and-paraphernalia-covered steps and rang Astroglide's buzzer. No response. He rang three more times, sweating underneath the vest, and then peered through the building's glass door and saw nothing other than apartment doors and littered hallways. He tried the handle. *Locked*. He pressed all the intercom console buzzers to get someone to open the front door.

A voice came over the intercom. "If you're not here to fix da air, *piss off!*" Next was a little kid who didn't make any sense. At last, a voice asked, "Who is it?"

"Police, ma'am." Lynch wanted out of the heat. "Can you buzz me in?"

There was a pause, and then, "Who you comin' to see?"

"Someone at another apartment who isn't answering."

"You ain't here for me?"

"Not at all."

Get me the hell outta this heat.

The voice laughed nervously. "Okay, just a minute, hun."

When the main door buzzed, Lynch walked in.

He made his way to Astroglide's apartment and found the door wide open. He walked in.

"Jesus fucking Christ."

Timmy "Astroglide" Rodgers was clearly deader than dead on the living room floor. Her corpse was naked, except for a pair of slippers and a pink negligee wrapped around her neck. She was facedown, except her actual *face* was twisted in the opposite direction, obliterated, featureless, and turned toward the ceiling with eyes submerged beneath a glaze of milky and coagulated blood. Someone had broken her neck and wrenched her head all the way around, *Exorcist*-style.

Reflexively, Lynch pulled out his .40 and pointed the gun straight ahead as he looked around the trashed living room. Coffee table turned over, narcotics strewn across the floor, along with the remains of a destroyed wide-screen television. He searched the other rooms—just a quick look-see for the killer or any other bodies. Nothing other than cheap furniture and piles of women's clothing in Astroglide's wardrobe.

Back in the living room, Lynch put his gun away and examined Astroglide's broken body and the battered mash that was once a face. The corpse in front of him wasn't going to give up any information about George Pallis's murder. And now Lynch had *another* homicide on his plate plus an unshackled murderer out there—and who knew what else?

Fuck me. Who did this to you, Astro?

Lynch walked out to his car and radioed a homicide crew to investigate and document the godforsaken scene. Within an hour, the street was filled with marked and unmarked police cars, forensic vans, and an ambulance. Lynch secured the crime scene with the first responding officers, who set up barricade tape and went looking for witnesses. Not a soul anywhere out on the block. While the officers knocked on apartment doors in Astroglide's building and the others in the neighborhood, Lynch went back into the apartment and did another, more thorough walk-through, documenting everything he observed. He briefed other investigators and the people gathering evidence with their crime kits, chemicals, and alternate light sources.

It was uncomfortable business, working inside the stuffy, hot confines of the apartment, and he couldn't wait to get back to his car.

"What's the deal with this one?" Detective John McRains said as he walked in the apartment door, arriving to assist Lynch at the scene.

Lynch shook his hand. He and McRains had been in the Academy together many moons ago and now worked out of the same area. They were around the same age and both Irish, but McRains was a head shorter, with black hair and a prominent porn-style stache.

"I'm trying to figure it out myself. She was a witness to a murder Monday morning and I'd come back to talk with her about IDing the perp."

Lynch had put polypropylene shoe covers over his leather wingtips and McRains did the same as they stood near Astroglide's corpse while an examiner photographed and inspected the body. "This is Timmy Rodgers, better known as Astroglide. This guy, sorry, this *gal*—as she wanted to be referred to—was into some deep shit. Drugs. Lots of 'em. There's shit spread all over this room. She got into other things, too."

"Queer, huh?"

"I didn't go there. Wore women's clothes. Preferred to be known as a gender-specific *she*. In any case, I'm trying to develop a general theory of the crime here. Someone rolled our victim real bad."

McRains nodded. "Looks like he got fucked. In all the ways you can."

Lynch noted how his colleague ignored the gender preferences of the dead—probably to annoy him. Lynch shook his head as he looked at Astroglide's body and then pointed at a woman in forensic scrubs and latex gloves. "Technician there broke out a sexual evidence kit. Collecting stuff now. She says—and you can see—someone destroyed this dealer and nearly tore off the head. She was also brutally raped ... and that was *postmortem*. Sodomized her dead ass so bad, her asshole looks like the Grand Canyon. There's DNA all over her and inside her."

"You're insisting on 'her'?"

Lynch turned to McRains. "What kind of person murders someone and then fucks the corpse?"

McRains shrugged. "Dunno. Accidental necrophiliacs? Crime of rage and passion, maybe. Once we brought in a woman who killed her cheating husband and his mistress. The wife cut her dead hubby's pecker off and kept it in her purse for a couple of weeks before we nabbed her. Remember that?"

Lynch nodded. Unfortunately, he did.

"Perhaps," McRains continued, "this was some Mexican gangland hit. Cartels have done some brutal OTT shit to those who've wronged them. And from what this living room floor looks like, old Astroglide was certainly doing business in those circles."

Lynch frowned. Sure, he knew Astroglide was a dealer, but she was pretty low-level. And if this was a vendetta for narc-ing or a drug-deal gone bad, he wasn't seeing the evidence. There were plenty of drugs all over the apartment.

He and McRains watched as another technician turned off the living room lights and flipped on a specialized black-light that illuminated biological evidence all over the room that had been invisible to the naked eye.

Astroglide's ravaged anus and buttocks radiated a dull red-white, the rectum an open cave inhabited by bioluminescent slime that indicated semen. The corpse, the couch, and the living room floor were peppered with hundreds of reddish-white dots, blobs, and trails glowing in the dark.

Lynch put a hand to his nose. The alkaline, chlorine-like smell of semen seemed to grow heavier—and to Lynch, unmistakable, even though the color was off. He pointed. "Is that what I think it is?

"Yeah. That's a constellation of pecker tracks." McRains scrunched his nose, tiptoeing backward over the floor that glowed with interspersed dots. "Weird, red jizz. Like some kind of blood and cum aggregate. Must've been gang-raped for all that spunk to be coverin' the place."

"Gang-raped? Maybe. I mean, I agree...no way one guy could spew all that DNA." Lynch turned to a technician. "Be sure to let Detective McRains and me know when you run the prints and semen. I wanna know what perps—and how many of 'em—that data might turn in."

The tech nodded.

McRains nudged Lynch. "Hey, you been in to see Tipton?"

"Yeah, this morning." Lynch was already feeling haunted at the thought of Earl, and the mention of his dying friend shook him. "He seems to be in good spirits. Still has his wits 'n' all."

"Good to hear. All the guys are praying for him. He was a good man."

"*Is* a good man." Lynch wasn't ready to use the past tense. He figured he'd never admit Earl was gone—even after his friend was in the ground with a stone marker six feet above his head.

"Right." McRains grimaced. "Sorry. He's one the finest detectives I've ever known, and he's been a great partner for you. Tellin' you what you already know."

"Thanks, John. Appreciate that."

McRains nodded. "I'm here if you need anything. As usual. And..." he cracked a grin. "we'll stay in touch about *her* case."

"Thanks." Lynch smiled back, shaking his head. He liked John McRains. Though the man rolled like some old-school curmudgeon, Lynch knew he was, at his core, one of the good ones. McRains was what Earl called a "detective's detective." And, hey, he was trying.

As Lynch walked McRains back out to the sidewalk, a beat cop approached them, pointing back at another officer who'd just walked up with a tall, emaciated Black man in a dirty pair of polyester pants and a ripped T-shirt. The two stood by the curb. "Do you want to talk with this guy we picked up down the street? He smells like skunk cabbage...says he witnessed something weird here."

"Give him a break, he's a product of this neighborhood," Lynch said. "Just look around. This place is a shithole...a trash-pit full of vice and despair."

The cop shrugged, not seeming to care about Lynch's defense for the dispossessed.

McRains raised an eyebrow at the officer. "Plus, it's a thousand degrees out. Kudos to a survivor."

The cop sighed. "Yeah, yeah, yeah. Ya wanna talk to him or not?"

"Of course." Lynch wanted to tell the cop to watch his tone, but he was too worn out to give a shit. He and McRains walked over to the man.

"I'm Detective Lynch; this is Detective McRains. You got something to tell us?"

The man squinted and looked Lynch up and down, then McRains.

"Yeah. I seen somethin' fuckin' wrong earlier, right here. Was just *wrong*. Don't know if it means shit, but ..."

"Okay, bud. I wanna hear." Lynch turned to the officer. "Bring me a bottled water, please."

The officer paused as if the request was beneath him, but the look on Lynch's face made him move. He ducked into his squad car and brought back a cold bottle. Lynch gave it to the man, who slammed it down.

"So, what's your name?"

The man wiped his mouth. "Tyrell Williams."

"Tyrell, tell me what you saw."

Tyrell hesitated, looking away in thought then piped up. "Crazy shit. Yeah, I's sittin' across the street there. Hotter 'n hell and hopin' for a cold forty or somethin'. Know what I mean? I seen this *big* white mutha comin' out the front of this building here." Tyrell pointed to the entrance door of Astroglide's apartment building. "Yo. When I's sayin' big, I mean the motherfucker was *huge*. Talkin' Hulk-huge...biggest fuckin' animal I seen. And he be sportin' wood...ready to hump anything, man."

Lynch raised his brows. "What d'ya mean?"

"I mean, this mutha had his big ol' rod hangin' outta his shorts. 'Kay? Y'know, playin' with it 'n' shit. He come at me, smilin' and sayin' he wanted to fuck me."

"What did you do?"

Tyrell looked around. "Shit, man. I ran like hell. I wasn't about to let the damn Hulk fuck my ass."

Lynch frowned and his heart jumped a little at the thought of Tyrell's encounter as his mind flashed back to Astroglide's remains. It would take inhuman strength to do that kind of physical damage.

Twisted Astroglide's head all the way around with bare hands...

It wasn't just brute force that created that level of desecration. Whoever did this harbored a truckload of rage and hate...and was out of his goddamn mind. The fact that the man's penis was exposed meant something else, too. Lynch began picturing some kind of homicidal sexual predator.

McRains pulled out a notebook. “What else can you tell us? Any distinguishing marks? What was he wearing?”

“Had ink, y’know? Tats from his face down to his fuckin’ kicks. Red goatee like the Devil. ’N’ like, black shorts and yellow tank top. Yeah, some shit like that.”

McRains got the rest of the physical description of the perp. The guy was a monster of a man, apparently. “Sounds like a professional wrestler with a perma-boner.”

Big, muscles, black shorts and yellow tank top, tattoos. Professional wrestler?

“No fucking way...” Lynch whispered to himself, realizing he had seen the guy who had to be the perp when he drove down the street to Astroglide’s apartment building.

Lynch asked McRains to return to the crime unit and brief the investigators with the description of the suspected murderer while he went out in his car to scour the neighborhood. Between new technology like Rapid DNA, speedy fingerprint results, and hopefully an All Call on the suspect, Lynch hoped they’d nail the sonofabitch sooner than later.

He reached into his pocket, pulled out two twenties and gave them to Tyrell. “Use that and get yourself some real food and water. No booze. And for Christ’s sake, stay out of the sun. Take a shower.”

Tyrell’s eyes lit up as he pocketed the cash and walked away. Lynch didn’t have much faith in where his cash would wind up, but Tyrell had done the right thing and given them *something*, and hey, one good turn deserved another.

Lynch got to his car and gathered his thoughts in the cool breeze of the air conditioning. He wanted to scream from the surge of frustration hitting him.

So close...fucking missed it.

Long gone, the killer could be anywhere. Lynch would cruise the streets just in case. The monster of a perp would be impossible to miss.

“Please show me your face...you unholy degenerate.”

Hoping the All Call would cover a sufficient radius, Lynch put the Dodge Charger Pursuit in drive and sped off down the street.

CHAPTER 18

It took Sid Hoffmann almost two hours to get things back to normal. Assisted by nurses, orderlies, and the security guards on the Peithos Labs floor of St. Cornelius, he'd pacified and sequestered the testing patients who had experienced erotic and emotional upheaval from their Libidonal doses.

Two patients were taken to the emergency room. One was a young man who'd suffered a mild heart attack. The other was fifty-two-year-old Henry Childress, beaten badly by Derek.

Now people were asking Sid questions about Henry and looking for the big man responsible. The Peithos staff wanted to know why Sid had let Derek go. So far, he'd dodged questions by working to maintain order on the lab floor, but he feared he was in deep shit with no way out. Back at his desk, Sid prepared a report on the morning chaos, desperately formulating damage control plans. His hands shook as he typed.

Derek...what have you done to me?

It had been horribly apparent to Sid for years that as a kid, Derek's heart and emotions had been broken down, ruined forever. Sid had watched the transformation happen. Primitive passions were the only things close to actual "feelings" that Derek had left. He hated the world.

All that pain and antipathy he carried had become unbearable in his adolescence. He may not have killed anyone, but little Sid had watched little Derek become homicidal by the age of ten, discharging his anger by punishing smaller neighborhood kids. As he matured, Derek began beating humans with merciless ferocity. Over the years, Sid had come to believe that someday his brother would indeed kill someone.

Jolted from his thoughts by a sudden knock, he looked up to see figures outlined in the frosted glass of his door. Whoever they were, they were ignoring the DO NOT DISTURB—WORK IN PROGRESS sign he'd placed on the handle.

"This office is off limits. Come back later."

The door opened and a nurse stood in the doorway. "Sorry, Doctor, but Officer Stedmann insists on seeing you."

The nurse moved aside. A short and stocky police officer stepped in. "Doctor Sid Hoffman?"

"Yes." Sid remained seated and tried controlling his shaking hands. A slight tic started up in his left eye.

"Couple questions for you." Stedmann looked around. "I'll make it quick."

"Okay." Sid swallowed and gestured Stedmann toward a seat.

"No thanks, I'll stand." Stedmann took off his cap and his bald, black scalp shone under the lights. "Can you tell me what y'all do up here?"

"Umm, lotsa things." Sid's words came out too quickly, so he paused and took a deep breath. "This is a pharmacology research unit. It's run by Peithos Labs and we test new, experimental, and unmarketed drugs."

"And you have folks who sign up to take these drugs, right?"

"That's right." Sid knew full well that Stedmann was asking questions he already knew the answers to. "We compensate all participants once they successfully finish the program."

"Kinda like paid guinea pigs, huh?" Stedmann smiled, showing a large gap in his teeth. The smile appeared false.

"Yeah, something like that." Sid wished he were with Gloria. He wished he were a million miles from here.

"Well, I understand one of your guinea pigs beat the tar out of another one and then left the building. Know anything about that?"

"Unfortunately. Many of our participants—around twenty men—suffered side-effects from the drug we cycled. We had our hands full trying to control them all." Sid looked away from officer Stedmann. Damn, if this cop didn't own relentless eyes. Sid looked back. "One individual became upset when a participant sexually assaulted him."

"Sexually assaulted?" Officer Stedmann's eyes narrowed.

"Yes. Mr. Childress had an encounter with a participant whose space he...uh, *violated.* The other participant didn't take it too well." Sid was thinking fast. What could he say? Yes. Dazzle him with bullshit. "Officer, you understand this is an environment where experimental drugs are administered. The potential consequences—whether a patient will become aggressive, passive, or extremely emotional—we can't predict."

"Don't you corral these people?"

Corral? They're not cattle, you moron.

"Not necessarily. We run an open, yet controlled environment here. People watch TV, read, and keep themselves entertained. We do study how an individual reacts to the drug during the duration of their stay. Most times, nothing extraordinary happens. Today, however, was a rare case where almost everyone spiraled out of control, and unfortunately, someone got hurt."

Officer Stedmann studied Sid for a moment, his hard stare seeming to pick apart Sid's story, looking for a crack. "Yeah, that guy got hurt all right. His face looks like a busted strawberry pie."

Sid tried to extinguish the vision of Henry Childress' obliterated face. "We'll take care of Mr. Childress. He'll be compensated."

"Compensated, huh? I'm sure his lawyer'll appreciate that. Now, I still wanna talk to that assailant. You wouldn't happen to have the man's name and contact info, would you?"

"I'd have to look it up."

Get me outta here.

"You don't remember?" Stedmann drilled his cop stare into Sid again. "Security guys told me the dude said his name was *Derek.* And they say you personally stepped in and let him go. Why would you do that?"

"I'm not the police here." Sid fantasized that Derek was right this minute being hit by a bus or a train, anything that would wipe him off the map. "Our usual procedure when anyone becomes violent or difficult, is to kick him out of the program with no compensation. That's what we did."

"Even when someone damn near kills a guy? He just walks?"

"I'm just following procedure."

"I see." Stedmann studied Sid's face. "Well, a *procedure* like that might put someone in jail. Sounds unethical, what you did. Even the security guards out there found it strange that you took personal responsibility for the guy."

"Officer, I had my hands full with a couple dozen patients who were out of control. I let the bad seed walk in order to calm the floor. I didn't know the extent of Mr. Childress's injuries." Sid tried to maintain a concerned face. He knew he wasn't anywhere as good a liar as Derek, but he was trying. "That's all I can tell you."

"Well, I'm gonna need to see a complete roster of all the patients in this program and their personal info." Stedmann placed his palms down on Sid's desk. "The security team here has a thorough description of the guy. Sounded like a really, *really* big ol' dude. That right?"

Sid thought he was going to get sick. He nodded. "Yeah, he was pretty big."

"Good. I'll expect you to give us a full description as well so that we can compare notes with all the security guards and patients who were near this guy. I'll be back at ya."

"Whenever." Sid hated Stedmann, hated Derek, hated life. "I'll dig up what I can for you."

"Good." Stedmann looked Sid over, the smile shifting into a sneer, and walked out.

Sid exhaled a heavy sigh, feeling an urge to crawl under his desk.

A hundred different ideas shot through his head. He had one glimmer of hope. The roster just might save his ass because he'd never put Derek's name on it. He'd made up a fake lab-sheet on Derek. Once he was in, Sid shredded the paperwork along with the blood and urine tests.

Sid's smile vanished when Officer Stedmann walked back into the office.

"Hey." Stedmann entered and shut the office door behind him. "One other thing you might wanna know. Something happened in the hospital downstairs. Something really bad, *Doctor...*"

Sid scowled, not wanting to know. "Officer, we lease this floor from St. Cornelius. Other than that, we're a separate entity. Anything happening in their world is irrelevant to us."

"Not this time." Stedmann smiled wide, his teeth bright in contrast to his ebony face and dark eyes. Then his expression darkened; his voice skewed angry, very much all police business. "Y'see, right around the time you were having your little horny-man rebellion up here, some sicko raped a woman in a coma. Walked right into her ICU and stuck it to her. He even took a bite outta her."

Nauseating fear coursed through Sid's veins. He blinked and his left eye spasmed. He opened his mouth to speak, but only dead air formed on his tongue.

"The only witness who saw the suspect was knocked out cold. Yeah, the rapist was a damn bull. An' *big*. Knocked out a big ol' Italian bodyguard with one punch. After that, he done helped himself to some powerless pussy."

Powerless pussy?

As awful and shocking as this was to Sid, he almost laughed at the hideous absurdity of it all. He dared not. Officer Stedmann might haul his ass in just for that.

"We're gonna review footage from the hospital security cameras. After our witnesses and y'all check it out, we'll see if we all agree it's the same dude from your little lab here." Stedmann stepped close enough that Sid could detect both the cop's aftershave and his B.O.

Sid gulped. "And if it was, we'll discuss compensation with them."

"Compensation? Shit. This wasn't no Henry Childress beatdown. This is *rape*. Be ready for some *major* accountability."

Sid's mind raced. "I can't answer to that. I'll have to refer you to our lawyers."

Officer Stedmann spit out a laugh. "Lawyer ain't gonna help you here."

Sid stood up, feeling anger now. "Is that a threat?"

"Nawwww." Stedmann shrugged. "Just a hunch. Y'see, I haven't even gotten to the good part yet."

This gets better?

Sid tried to swallow. His throat closed up. "What's that?"

"You sure you don't have the paperwork on that predator? Because it will be a lot easier on you if we find him before the girl's family figures out what happened."

"What are you talking about?"

"The woman who was raped is the daughter of Tico Tortellio."

Sid had heard that name somewhere. *Tortellio*. But he couldn't figure out where he'd heard that surname. Sounded Italian. He stared back at Officer Stedmann with what he hoped was an indifferent expression.

"Tico fuckin' Tortellio. Y'know, the Meat Grinder?" Stedmann shook his head. "Doc, he's the most vicious Chicago Outfit boss that ever existed. He feeds guys like you into a grinder—and out comes burgers. Sausage links n' shit."

Sid eyed Stedmann, his composure crumbling. "What's this got to do with me?"

Stedmann grinned. "You're the one who let that maniac loose. You may as well have done the deed yourself."

Sid's stomach flip-flopped and his voice cracked. "You're a cop and you're telling me that a mobster might kill me. If that's true, I can report it and demand protection from you or any other cop." He sat down and pretended to look over a file.

"Hey...I'm just speculating. And we don't have to do shit, Doc. We ain't bodyguards." Stedmann flashed his bright teeth and leaned onto Sid's desk.

"I told you, we're not responsible for someone's actions after we cut them loose from the study. Why are you hounding me?"

"You're in deep. Looks like you aided a criminal here. We'll help you when you help us."

"I told you; I don't have that information...uh, here at least. I gotta dig through some stuff"

"Suit yourself," Stedmann said. "But you know, the other, nastier side of this coin is the Meat Grinder—he's not gonna be as nice as we are. Bet your ass he's doin' his own diggin'. You're not gonna be worth spit when he connects the dots between his girl done wrong and you. Whether you're on the street or behind bars, there's some things you can't hide from."

Sid slid his chair up closer and sat on his shaking hands. Looking up at Stedmann, he did his best to appear calm. "I'd like you to leave. I need to call my lawyer."

Stedmann frowned. "Do what ya gotta do, Doc. Lawyer up all you want. But I'm getting that roster and all your patient paperwork, y'hear?"

He sauntered out of the office and shut the door behind him. Sid heard him whistling in the hallway, and then, before Stedmann walked away, Sid heard him say, "We gots a dead man walkin' over here."

Sid's mind turned upside down. "Oh God, Derek. What did you do?"

He feeds guys like you into a grinder—and out comes burgers. Sausage links n' shit.

"No, this is all wrong."

You're the one who let that maniac loose. You may as well have done the deed yourself.

Stedmann's words tumbled in his head. Sid lurched and put his head over a small trash can. He vomited bile, hard, over and over, until there was nothing left but dry heaves.

Leaning back in his chair, Sid wished for his office to swallow him up. His stomach cramped, his eyes streamed tears. He thought of

Gloria, his everything. Why hadn't he just come clean in the first place? It wasn't his fucking fault; Derek had drugged and then manipulated him. Would Gloria have understood?

He wondered so many things.

One thing Sid didn't have to wonder about was how much he hated his brother.

Derek...the gift that keeps on fucking giving.

When the dust settled from this nightmare, this druggie...this punisher...this criminal...this beast...this predator...this *rapist* would cost him his upcoming marriage, his career if the Data Safety Monitoring Board or Institutional Review Board opened an investigation, maybe even his freedom if Peithos leveled charges against him. And if that wasn't enough, Derek had induced the wrath of a sadist who turned people into shredded beef as part of his job profile—and that sadist wouldn't hesitate to slap a death sentence on Sid's head if he determined Sid's negligence was responsible for his daughter's harm.

Sid sat shivering at his desk for another half-hour. He tried to think about escaping with Gloria. Maybe things would end up all right. He laughed out loud at that.

Sure, Sid. Sure, it will...

Derek.

You fucking dumbass...you let him go.

Sid managed to collect himself and summon the courage to stand up. He moved discreetly through a few offices until he arrived at the Records Room. He found and pulled a few more documents on Derek's falsified application—papers that would've gotten Derek *paid*. He went back to his office and put it all through a shredder.

When he was finished, Sid grabbed his belongings and shut his office down. With the hospital buzzing and Officer Stedmann likely lurking somewhere nearby, Sid snuck out of Peithos Labs and left St. Cornelius Hospital without telling a soul.

CHAPTER 19

Derek stood in a bleak alley somewhere in Chicago. He stared directly into the glare of the sun. It was a pissed-off and angry star, driving its merciless heat down on him and the rest of the city, wanting to cook everything in its fiery rays.

The sun could try, but it couldn't kill him. He'd fuck it and extinguish it with an ocean of cum.

Derek looked down, his vision taking a moment to clear and focus. Crimson lightning bolts flashed in the corners of his eyes. He was mesmerized by wave after wave of shimmering heat rising up from the torrid sidewalk and road in front of him. Buildings on the block and in the horizon took on distorted shapes as the heat waves twisted and baked the air around him.

He felt combustible inside and out. Sex-stimulants tore through his circulatory system as his skin blistered from exposure to the sun. His insides a furnace of passion and rage, loins ablaze, Derek envisioned himself a walking human flare, morphing into an erection with legs.

The intense heat transported Derek back to himself at seven years old, halfway into his summer vacation. Triggered, his fists balled up on reflex and he began punching at demons that weren't there.

Little Derek didn't have many friends—he never played well with others, period. There was Sid...*that little jagoff*...who was too young to play with anyway.

The Libidonal and the other drugs, and the melting sun, distorted everything in his head. Flashbacks came and went.

Heidi.

Yeah...it was Heidi. The one kid who was nice to him. Heidi, a light blonde, pigtailed girl who lived next door.

The heat...

The heat had been unbearable one particular summer afternoon. Heidi had come by and asked Little Derek if they could play at his house rather than hers because her parents were fighting.

"They sometimes use me against each other." Heidi had looked forlorn. "Screaming about divorce and custody and stuff. I don't wanna be there."

Parents...are evil.

Yes, he told himself, when he was a kid, his father only triggered Little Derek's fear—the rage would come later in his youth and then intensify when he became a man.

He was surely a man and much more today.

That day, though, Dereks's dad was at work, and his mother was inside, busy with housework and Little Sid.

A couple of hours into their play, Heidi said she needed to pee and asked if she could use Derek's bathroom.

"No. No one is allowed in our house, Heidi."

"Please, Derek. I really have to *go!*"

Adult Derek's eyes fluttered and Dad Hoffman's face appeared in front of him for a moment.

Shut up! Shut up, little bitch. He might hear you.

Derek impulsively shadowboxed the air. Then, as crimson lightning bolts lit up his eyes, Dad's face disappeared.

Derek shook his head...In his drug-addled mind, he could still hear Heidi's voice, and himself talking to her.

"Just go out in the backyard here." Derek had waved his arm towards the lawn at the back of the house.

Heidi had shaken her head. "No. I won't go out in the open."

“Then go inside the machine shed and get it over with.” He had himself peed on the dirt floor in the corner of the shed many times while playing in the yard or hiding from Dad Hoffman.

That fucking shed...the bad place.

Heidi had said she wouldn’t go into the creepy, old machine shed unless Derek went with her. Derek had never been in the same room with a peeing girl—not even his mother—and the request had struck him as odd. But she said the shed spooked her.

I went inside. Into the...

The dilapidated shed had been the size of a one-car garage and the inside temperature that day was equivalent to that of a sauna. It was also dark, thanks to the plywood Dad Hoffman had nailed over the windows. Still, small rays made their way in through cracks and holes in the old walls, catching dust particles in their narrow light.

As he stood sweating in the alley, Derek envisioned that filtering light of long ago, as if it were dancing in his eyes this very moment, and he remembered the intermingling smells of dirt, oil, mouse shit and sawdust permeating the old shed. His burning mind and memories nearly made it real again.

Welcome back...you piece of shit.

He punched at the air again with all his might, connecting with nothing but the past.

The shed had been filled with old barrels, yard tools, tires, and dusty beer cases packed with empty bottles. The rafters above were bad news; that’s where bats dwelled and wasp nests were built. Boxes containing miscellaneous items sat stocked across the beams.

Heidi had found a space in the dark corner of the room. “I’ll go right here.” She squatted to do her business.

Little Derek had turned away, looking toward the door to give her privacy. He had hummed to himself—*he hummed to himself now*—and listened to the soft sound of urine hitting dirt. The sound had made him want to urinate, so he had walked to his own corner of the shed.

So fucking...bright.

Derek was gazing up at the sun again. That pissed off, the angry star was aiming everything it had at him.

Fuck you, sun. Fuck you, Dad. The sun...the son.

The sunlight of the *now* triggered Derek into the sunlight of back *then*.

Little Derek had begun to relieve himself just as the wooden door of the shed burst open with a flood blinding sunlight. When Little Derek's eyes focused, he was horrified to see his father in the doorway.

The mother...fucker.

"What the hell's goin' on in here?" Dad Hoffman had stepped menacingly toward the two children. "I come home from work early and find you two in the shed with no pants on."

Heidi had squealed, pulled her underwear up and hidden behind Derek. He'd been standing frozen in fear with his pants and underwear down.

Go for it, motherfucker. Just try it...

"I said, *WHAT* the fuck's goin' on in here?!"

Little Derek was not yet good at deceit—not like the lie-master he'd become. His childhood mind made simple thoughts and produced simple answers.

"We was goin' to the bathroom, Dad."

"You went to the bathroom in the shed here? *My* shed?" Dad Hoffman's voice had quieted.

"Uh-huh."

Dad Hoffman hit Little Derek across the forehead with the back of his hand. "You're a dirty fuckin' animal!"

I hate you!

"I hate you!" Derek blurted the words in his head and out to the alley. He threw blows in the summer heat as if he were punching a speed bag. *I'll kill you, motherfucker!*

Back in the shed, Little Derek, with his jeans wrapped around his ankles, staggered from the blow. He began to fall, but Dad Hoffman caught him, grabbing him by his hair and setting him on his feet.

"Piss in my shed, huh?" Dad Hoffman's breath reeked of whiskey. "You probably shit in here, too. Just like the pig you are. You and that dirty little bitch using my shed for a goddamn toilet." He had slapped

Little Derek's face then. "Take your clothes off, boy. And little missy, you get the fuck outta here!"

Run, Heidi. Run!

Heidi had run out, never to return. Little Derek didn't want to strip, but the look in Dad Hoffman's eyes had chilled his blood, so he'd kicked off his gym shoes, pants, and underwear, and pulled his T-shirt over his head. He'd stood naked in the heat of the shed, clutching himself about the middle and wondering with terror what Dad Hoffman might do next.

"You showed each other your hairless little parts and now you know what they look like. You got a worm and she's got a hole. You want a hole, too? I'll lop off your willy and make you into a little girl. Would ya like that?"

Little Derek had shaken his head and held himself tighter. He wanted to pee again.

I piss on you, Dad.

"No? I just might do it. Or I might tie it in a knot so you don't piss in my fuckin' shed again." Dad Hoffman looked down at Little Derek in disgust and shook his head. "Gonna teach ya not to use my shed as a latrine."

I piss on you...Daaaad.

"I'm sorry." Little Derek had tried not to sob. "I won't do it again."

"Oh, I know you won't." Dad Hoffman had raised one of his grime-caked work boots and, with a hard kick to his small chest, sent Little Derek flying into a stack of beer cases. He'd then bent down and picked up Little Derek's clothes. "You wanna act like a pig? Okay. You're gonna stay here like an animal, with no clothes, no food, and with your nasty little prick out in the open."

The bad place...

Little Derek had crawled out from under the upended beer cases and empty bottles, pulling himself up onto unsteady feet. "Please, Dad. Don't do it. Don't leave me here. I won't do bad again."

"Too late for sorry, boy." Dad Hoffman walked to the door. "I know you won't do it again, because if you do, I'll kill you. Stay in the shed and sleep in the dirt. Think 'bout what you did, you goddamn idiot."

With that, Dad Hoffman had pulled the door shut and locked it.

He didn't come back for three days. Little Derek had lost his mind.

The bad place. You put me there, you motherfucking cunt.

The darkness of the shed had brought out all Little Derek's fears of bats, rats, spiders, wasps, and assorted monsters. He had heard nightmarish things rustling in the dark and had panicked when he felt small stings and bites. During the day he had peeked out through the various cracks and holes in the walls of the shed but couldn't see anything other than foliage and weeds.

His sequestered days had been filled with unforgiving heat that roasted the shed and brought the temperature inside to agonizing highs. Dizzy and parched, Little Derek felt like he was broiling alive.

I'm burning now. Burning red.

On his last night inside, the temperature dropped. Little Derek's unclothed body became chilled. He had curled into a shivering ball on the dirt floor and cried himself to sleep—ashamed, claustrophobic, exposed.

Where was bitch mother? Where were you?

Little Derek's mother had never checked on him. No one had brought him food or water. He had fed on the sparse weeds growing from the soil in the shed. What matter he'd shat, he had buried in the dirt like a cat covering its stool. Little Derek hadn't wanted to imagine Dad Hoffman's wrath if he should find his turds in the loam.

Come to me now, Dad. I'll bury you...bury you like my shit.

On the third day, Dad Hoffman had opened the door to the shed. The bright daylight pouring in seared Little Derek's eyes.

The light hurts my eyes now...

"Get up, boy. It's Saturday." Dad Hoffman had sounded almost jolly. "Forgot you were in here. Lucky for you I had'ta bring a case of empty beer bottles out here."

Little Derek had pulled himself to his feet and hobbled out of the shed, body and hair black with dirt and dust, filthy face encrusted with snot and tear trails, eyes turned to gunk-caked slits.

Out in the summer air, Little Derek began coughing out globs of dirty mucous. His chest, already weak from Dad Hoffman's boot, had picked up an infection from the dust and unclean air in the shed. He'd ended up with a nasty head and chest cold that had knocked him down for a week.

Fucking prick Dad. Motherfucker.

"Stand there and don't move." Dad Hoffman disappeared around the side of the house.

Little Derek hadn't wanted to move. He'd wanted to collapse in the middle of the backyard. He'd waited, staying rooted to that spot until his dad had reappeared with a dripping garden hose in his hands, a fresh cigarette tucked into the corner of his mouth.

"Gonna clean you up before you go in the house, ya fuckin' pig." Dad Hoffman aimed the nozzle at Little Derek.

The water was scalding at first as it blasted through the sun-cooked hose.

Everything burns...

But the water soon turned frigid. Little Derek stayed put, shivering and coughing, as Dad hosed him down while insulting the size of his prepubescent genitalia.

Everyone sees me. Everyone sees my cock.

Little Derek had been mortified to see a neighbor pointing and laughing as he stood naked under the frigid spray. The noise had drawn a few more neighbors, and they'd appeared to be disgusted, maybe even angry. But none of them had been concerned enough to call Child Protective Services. Little Derek had turned away to minimize his nakedness, and through the water, he'd seen his mother in a window, looking down at him and his father. She'd put her hands to her face and then, suddenly, she was gone. Broken and humiliated, Little Derek had wished he could die right there.

Mom. Mother...you fucking cunt.

For Little Derek, the humiliation was an eternity until Dad Hoffman finally turned off the hose and tossed it to the ground. Dad took a drag off his cigarette and exhaled as he examined his first-born. "You can go in the house now, ya twat."

Now, the adult Derek Hoffman pushed himself free of the helplessness of the past. Big Derek was here—and he was angrier than ever.

Violence and rage were Derek's inheritance; hate was his heirloom. The seeds of the bad apple known as Dad Hoffman had germinated and then flourished in his psyche. And now, in his aroused and inebriated state, he felt them growing deeper.

As the sun pounded him with malicious, unforgiving intent, Derek shoved himself away from the wall and out of the alley. He moved through the streets, his body and mind filled with a lust for flesh and blood—and to do unto others ...

CHAPTER 20

After cutting Charlie Reynolds down to size, Tico sent the twins straight to St. Cornelius hospital and raced home to pick up Valentina, who readied a lightweight, charcoal-colored suit for him while he quickly showered. When they arrived at St. Cornelius, the hallway around Annabella's room was frenetic with police officers, hospital staff, and several Tortellio associates.

Tico, his wife and sons, and his two enforcers were forced to wait as the police sexual assault techs finished their examination and the doctors tended to Annabella's immediate needs.

The techs had told him Annabella may have been raped by a couple of men, as evidenced by the copious amounts of semen obtained from the scene. But before his release from Tortellio employment and his mortal coil, Giorgio—now posthumously dubbed, "Fredo" by his *Godfather*-obsessed, nickname-giving sons—said he had only seen one guy before his lights were punched out.

Tico's infinite rage at the delay overwhelmed him. He lashed out numerous times, threatening to kill two doctors, a number of nurses, and a few hospital security guards. He had to be restrained by his wife and sons more than once. He got himself under control and stifled the horror inside his head. With a deep breath, he gathered himself and demanded that he, his wife, and sons have a moment alone with their beloved girl. The Tortellio enforcers and a few police officers kept everyone—including the hospital staff—outside of the room while Tico put his arm around Valentina and walked her in to see Annabella with their sons following behind.

It was quiet in his daughter's room, and Tico could feel the misery emanating from his family as he leaned over and kissed Annabella's cheek. For a micro-second, he visualized the debaser spilling his seed across his daughter's face. He blinked the image away as they stood around her bed. Valentina stood at his side, stroking Annabella's forehead. Liuni and Vito stood behind them, their arms hanging helplessly at their sides. Annabella lay silent and motionless, attached to the beeping machinery around her bed.

Tico squeezed Valentina's hand. He had always considered her to be a strong woman, yes, and also sweet-natured, reserved, and soft-spoken. Within seconds, however, he watched his wife roused to a level of anger rivaling his own. She exploded, screaming for the heads of anyone involved in the desecration her daughter had suffered.

He put his arms around Valentina, trying to calm her, but she kept screaming, clawing at her hair and face as she sobbed. He held her closer, took her handbag and found an Alprazolam in a pill container. He motioned to Liuni to fetch a cup of water and then he forced the pill down her throat. After Valentina swallowed it down, he instructed his sons to take her home. "Rest up at home and come back here to the hospital when you're ready. I'll be home as soon as I can, my love." Tico held her close. "But I need to handle *this* for us first. Know what I'm sayin'?"

The twins walked their mother out. Left alone to agonize, Tico grasped his daughter's limp hand. "Anna, baby. I want you to know, I'm gettin' the bastard whose done all this to you. I already took care of one of 'em. I promise you, they'll all pay." Wet trickles coursed down his pit-scarred cheeks. A rare sting hit his eyes. He hadn't cried since childhood but his daughter's pain had become his own.

Tico straightened Annabella's gown and discovered the bandage on her shoulder.

An involuntary growl escaped him.

Fucker sank his teeth into my baby...

Where to begin? How? Now wasn't soon enough.

Once this beast was in his hands, he planned to do so many painful and bloody things to every inch of him.

Bit by bit.

Piece by piece.

He had lots of ideas.

I'm gonna start with his cock and balls.

He spoke to his daughter in Italian. "A woman who is young and beautiful is never poor. Angel Face, God bless you and keep you. Your family loves you, and I love you. May God open your eyes and let you speak my name again."

Tico walked to the doorway and motioned for his enforcers to come in, then asked his security guards to close the door to her room. "These cops out in the hall are in our pocket, right?"

They nodded.

Sammy said, "Yeah, once they run the security footage, do their DNA tests, prints...whatever else they've collected, they're gonna get us pictures, personal info, and all the other shit they have on record."

"Whaddabout that video?" Tico folded his arms.

Sammy shrugged. "Can't get the hospital surveillance video, right now, Boss. It's in other hands. Hospital security got it."

"I wanna see what this fucker looks like!" Tico threw his hands in the air. "I wanna see what he was wearin' and make sure I see him walkin' in and out. Gotta be sure."

"Don't worry..." Sammy stepped back. "They say that cum-DNA is gonna get done real quick through some tech. Let's hope he has a record. We'll see what he looks like if he has mugshots. And if the prints get matched, our cops are gonna tell us who he is and where to find 'im."

DNA. Cum.

Tico didn't want to even think about it, but horrible visions already swirled around his head. He looked at Annabella, serene, her mind gone somewhere else. She had no idea her honor had been destroyed. Even if she did recover, people would talk about what had happened. What kind of life would she have after this? Tico's blood began to run cold as he pondered ideas of putting his daughter out of her misery—and for being damaged goods with a Tortellio name, which was a hard pill for Tico to choke down.

"You paid our pigs? Paid 'em double, right?" Tico tried to control his voice. "I wanna make sure I get a big head start before the fuckin' cops start lookin' for him. He's *mine.* He goes into my hands to be sliced, diced, cubed, and made into shark chum. Got it?"

"Yeah, Boss." Both Sammy and Grotto nodded. "It's one copper working this for us. Vito knows him. He's been taken care of. And we'll be privy to all the info before anyone else. By the time the cops decide to go after this guy, he'll be dead."

"Good. You sure Giorgio's a done deal?" Tico wanted to make sure the enforcer who'd let himself get duped had been dispatched.

"Fredo? Oh yeah. Had a couple of our guys give him his *severance pay,*" Grotto said.

Tico nodded. "Let's go pick up my boys."

The Tortellio men were escorted out of the hospital by the police officers in the hallway.

As soon as they got to his car, which Mickey had pulled up to the curb, Sammy and Grotto put word out to every Tortellio soldier and crew member to scour every block of the city for the guy as soon as they knew who he was. Then they drove up to the North Shore to check on Valentina and to pick up Vito and Liuni.

His boys. Make men out of them? No better opportunity to do just that than by showing them how to avenge their sister's defilement.

I'll make them men before this day's over.

An hour later, Tico and his sons sat down for lunch at an old-school Italian restaurant on Taylor Street where the menu had always reminded Tico of a place he was fond of in Taormina. Grotto, Sammy, and Mickey sat at a table next to the three Tortellios.

The restaurant was gently lit and the temperature was a comfortable cool, a nice break from the heat and disturbing events of the past day. But he didn't allow himself to relax. Most days, Tico was voracious by noon. After seeing Annabella in such a bad way, however, he didn't have an appetite. He called home to check on his wife, told her he loved her, then drank a couple of glasses of house wine.

It was midafternoon when Vito's phone rang. He answered and nodded.

"Okay ... really? Wow." Instructions were given and then Vito hung up. "We got 'im, Pop. One of our cops given us somethin' real special. He got this guy's wallet from the hospital lost and found. Can you believe it? The dumbfuck left his wallet, ID, everything in a gym bag. We gotta go meet our cop."

"Boys, get the check. Time for us to move."

Half an hour later, Tico and his crew pulled up at the hospital behind a marked CPD car. Tico sat in the back of his Lincoln with Vito, Liuni was up front with the driver. The enforcers in their gray Chevy sedan pulled up and parked behind the Lincoln.

A middle-aged officer with a chunky build got out of the squad car, gave a cautious look around, then went to the rear passenger-side window. When Vito opened the window, the officer gave him a padded mailer. In exchange, Vito handed the cop a thick envelope. "Great job. There's an extra two-large in there. Don't blow it all at the OTB."

No reply. The policeman smiled and walked back to his cruiser.

"Gimme that." Tico swiped the package from Vito. He looked up at Mickey. "Drive somewhere."

The Lincoln pulled away from the curb and Tico opened up Derek Hoffman's wallet, checked his ID and then scanned the police info-sheet their cop had printed for them, which included his social security number, last known address, fingerprints, rap sheet, and mugshots from over the years. He shuffled through all of it over and over again, committing every detail to memory. "Mister Derek Hoffman. Deadfuck."

Hoffman's ID said he was six-foot-nine, 330 pounds. Bigger than Tico...probably bigger than any man he'd known. The spiky hair, the pointy red goatee, the crazy tattoos all over, and the razor-scarred face made Tico sick with anger as he thought about how this vile cocksucker had forced himself on his daughter.

Big and bad, Huh? Wait 'til you getta load of me, head bait.

Tico turned to his sons and shared Derek's arrests for battery, sexual assault, disorderly conduct, DUIs, restraining orders, and other offenses , then passed the documents to Vito. "Memorize these, then share them with your brother." He tapped his driver on the shoulder.

"Hey, Mickey. You know where VanMeter is?"

"Yeah, Boss." Mickey nodded. "It's South Side-ish."

"1666 VanMeter Avenue, Apartment B."

"I'll GPS it."

"*Now*, goddamn it." Tico turned to his sons. "Boys, make sure our attack dogs stick close. This guy's big and bad, reports say, so we'll need the extra muscle."

"No problem, Pop," Liuni said. "I've got 'em on the cell. We won't lose 'em."

Tico was hyped, fixated on Derek Hoffman's photos. He leaned back in his seat. Tools and implements were coming to mind. Clawhammers, blowtorches, razor blades, bolt-cutters, chainsaws, pliers, and assorted utensils. "Got you now, Deadfuck."

He looked out the passenger window. The sun was high, bright, and hot. A red halo circled it. Tico thought of it as a harbinger for the blood and flesh he planned on collecting from every fiber of Derek Hoffman's body.

"Vito, gimme a piece."

Tico never carried a gun. Today, however, having a gun in hand was a must—just in case he needed to blow out Hoffman's kneecaps. He enjoyed imagining what a gun barrel would look like stuffed down Derek's mouth and through his broken teeth.

Vito reached under the passenger seat in front of him and pulled out a black gun case. He put it on his knees, opened it, and took out a stainless-steel Smith & Wesson .44 Magnum with a six-inch barrel. He handed it to his father.

Tico held the revolver, liking its weight and the feel of the walnut combat-grip. He checked the cylinder to make sure it was loaded before setting it down on the seat between himself and Vito.

CHAPTER 21

The world was glowing red. It was like gazing through rose-colored glasses, thanks to those oval, colored pills.

I put the libido...in Libidonal...

Derek had covered a lot of ground since leaving Astroglide's apartment. Block after block brought him new sensations. His emotions were stripped down to elation and rage. His stimulated receptors for sight, smell, touch, and taste made everything he encountered vivid and intense. He detected the scents of decomposing garbage in cans half a block away. The slightest touch of sun, wind, or the fabric of his clothes aroused him, sending him into throes of ecstasy. Every step was a tread into rapture—it was almost too much to bear.

His body had morphed into a single, gigantic, erogenous zone, a six-foot-nine-inch walking erection. Derek touched himself over and over, his penis pointed upward, swollen, bloody, and rock-hard. He thrilled to the sight of his ever-dilated, blood-filled member, shiny with ejaculate. It blinked light and dark reds from the increased blood flow, reminding him of a moody, color-changing octopus.

Cocktopus ...

With the arousal had come extreme aggression. His heartbeat jacked, muscles coiled, and blood pressure soared. Hot and pumped up, trembling and slick with perpetual sweat, he wondered if his body and mind were melting down.

Derek skulked through housing projects and along alleys behind house and businesses as he made his way across the city, seeking shade and relief from the merciless sun that lit up his electrified flesh.

He thought the alleys gave him invisibility, thought the sun still found him. He liked the idea of being invisible—which wasn't easy given his unsettling size and strangers giving him startled glances and a wide berth.

Derek found himself behind a seedy strip mall with a Dollar Store, a pizzeria, a Currency Exchange, and an off-brand mini-mart. Smells of pizza and rotting food waste in the various garbage receptacles made his insides violently stir.

Fucking need ... to eat...something.

A greasy pizza box offered up chewed crusts, bits of cheese, and stray pieces of pepperoni. Without a thought, Derek scarfed it all down as fast as he could. Still hungry, he dug through more dumpsters and bins and devoured handfuls of compost. His rotten eats reeked, ripe and strong, and tasted bitter, tangy, dirty. The foul scent exploded through his senses and he luxuriated in the repulsive flavors on his tongue.

Suddenly, Derek grabbed his abdomen. He moaned from what he imagined were a million razors in his intestines. Something was wreaking havoc on his bowels, and his guts began to revolt. Hastily kicking off his sweat shorts, he squatted next to a dumpster, and evacuated the sharp fire inside him, releasing everything in a noisy, burning, watery blast. It was like shitting napalm. His nostrils flared at the stench of his feces mingling with the odors of the alley. He let out a long, loud, and smelly belch, which calmed his insides. He stood and pulled his sweat shorts back on.

Thirsty ... so thirsty...

As Derek continued behind the buildings into the next block, he encountered a teenager wearing a hairnet and food-stained clothing, spraying down a spill in the alley with a hose.

The teen looked up, startled, and muttered something in Spanish.

Derek growled and flexed.

The teen dropped the hose and fled inside.

Derek grabbed the running hose. The water was cold and refreshing, hydrating his insides like a cool, sensuous kiss. He filled his mouth, slurping, sucking, and taking long swallows, engorging himself with it.

His bladder suddenly screamed. He pulled out his penis to go but the water had aroused him, and he found it difficult to relieve himself. His pounding member remained upright and rigid, and the urine sprayed straight up like a fountain, hitting him in the chin and soaking his goatee with piss.

As he urinated, Derek's peripheral vision caught the teen and four older men dressed in kitchen garb emerging from the back door of the restaurant, yelling in Spanish, wielding kitchen knives. They emptied into the alley and shook their blades as they approached him.

Derek turned to face them while still discharging a vertical stream. He bared his teeth and confronted them, pissing away as he advanced.

The men hesitated, nervously exchanging looks at each other as if figuring out what move to make. Derek could smell their fear. He took another encumbered step to see if the men wanted to play, but they ran back into the restaurant and slammed the door behind them.

Derek continued his journey and soon found himself on a street busy with cars and people. On a day of intolerable heat, where nary a soul had been seen outside, Derek's defenses shot up as he began to mingle with people. Across the street, men and women bustled around a liquor store. To his immediate left, a group of laughing kids played in the water shooting from an open fire hydrant. What an amusing thought—grabbing the kids and maybe throwing them into traffic or into a wall.

His attention turned to something more alluring: *sound.* Music, laughter, and chatter came from the buildings in front of him. Then, smells perked up his senses. The odors of food, exhaust, and marijuana came to him ... and something else.

He cocked his head to the left and then right, his olfactory lobe on overdrive. He sniffed again and again until he identified the odor. It was the smell of sex—hot, wet, and musky, coming from a decrepit tenement next to the liquor store, bringing back to life the debauchery he had committed on the comatose girl at the hospital and the ways he had defiled Astroglide.

He wanted more.

Excited, Derek watched as women of all colors and sizes and shapes wearing thongs, negligees, fishnets, and assorted high-heeled pumps, approached men on the far sidewalk, poked their heads into waiting cars, and escorted concupiscent tricks into the apartments.

Derek slowly ran his tongue over his lips. "Gonna fuck you all."

Following his nose and eyes, he crossed the street. Cars on both sides of the street locked their brakes, blared horns, and stopped inches away from hitting him as he walked into traffic and across the street, oblivious to the danger, the blacktop squishy and melting beneath his feet. Drivers screamed obscenities at him. Derek ignored them as he prowled for his next conquest.

All around him were people he regarded as scumbags. Sweaty men in flashy suits and loud jewelry. Some guys toking up, others peddling all forms of powder and rock. Bums begging for change. Whores. Everyone moved aside as he walked by. He smelled them all, ate them up with his eyes, absorbing their stunned expressions as they took in his appearance.

Close to the tenement, a young woman in red hot pants, a matching half-shirt, and black pumps with clear, plastic, spiked heels approached him. Her light brown hair hung in long braids, and makeup was smeared all over her pale, sweaty face. She looked up at Derek with a twitchy smile. "Whatchya lookin' for, babe?"

Derek gave her a once-over. She was on the scrawny side, but her sallow skin was flushed from the heat and her breasts and buttocks flopped out of her clothing, teasing him. He could smell every molecule of her, including the codfish odor of semen on her breath and from between her legs. He throbbed like a powerline.

"I want *fuck*."

"Oh, I can see that, babe." The woman laughed and looked down at the pitched shape in Derek's shorts. She reached out with her hand and squeezed his cock. "Good lord, what the hell you got between your legs? A third leg? How 'bout we get outta this heat and I take you to the best little whorehouse in Chicago? I'll rock your world, big boy. You got Benjamins somewhere in those shorts?"

Derek nodded, not actually acknowledging the woman, only focused on the sensation of something trickling out of him from her touch.

Break you...into pieces, cunt.

No.

Some rational part of his mind stopped him from punching the whore in her face and crotch. Not on this busy street, he wouldn't. He'd wait. Just a little longer ... until they were alone.

"Well, let's go, baby." She beckoned Derek to follow her, which he did as a fury blossomed up inside him like a mushroom cloud. With each lurching step, his restraint failed further. He welcomed whatever savagery would follow once his desires were unleashed.

CHAPTER 22

Lynch drove around for an hour, patrolling streets around Astroglide's apartment for several blocks, asking people if they'd seen a monster of a man strolling through their hood. Obsessed with finding the suspect who'd killed his informant so brutally, he also felt hot—both in temperature and disposition—as the day turned worse on all levels. The entire week had sucked—and he was only three lousy days into it.

He should never have called Sandy. It was time for him to just leave that whole scene alone and move on.

She divorced you, remember?

He was glad she hadn't picked up.

His heart ached.

"Whatever." Lynch spoke to his car, disgusted with the way events were panning out. Nothing could turn his frown upside down. Sure, if Earl were cured of cancer by some miracle, that would make everything better. And catching that perp would set his mind at ease. Also, a Cubs victory and a winning Lotto ticket wouldn't hurt.

The police radio yapped with a report of a nearby car crash. A late-model Lexus. Requests for paramedics and a tow truck. Reports of gunfire. It was early; he figured there'd soon be more shootings across the city. He turned his police radio down to clear his head.

His mobile phone went off. He answered it via a Bluetooth button on his steering wheel. "Yeah?"

"Donnie, it's John." Detective McRains was on the phone and sounded excited. "Got some info for you on our perp, as well as some shit you ain't gonna believe."

"I'm listening."

"We got a match on the prints already—thank you, Rapid DNA. It's all from one guy. But that weird jizz is still getting worked over at the DNA lab. Even with Rapid DNA, it's gonna take a while, maybe a couple hours. I'm pushing it through as fast as possible. The guy we want has a long record with the law over the last decade. Disorderly conduct, a lot of battery and violent stuff. Minor drug offenses, too, and a sexual assault charge that was dropped three years ago."

"What's the name?"

"Derek Hoffman."

"Stats? Description?"

"Lessee, looks like he's twenty-nine, six-foot-nine, bodybuilding type. Sounds like the big, bad boy Tyrell Robinson described at the scene." McRains paused. "He's got short, spiked-up blonde hair, a red-dyed goatee, blue eyes, tattoos from his face down to his toes, and some gnarly facial scars."

That's gotta be the asshole I spotted near Astroglide's place.

"Address?"

"Yeah. All the way down on the South Side, at 1666 VanMeter Avenue, Apartment B. That's the last known. Nothing on a work history or current employer."

"Great. Text me that address." Lynch finished writing. "I'm gonna go and—"

"Wait, Donnie, I told you I've got some other info for ya." McRains cleared his throat. "It's crazy."

One thing Lynch knew about McRains, the man sure liked to talk. Whenever there was dirt or over-the-top news filtering his way,

McRains was thrilled to dish it out to anyone who would listen. "Is it relevant, John, or are we just gonna shoot the shit?"

"Oh, you're gonna want to hear this."

"What's the story?"

"You heard about Annabella Tortellio? The Meat Grinder's daughter? The one who got hit by a drunk?"

"Yeah. I read the *Tribune* article. And it's been the main subject of watercooler talk ever since it happened. Word on the street's that the drunk driver's gone missing."

"Gee, surprise! An idiot coulda seen that comin'. That drunk's probably been processed into ragù Bolognese somewhere. But in the meantime, Annabella Tortellio was admitted to St. Cornelius Hospital. She's in a coma, right?" McRains paused. "Turns out she was raped in her hospital bed this morning. Some transient dipped in 'n out of ICU."

Lynch sat up. "You're shittin' me."

"Swear to Christ."

"What the hell happened?"

"Nurses discovered a clear rape scene and an unconscious Tortellio enforcer in Annabella's recovery room. CPD was called in with a sexual-assault tech. That tech works in the same lab as our girl."

"You mean the tech who worked the forensic scene over at Astroglide's?"

"Yeah." McRains continued quickly. "The cops at the hospital kept quiet about the rape. I suspect they're Tortellio-friendly. Surveillance footage is also MIA, so there ya go. Anyways, when our lab girl called to report Hoffman's ID on the prints from Astroglide's, she mentioned her co-worker told her about working Annabella Tortellio's rape."

"And I thought Monday was bad."

"Two nasty crime scenes, and I haven't even told you the good part yet."

"C'mon, John. Really?" Lynch, idling at the curb, was growing weary of everything.

"The techs ran their prints—from both scenes, right? They say we're dealing with the same guy."

Lynch blinked and pulled the car over to the curb, his mind trying to piece the two crimes together. "Are you sure the techs didn't mix shit up? I mean, that's one hell of a perp. He'd been a very, very busy guy this morning between what happened at St. Cornelius and then at Astroglide's."

"Tell me about it. Both crime scene techs thought there was more than one perpetrator, 'cause of the large amounts of cum that ended up everywhere at both scenes. But the lab's saying they're certain it's only one guy, and the semen is that same crazy red color and consistency. That's our boy, no doubt."

Lynch resurrected the sight of Astroglide's battered, bioluminescent, and semen-covered body glowing under the black light.

"Even with the ongoing DNA work, it's a no-brainer far as I see. The damn prints are a match. The techs aren't sure why the jizz is red, or how one man could produce so much of it." McRains took a breath. "He must have back-up balls or somethin'."

"Sounds like it." Lynch wished he owned a pair of back-up balls. Rather, he wished his scrotum had two normal, healthy testicles inside it. Lynch likened his balls to his partnership with Earl.

Once there were two, now there was one.

"The Chief of Detectives wanted all DNA evidence pushed through now rather than later." McRains paused. "Gotta push it. He wants to see someone get their money's worth out of that Rapid DNA processor."

"Rapid DNA is really something, though," Lynch said. "So many more cases are getting solved now—even some old cold cases where we thought it would have taken a miracle for that to happen."

"It had better work wonders for the price. I heard each one costs around $100k."

Lynch whistled loudly.

"But you're right, it's a miracle machine," McRains continued. "We can identify a serial rapist or murderer in something like ninety minutes now, which can help us stop perps like this insane fucker from slipping through our fingers."

"Hey, in addition to the DNA, did you ask for them to check if any drug traces have been detected in this guy?"

"Oh, yeah. I was about to tell you that. I'm getting a play-by-play as the Rapid DNA results come back one by one, and you're right, there are plenty of drugs tagged in his spunk." McRains paused. "All kinds of shit: hallucinogens, anabolic steroids, Ecstasy, coke, and something else they can't identify, but they said the compounds were like Viagra's sexual stimulants. His body's a chemistry experiment."

"Hmmm ... so this Hoffman massacred Astroglide and raped Annabella Tortellio, which means that right now Tico Tortellio's lookin' for the guy?"

"No doubt, D. We're on the same trail, though, and might even have a head start thanks to your All Call, our criminal records and mugs of Hoffman—and the description that bum gave you over at Astroglide's."

"But right now, no officers have been given Derek Hoffman's address?" Lynch put his car in drive.

"Nope. Waiting to see what you wanna do."

"Hold tight." Lynch pulled away from the curb and forced himself into a busy street. "I'm gonna fly over to Hoffman's place. I'll need reinforcements. Meet me there."

"You got it, Don."

Lynch tapped the .40 on his hip. "John, be sure I get that backup. If Tico's on the hunt, I might be dealing with two fucking maniacs."

"I'm hearin' ya and I got you."

"Thanks." Lynch hung up.

He turned on his police lights and flew down side streets, passing cars that pulled over to let him by. He zipped, turned, and floored his way toward a part of the city he never looked forward to visiting—even *without* Hoffman living there.

He turned a corner and looked up through the windshield. Though the burning sun had kept the sky bright and clear blue, he could feel unseen clouds massing above him.

CHAPTER 23

As the Lincoln sped toward Derek Hoffman's home, Tico sensed a nagging familiarity—the stakeout, the group of thugs waiting for their mark, the location—as though he'd been in this scenario before.

"Y'know, I'm havin' déjà vu right now."

"Déjà what?" Vito said.

Liuni turned around in his seat, lifting his hand in a mock threat to slap his brother, "Déjà vu, *finocchio!* It's foreign. French or somethin'. Means ya feel like ya been in this same place before."

Vito shrugged. "Okay, Einstein, I've felt like that before. Sometimes."

Tico rolled his eyes. *Annabella got all the smarts out of this batch.*

"I remember now." Tico nodded as the car passed a familiar building. His sons turned and looked at him, ready to hear it. Mickey, the driver, sat silent, ever-alert at the wheel. "Back in the seventies, when I was about your age, I was getting my hands dirty working my way up for your *Nonno*, Carmine." Tico made the sign of the cross. "I busted my ass, unlike you two who've had the luxury of moving right into the throne without so much as hijacking a Yugo."

Liuni and Vito grinned into their collars. Tico knew they were spoiled. They'd been through Tico's ball-busting and scolding a million times and it always rolled off their shoulders. Nothing ever *really* changed and that's how they liked it.

"Time for you boys to grow up and that's why you're in bootcamp with me." Tico looked at his sons, appraising their weaknesses and ignorance. He sighed, knowing any qualities they lacked in leadership, courage, and ruthlessness were his fault. Well, too bad. He wasn't going to beat himself up about it anymore, now that he was trying to effect some actual change.

"When I was in my twenties, there was a guy in our crew named Shotgun Jimmy. Shotgun Jimmy used a *lupara*, a sawed-off Sicilian shotgun—something you two *chooches* should already know. Jimmy had a girlfriend. Her name was ... Tammy, I think. Anyways, this chick was hot and classy, not like these tramps you guys bang."

Vito laughed and held up a hand. "Hey, one of these tramps might be your daughter-in-law someday."

"Don't get smart. You marry one of those wanna-be porn stars and I'll have you out in Vegas, emptying ashtrays at the Golden Nugget." Tico glanced over at Liuni and pointed a finger at Vito. "Now shut your fuckin' hole and let me finish my story."

Vito frowned and sighed, his eyes on Tico.

"So, Jimmy's girl. She looked like a young Angie Dickinson, not that you know who that is." Tico smiled at his memory. "She had great legs. Was a great cook, too. She still lived at home, used to come by the club on Saturday with a big pot of homemade pasta and gravy she made with her mamma.

"Anyway, this girl had a stalker, a real low-life scumbag. We called him 'Herman,' because he was big and ugly like that Munster guy on TV—Herman Munster."

"Yeah, we remember that show. Vito and me watched it a lot when we was little." Liuni said.

Tico nodded, surprised his sons remembered anything before iPhones and partying killed their braincells. "This Herman, he used to hit on her all the time and ask her out. She'd tell him to leave her alone, but he'd still keep comin' back like a rash. He lived in her neighborhood, down the street from her parents' house in Niles. Jimmy had already rolled him over lotsa times. Beat the living shit out of him once, too, when Herman was caught stealin' this girl's panties off her clothesline in the backyard."

"Sounds like somethin' Liuni would do," Vito said.

"Hey! Fuck you. You're the pervert of the family." Liuni threatened Vito with a mock slap.

Tico ignored his sons. "Even with all the threats and the ass-kickings this guy got, he still kept harassing the girl. Wouldn't stop. He had a real problem, and then it went too far. Cocksucker ended up rapin' her one night, right in her front yard."

Tico looked at his sons, their faces had turned grim as this story no doubt hit close to home.

"She was beaten and soiled like a blow-up doll." Tico cleared his throat, no longer smiling at his recollections. "When she finally called Jimmy, it was from her hospital bed. He rushed to see her and she told him the whole story best she could. Y'see, her mouth was wired shut. As you can imagine, Jimmy went fuckin' berserk. Called in to me and my crew. Within an hour, we were up in Niles. We nabbed Herman, threw him in a van, and brought him back to my old club—kinda like the one you jamokes are mismanaging now."

Liuni and Vito flushed red.

"We took Herman down into the basement." Tico shook his head; he could still see the bastard's face. "We had six guys down there with him. Stripped him down to his bare ass and laid him out on a folding table. Had his arms and legs tied down. Cocksucker fought like crazy, but not for long. Not after all six of us punched him into submission."

Tico swallowed. He looked down and found his fists were clenched.

"I had a workbench down there, laid out with a buncha tools, utensils, and devices that me and Shotgun Jimmy used on Herman. We had a stereo down there, too. Me 'n' Jimmy argued about what music to play to drown out the sound of our work. I wanted Sinatra, he wanted Tommy James and the Shondells or some shit. I had a buncha records down there and Jimmy dug up a 45 of *I Think We're Alone Now*. I finally gave in. I mean, we were carvin' Herman up for Jimmy's girl, after all.

"So, the whole time we went to work on Herman, we cranked that tune loud. We played it over and over again in the fuckin' basement to drown out the screamin' and hollerin'. It got stuck in my head. Every time I hear it, to this day, I think of goin' to town on old Herman." Tico chuckled in a musical tone, "Oh Herman, *I think we're alone now*."

Liuni and Vito smiled.

"Talk about doin' a number." Tico shifted in his seat. "I took a scalpel, cut off his ears 'n' nipples. Jimmy pried his mouth open with a screwdriver and then pulled out his teeth with a pair of pliers. We yanked fingernails, then took the fuckin' fingers. We broke bones, drilled his kneecaps, electrocuted his fuckin' gonads, and burned his toes off with a torch. Oh, how that cocksucker screamed." Tico's memories came back fresh, and the excitement picked up in his voice. "Herman never passed out, though. He was a tough prick; I'll give him that. One of the toughest I've seen. He kept begging for death, but we wouldn't drop him." Tico shook his head and smiled. "I swear, Jimmy could've been a surgeon. He took that scalpel and sliced off Herman's face, so he looked like one of them German models they had at the Museum of Science 'n' Industry. Y'know? Like those Body World things where ya see all the facial muscles 'n' shit?"

"Skinned him raw for the Meat Grinder, huh?" Liuni smiled, then he and Vito snickered as they teased their old man with the forbidden nickname.

"How many times have I warned you boys about callin' me that? Maybe I should stop the threats and just slap the fuck outta youse. Ya know you do *not* call me nothin' but Pop or Dad. *Capisce?*"

My two punks...gotta learn. Respect. Responsibility. So much real bloodwork ahead for them to do...

"Anyway, after we'd reduced Herman Munster to a miserable pile of bloody horseshit, Jimmy cut Herman's balls and cock off with one of them electric bone saws. One of them little circular jobs they use to open someone's head with." Tico clapped his hand once. "And that was that."

"Bled to death, huh?" Liuni said.

"Naw, asphyxiation." Tico paused. "Sure, he was bleedin' out a bit, but Shotgun Jimmy stuffed Herman's family jewels down his own throat while he was still wide-eyed and bleedin'. Suffocated on his own privates."

"What about Jimmy and his girl?" Vito asked.

"Well, first Jimmy got rid of Herman Munster. His remains are somewhere in a concrete slab in the water between Soldier Field and the old Meigs Field airport," Tico said. "Then Jimmy went to the hospital, told his girl that the scumbag wouldn't be around any longer. And then he let her go. Broke his heart, but he had to do it."

Liuni and Vito both said, "Why?"

"She was damaged goods. Too damaged and defiled to ever make a wife." Tico sighed. "Even if Jimmy had stuck with her, it didn't look good to all the friends of *ours*. It woulda made things tough on Jimmy with all that nasty talk and such. He was a *capo*, after all. Don't matter anyway, Shotgun Jimmy was whacked at a sit-down in New York, and that old girlfriend of his ended up killing herself a few months after the rape."

Tico's sons were silent.

"This story hits close to home today. That's why we do what we do for Annabella. This is *beyond* personal. This guy is gonna be fucking deader than dead, *capisce*? Anna...she's gonna have her honor avenged. Got it?"

Liuni and Vito nodded. They might not be as sharp as Tico wanted, but he knew that they believed in and cherished the preservation of their family's name and reputation.

We'll avenge her honor. But what kind of life would she be able to have now, after this defilement, even if she recovers? How in God's name did it to come to this?

Tico shivered as he began to consider the unthinkable. It would be the worst thing he'd ever have to do but he couldn't bear to have anyone treat his beloved baby girl as something damaged, soiled—or even worse, perhaps, to regard her with pity.

Was this the only way he could prevent her from being harmed again? Was there another way?

He held up a finger. “This guy … this Derek Hoffman…he’s our own Herman Munster.”

“I prefer callin’ him Arnold. As in, Schwarzenegger,” Liuni added. “He’s got those Terminator muscles ‘n’ shit.”

Vito chuckled. “Yeah, the *‘I’ll be back’* dude.”

Tico rolled his eyes and shook his head, but he was grateful for the distraction.

“You guys and your fucking nicknames for everyone. I pray for a day when you’re no longer acting like a pair of goddamn idiots.”

CHAPTER 24

"Name's Cortnee." The prostitute led Derek up a rickety flight of stairs in a tenement that was a spark away from a fireman's worst nightmare.

The building had no air conditioning or open windows, causing Derek to exude moisture from every pore.

Hot. Hot 'n' wet.

He followed the new prize of his desire.

A bare bulb hanging from a wire made odd shadows in the dark stairwell, which animated themselves in Derek's over-stimulated mind as Cortnee led him down a hallway covered with threadbare carpet, abandoned clothes, soiled condoms, garbage. The walls were cracked, peeling, and covered with graffiti. Odors of piss, smoke, and a thousand recent sex acts bombarded his olfactory lobe.

Derek followed Cortnee into a hot and stuffy studio apartment. She flicked on a light. The blinds were drawn over the windows and the only furniture he saw was a beat-up kitchen table covered with dirty dishes, the carcass of a cooked chicken in pieces on a cutting board, and utensils. Flies landed on the table and orbited the lone light in the ceiling. As he looked past the table, Derek saw a stained mattress in the middle of the apartment. Engulfed by the cat-piss stench of meth soured by old chicken grease, mingling with the smells of numerous sweaty men, bodily fluids, and latex, Derek's exhilaration rose.

Cortnee shut the door and posed in front of him. "Do you talk?"

Derek stayed silent.

She laughed. "Oh yeah, you want *fuck*, right?" Cortnee winked, playing with her long braids. "Well, I want cash. Gonna need to see that green first."

Derek nodded. He stared at her body ... taking in every luscious part of the camel toe that was pushing through the red hot-pants.

Fuuuuck ...

Here was desire incarnate, a living, breathing, fuck-doll if Derek ever saw one. She was irresistible.

His impatience simmered up; he needed to penetrate her now, in every possible way, to satisfy his lust. He also wanted to tear her limb from limb to vent his mounting aggression and sate his growing hunger for violence.

Cortnee wrinkled her nose. "You don't smell so good. You're wet and smeared with all kinds of nasty shit. Need you to wash up before we get down to it."

Derek stared into her.

"I'll clean you up ... but it'll cost you extra."

Derek grinned.

"You're one big and scary-looking boy. You ain't gonna hurt me, right?"

Derek breathed deeply, his heartbeat quickening, his muscles tensing up to attack. But just as he was about to move on her, an insistent knocking came from the door.

"Yo! Fuckin' workin' in here." Cortnee stomped a foot. "Come back in thirty."

The door flew open with a bang, revealing a tall, slender, Black man with long, straight hair, wearing a white suit, white leather shoes, and gold sunglasses. Flashy, bulky gold rings covered his fingers and thumbs. His fingernails were extremely long. He didn't seem bothered by the heat.

Derek wanted to destroy him on sight.

"I ain't comin' back in thirty, when it's you who's owin' me." The man frowned and flashed a grille full of gold teeth. "Got my money, bitch-bag?"

"Scatt-Dogg, sorry. Shit...I thought I'd settle with you on the hour. Been busy here." Cortnee stepped back.

"Busy, my ass. I seen ya workin' your jaw with the girls out there, shootin' the shit with no dick on your tonsils." The man took his sunglasses off and glared at Derek with a degree of awe. "Jesus H. Christ in hell...if you ain't the biggest motherfucker I ever seen. Imma call you 'Bicep.' What funhouse did you roll outta, boy?"

Derek didn't respond. He stared at the pimp with deep contempt.

"You eyeballin' me, boy?" Scatt-Dogg pulled his suit jacket to the side to reveal a small chrome handgun stuck in his waistband. "Tha's right, you overgrown cracker. Keep givin' me stink-eye and I'll give you a cap or two to remember me by."

Derek balled his hands into fists as Cortnee stepped in front of him.

"Scatt. He's just hot and bothered. Take it easy and let me take care of the man."

Scatt-Dogg gave Derek a hard look. "He's hot and bothered all right. His pecker is bustin' through and he's greasy as all get out. Fuckin' stinky, dirty fucker."

Cortnee nodded, her hand rising up over her nose. "I'm gonna wash him up."

"Good. Charge this gorilla for *my* water. I ain't runnin' no bath house." Scatt-Dogg jabbed a long-nailed finger at Cortnee. "You need to be doin' less talkin' and more ass-pushin' up here."

Derek took in the tension between Scatt and Cortnee. His senses lit on the unpleasant electricity, the anxiety and anger in the baking air, and all of it irritated him.

Fuckin' stinky, dirty fucker.

Scatt-Dogg's words took Derek back ...

You're a dirty fuckin' animal!

Dad Hoffman...

Derek wanted to kill the memories and kill these two in front of him.

"Here's what I've got since noon." Cortnee pulled out a wad of crumpled bills and handed it to Scatt.

Scatt-Dogg took the cash, counted it, and shook his head before putting the money under his suit jacket. "Little short." He glared at Cortnee. "If you didn't have my cash and a trick here, I'd crack ya. I don't know what you been doin' with your time up in this apartment, but I want your ass on the street all day, not up here tweakin' on the rocket fuel. Dig? I'm hittin' the salon, gonna be out for about two hours. I'll be back to check the street, so you better be down there with twice this amount or else..."

"Scatt, baby, I done give ya everything I made today." Cortnee's words poured out quickly. "I got this dude here but no tellin' who else is gonna be around. It's too damn hot even for regulars wantin' to blow a load."

Scatt-Dogg put a hand up. "I don't wanna hear it, 'kay? I'm givin' ya twenty minutes t'do your thang with Bicep here—" He paused, looking Derek up and down and sneered. "—then I want your ass down on that street makin' up for lost time. Dig?"

Cortnee nodded.

"Well, quit eyein' me and get to fuckin', bitch." Scatt-Dogg shot a final glare at Cortnee and then at Derek, straightened, and spread his fingers out as if taking inventory of his rings. He put his sunglasses back on and sauntered out as Derek's urge to brutalize him came burning to the surface.

Cortnee turned to him as the door closed. "Don't mind Scatt-Dogg. He works all of us girls down below. He can be a real mean fuck."

"Mean fuck." Derek touched himself and locked eyes with Cortnee as the blaze inside him grew fiercer and his vision surged crimson.

I am burning red...

"Big boy, you're ready to go, ain't ya?" she said.

Derek dropped his shorts and grinned as he gripped his erection.

"Damn, boy. What you want, then?" she said as he groped himself. "Usual tricks like a blowjob 'n' lick your balls without a jimmy's gonna be thirty bucks. And believe Imma wash your junk with a washcloth before goin' there, 'kay? You wanna fuck my vajayjay—you're wearin' a jimmy for sure—that's gonna be fifty. And if you think you're stickin' it up my ass, then you better cough up a Benjamin and *two* jimmys goin' on that crazy third leg in your hand."

"Mean fuck." Derek stroked himself and ground his teeth, looking at Cortnee with a mind full of horrific intentions.

"You can jerk all you like, but that's gonna be twenty." She licked her lips. "Twenty-five if you want me completely naked."

Derek continued his mute masturbation.

"Gimme some money, fool." Her tone turned unfriendly. "I ain't lettin' ya jerk here for nothin'. Scatt-Dogg's watchin' the clock, too. So, pay me or get the fuck out!"

"Mean fuck." Derek's eyes fluttered and he ejaculated a stream of white and red.

"Aw, hell no!" Cortnee's voice grew louder. "I can see you don't got money in those fuckin' nasty-ass shorts. I'm gettin' Scatt-Dogg." She turned away from Derek, walking toward the door. She began yelling. "Scatt! Scatt-Dogg!"

As she reached for the doorknob, Derek's arms shot out and grabbed her from behind. She cried out as he clenched her braids in his fists and yanked her off her feet, then immediately threw her down. She hit the floor with a hard thud and a deadened scream.

Naked and grinning down at his prey, Derek stood above her, straddling her prone body. She cursed and kicked him hard in the testicles. Derek didn't even blink. No pain for him, only pure pleasure rocketed through him.

"Do it...again...I want it."

Cortnee shrieked and scooted back as fast as she could, her high heels kicking away. But Derek was on her. He grabbed her throat and picked her up with a vein-pumping hand wrapping around her neck. He held her, squeezing her trachea and jugular while she squirmed and struggled for breath. He punched her in the face, and her lips detonated into a red explosion. He dropped her on to the kitchen table and it collapsed, sending chicken bones, aluminum foil rolls, disposable lighters, plastic straws and assorted other paraphernalia clanging and scattering across the floor.

Derek snorted like a Cape Buffalo as he looked at the helpless creature before him. Cortnee crawled, sobbing and spitting out gobs of blood, hands flailing as she reached out for items on the floor. Derek squatted behind her, grabbed her waistband, and began tearing at her shorts. He smelled her fear. He smelled her sex. It hit him in waves and made him mad and insatiable.

As he tore her shorts off, he flashed back—

The school.

The Bradley Davis School for Delinquent Boys and Young Men where the older boys—

Raped me. Cornholers ... all of 'em.

Derek pictured himself being held down and sodomized.

His father.

Dad. The real *MEAN FUCK...*

He pictured Dad Hoffman making him strip then beating him within an inch of his life.

Vivid...oh so vivid now. The memories were as intense as if they'd just happened.

Do unto others. Women. Men. EVERYONE...

Overwhelmed by shame and rage, along with images of the older boys laughing and defiling him, his hands turned into fists as fury filled him and fused with his erotic arousal.

Derek stood and looked at down Cortnee as he did every other woman: an object for getting off, a punching bag for his frustration and anger. His eyes rolled back into his head. In his distorted, drug-marinated mind, desire to do more than just fuck or beat the bitch began to take root. He wanted to see what she looked like on the *inside.*

An audible *thump* was followed by Cortnee's high-pitched, *"Motherfucker!"*

Derek's eyes opened and he looked down and discovered a small butcher's cleaver stuck hard in his left hip, its square blade wedged at least an inch into his bone. His blood pooled thick across the metal, dribbling in a scarlet stream down his bare, muscled leg.

Cortnee moved away, scooting backwards on her hands and butt across the floor toward the door as she cursed him, trembling.

For a moment, Derek ignored her, fascinated by the cleaver embedded in his body and the sight of his own blood. Then a sliver of pain crept up from his hip. He could feel the slice, the wound, and the hurt from the blade.

He bellowed, furious and insulted that this *bitch* had caused him pain and broken the erotic and violent spell that had dominated his every move with pleasure.

"Fuckin' ...! Cuuuunnnnnnt!" Derek roared. He ripped the cleaver from his hip and turned to her. "I...am...the...*mean fuck!*"

Cortnee screamed, mouth wide. She raised a hand as if it would halt the driving blade, but the cleaver came down. With a crunching, irriguous sound, it split her hand in half between the index and middle finger, down through the palm to her wrist. Derek pulled the cleaver out, yanking it to free it from her bone. He drew it back again and raised it high.

Crossing the threshold into butchery gave him a release as ecstatic as a sexual climax. Hacking and mutilating, coming and coming. His afterglow arose from the lingering pleasure of the bloodbath.

"Gooood...so, so, sooooo good." Derek smiled as Cortnee screamed again, her cry interrupting Derek's moment of bliss. He cut her wail off, slicing the cleaver down hard and burying the thick blade deep in her face, sideways, from the right side of her chin, across her mouth and nose, and into her left eye-socket and brow

From toe to temple, Derek's skin was smeared with hot blood that mingled with his sweat. He dripped, burned, and gulped air like a jackal in heat as he loomed over his prize. With the cleaver still embedded, Cortnee's body convulsed as if surges of electricity were pumping through her.

One final wracking shudder and Cortnee went still.

He wanted to give this whore everything he had. He pulled the cleaver from Cortnee's splayed face and touched himself, finding his sex ossified.

Petrified.

Ever-hard.

With a groan of pleasure, he raised the cleaver and came down on her again, and again. Blood rained and flesh separated from bone. But rather than satisfying him, the hacking only fueled his blood lust. He wanted more.

CHAPTER 25

The unmarked Dodge Charger Pursuit wove in and out of traffic as Lynch barreled toward Derek Hoffman's apartment. McRains had texted him the address along with police photos of Hoffman and his rap sheet.

Lynch's gut ached. He cursed to himself as he drove recklessly, desperate to stop Derek before he did something that Lynch wouldn't forgive himself for.

Lynch had seen enough of Hoffman's actions back at Astroglide's crib, and between that and the Annabella Tortellio assault, it was clear Hoffman was an out-of-control lunatic with no apparent method to his madness. He thought about Hoffman doing something else horrific this very moment while the overextended CPD scrambled. Hell, Lynch was overextended, too. On top of finding Hoffman, he still had to find out who killed that john on Monday morning.

Lynch had seen his share of carnage over his years with the CPD. Ritualistic gangland hack-and-saw jobs, decapitations, infants in microwaves, suicides where victims ended themselves in front of eighteen-wheelers doing eighty on the Expressway. And this Hoffman and his crimes were just as ugly, but the fact that he'd attacked people one after the other—and was high on just about everything you could ingest—heightened the likelihood that more destruction was in store.

Goddamn, I need to get this bastard now.

A dump truck cut him off and he switched the flashing headlights and dash lights on, pressing on his horn and swearing at his windshield.

"Get outta my fuckin' way!"

Who was Derek Hoffman? What else was he capable of? Though Lynch didn't consider himself a Jedi-level criminal profiler, Earl *was* that good. Lynch knew enough, and had worked with Earl long enough, to study a crime scene and put together a psychological profile of a sexual predator and a killer. He'd taken courses in abnormal human psychology and had friends in the FBI who handled serial killer cases—a couple of which Lynch and Earl had been involved with over the years. Lynch had gleaned what he could from their knowledge and his own experience. When it came down to it, though, a profile could help an investigation, but it couldn't *replace* an investigation.

You still have to get out in the field and play in the mud.

As he drove, Lynch ran Hoffman's stats through his head: White male, late twenties, muscular build, bigger than any man he'd ever laid eyes on. Long history of everything from theft and disorderly conduct and drug possession to domestic violence and barbaric assaults. No current employment. And now a murder and two violent rapes, with seemingly no rhyme or reason.

Mental illness? Definitely. Psychosis, for sure. Lynch theorized Hoffman was also a loner who didn't associate well with men or women. He figured he must be getting money from family or illicit activities. Who the hell would hire him?

In his experience, it was males in their twenties and thirties who perpetrated these crimes. They committed their deeds on their own race. White killer on white victim. Black killer on Black victim. And so on. So, what was this guy's MO? Hoffman had raped a white woman then killed and sodomized a Black trans woman. Sure, Astroglide may have identified as a woman, but she still had all her male equipment intact. Lynch figured Hoffman hadn't given a shit as to Astroglide's gender. It seemed that the perp just wanted to stick his custard-launcher into any orifice that would accommodate it.

Any port in a storm, they say...

City blocks flew by, and nothing got in his way. The traffic gods were smiling on him. Lynch drove and continued to ruminate.

Hoffman's crimes appeared to be disorganized, unmethodical, unplanned, and not accompanied by the careful disposal of evidence one sometimes saw in organized sociopaths. Lynch saw him as confused and spontaneous. He had never seen a killer so straight-up sloppy. Hell, Hoffman had walked all over the crime scenes, leaving enough DNA and prints to earn him a thousand-year sentence. He seemed to lack the mental clarity to cover his tracks.

And Hoffman had committed horrors Lynch had never imagined.

Postmortem anal penetration?

Another sick crime Lynch hadn't seen before. It disturbed him.

What evil lurks in the heart of Hoffman?

Lynch figured a killer capable of committing such senseless and brutal sex crimes must be in the grip of one or more forms of the deep psychosis he suspected. Sure, losing one's mind on hallucinatory drugs could lead to murder—Lynch and Earl had seen it before. Those cases, however, usually involved killing someone close, by accident, with the killer exhibiting remorse afterward.

The biology of violence had always interested Lynch. Why were some people capable of doing the worst possible things to others? Whatever Hoffman's life might've been before, he was clearly now damaged beyond repair—a vengeful and sadomasochistic sexual predator, driven to assault, degrade, and kill others, apparently without emotion or remorse.

Hoffman seemed to be going for broke. What was wrong with his head? Lynch knew that the brain was fragile. Even the slightest trauma to the amygdala—the small, almond-shaped clusters of gray matter stuck deep in the temporal lobes—could make someone homicidal or cold-as-ice insensitive or consumed with uncontrollable sexual desire.

Are you there, God? It's me, Donnie. Please get me Derek Hoffman before things get worse ...

As he continued to speed south, Lynch began bracing himself for resistance. Given Hoffman's huge size, deranged mindset, and the violent crimes in his arrest record, there was a good chance that Hoffman was not the type of guy who would allow himself to be handcuffed.

As he cruised closer, his mobile phone rang. He hit the button without looking at it. "Detective Lynch."

The caller hesitated. Lynch heard breathing on the line before a female voice spoke. "Hi, Donnie."

Lynch swallowed hard. His face flushed by the surprise. He hesitated. "Hey, Sandy. How's things?"

"I'm fine." The response sounded stiff. "What's up with you?"

"On the job at the moment."

"Ah, the job. Of course."

Was she being insulting? Don't be defensive, Don.

"So, what's up with you?"

"Well, Donnie, I saw your name on my caller-ID. Missed call? I was wondering what you might've wanted. You didn't leave a message, so ..."

Shit.

He'd forgotten about the earlier call. His mouth went dry and a hundred different things invaded his mind. There were things he wanted to say, but he found himself blank. "I, uh, don't remember."

"Figures." Sandy paused. "Probably wanted to know if I'd give you back your air fryer."

He wanted to talk to her so badly, but the goddamn timing was horrible. He took a left, closing in on Derek Hoffman's street, mere blocks away. "Now's a bad time, Sandy. But I really want to talk. I want that much, okay? I'm in a bit of a hurry here."

"What's the big deal this time? Gang shooting? Vengeful man killed ex for TV?"

Lynch smiled. He missed Sandy's sarcasm and it was wonderful to hear again. "You know I don't go there with you. What happens out here, stays out here."

"Oh, I know it all too well. You don't talk about shit."

"Look, I'll call you later, as soon as I get a chance." VanMeter Avenue came up on his left. "Would that be all right?"

There was a long, exasperated, exhalation. "Sure. I'll be waiting here for you with bells on. Watching the phone and praying, 'Oh, sweet Donnie, please call me.'"

Ouch.

"Hey, Sandy...I really do want to talk. I'm sorry for the bad timing."

"Call me when you have the testicular fortitude."

Lynch squeezed his eyes shut. "Jesus, Sandy...that's low."

A couple beats went by, then a sigh. "Sorry, Donnie. That wasn't cool. I'm not trying to be a bitch. I have mixed-up feelings here. Call me when you can."

Sandy hung up. Lynch smiled. That was Sandy, always a bit temperamental and sassy. He hoped this was one step closer to having a real heart-to-heart with her. As soon as he caught a break, he'd call her back. He couldn't wait to talk to her.

Lynch parked his car in front of Derek's apartment building, turned off the ignition, and prepared for a confrontation. He pulled out his .40, checked it, and put it back in the holster on his waist. He put on his bulletproof vest, dreading its weight in the rising heat.

Although he had asked for backup, there wasn't a CPD car in sight. He thought about waiting for a police cruiser to pull up but changed his mind when he noted a Lincoln with limo-black tint on the windows nearby, idling with its rear lights on and a driver behind the wheel. An empty, nondescript gray Chevy sedan sat behind the Lincoln. Lynch figured pestiferous visitors were crawling through the building in search of Derek.

This isn't fucking good at all.

Lynch pulled his car around the corner, out of view of the Lincoln. He stepped out, looked around and walked with a nonchalant-yet-cautious stride across a yard, and then around to the back of the two-story apartment building, pulling out his gun.

Standing amongst the neglected weeds in the small back parking lot, Lynch saw no signs of life, just a few tenant' cars, dumpsters, kids' toys and bikes, air conditioners humming in apartment windows. He approached the rear entrance and looked though the grease-smeared window. There was a door straight ahead for the first floor, a flight of stairs for the second floor, and another going down to the basement level.

The Paradiso, the Purgatorio, or the Inferno. Which do I choose?

Lynch gripped his gun with a sweaty hand. The sun bore down and roasted him.

I'm already in the Inferno.

CHAPTER 26

"I used to crack a lotta heads down here." Tico looked at his sons as they pulled up to the curb. "This neighborhood was bad news back in the day, when I worked for your Nonno, and it's even more rundown now. Gangs. Shootings. Drugs. Lotsa tough guys, and lotsa thugs tryin' to move in on the family turf. Not to say any of that shit worries me because I'll eat gangbangers for breakfast."

"We're gonna do more than kick heads in today." Vito sounded confident.

"That's right, son. Once we get a hold of this fuck ... I'm gonna force feed 'im select chunks of himself."

"So...what're we waitin' for?" Liuni asked from the front seat.

"We're surveyin'. Chilling to see who and what comes 'round. Just for a few minutes." Tico noted a lack of activity on the street. That was a good thing. He figured the smart people were staying inside, anywhere cool and out of this hot Chicago skillet. "Then we're gonna go to Apartment B. Just wanna get the lay of the land first. *Capisce?*"

Liuni nodded. "He won't be hard to miss, Pop. He's one big, ugly sonofabitch."

"Knocked Giorgio out with one punch." Vito shook his head and crossed himself. “Giorgio was a badass, may he rest in pieces. Anyone who could lay him out has to be superhuman.”

“Well, Mr. Derek Hoffman hasn’t met *me* yet, has he?” Tico frowned. “You two gotta start thinking like cold-blooded killers. That’s the only way you’re gonna achieve respect when you take over the family business.”

Tico had been hopeful about Liuni and Vito when they’d made their bones on a few sanctioned hits, which had been supervised with Tico keeping a *capo* nearby to guide them, like a veteran hunter taking his green sons out for their first shot at deer season. But he’d since had to face it; his twins weren’t *street.* He doubted they could kill on their own without losing their nerve.

“Speaking of business, we gotta talk about this new load of *babania* and fentanyl we got sittin’ in Chinatown,” Vito said. “It’s gotta move quick, Pop.”

“Not to mention a container of cars and laptops my own crew just picked up,” Liuni said.

“Hey, I don’t wanna talk business right now.” Tico absentmindedly wound his Rolex. “That shit can wait ‘til we’re done with our fuckin’ *job*. Can we keep the focus on what happened to your sister?”

The twins nodded and grumbled and said of course they were and blurted out how badly they wanted to avenge Annabella and go all *Saw II* on the rapist.

Tico raised his eyebrows. “*Saw II?* That supposed to be a movie or somethin’?” He didn’t get the reference and didn’t care. Tico straightened up in his seat. “You guys ready to take care of this prick?”

The twins nodded.

Vito said, “This Derek Hoffman’s a real monster. Like, an actual fucking *monster*.”

Tico’s rage swelled up again. Hoffman *was* a monster all right, a nightmare unleashed to ruin Tico’s life and destroy his most precious blessing. “Check your fuckin’ pieces. Chamber rounds.”

The twins inspected their handguns and prepared for action as Tico did the same with the .44 in his large hand.

“Have the soldiers follow us inside. Mickey, you stay put until we come back. You see a cop, you call our cellphones, *capisce*?" Tico squeezed his driver's shoulder.

Mickey nodded as he gripped the steering wheel and continued looking straight ahead, scanning the street.

"Let's get this cocksucker." Tico exited the Lincoln with the twins. "I wanna have 'im in a torture chamber before dinnertime."

The hallway glowed under dirty fluorescent lights. Tico, his sons, and Grotto and Sammy walked quietly through the first-floor hallway and up to Derek Hoffman's apartment door. Tico didn't see any signs of life aside from flies; he heard only the smothered sounds of televisions and Mexican pop music coming from elsewhere in the building.

"This is Apartment B?" Tico tried to whisper and it sounded like a hiss.

Vito nodded.

"Okay." Tico turned to Grotto, who was one of the best safecrackers—and auto thieves—in the family business. "Try the knob. Pick it if it doesn't budge."

Meanwhile, Sammy scanned the hallway and Tico indicated to the twins they should fix their eyes on the entrances at each end of the hallway.

Grotto tried the knob. When it didn't turn, he pulled out a small metal tool and shoved it into the lock.

The anticipation of surprising Hoffman charged Tico's every nerve. Geared up for the kill, Tico knew if he didn't control himself, he might end up doing Hoffman on the spot. That would be messy—and he'd miss out on the wonderful forms of torture he was planning. Tico sucked in a deep breath and checked his hostility.

Relax ... gotta take this cocksucker in one piece.

He watched Grotto working the lock. "You just about done there?"

"Yeah." Grotto whispered as he worked the lock. "But Boss, we'll hafta bust this door down if it's dead-bolted from the other side."

"I'm not worried." Tico grinned and kept his voice low. "I'd ram my fucking head through the wall to get the sonofabitch."

There was an audible click and Grotto stood up. "Got it."

Grotto and Sammy drew their guns and waited for Tico's word. Liuni and Vito did the same, but only after Tico glared at them. Vito yawned.

Tico shook with rage at that yawn and slapped Vito's face. "You fuckin' bored? You two better step up and get with the shit we're doin' here." He kept his voice low while wanting to erupt as loud and violently as possible. He jabbed an index finger at his sons. "I shouldn't have to give youse a lecture in order to get this job done. You both just keep talkin' with no action. Fuck that. You should *wanna* do this. That piece of shit in there ruined your sister's life. You got that?" Liuni and Vito stared at their shoes.

"Heads up. Grotto, open the door."

All five men pointed their handguns into the darkness ahead. Tico jerked his head toward the door, in a silent command for his enforcers to move inside. As they did, they were startled by the abrupt sound of a door banging open. Tico yelled in surprise as an object bounced off the back of his legs.

Fueled by adrenaline, all five men whipped around and leveled their guns at the head of a young boy with black hair, whose bewildered brown eyes widened in terror as he focused on the stainless-steel barrel of Tico's .44, only an inch from the tip of his nose.

Exhaling deeply, Tico lowered his gun and nudged the soccer ball that had hit his legs back toward the boy.

"Whatchya doin' here, little guy?"

He reached down and tousled the boy's hair, engulfing the top of his head with a large and gentle left hand while his right hand maintained its grip on the .44.

"Felipe!" a female voice cried out, as a young woman with long black hair stepped halfway out of an apartment two doors down. *"Ven aqúi!"*

"Mamma, si!" The boy snatched up his soccer ball and ran to the woman, who pulled him to her while keeping her eyes on the men.

"Hey, lady." Tico offered a smile. "You seen the guy who lives here? You know him? Big and ugly fucker?"

The woman shook her head. "*No hablo Ingles.*"

Tico frowned. "Right."

The woman held the boy close and led him inside the apartment. As she slammed the door, Tico heard the sound of locks being hastily buttoned up.

"'Nough bullshit." Tico turned toward his crew. "If the cocksucker's home, he's heard us. Let's go."

Grotto nudged the door open with his foot. It opened with a slow creak. Tico and his crew raised their guns, arms extended in front.

The group stopped dead as the door to the building's rear entrance banged open and a voice called out. "Tortellio. Move yourself and your guys into the hall."

Tico and his crew whirled, their weapons pointing at a solitary man standing with a handgun raised and aimed at them.

Grotto and Sammy cursed in Italian, lowering their hands as Liuni and Vito waved their guns with feeble, amateurish sweeps.

Vito yelled, "Who the fuck're you?"

Ignoring him, the man spoke to Tico. "Tortellio, last chance here. Get your goons away from the door and put those guns down before shit gets ugly."

Tico clenched his teeth as his memory suddenly clicked the connection in place. He turned to his sons. "Put your guns away, goddammit."

"Why, Pop?" Vito maintained his unsteady aim. "Who the hell's this?"

Tico pocketed his piece and slapped Vito's gun hand down. He turned toward the man in the doorway. "He's a fucking cop."

CHAPTER 27

Gripping his .40 with a steady hand, Lynch addressed the group, all of whom he recognized.

"That's good, keep those guns down," he said as the men lowered their weapons. "Now, I know you boys probably don't wanna relinquish those guns—"

Grotto spit out a laugh and Sammy glared.

"—but I'd sure feel a lot better if you'd put 'em away." Lynch kept his tone easy. "Do that, and I won't bust any of your asses for illegal possession of firearms. I don't give a fuck about concealed carry or FOID cards right now."

The mobsters tucked their weapons away.

Lynch glanced toward the open apartment door "What're you doing here, Tico?"

"I'm lookin' for a new apartment." Tico smiled. "Somethin' a little cozier for me and my family."

"Downsizing?" Lynch twisted his lips.

Tico looked ready to spit railroad spikes. "Maybe. What the fuck's it to you?"

"Breaking and entering's against the law." Lynch kept his gun on the men.

"Gotta prove it first, Detective." Tico smirked; his crew snickered.

Lynch ignored them. "Tico, you're not supposed to be here."

Tico stepped forward and rubbed his knuckles. "It's a free fuckin' country."

"Not when you're trespassing. Do yourself a favor and stand still."

"You think this is your turf or somethin'?" Tico laughed and looked at his grinning gang before turning back to Lynch. "Y'know how much property I own around here? I just might own this rat trap, for all you know." Tico aimed a finger at Lynch. "Cocksucker, this was *my* turf before you was ever a speck of flyshit on the tip of your daddy's prick."

"Cut it, Tico. We're all here for the same guy, except Derek Hoffman's leaving with me and you're gonna forget about it."

"Fuhgeddaboudit? Fuck you. I ain't forgettin' shit." Tico jutted his chin at Lynch. "I've got my reasons for bein' here and it don't concern you, *capisce*?"

"I know why you're here." Lynch said lowered his gun a few inches. "I'm sorry about your daughter."

Tico visibly stiffened at Lynch's apology.

"But you need to stay away from Derek Hoffman and let the law handle this."

Tico threw his hands up. "Lemme tell ya about laws. Laws get bent, they get broken, and the guys who make 'em turn the other way when a carrot's dangled in front of 'em."

"Not everyone breaks the law or gets corrupted."

"*Au contraire*, Detective." Tico smiled. "Everyone's corrupt. Just ask your Daddy; he knows all about it."

Now it was Lynch who stiffened. "I don't know what you're talking about."

"Yeah, your dad ... Jake fuckin' Lynch. You look just like him. You're Donnie, right?" Tico scratched his nose. "You busted some of my crew before."

"You've got a great memory." Lynch raised his .40 a little higher.

"Your old man and me go back; you know that?" Tico sounded friendly.

Lynch frowned, saying nothing.

"I knew your dad when we was younger. He became a detective, hell, even arrested me once, but that was all for show. At the heart, he coulda been one of *ours* if he wasn't a mutt."

"You might've been acquainted with my dad, but you don't know him."

"Knew him well enough to know he was on the take."

Lynch swallowed. His dad had admitted once over a twelve-pack that he had sometimes looked the other way or done "favors" here and there for some dirty cash to help put food on the table.

"I assure you, I can't be taken. You can bank on that."

"You sure? Leave us here to take care of Hoffman and I'll make sure it's worth your while."

"No."

Tico smiled. "Cops like you are no fun. You go through life thinkin' you're better than everyone, don't ya? Well, you ain't shit."

"Save it for someone who gives a flying fuck." Lynch frowned. "This is one rare time where if you leave now, I'll look the other way. Get outta here or I'll bust ya for interfering with police business."

"This is *my* fuckin' business." Tico's voice grew louder. "And if I don't leave, what you gonna do?" Tico stepped forward. So did his crew, slipping hands under their jackets. "You ain't the first detective I've run over."

Lynch almost laughed. He'd received threats from countless disgruntled criminals over the years. From dead cats in his mailbox to thugs firing pop shots at his car, he'd tangled with the worst that Chicago's substratum offered up. Threats never bothered him, and he'd learned not to blow his top. *Never take things personally*, that was another gem of wisdom that both Earl and his father had instilled in him. This new confrontation was just another test, Lynch thought. He wanted to defuse this underworld king, the thug who thought he and his mob would take Derek Hoffman down—and maybe Lynch too.

Lynch wasn't going to step aside.

Not today. Not ever.

He stepped forward, his right arm straight out, and pushed the barrel of the .40 into Tico's forehead. "You wanna run me over, asshole?"

Tico froze as each of his four-man crew drew their guns. Liuni and Vito yelled and pleaded for their dad to tell them what to do, Grotto and Sammy cursed at Lynch in Italian.

"Better call your dogs off, Tico." Lynch forced the barrel harder into Tico's brow. A combination of anger and nervous exhilaration coursed through him. "I don't like you and I won't hesitate to blow your brains all the way to Palermo even if I go down with ya."

"My boys might cap ya before you get a chance to pull that trigger." Tico was red and snapping. "No one's pulled a piece on me in thirty years. You got some fuckin' balls."

Some fuckin' balls? If he only knew, today I got more audacity in the one ball I have left than he has in both of his...

"Well, let's just wager on that, then." Lynch stuck out his jaw and fingered the trigger of his gun. "Me and you die, backup'll show any minute. Your goons can explain how they got caught with our dead bodies in this hallway."

He pushed the .40 harder into Tico's forehead, knowing the barrel was going to leave a mark. "Last chance, Tico." Lynch dug his heels in. "We could stand here all day until my backup comes. We could also kill each other. Or you can leave, without arrest or injury, and I'll conduct my business."

Tico glared at Lynch. Then he blinked a couple times and drew a deep breath. "Stand down, guys. Put your shit away."

"Fuck this guy, Pop." Vito danced around, waving his gun at Lynch's face. "We can take this pig down!"

"Boss?" Grotto spoke in English as he got in Lynch's face. "He ain't Dirty Harry. He's just a fuckin' *mameluke*."

Tenants opened their apartment doors and peered out.

Lynch didn't flinch or blink, just kept his eyes and gun on Tico. "Your guys better back off me right now, or so help me God, I'll fucking kill you as soon as the backup arrives and have the DA buy me dinner."

Tico roared. "Guns down, goddammit!"

His men hesitated, grumbling and frowning as they put their guns away. The twins pouted and complained, making Lynch wonder how these Tortellio heirs would ever make it through life.

"All you guys, out to the cars." Tico nodded toward the exit door. "If that fuckin' rapist was here, he's long gone. Stupid cop-fuck and all of us made enough goddamn noise to rile up the whole building."

Tortellio's mob walked to the end of the hallway and waited by the door, keeping watch on Tico and Lynch.

"You can go now." Lynch kept a firm aim on Tico.

Tico backed away a few steps, muttering something in Italian. He spat a gob of phlegm at Lynch's feet. "You done fucked up, Detective. I'm gonna find that cocksucker and he's gonna disappear. Simple as that. My daughter, she's ..." Tico choked and swallowed. "I'm inclined to taste some retribution and nothin's stoppin' me."

"Tico, don't even—"

"Don't say a goddamn thing." Tico pointed a finger. "Just shut your hole and watch your back. I'm not forgettin' what happened here. Got that?"

"Keep threatening me, Tico." Lynch stepped forward. "There's witnesses here now looking out their doors. You wanna kill a police detective? You'll get a shitstorm like you've never known."

"Like I said, you ain't the first detective I've had to run over." Tico spat again, then turned and walked to his waiting crew. He ushered them out while looking over their shoulders at Lynch.

All was quiet again. Tenants had closed their doors. Lynch stared down the hallway for a few minutes, listening, until he was confident the men were gone and the pulse in his temples quieted to a normal, undetectable beat.

Goddamn, that escalated. Lost my cool...

He turned toward Derek Hoffman's lair, which appeared almost pitch-black from the doorway.

Where's my backup?

Had Tico put a word out to his connections in the CPD in order to keep the law away? Where the hell was McRains? Lynch waited a moment longer and then entered the apartment.

No lights were on inside. Black garbage bags covered the windows.

Lynch's sweat cooled. He heard an air conditioner rattling somewhere in the chilled dark. The space smelled of rotting food and old incense.

He pulled his gun out, flicked on a kitchen light, and crept along until he found and turned on a living room lamp, easing his way from room to room. The leftover adrenaline from his Tortellio confrontation began to surge in his bloodstream again as thoughts of Derek Hoffman, hulking, fried, and potentially lurking somewhere in the apartment, hyper-sensitized his nerves.

The place looked like a hundred squalid holes he'd been in over the years. The kitchen was a disaster: garbage from an overflowing trashcan strewn across the grimy tile floor; sink full of crusty dishes, counter and tabletop covered with bags and containers from fast-food restaurants. The cabinets and appliances were smeared and filthy and the rank smell of decomposing food choked his nostrils. The living room carpet was littered with dirt, miscellaneous stains, food particles, and hair. The battered and cut-up black pleather sofa and chair looked like victims of Derek's anger. A pair of legless and chipped wooden tabletops sat on cinder blocks at each end of the sofa.

You are now entering the White Trash Zone.

Free weights were scattered across the floor, along with miscellaneous heavy metal CDs and porno DVDs. The dented and cracked components of a home-theater system sat in disarray against a wall next to the dirt-covered TV. An unsecured, cobweb-covered ceiling fan hung by electrical wires above his head. Nothing decorated the walls other than a tattered promotional poster from a Toughman competition and a crooked picture with a broken frame and shattered glass.

Inside the refrigerator were jugs of expired liquids, old take-out, and a moldy, unwrapped package of deli meat. An open can of dog food with a spoon in it was inside the door—but there didn't seem to be a dog in the apartment. Lynch shut the door, gagging at the stench. He wiped his eyes.

Lynch walked up to the picture and studied it. A family portrait of some sort, and judging by the clothes and hairstyles, Lynch figured it was taken decades ago. Two young boys, a man, and a woman—and not one smiling face among them. Lynch couldn't make out the face of the man because a large nail had been hammered through the glass and into the photo where his face used to be.

Someone's got a problem with Daddy.

He went back into the bathroom—a rust and lime-covered shower stall, a broken bathroom mirror hanging over a dripping sink, and a dirty toilet Lynch deemed worthy of a BIOHAZARD sign.

The bedroom was grotesque, its walls papered from baseboard to ceiling with a grisly collage of pictures from hardcore fetish magazines, S&M shots, and professional muscle and body-building circulars. Cutouts of women with their legs and asses spread. Penetration. Bondage. Torture. Swollen cocks and cum-shots. And then pictures of bodybuilders, biceps, sweaty tan torsos, vein-infested muscles, and arms pumping iron.

Lynch shook his head, overwhelmed. On a pegboard crudely nailed to the wall were hooks and small shelves with dildos, anal-beads, phallic objects made of glass, a whip, a cat-o-nine tails, gag-balls, tubes of lube, various restraints, handcuffs, and a couple of bulging things in small satin bags he dared not open.

A decrepit dresser, covered with bottles of body supplements, protein powder, and dirty clothes rested against a wall. Next to it was a pile of well-worn kink and muscle magazines, and in a corner stood a baseball bat wrapped in barbed wire.

He took a step.

Crunch.

Lynch looked down. The bedroom carpet was covered with food remnants, used syringes, steroid ampules, coke vials, and spent condoms.

The bare mattress on the bed was soiled with myriad mystery substances. A grimy pillow and a threadbare red blanket had been tossed in the corner.

Startled, Lynch caught glimpse of the limbs of a female victim...

...which turned out to be mannequin legs.

Lynch startled at the sound coming from the apartment's front door. He drew his gun as he crept toward the living room with his finger on the trigger.

"Hey! Whoa!"

Two young police officers recoiled at Lynch's entrance into the living room.

"Bang. You're dead." Lynch put his gun away as he looked them over—one male and one female officer; both had the bearings of rookies. "If I was a perp, I'd have just bagged two green cops. Why aren't your guns out?"

The cops looked at each other, embarrassed, then shrugged.

"You were supposed to meet me here. What kind of backup is this?"

"Sorry, Detective," the male officer said. "We were dispatched to do a follow-up to your original backup request."

"No backup arrived?" the female officer asked, looking surprised.

Lynch sighed and rubbed his eyes. "No, nothing."

"Everything okay?" the male officer asked.

"Yeah." Lynch looked around, irritated. Either the department had its lines crossed—which often happened—or nobody was available due to inadequate manpower, which was commonplace in the CPD these days. Or, Tico's influence had kept the police away long enough to provide a window for the Outfit boss to try to get his paws on Derek Hoffman. "I found the door open and poked my head in. I want more personnel down here, and forensics, too. There's evidence in this place."

The female officer nodded and spoke into the radio on her shoulder. The male officer asked, "Do you think this guy's coming back here?"

Lynch shrugged. "Hard to tell. He's operating in a way that's completely unpredictable. I can't even begin to tell where his head's at."

"Heard the dude raped the Meat Grinder's daughter while she was in a coma," the male officer said. "They say the mob's after him."

"The proper term for the Chicago mob is 'The Outfit.'" Lynch laughed to himself as the officer silently raised an eyebrow, realizing he probably sounded like some cranky old geezer to these two. "Go assist your partner and get this place secure."

As the officer walked back to his partner, Lynch turned toward the kitchen, recalling something he'd noticed earlier on a cabinet above the kitchen counter. Breathing through his mouth, he retraced his steps and picked up a mustard-colored, weekly/monthly planner. It was an A5 hardcover festooned with smudges and scribbles. It was open to August. Almost every day of the month was marked with notes on workout routines—different body parts on alternating days. Then he noticed a name, *"Astroglide,"* noted on each Saturday. Lynch nodded. *Keeping those drug deals on schedule, huh, Derek?* There it was. They'd known each other. Another piece of this abominable puzzle confirmed.

One more scribble pattern landed on Wednesdays: *Dinner @ Mom's.*

That was a start.

Who is Mom and what's her fucking address?

Lynch rummaged through papers and mail to find anything with Derek's mother's address and info.

Nothing.

Lynch scratched out a few notes, knowing he had to move fast.

He dialed McRains and rattled off a succinct breakdown of his arrival at Hoffman's and chasing Tico and his goons off, without mentioning that guns had been drawn.

"It was fucked up." Lynch rubbed his temples. "And what happened to my backup, John? The CPD isn't *that* understaffed."

"I had officers dispatched right after I got off the phone with you." McRains sounded agitated. "No one showed?"

"Yeah, like forty minutes later. I was ready to ream someone."

"You all right?"

"I've got two rookies down here. Hoffman's door was kicked down so we went in. They're getting me more officers and a crime scene crew. Being caught with Tico and his guys all alone with my dick in my hand didn't make me feel real confident in the backup. And why the hell aren't you here yet?"

"Don, I'm in gridlock. Construction season and shit. No one cares how loud my siren is. I got lights, sirens, and I still can't move."

Lynch exhaled in frustration. "Listen...I got a tip here from Hoffman's calendar planner. Says here that every Wednesday, he has dinner at his mom's place. Get me the info on Hoffman's mother for me."

"On it. Hope to get you a name A-fucking-SAP. In the meantime, want me to send squads up north to Tico's house? Try and sniff him out if he stops at home while he's hunting down this Hoffman?"

"Not worth it. Tico's probably gonna keep his head low since he knows cops are aware that he's been over here. And anyway, the one we're really after is Hoffman."

"Anything else?"

"Yeah." A sense of unease made Lynch tingle. "Hurry up. If Hoffman shows up, I don't want to face him with just these two newbies here. I'm not so sure we can handle that fucking brute."

CHAPTER 28

Scatt-Dogg posed in front of the full-length mirror inside Sweet Stylz Salon. He admired his look—tall and slender frame, swathed in a spotless white suit, white leather shoes and twenty-four carat gold-framed sunglasses.

"That's tight, man. *Tight*." Scatt-Dogg spoke under his breath, feeling fly with his new, neat, straight cornrows and a fresh manicure. He spread his fingers wide and admired his fingernails. Each nail was polished and glossed, his left pinky nail an inch long, honed for use as a spoon for all kinds of powder. He tipped the ladies who did him right —even though a ten-spot was too generous, they were sweet to him. Unlike the street bitches working under his thumb.

Both of his hands were full of next-level, gold and diamond-laden bling that reflected real estate and the flashy pride he had for two cities near and dear to his corrupt heart.

Scatt-Dogg's left hand represented where he now made his bread and butter: Chicago. This hand was decorated with bejeweled, gold rings: on his index finger, the John Hancock Building; on his middle finger, an inch-tall Sears Tower—he'd be damned if he ever called it "Willis Tower." On his ring finger, the Chicago city flag. A tiny gold top hat adorned his special pinky. This was his "Windy City hand."

He checked out his right hand, which was covered with jewelry devoted to his original home: New York City. His index finger featured the Statue of Liberty; his ring finger, the Empire State Building; his pinky had the tiny ring letters NYC in micro-diamonds; and on his middle finger was his absolute favorite: a one-inch tall, solid-gold, diamond-capped tribute to the World Trade Center towers. Each side of the towers was inscribed with *9/11 ... NYC Strong.*

Man, he cherished his WTC ring; it beamed his status and kept his pimp-hand—his "Big Apple hand"—strong. He'd used it numerous times to perforate the faces of whores or johns who'd tried to fuck with him.

He was a fourth-generation pimp whose father, paternal grandfather and great-granddad had, since the early 1900s, all managed the skin trade in various boroughs. Coming up, Scatt-Dogg had been known as Reggie. He'd despised the name, dropping it years ago, but never forgot where he came from, as his jewelry proved.

Chi-Town had become his home decades ago when he came to help out his cousin. They owned this hunk of turf and had fought tooth and nail against every Latin and Asian gang that the city sent their way. His cousin was long gone—victim of a gangland hit—but Scatt-Dogg was still tickin'.

He grinned into the mirror, flashing a gold and rock-encrusted grille at his reflection. Smoothing out his suit jacket and pants—which concealed the small, chrome-plated gun in his waistband—he walked out of the barber shop, feeling like cock of the walk on the blocks he reigned over.

As he stepped onto the sidewalk, Scatt-Dogg did his best to shrug off the sweltering motherfucker of a day, which was trying to cook him alive, but there was no escaping the intense humidity. He looked down the block—his block—and saw his stable of whores mingling, fanning themselves, talking to men in their cars, and letting their shit hang out for all to see.

He studied the bustle of activity, searching for Cortnee. Her absence got his anger churning. With a cool, deliberate stride, he made his way over to that stretch of sidewalk.

The first girl he reached was Lolinda, a busty nineteen-year-old brunette he'd recruited from Brooklyn last November. Her back was to him but he grabbed her attention by slapping the cigarette out of her mouth with the palm of his Big Apple hand.

"Where the fuck's Cortnee?"

Lolinda held her trembling mouth as she squinted up at him. "Damn, Scatt, I don't know. Haven't seen her in a while...not since you gone over to Sweet Stylz."

Scatt-Dogg considered Lolinda's reply. He leaned down into Lolinda's face. "I know that bitch be tellin' you to lie to me? She hiding up in the apartment? She up there smokin' that ice, or what?"

"I don't know, Scatt. She busy?"

"Busy with who?" He grabbed a fistful of Lolinda's hair and pulled her close. "She been upstairs last time I seen her, and she know I wanted her on the street all fuckin' day now. No way she been doin' dicks up there since I left for the salon. She knows to be on the street."

Lolinda shrugged and he yanked her hair harder, causing her to shriek. "Swear, haven't seen her for a couple hours. Last time I seen her, she was headin' up to her crib with some big fuckin' fool. And I mean, *big*. You can't miss 'im."

That Bicep motherfucker!

"You sayin' she ain't been down since?"

"'S right." Lolinda said, squirming. "You're hurtin' me, Scatt!"

Scatt-Dogg shoved her away. "If I find out she's up there slackin' off or tradin' freebies for a fix, 'n' you knew 'bout it, I gonna beat your big ass silly. Feel me on that?"

Lolinda nodded as she tried to smooth down her hair.

Scatt-Dogg spat in her face. "Get back'ta work, bitch."

Lolinda's eyes turned wet and she quivered as she wiped his slobber from her nose and cheek.

Scatt-Dogg strode toward his tenement-turned-brothel. He'd regarded Cortnee as a reliable hooker. She knew better—for fear of a bludgeoning. Why'd she be gone from the street for two hours? He loved the green and if she kept him from it, she was gonna get a lot more than just a slap-around.

He walked into his building of debauchery and stood in the hall, watching and listening for anything strange. One of his older girls, Fuenta, squatted in front of a fat white guy whose shrinking penis hung out of his zipper. She looked over at Scatt-Dogg and spat the contents of the fat-guy's drained balls in his direction.

Uncouth bitch.

"Nasty hoe, I oughta brain you."

Fuenta giggled, shrugged and turned back to the fat guy's flaccid member.

Scatt-Dogg raised his Big Apple hand but didn't use it. Instead, he cursed at Fuenta, ascended the stairs, and stood at the top with his ears open. There were faint sounds of someone getting laid in an apartment down the hall, but not from Cortnee's place. He eased up to Cortnee's door but as he went to grab the knob, a scratching and thudding sound came from within the apartment.

Scatt-Dogg lowered his hand and put his right ear up to the door. He could make out the sounds of something metallic and someone panting. He heard a sudden snorting, like a pig, but made by a man. What the fuck was going down in there? It was wrong, whatever it was. And what the hell was going on with Cortnee? The long, low animal-like bellow-moan that came next sent a quick shiver down his spine.

She be fuckin' a bear in there?

Scatt-Dogg grabbed the handle of the chrome .380 tucked into his pants and drew it out. Somethin' was off for damn sure. Sweat broke out all over his body. Beads of perspiration ran down his face—and it wasn't from the heat. He tried to keep cool, but his nerves and the humidity weren't cooperating. It made him angry.

You can handle that big, mud-clutch Bicep fucker ...

Scatt-Dogg figured he'd take that big 'ol, ugly sonofabitch out with one gunshot to the eye. Hell, he'd done it before, capping plenty of tough fucks from Brooklyn to Chi-Town who'd gotten in his way. Still, he'd never seen anything like the overgrown and crazy-looking son of a bitch he suspected was still behind the door. The john looked like something straight out of a horror movie. No doubt, that white boy would die hard once Scatt got rollin'.

Muthafuckah's eyes wants'ta eat ya.

Gun in hand, Scatt-Dogg reached out, quiet and careful, and grabbed the doorknob to Cortnee's apartment.

CHAPTER 29

Tico winced as his wife went crazy in his ear, screaming down the phone. He had called to check on her, and it sounded like her Alprazolam was wearing off.

"Did you find that monster yet?" Valentina's voice rose and dropped with each trembling word. Up and down. "The hospital called and I'm going over to be at her side. And did you think about the fact that our girl could be pregnant. What if that happened?! Pregnant! Can you imagine? You have to find him, Tico. Find that raping fuck and that drunk driver. Make things right again, for Anna!"

Sitting alone behind a desk in the back office of the Tortellio private club as his twins and the enforcers waited out in the front, Tico closed his eyes. There was no coming back from that news. Annabella, his beautiful Annabella...her life was over now.

He took a breath. He couldn't bear to hear his wife carry on this way. Soft-spoken, sweet, and passive, she stayed close to God and never wished anyone harm. But this raping prick and the drunk driver had pushed her over the edge. She was heartbroken, as much a victim as her own daughter. And now, it was only going to get worse. He would make sure her honor was avenged but there was no way to stop the downward spiral. He tried to think of something to distract her, but he didn't want to mention over the phone that the DUI was now DOA.

"Shhh, please, honey." Tico's words softened. "Are you on the home phone?"

"Yes, and I don't give a shit who's listening." Valentina's voice rose. "Hello? Police? Go screw off. Are the police doing anything to bring justice for Annabella? No? I didn't think so. The police can die and burn in hell along with that drunk and the rapist!"

Tico bit his lip. He never really knew if his home phone was tapped. If it was, it was tapped outside at the box. Sure, he'd had the box checked and he'd arranged for weekly sweeps at his house, but he trusted *nothing*. He certainly didn't want anything about killing people or threats to the police mentioned over the phone.

"*Bella, please.*" Tico cooed as gently as possible. "Don't do this to yourself. Annabella needs us to be strong. We need to be here for her. If there's a God above us, he will grant our family the justice it deserves. Have you ever doubted me?"

A brief silence then sniffles followed by Valentina's trembling words. "No, I've never doubted you, Tico. This monster will be punished by God...I just don't want to wait that long."

Tico almost laughed at that. His wife sounded like him. Aside from Derek Hoffman's head, Tico wanted nothing more in the world than peace of mind and a strong heart for her. "You know how much I love you?"

"More than your Rolex?"

Tico laughed, surprised. "Yes, my *bella*. I love you more than my Rolex, or anything else in the world."

Valentina allowed herself a small laugh that warmed Tico's heart. "Be careful out there, Tico. If you need me, call my cell. I told you that I'm going back to the hospital to sit with Annabella soon—and I won't be leaving her."

Oh, shit. He needed the hospital room to be clear. There was no way he could do what he was going to have to do if his wife were anywhere nearby.

He needed to buy time until he could get to the hospital himself first. "Wait for me to come pick you up."

"No need. My sister Cecilia is taking me. I need to be with Anna, not all by myself in this big, lonely house. You and the boys should be with me, too ... staying with her."

She succumbed to another round of uncontrollable tears.

"Honey, please." Tico vainly tried to calm her. "I'm sorry, *bella*. Please, be strong. I'll be with you. So will the boys. Just have your sister stay with you at the house and we'll come get you later."

As Valentina wailed louder into the phone, Tico squeezed his eyes shut, almost crushing the phone in his large hand. *Annabella, pregnant?* There was no way to keep her honor now. He knew it was his vanity and his old-school mentality that made him consider this horrific option. This motherfucker of a rapist was now forcing Tico to do the unthinkable, which would destroy his already-broken wife's heart, not to mention his own. Her cries tore him apart.

"She can't be there alone," Valentina wailed. "And what will we do when she finds out what happened to her and if she got knocked up by this rapist? Is she going to be normal? Would she keep a baby?

That's never going to happen.

"We'll take care of all of this," Tico told her. "But you can't go to the hospital in the shape you're in. Take a pill and get straight for Annabella before you go."

Valentina sobbed into the phone. "Our daughter needs her mother. And she needs you, goddamnit."

Tico exhaled. "It may be a while. We have some things to take care of. I'll be there for you and Annabella as soon as I can, *bella*. I promise."

After a moment, Valentina got herself under control, breathing deep, forcing out her words. "If you're going to stay out, don't come back until you've taken care of the *stronzo* who got her sent to the hospital in the first place, and also this..." Her voice cracked. "...this... animal. I need to know that fucking *cazzavo* is dead."

Valentina's cursing signaled to Tico in that she was gonna be reeling with no end in sight, close to the edge. He'd never heard her use foul language. "Please, relax. I'll be with you before long, okay?"

"Okay, but I can't just sit at the house. I'm having Cecilia take me to the hospital as soon as she gets here."

No. She can't be there.

Tico clenched his back teeth to control his voice. "Just wait, *bella.* I don't want Cecilia to have to take you there if you're gonna be out of control."

Valentina's voice came through the receiver, ragged but unwavering. "If I have to stay there all night so that she knows she's not alone, that's what I'll do. I'm packing a suitcase and I'll take it with me."

Tico ground his teeth but he knew there was no talking her out of her determination. He'd have to send her home with the boys later when it was time for him to be alone with Annabella. His heart constricted in his chest.

"Valentina, my *bella,* I love you." Tico said to her and hung up the phone. He shouted for his sons.

Liuni entered the office. "How's Mom?"

"How the fuck d'ya think she is?" Tico didn't mean to snap at his son. He sighed and calmed himself. "Emotions are high. We're all upset about Annabella. We need to pull together and do right by her, *capisce*?" Tico stretched as Vito arrived in the doorway. "I want the names, numbers, and addresses of every relative of this Hoffman fuck. Mom, Dad, sisters, brothers, cousins, long-lost uncle, I don't care. Just give me someone who shares blood with this animal. With a name, we can get info. And when *I'm* working, they'll give him up. That's an ironclad guarantee."

"Already working on it," Liuni said.

Vito waved his mobile phone at Tico. "Just waitin' on some friends in the CPD to ring me back, Pop."

"They better not take too fuckin' long." Tico cracked his knuckles. "I could use a caffeine boost. Why hasn't anyone replaced that espresso machine yet?"

Liuni looked up from his phone. "Pop, we've been busy."

"I didn't say you had to go buy one yourself. But why hasn't one of your *pigros* out on the sidewalk taken care of it?"

The twins looked at each other and Vito walked outside.

Tico flexed his fingers until his knuckles cracked again. Thanks to

Lynch jamming the goddamn gears, Tico had to come up with a new strategy.

The bastard rapist was roaming free and he needed to somehow move Lynch to the back burner so that he could nab him before Lynch did. He wanted Hoffman's blood, and his screams, and he'd never rest or be satisfied until Derek was in his clutches—mutilated and begging for death.

He knew in his Sicilian heart that whatever black, unlit fissure Derek Hoffman was hiding in, he'd find him. And when he did, he'd extract Hoffman—the wriggling snake—and gnash the fucker between his teeth.

"We got a bite. Hey, Pop!" Vito chattered into his mobile phone and jotted notes on a pad. He hung up. "There's a brother. So far, he's the only relative my guys could come up with."

A brother? Good.

Tico's mind raced. "Where's this brother live?"

"Near North Side." Vito examined his notes. "Got the street address right here."

"Give Mickey the address. Let's fuckin' move it." Tico caressed the .44 Magnum in his pants pocket.

They rolled out in two cars. Vito passed the address to Liuni, who instructed the driver where to go.

Tico turned to Vito. "So, tell me about this brother."

"The cop I talked to is pals with another cop who was at the hospital earlier today." Vito checked his scribbles. "There's some drug company that rents a floor at the hospital. Peithos Laboratories. Big pharma shit. They make drugs and do experiments on people, somethin' like that. That rapist was a test subject. He beat the livin' shit out of someone in some lab—and that's why the cops were there. Turns out the main guy—doctor or somethin'—manages the department for the drug company ... and he's the fuckin' younger brother of Derek Hoffman."

"No shit?"

"Yeah. When the big lummox was nabbed by security, the younger brother stepped in and talked security into lettin' him go."

Tico's eyes narrowed as he listened to this.

"After that, it's a good guess that the fucker went down and did ... y'know."

Silent, Tico's insides filled with black hate. This scumbag was apprehended...and then released? He wanted to scream, vent, take out the .44 and empty it into the roof of the Lincoln.

"What's the name of this kid brother?"

Vito checked his notes. "Sid Hoffman."

Tico yelled to Mickey and Liuni. "You guys better know where you're goin'."

The driver nodded and Liuni said, "Yeah, Pop. We got his address and it's in the GPS."

Tico couldn't get there fast enough. "Maybe these Hoffman brothers are close. This brother protected Deadfuck from getting arrested; maybe that's where he's hiding out."

"Fucker might be there." Vito said.

"Either way, we're getting traction." Tico took out the .44 and held it in his hands. He thought about the ways he could use it to blow off some precious body parts. "This brother's as good a place to start as any."

CHAPTER 30

Derek's skin glistened dark red—every inch of his limbs and torso slicked with blood.

I am a red Hulk.

Everything in his eyes was red, velvety. Black oil would look like crimson honey to him.

I am burning red...

I am the mean fuck!

The coppery smell of fresh blood filled his nose. His mouth watered.

The woman was most un-womanlike now. Derek had transformed her. He'd lost track of time as he'd ripped her and cut her apart, spreading her remains out and around him. Numerous pieces of her body covered the floor like a processed hog. Naked, on blood-covered knees, he was holding her lifeless rump up to his throbbing penis. Snorting and moaning, he greedily inhaled the aromas of blood, sex and death.

I feel...feel so out of my fucking mind.

Cortnee's body was crisscrossed with gashes and deep lacerations from the cleaver. Her left leg was cut off from the knee down. Derek had dismembered her upper body—ripped off her arms, bitten off her nipples, taken chunks out of her back, and torn away a mouthful of her right buttock. In his fury, he'd planted the cleaver in her sternum, removed the blade, and with his powerful hands, cracked her ribcage open to remove her lungs and heart; to dig in deeper for whatever meaty gems were hidden in her recesses. He needed to see what she looked like on the inside.

Mission accomplished.

He was so high in so many ways, riding on waves of euphoria and madness. With Cortnee's torso splayed on a pile of fly-covered gore, Derek wanted to dive into her viscera like a stench-hungry hound driven to roll in a mound of excrement.

Cortnee gazed at him with glazed, dead eyes from a cheap nightstand where he had placed her severed head. He had lopped it off with one cleaver blow to the neck and now he wanted to look into her contorted face as he fucked her dead holes, befouling her headless, eviscerated, nearly limbless corpse.

Derek rested for a moment, awash in carnage, and looked around at the blood and body parts in the apartment he'd turned into an abattoir.

I am becoming...be-cum-ing...

He'd become a murderer this day—and so much more. The butchery brought him *pleasure*. In his red-lit mind, he embraced what he thought was his *purpose*—to live only for the pleasures of the flesh... for the joy in the fucking, in the killing.

A sound at the door momentarily brought Derek out of his hyper-stimulated, scarlet world. He smelled the man before he entered the room and knew it was the pimp who'd visited earlier.

Derek watched the tall, slender, Black man in the white outfit and gold sunglasses step into the apartment with a gun in hand. In the faint light, the gun shone, along with the gaudy rings on his fingers. Derek couldn't see the eyes behind the gold sunglasses. He watched the pimp's jaw drop and his expression curdle.

The pimp. She called him something...Scatt-Dogg.

Derek had wanted to attack Scatt-Dogg when he first saw him

earlier. Now, he really wanted to rip him apart for disturbing the pleasure he'd been taking in the erotic carnage he had created.

Derek rose to his feet, the meat-cleaver clutched in his right fist, Cortnee's rump dropping from his left hand as he stood. Blood and semen dripped from his naked body. He flashed a raptorial grin full of craggy teeth and belched a low growl from deep within.

"Sweet mother of fuck!" Scatt-Dogg raised his gun and fired repeatedly.

Four rounds hit Derek in the right shoulder. He felt small stings, as if a wasp had nailed him. The pain was gone as fast as it came. Scatt-Dogg kept firing and shouting. The shots sounded to Derek like a little cap gun—and they missed. Derek lunged at Scatt-Dogg, but the pimp was quick and slipped past his lethal arms.

"Gonna kill ya!" Scatt-Dogg slid behind Derek.

Derek whirled around. "I will...eat your heart ... *out!*"

"Naw, bitch. You dead!" Scatt-Dogg skidded to a standstill among the greasy innards, which stained and ruined his white leather shoes. He raised the gun and fired at Derek's face. The gun made repeated, hollow clicks. No bullets. Scatt-Dogg grimaced, looking at the pistol. He chucked it at Derek. "Fucker!"

The gun hit Derek in the forehead, but in his orgasmic rapture, the impact of the flying firearm was as harmless as the rounds that had come from it. Roaring, he bolted forward. Scatt-Dogg tried to dodge him again but slipped on the gore-slicked floor. His legs kicked in a wild jig and his arms spun into pinwheels as he tried to hold his balance. He fell on his back with a hard, wet thump and floundered in the thick, stinking veneer of Cortnee's blood and entrails.

With adrenaline pumping through his inflating body, Derek stepped over Scatt-Dogg and looked down at him as he squirmed, his white suit soaking to a dark scarlet, reminding Derek of a used tampon.

"I'll kill ya, I'll kill ya," Scatt-Dogg screamed over and over while thrashing around, tangled in intestines. He tried to get up but slipped again. In a desperate attempt to struggle to his feet, he reached up and grabbed Derek's greasy erection with his hands but lost his grip on the blood-lubricated shaft.

Derek dropped and landed with his knees on Scatt-Dogg's chest. He heard and felt Scatt-Dogg's ribs break and the pimp squealed in pain as Derek forced the air out of his lungs. Before Scatt-Dogg could inhale, Derek punched his face, obliterating his nose and gold-framed shades in an explosion of blood, broken glass and plastic. Grabbing the cleaver and raising it high with his right hand, he brought it down with all his weight, driving the blade deep into Scatt-Dogg's shoulder.

Scatt-Dogg released a wild scream as the cleaver connected, his eyes wide and his eyeballs rolling. Derek stood, grunting in pleasure as he lifted Scatt-Dogg as he rose. Derek held the pimp by his throat and lifted him up over his head. The man was weightless to Derek...lighter than the dumbbells he used in the gym.

Derek threw Scatt-Dogg across the room, airborne for a second before the pimp slammed into a wall, caving in the drywall. Scatt-Dogg slid down the wall and curled into a battered ball. He didn't move. Derek breathed heavily and waited. Soon Scatt-Dogg moaned and began to stir, straining to crawl away, toward the apartment door, his swollen eyes focused on Derek.

"Derek had a little lamb...little lamb fucker." Derek snarled as he walked over to Scatt-Dogg and squatted in front of him. He grabbed the pimp by his cornrows and lifted his head, the tip of Derek's penis brushing against the pimp's face.

Scatt-Dogg sobbed. He managed raspy and weak words. "Fuck... fuck you, bitch."

Derek grinned. "Mmmmmm. Fuck *you*, lamb. Fuck-toy."

Scatt-Dogg howled as Derek dragged him by his cornrows to the gore-pile in the middle of the room. He continued to cry out as Derek turned him over and then slammed him facedown. He straddled Scott-Dogg's back, pounding the back of his head with a hard and heavy right fist. Scatt-Dogg's cries gave way to silence.

Eyes closed, Derek took in a rush of sexual desire and anger.

Red bolts of Libidonal-lightning crackled across his eyelids.

Scents of blood, sex, and death overstimulating his hypersensitive olfactory senses.

His overdriven heart pounded with relentless passion...the beats, fast and high.

His every vein filled with adrenaline, recycled anabolic steroids, and man-made rapture elixirs only worthy of gods...

His limbs and torso pulsed with bulging, blood-filled branches that crisscrossed beneath his paper-thin flesh.

He opened his eyes and looked down, admiring his sex, now grotesquely swollen, dark, and throbbing, a red-filtered purple.

"I am unstoppable. You can't kill...the god of fuck."

Derek was immune to pain. He realized this, and it compelled him to do more damage. He wanted to tear the *world* a new orifice.

Gazing down at Scatt-Dogg, Derek decided the tearing would begin with the dirty man-toy at his feet.

CHAPTER 31

Lynch drove, talking hands-free to McRains.

"Okay, here ya go," McRains said. "The name of Derek Hoffman's mom is Melinda A. Hoffman, and she lives at 29 East Coltrane Avenue. Not far from Derek's place."

Lynch pulled over and jotted the name and address down. "I know that neighborhood. It's pretty nondescript; a lot of cheap duplexes which almost guarantee frequent residential turnover. People around there tend to mind their own business, so I assume even someone like Hoffman will blend in while standing out. I'd guess his mother's neighbors have seen him plenty—and avoid him plenty. Did anyone contact her yet?"

"There's been a couple calls placed, but no answer or voicemail." McRains sighed. "We'll keep trying."

"Hold off on the calls; I have an idea." Lynch eased back onto the street. "I don't wanna spook her and possibly have her tip off or hide her son. I wanna scope her place out and then see what she's got to say. Maybe Hoffman will show up while I'm there."

"Yeah, or maybe Tico and his guys will pop up. You need backup, pal."

"Backup? Ha! I'm sick of that word. That's a good one. Backup didn't help me earlier, asshole."

McRains was silent for a moment. "Listen...we got two crazy bastards out there. I won't leave you holding your dick again."

"Please...the CPD is spread thin as fuck and so is my patience. I won't get my hopes up, so I won't be disappointed. I agree, I don't want surprises. I don't wanna face Tortellio and his posse alone again but I can feel Hoffman at my fingertips and precious time is dwindling. You know Tico's watching the clock, too, and he's a desperate motherfucker."

McRains piped up. "Hey, Don ... sorry ... wait a sec. I'm getting another call."

Lynch continued driving, heading in the direction of Melinda Hoffman's address.

After a long hold, McRains returned. "Check this. Hoffman has a brother in the city."

Lynch was all ears. "Really?"

"Yeah, lemme see what I scribbled here. Name's Sid Hoffman. Turns out he's an employee at a company called Peithos Laboratories. Get this: He works in a division of Peithos on a leased floor at St. Cornelius Hospital." McRains paused. "That's where the Tortellio girl's rape occurred. And on top of that piece of intel, a police report was filed earlier for an assault on the Peithos Labs floor. Turns out it was Derek Hoffman. He beat some guy over there and then left the building."

"No one arrested him?"

"Apparently the security guys let him go before any CPD came around. Hoffman's brother—this Sid—stepped in and got him out of there before the heat really came down." McRains paused as Lynch whistled. "Guess Derek Hoffman was doing something up there in the labs, not sure what. We sure as hell know what he did after he left the lab, on his way out of the hospital. The police didn't have his name at the time of either the attack at the lab or the assault of Annabella Tortellio. His name wasn't on any paperwork at Peithos. He was a mysterious, unidentified perp until some lab folks, hospital staff, and

CPD officers linked the Hoffman brothers together and then we got Derek's name."

"So, Derek Hoffman was visiting his brother for some reason..." Lynch mulled over ideas in his head. "He got in a fight, got away ... and made a pitstop to rape Tico's daughter on his way outta the hospital."

"That's the gist. Security said they found a gym bag and wallet at the ICU. They only had it for a minute in their Lost and Found before a CPD cop took it away. Security never got a chance to rifle through it and get an ID. They assume the bag and wallet were Derek Hoffman's. And we don't know which cop took that wallet and where it is."

"And now we've got another layer of shady shit added to the rape case."

"Why would Hoffman risk raping a woman in broad daylight? Especially right after assaulting someone and getting heat on his ass?"

"Not sure what made this lunatic go off." Lynch had many thoughts. "I could speculate the motives of rapists and killers all day. Do they ever make sense? Not sure they have a reason other than some turmoil goin' on in the old attic. Whatever it is, Hoffman's got major issues."

"Uh, that's putting it mildly, Donnie." McRains chuckled. "After seein' what Hoffman did to Astroglide's body and the condition of Hoffman's apartment, I file him under: Super Twisted Fuck."

"Did officers interview his brother?"

"Yeah, from what I was just told, a cop went to his office, asked some questions."

"Like what?"

"Oh, general questions about the beating at Peithos and the rape downstairs but he didn't give up his brother's name. Just played stupid."

"You know if the brother's still at Peithos Labs? We need CPD to keep him there. I want to talk to him."

"He left sometime after the police interview."

"Where?"

"Dunno. He didn't tell anyone he was leaving. We all wanna talk to the guy. Bring him in."

“I’m heading toward the mother’s house,” Lynch hoped Hoffman might show up there for Wednesday night dinner—the clue his calendar had offered. “He’s not rational, so who knows where he’ll pop up—but it’s as good a lead as any.”

“What about the brother?”

“Verify his address, send a couple cars over there. Bring him in for questioning. Also, Derek Hoffman might turn up at his brother’s place for all we know. And if Tortellio’s crew finds out where he lives, they’ll be over there looking for Derek, too. Tell *everyone* going there to exercise extreme caution.”

CHAPTER 32

Back on the hunt and in another hallway in another residential building, Tico stood with his twins and enforcers in front of a condo door as Grotto pulled a roll of duct tape from a paper bag and applied a strip over the peephole. Grotto and Sammy rapped their large fists on the door, the sound echoing down the hall. No one answered. They knocked again, their knuckles heavy and hard on the door.

A cautious male voice spoke up from the other side. "Who are you and what do you want?"

"Police," Grotto said.

There was a beat or two before the voice returned. "Okay. And what do you want?"

"Mr. Sid Hoffman." Grotto's accented voice adopted a tone of formal authority. "Sir, open the door so we can talk."

"Not here," the voice said.

Grotto's tone turned impatient. "Open the goddamn door or we knock it down."

Bolts and locks clicked and turned. The door opened and a young man stuck his head out, looking Grotto and Sammy over with an expression of suspicion and fear. "You have identification?"

Grotto grinned. "Sure, fella. We got badges. Now, stop fuckin' around...*Sid*."

The man caught sight of Tico and the twins standing to the side and the color ran out of his face as Tico locked eyes with him. "Okay. I'm Sid Hoffman. Oh no, please don't—"

Grotto cut him off with a right jab to the mouth. Sid, who was wearing nothing but a pair of black Loyola University running shorts, stumbled and fell backwards into the condo. Grotto and Sammy jumped through the door, each landing on either side of Sid.

Sammy grabbed Sid by his hair while Grotto punched him hard in the stomach. As Sid doubled over, Sammy yanked him up with a scalp-tearing fist and Grotto slapped him across the nose.

Tico and the twins followed the enforcers into the condo and locked the door behind them.

"Look out." Tico stepped between Sid, Sammy, and Grotto and squatted in front of Sid as he lay on his side, gasping and choking. "There anyone else here?"

Sid shook his head fast.

A woman's voice echoed from the back of the apartment. "Sid, who's here?"

Tico slapped his hand over Sid's mouth as the enforcers immediately followed the sound of the voice. He nodded as he heard shrieks coming from the back of the apartment.

Tico stood up as the two walked into the living room clutching a small, howling, kicking redhead in a pink bathrobe.

Grotto said, "She was in the bathroom. Where d'ya want her, Boss?"

"Shut her up. Tape her and her boy to those chairs there." Tico pointed to four wooden chairs tucked beneath a dining-room table.

Sammy pulled the woman's head back by her hair and Grotto told her he'd disfigure her if she didn't shut up. The woman subsided into quavering sobs as she was led to her seat.

Tico looked at his sons, jerked his head. The twins stepped forward, picking Sid off the floor and sitting him down in a chair next to the girl.

"Please, don't hurt her." Sid's voice cracked and his breathing accelerated. "She didn't do anything wrong."

"No...but you did. And she's a casualty of your fuck-up." Tico watched as his four thugs duct-taped Sid and the woman's arms and torsos to the chairs. Seated side by side, the couple's legs were bound together, their bodies wrapped with silvery, mummifying bands.

The woman began sobbing again and Grotto put a gun to her head. Tico leaned in toward her. She looked down to avoid his gaze. He could smell the perfume and lotion on her skin. He watched tears rolling down her cheeks and onto her cleavage.

Tico smiled at her. "What's your name, hun?"

The woman stared at the floor. She took a deep breath. "Gloria."

"Pretty name, doll." Tico flashed a tiger's smile and sang. "Glooor-ee-uh, G-l-o-r-i-a, Glor-ee-uh."

Gloria sniffled and continued staring at the floor.

"Nice place." Tico straightened and looked around, noting the bright room and the tasteful pieces of artwork on the walls. Gloria must've decorated the condo. It had a woman's touch. "Vito, Luini... tear the place apart, see what you can find out about Derek."

He turned to Sid. "Fuckhead, you need to answer every question I come up with or else you and G-l-o-r-i-a here are gonna start losing p-a-r-t-s of your bodies." Tico grabbed Sid's face with a mammoth hand and squeezed it hard. "You wanna keep yourself together? Do ya?"

Sid mewled through his constricted mouth. "Yuh-yuh!"

"Good. Time to get right to it." Tico let go of Sid's face. "Where's your fucking brother?"

Sid shook his head. "I don't know."

Tico pinched Sid's bloody nose. "Get with the program, jagoff. Time's ticking and that asshole's out there somewhere. I need to find him before the cops do. Think hard, 'cause it's not only important to me—it's goddamn mortality in the balance for you and your *puttana* here."

Sid groaned. Blood ran from his nose and mouth and he looked over at Gloria with a hopeless expression. She didn't meet his gaze or speak. She just shook, keeping her eyes focused on the floor. Sid turned back to Tico. "I don't know, man. I'm sorry. I'm so sorry."

"That's true. You *are* sorry." Tico leaned closer to Sid's face. "Do you know who I am?"

Sid shook his head.

"Tico Tortellio. Do y'know what else they call me?"

Sid shrugged, but his expression told Tico this guy had some inkling of who Tico was.

"They call me the 'Meat Grinder.' Y'know why?"

Sid choked on his words. "Mister, please. I don't wanna know."

"What you don't wanna know don't matter. This is all about what I wanna know." Tico's spittle peppered Sid's face. "They call me Meat Grinder 'cause I take fuckheads like you and your rape-fuck brother, and I turn you into fuckin' *Snausages*."

Sid's face twitched and he groaned. "God ..."

"I'll grind Gloria here six ways to Sunday. You and your bitch wanna be turned into doggy treats?"

"No, no, please no." Sid shook his head violently.

"Then where the hell's your brother?" Tico roared in Sid's face.

"Please, mister. I don't know where he's at. If I did, I'd tell you. I don't like my brother. Really!" Sid shuddered. "I know he's probably done some bad stuff and you gotta do what you gotta do to him. But I don't know what he's up to or where he's at. We hardly talk."

"Fucking liar!" Tico punched Sid in his already battered mouth.

Sid's eyes rolled back into his head. He spat up a mouthful of blood and a tooth that he held tight between his lips before letting it drop into his lap. He began to sob.

"I know your brother was at that hospital. He was up in that freak lab you run. Then he beat up a guy and you...*you* got him out before the cops could take him away." Tico bent down and plucked the bloody tooth from Sid's lap. "Now," he said, rolling the rogue incisor between his fingers and thumb, "I'm not gettin' what I want from you. Guess the punches to your noggin' aren't motivating you." He looked at the tooth without interest before tossing it across the room. "Sammy! Gotta up the ante in the damage department. You got the big bag?"

"Naw, thought Grotto was gonna get it," Sammy said.

"Grotto?" Tico turned to his other enforcer.

"Sorry, Boss." Grotto frowned. "We was in a hurry to get in here. Left it in the car."

"See what happens when you get excited about meeting new acquaintances? We forget our heads." Tico smiled at Sid and Gloria and stroked his chin. "Well, I'd hate to trouble my boys and make 'em go out in this crazy heat just to get a bag of fun. Plus, other tenants seeing us comin' and goin' might get 'em curious. Best we stay put." He looked over at Grotto and Sammy. "Got anything flammable?"

"Got Vito's breath, Pop," Liuni said.

Vito flipped off his brother. Tico let out an irritated snarl and the twins straightened. Tico looked around. "Get me somethin'!"

Grotto and Sammy pulled out a couple of lighters from their jackets and threw them on the table. Tico turned toward his sons.

"See anything in those drawers you were snoopin' through?" Tico asked.

"Looking, Pop," Vito said.

"Not sure," Liuni shrugged. "See stuff."

Tico shoved Liuni. "Every passing second here is making me more 'n' more ornery."

"Got some kinda lighter fluid, here." Vito shook a small plastic bottle of Ronsonol.

"Give it here." Tico held out his hand and Vito handed over the yellow bottle. Tico looked the bottle over, shook it, and turned to Gloria. "I'm gonna do your nails for ya."

Gloria broke her gaze away from the floor and turned her colorless face to Tico. "What...what do you mean?"

"I'm gonna do you a favor and remove that hideous red shit you got lacquered on your toes." Tico tossed the bottle from one hand to the other. "Gonna light those little piggies right up."

Gloria whimpered, begging Tico to leave her alone. She strained to look at Sid from her duct-taped place in the chair. Her voice went from fearful to angry. "What did you and Derek do? *What did you do*? Sid? Goddammit!"

Sid flushed, looking back and forth between Gloria and Tico, who were both staring at him. "I didn't do anything, honey...swear."

Gloria's voice rose to a new octave. "Derek! This is all because of him!"

Tico spoke up. "You know," he said to Gloria. "I admire you. For a small woman, you command a lot of anger. And you know how to channel that into power."

Gloria didn't reply. She stared at Sid with a dumbfounded and hurt expression.

"Yeah, Gloria...Derek..." Sid shot a shamefaced glance at Tico, "Derek did some things, bad things he got me into. He ... uh, he—"

"Bad things? That fuck raped my daughter." Tico interjected and backhanded Sid's jaw with a loud crack. He stared down Gloria. "And your boy here knew all about it. Didn't ya, cocksucker?"

Sid's head wobbled as if all these brutal truths and pain were all too much to process. "No, I...I mean, I didn't know exactly about *that*."

"Sid? Sid!" Gloria squirmed in her chair.

"This piece of shit's big brother was over at that lab at St. Cornelius for some reason. They had some kinda get-together there before Sid sent that monster on his way," Tico shook and his voice grew louder. "And on his way out, Derek-fuckin'-Hoffman made a pit-stop and raped my daughter. She's in a fuckin' coma."

An intense fury suddenly overtook Tico. He lunged at Sid, his large hands out and ready to throttle, his body filled with murderous intent. He wanted to rip Sid apart and hear him scream in agony.

Then Tico pumped his brakes just as he was inches away from ending Sid.

Tico composed himself. He needed more info.

Wait. Just wait...

Gloria's head swayed. Tico thought she might pass out, but she recovered herself and tossed her gaze at Sid. Her voice was weak. "You told me you weren't ever talking to Derek or seeing him again."

Appearing abashed and spitting blood, Sid looked past her. "Yeah, I know, baby, but he came to me."

"For what?"

"Needed money. Trouble as usual."

"What did you do? Did you help that bastard?"

Sid looked down. Blood bubbled from his mouth. "Yeah."

"Why the hell would you do that after everything we discussed?" Gloria's voice rose again, demanding.

"I had to." Sid's voice cracked. "I...owed him a favor. He came to me for help. That's all there is to it."

"Why did you owe him a favor?" Gloria was shouting. "What could you possibly owe that asshole?"

"This isn't the time." Sid looked away.

"That's right, you fuckin' liar. Not the time." Tico spoke before Gloria could hit Sid with another question. "I don't have the time or patience to listen to fuckhead Sid explain why he's in big brother Derek's service. I'm gettin' really sick of sayin' that I'm in a hurry here. *True* answers now. And I'll get 'em while I'm putting some shrimps...I mean, *toes*...on the barbie."

Tico squatted down in front of Gloria and enveloped her small left ankle in his beefy left hand. With his right hand, he flicked the nozzle of the lighter-fluid bottle and sprayed the tips of Gloria's polished toes. He savored the fumes from the fluid filling his nostrils.

Gloria let out a scream that was abruptly cut when Sammy slapped her.

"Don't do this, please." Sid cried and spat out blood, straining in his chair, leaning towards Tico. Grotto punched him back in place.

"Sammy, the lighter." Tico considered Gloria's foot. "You know, I'm not much of a foot guy, but I think yours are cute. Shame I'm gonna ruin 'em."

Sammy tossed Tico a chrome Zippo lighter engraved with a large letter "S." Tico caught it and flicked it open in one motion.

Gloria turned to Sid, her voice breaking. "Tell him what he wants, Sid. Tell him anything. Don't let him hurt me. *Please*."

Sid coughed. "Mister, please. Don't hurt her. I swear I don't know where Derek is. I *want* you to get Derek. Believe me. Please, I really, really wanna help you. I...can go with you to look for him, but I just don't know where he is."

Tico glared. "I don't believe ya. Your big, bad brother 'n' you were at the hospital together. He was in some program you were running over there."

Sid's face dropped. "Yeah, but ... how'd you know all this?"

"I know everything." Tico frowned. "So, he must've told you where he was goin' once you sent him on his way."

"No-no-no. That's not right." Sid blurted his words. "He assaulted a guy and was kicked out of the Peithos Labs floor. We didn't speak after that. He didn't say where he was going."

Tico tested the air. "Why does it suddenly smell like bullshit in here?"

"No bullshit. Derek was out of his mind when I threw him out of the labs. I didn't care where he went; I just wanted him gone."

"Hey, boys," Tico said to the twins, who were lolling by the sink. "Quit relaxing and throw me a towel."

Liuni grabbed a small dish towel and threw it to Tico. He stuffed it inside Gloria's mouth. Her face reddened as the towel smothered her protests. Tico turned to Sid. "One last shot, fuckhead. Where's your brother?"

"His apartment, maybe?" Sid said.

"Nope." Tico kept his composure while itching to create some pain. "Been there already and so have the cops. He's running wild."

Sid hung his head. "I don't know where he's at." He snapped up as Tico leaned down to Gloria's feet. *"No! Please don't hurt her!"*

The toes on Gloria's left foot blazed with a *whoosh* as Tico put the flame of the lighter to her nails. Gloria bucked in her chair, vainly trying to kick despite the thick duct tape around her legs and Grotto's hold.

Her towel-muffled screams echoed like a revving motor as the stench of burning flesh and fluid overtook the room.

"Staaaaaap!" Sid begged. Tears rolled down his face as he watched his twitching fiancée and her burning toes.

Tico squatted down, slapped his hands over Gloria's foot, and snuffed out the fire. Gloria's chin dropped to her chest, and she trembled, moaning. Tico looked up from her burnt foot and into her tear-

and-snot-covered face. "Well, I got the polish off, but those cute little toes are gonna be blistered and black. I'd recommend a pedicure at one of my daughter's nail salons—but that's a stretch."

Gloria bucked in her chair again and glowered at Tico. Small veins popped out in her temples. She muttered an angry nasal noise that sounded like, *Fuck you*.

"Take it easy little lady, else I'll light up your tits next." Tico stood and turned to Sid. "Okay, fuckhead. I paused the barbecue. You got somethin' for me?"

"I'm thinking!" Sid said.

"Don't start gettin' pissy like that with me." Tico dug around in his pants pocket.

"I'm sorry." Sid's tone sounded desperate. "I'm trying to help you. Trying to think of where my brother could be."

"Maybe this'll jog your memory." Tico pulled his right hand from the pocket, his fist now accessorized with brass knuckles. He looked down at Sid's bare legs, bound together from his ankles to his knobby knees. With a wind-up and a hard punch, Tico used all his weight into the blow as he came down on Sid's left kneecap.

An audible crunch sounded through the room as the bone shattered. Sid screeched with a pain-filled yelp. Sammy leapt forward, squeezing his mouth shut.

"Now the other one." Sammy kept his hands clamped on Sid as Tico came down on the right knee, again using all his weight. Sid writhed and forced out a scream as Tico whacked the kneecap out of place, sending it bulging to the right side of Sid's leg joint like a giant wart.

Sid rocked his head back and forth, his eyes shut tight, whimpering in pain.

"Open your eyes." Sid opened his eyes slowly, and with difficulty. Tico raised his brass-adorned fist. "You know this baby destroyed your knees. Just think what it'll do to your face." He glanced over at Gloria. "Or to *her* face. I will fucking kill her with my fucking fist right now if you don't give me something, you little shit!"

Sid struggled to talk, hyperventilating. He half spoke and half wept. "Derek. I got an idea ..."

"What's that? Spit it out, already." Tico grazed the brass knuckles across Gloria's shoulder. "Speak *finocchio*, speak!"

Sid gasped and moaned, managing to eke out, "He might show up at my mom's house. He usually always goes there every Wednesday night for dinner."

Tico digested the info. "What time they do din-din?"

"Seven. Somethin' like that."

Tico looked at his watch and saw it was after six. He knew it would be dark before long. "What's Mom's address?"

Sid grimaced and didn't reply.

"Okay, asshole..." Tico bent down and picked up the bottle of lighter fluid. He squeezed, showering Sid and Gloria's heads and bodies then pulled the lighter out of his pocket and roared. "Gimme the fuckin' address! If you don't tell me now, I'm gonna burn both you miserable cunts alive!"

Gloria rocked and screamed through the hand towel. Sid let out a moan of defeat and anguish. "29 East Coltrane Avenue! Melinda Hoffman. Sid's mom. Please ... don't hurt her."

"What the fuck do you think I am? I don't kill mothers. I only kill the sons of mothers." Tico smiled big. "Okay guys, we're outta here. Tape 'em shut."

He watched as Grotto and Sammy placed duct tape over Sid and Gloria's mouths. His icy stare met Gloria's intense gaze.

Firecracker, that one...

Tico turned to look into Sid's soul, but Sid's eyes were squeezed shut, his left nostril oozing a large bubble of blood.

"That tape's gonna hurt when it comes off." Tico looked at his captives. "That shit'll tear off your hairs and even some skin if you're not careful. You're lucky I didn't wrap your *cogliones* with it."

He walked to the door and on his way out he turned to the betrothed couple and addressed their backsides. "I'm goin' to your mamma's house now. Better hope I find your brother before the cops do. I'm gonna do stuff to him no one's ever dreamt up. And if he's not there, I'm comin' back for you two and there won't be any Q and A next time. I'll end both of you on the spot. *Capisce?*"

Sid nodded but Gloria didn't move.

"Understand, goddammit?"

They nodded together.

"Better not even think of callin' the cops about our little visit here. I'm gonna do Derek up and no one's gonna ever find your big brother when I'm done."

"Hold up, Pop. You're not gonna just let them walk, are you?" Liuni looked disgusted. He pointed at Sid. "If this asshole hadn't let his brother go, our sister wouldn't have been, you know, *violated.*"

"Yeah!" Vito pulled an extension cord out a drawer. "They seen us, too. You taught us was not to leave witnesses 'n' shit."

Tico raised his eyebrows.

Well, isn't this a surprise?

He welled up with a paternal love at this unexpected initiative. "Oh? You boys are gettin' with the program, huh? Color me fuckin' impressed. Gonna step up?"

The twins looked at Tico and nodded.

"Yeah, Pop." Liuni took the extension cord from Vito.

Vito nodded. "We know what to do."

Tico smiled. "Then by all means...*really* earn your bones."

Tico and Liuni stepped behind the two chairs as Sid squirmed and Gloria attempted to throw herself out of her chair. Both of their moans muffled by duct tape, their breathing labored. Sammy and Grotto grabbed Sid and Gloria by their shoulders and forced them back as Vito and Liuni threw the cord around their necks one at a time—with Gloria first. The twins pulled the cord up in unison each time, quickly cutting off their air supplies and snapping their necks.

Tico was pleased. He liked seeing Sid's horrified face as he was forced to see his girl murdered before him.

With a huge, proud smile, Tico patted his sons on the back and handed Sammy and Grotto the lighter fluid, motioning for them to spray it around the room and over the garroting rope, which he then pulled across the room.

"We need to make sure we're not leaving any DNA behind here," he said as they all stepped to the doorway and Sammy leaned down to set the soaked rope on fire. He jerked his head, motioning his men out of the condo and took one last look at the motionless pair as the flame crept across the room and ignited their wooden chairs.

"Goodnight, lovers."

Tico flicked the lights off on his way out and got in his car before the fire alarms went off.

CHAPTER 33

Lolinda Watson had run out of cigarettes an hour ago and was jonesing for a smoke. She'd bum one, but all the working girls were talking to johns, leaning over into the cars to handle business. The last couple of johns Lolinda had serviced didn't smoke. She looked up at the building of ill repute and wondered if maybe Cortnee had cigarettes up there.

Cortnee...girl must be havin' a poppin' party up in her room.

Lolinda hadn't seen her street colleague in some time. Either that or Scatt-Dogg wasn't done tearing into Cortnee for some bullshit transgression.

Scatt-Dogg...

Lolinda reflexively put a hand to her lip, touching the place where Scatt-Dogg had earlier slapped the cigarette out of her mouth earlier with his Big Apple hand. Her face and lips were swollen—and her jaw was sore from the half-dozen hummers she'd given in the last hour.

To Lolinda and the other girls who tricked for him, Scatt-Dogg was a nasty leech. She hated him and cursed the day she'd met him. She'd just started hooking in Brooklyn last November for T.J., who, as pimps go, wasn't bad. He had taken her in when she ran away from a predatory stepfather back in Buffalo; T.J. showed her the ropes and actually looked out for her. Once she started sex working, she actually *made* money. But then, two weeks into her new career, Scatt-Dogg came to visit his old Brooklyn neighborhood. When he saw Lolinda, he told T.J. he wanted the *big-tittied, nineteen-year-old piece of ass* for his *stable*. T.J. owed Scatt-Dogg some money or some shit, and so the next thing Lolinda knew, she was giving head in Chicago for twenty bucks a pop with nothing to show for it.

A brown Toyota sedan pulled up to the curb with two young white guys inside, motioning her over. Lolinda walked to the passenger-side window, flashing skin. "What up?"

"Not much." The driver, a skinny dude with red hair, leered at her.

"Lookin' for fun." The passenger, who had a shaved head and a pierced septum, gawked at Lolinda.

"Well, y'all came to the right place." Lolinda smiled. "I got lots of fun."

The guys looked at each other and started giggling, their eyes watery-red.

These fools are baked...

"You guys gotta smoke?"

The passenger shook his head. "We don't smoke, honey." That statement started another round of giggles.

Lolinda rolled her eyes. "You wanna date, or what?"

The driver said, "Yeah, but I want some prices first."

Lolinda crossed her arms.

"Yeah, wanna know what we're getting for our money here," the passenger said.

"Whad'ya want?"

The guys looked at each other with impish, shit-eating grins.

Lolinda hated this game.

The driver asked, "How much for a blowjob?"

"Twenty," Lolinda said.

"Yikes," the driver said. "That's kinda steep. You swallow?"

"Fuck, no." Lolinda

The passenger asked, "How much to toss my salad?"

Lolinda was sweating from the heat while losing her cool. *Damn these losers fuckin' with me.* "I don't do that."

"How about doin' you in the ass?" the driver asked.

Lolinda scowled. "Five-hundred a minute."

"Okay, okay." The passenger tried to control his laughter. He wiped his eyes. "Okay, listen. How much to take a corncob, right? And we shove it in your ass while I recite the Pledge of Allegiance?"

The guys cried with laughter, rolling in their seats as if they were having seizures.

"Hillbilly fools." Lolinda stepped back onto the sidewalk, adjusting her skimpy outfit. "Get the hell outta here 'fore you get *your* asses fucked."

The guys continued laughing. The passenger reached down and pulled out a thirty-two-ounce Slurpee cup. Then he threw it, the contents splattered and soaked Lolinda's top.

"Whore!"

Lolinda let out a scream of surprise and anger as the cold, pink slush hit her. "Assholes!" She flipped the guys off as they peeled away, laughing and hollering.

The Slurpee's icy relief provided a momentary break from the intense heat of the day—but it also felt gross as hell as it clung to her skin and clothing. Now she needed to wash off the damn heat, the Slurpee, and the smell of the anonymous, unpleasant men she'd finished off all day.

Lolinda opened the door into the derelict building, hoping Cortnee was in her apartment so she could bum a cigarette and hose down with a quick shower. She could rinse out her clothes and put something fresh on before going back out into the muggy evening.

Inside the dim hallway, two crackheads were sharing a glass pipe. They paid her no mind as she walked to the stairs, curling her nose against the fetid smell of calcified shit that mingled with the odors of stale semen and dried-up malt liquor. Somewhere in the building, a man's voice said, "Put it in yo' damn mouth." Somewhere else a female voice bawled joyful sounds of sexual pleasure. Lolinda wondered if she'd ever experience such pleasure. Men got it, she figured, she sure as hell didn't.

Scatt-Dogg had always told her it was a *man's world*, but as far as Lolinda knew in her experience, it was a woman's world. Scatt and all the other male trash weren't shit without women.

Buncha frontin' bitch-boys. Gonna turn this game around on these fools one day...

On Cortnee's floor, Lolinda could make out some graffiti and garbage, but the walls and doors disappeared into blackness.

Her skin prickled at some strange noises wafting down the hallway. Sucking in a deep breath, she walked forward, kicking filthy detritus with her feet until she came to the door of Cortnee's apartment.

Lolinda raised her hand to knock and froze. An odd sound was coming from behind the door. Listening close, Lolinda heard grunting and groaning, along with a man's voice screaming.

"No! Gonna kill...fuck! Fucking stop! Stop nig—"

The voice abruptly cut off.

Knowing she shouldn't, yet unable to stop herself, Lolinda used a cautious hand to turn the knob and slowly opened the door, wincing as the hinges squeaked. Cortnee's apartment smelled rich with blood; the slaughterhouse stench of a fresh butchering and worse wafted out as the door swung inward.

Lolinda found two men locked together in the middle of the apartment's main floor in what looked to her like some fucked-up wrestling match. One of the guys was Scatt-Dogg, and he was locked together with the monster of a man she'd seen being escorted by Cortnee earlier. Scatt and the other guy were writhing in a pile of what she could only think of as roadkill. Whatever it was, it sure stank and reminded her of the splattered remains of deer she'd seen on the highways of upstate New York and along the highways she'd taken to Chicago.

Like all them poor Bambis turned inside-out by them big rigs...

It was then Lolinda noticed the limbs. A pair of woman's legs and a lower torso stuck out of the heap of butchered blood-meat. A scream tried to force its way out of Lolinda's mouth but froze in her throat as she recognized Cortnee's decapitated head resting on its neck stump on the nightstand. The horror of the scene snuffed out her ability to make a sound. She could barely produce a breath.

The cruor-imbrued, muscle-bound creature whom Cortnee had solicited earlier stared at Lolinda with dire intent as he jackhammered himself into Scatt-Dogg's upended rear. Scatt's face kissed the floor as the muscle man held Scatt up by his hips. Scatt struggled and got up on his elbows. A flash of surprise shown on Scatt's face as his gaze met Lolinda's. He groaned as he stared—along with the big man—directly into Lolinda's wide eyes. The two men bounced back and forth off each other in a depraved rhythm.

Lolinda could see Scatt had been worked over *real* good—split and bloody lips, swollen eyes, and bloody divots in his scalp where the cornrows had been torn out. His once fabulous and flashy gold and rock-encrusted grille had been pulverized out of his mouth.

She stood frozen, suddenly realizing for the first time how small and ridiculous Scatt-Dogg looked; his pants torn off but his leather shoes and dress socks remaining on his feet. His fancy shirt and suit jacket still covered his upper body, the once white and meticulously groomed clothes now transformed to a dark, splotchy red that crept up his left sleeve from a pool of blood seeping across the floor.

She looked closer at the lake of red and discovered that Scatt-Dogg's Windy City hand had been chopped off and lay disconnected next to the bloody stump of his wrist—palm-down on the floor, its long nails and the sparkling, mini-skyscrapers rising above the blood, making it look like some a five-legged and bejeweled insect.

Lolinda opened her mouth to scream and again produced nothing.

"Help me ... *bitch*." Scatt-Dogg croaked as his buttocks bounced off the muscle man's lower abdomen.

She looked away from Scatt-Dogg's sniveling face and connected with the mad eyes and teeth-grinding grin of the muscle man.

"I can smell it. Your sweet cunnus." The muscle man licked his lips and glared at her as he continued to plow balls-deep into Scatt-Dogg.

Lolinda backed up to the doorway, keeping her eyes on the grotesque scene in front of her. Scatt-Dogg collapsed, his shoulders twisting sideways as the muscle man reamed away, sweaty, and drooling, exhaling with deep groans, his eyes remaining on Lolinda.

She tore her eyes away from his but as her gaze landed on Cortnee's decapitated head, she squeezed her eyes shut. She opened them again and, glancing at the floor near her feet, she saw Scatt's gold sunglasses —now twisted and smashed—and his chrome .380, streaked with blood. For a second, she thought of grabbing the gun and shooting the monster in the head, but what the hell did she know about a gun?

Nothing.

However, she spied something she actually would risk her neck for: Scatt's money clip, which was stretched wide by a folded wad of green.

Lolinda flicked her eyes over at the beast whose libidinous gaze continued to bore straight through her, but he didn't make a move to come after her.

Just keep Scatt-Dogg...keep him all to yourself and leave me alone...

She snatched up the clip of bills and, keeping her eyes on the muscled nightmare man, she slowly walked backwards, thinking every second determined her fate. Her hand found the doorknob as Scatt-Dogg's eyes met hers one last time. He mumbled, trying to tell her something, but she backed into the hall, easy and quiet, as the muscle man punched Scatt-Dogg in the ribs.

God, don't let this monster come after me...

Lolinda sprinted through the hall and leapt down the stairs, stumbling as she cleared several steps at a time in her high heels. She burst out onto the sidewalk, startling two prostitutes who'd been fanning themselves with newspapers while waiting for the next guy with fuck-money to come along.

She grabbed the arm of the closest one, a plump girl in a yellow negligee and red wig, who dropped her newspaper fan. "Lolinda! Girl, lookit you. What's wrong with yo ass?"

Trembling, Lolinda moved her lips, but no words came out.

The hooker in yellow stepped back. "You seen the devil, or somethin'?"

Lolinda finally managed to muster words. "Crazy shit goin' on up there. Cortnee ... she, uh, doesn't have a head no more. Scatt-Dogg... he's soon dead as shit. Like...ah, damn..."

The hookers shook their heads but stood up straighter. "The fuck you say? Sure 'bout what you say, girl?"

"I'm too sure. Don't believe me? Take a look your damn self. But ... you go up there, take everyone on the block with you or you might not come back. There's...there's a real *monster* up there."

She shivered, and despite the heat, kept shivering, couldn't stop herself. The women looked at her, then at the building, and hustled down the block.

Yes, a monster. He could appear at any moment and grab her.

Could he? Would he?

She turned and ran as fast as she could down the street.

She knew there'd be no more tricks happening in that building for a long time—if ever again. The muscle man had tainted the entire block. But he'd also freed Lolinda and the others from Scatt-Dogg, hadn't he?

Was he a savior?

Savior or not, she knew he would drag her back up there and carve her up if he got his hooks in her. And even if someone spotted him, who would stop him?

Lolinda kept running.

Outta here. Tonight!

She clutched Scatt's cash tightly in her small hand as she ran toward the ratty room she rented and the little money she had stashed away there. She would find a decent hotel and take a long, cleansing shower.

Maybe I'll sleep well for once.

After what she saw, Lolinda doubted she'd sleep anytime soon. One thing she'd do for damn sure was buy the damn cigarettes she'd been hankering for all afternoon, even before she'd discovered the bloodbath.

Then *tomorrow,* she'd hit that big-ass Greyhound station underneath the expressway she'd always dreamed of leaving from. She'd grab a bus to a normal place, somewhere far, far away from Chicago.

CHAPTER 34

Evening crept slowly over the city. When the blazing sun sank at last, it went down red and miserable, leaving suffocating heat and humidity as a parting gift.

Lynch had been speeding down to Melinda Hoffman's residence when he'd had to pull over yet again to talk to Earl's wife, Angela, who'd called to tell him that his former partner had succumbed to the cancer. Lynch's head dropped to the steering wheel and he pounded the passenger seat with his right hand as she gave him the news.

The wake and funeral arrangements were being booked for Sunday night and Monday. Lynch would be a pallbearer at the funeral. He knew the morning service would be long and would bring out an army of cops. He was already planning to duck out after the service and skip the lunch at the banquet hall. He hated funerals, period.

Was hoping you wouldn't go this fast, Earl.

Lynch's eyes blurred with tears. He dabbed at them with his knuckles. This day was turning into one of the shittiest he'd ever experienced.

Suck it up...

He swore he wouldn't fall into that dark place again. Had this all happened before he sobered up, he'd be drinking and pill-popping his emotions into submission. And it had lost him Sandy.

Forget that shit.

Lynch liked himself better now. *The new Lynch.* He had to remember that, embrace his reinvention. Doing so would give him reason to celebrate his survival. And maybe it would earn him another chance with Sandy, but either way, despite everything, he really was grateful to be alive.

His car sped through the city. In the distance, he saw Lake Michigan and, as he turned a corner, the skyline he loved so much loomed up to the north. It wouldn't take him long to get to Melinda Hoffman's house on Coltrane Avenue.

"Where in the world are you now, Earl?" Lynch asked out loud and he choked down the sob threatening to escape. The police radio crackled without an answer, and he turned it off. His heart hurt. He collected his thoughts. He'd have to tell Sandy that Earl was gone.

Sandy...

On his mind now and always, ever since their first meeting outside Wrigley Field almost twelve years ago. Lynch recalled Sandy telling him that she'd been dating a guy who was cheating on her. Suspicious, she'd tailed him to a Cubs game and caught him sucking the lips off a brunette with fake boobs and a bad complexion. Sandy confronted the couple. The boyfriend went into defense mode, started cursing Sandy, and slapped her face.

Lynch, who was on his way into the game, had had his eye on Sandy even before the confrontation. And when the boyfriend slapped Sandy, Lynch stepped in immediately. Sandy's boy got in his face, trying to get tough, and Lynch pushed him onto the pavement face-first, shouting at some bystanders to call the police. The woman who'd been making out with Sandy's boyfriend threw a tantrum, screaming at Lynch and hitting his backside with her purse as he held Sandy's cheating boyfriend down. Lynch ignored the hostile woman and tightened his hold on the guy's arms, which were behind his back, until police officers arrived and took Sandy's boyfriend away along with the other woman.

Sandy thanked him for defending her honor and introduced herself. Lynch remembered being lovestruck. It was weird and surprising to him. Something had immediately clicked. Her beauty overwhelmed him, and his heart became almost too large to contain. That first encounter was—even though he knew it sounded corny—love at first sight.

Lynch didn't want to let her go, so he suggested she catch the game with him since she was already there, and he had an extra ticket because Earl had backed out at the last minute. Sandy confessed she wasn't a sports fan—had never even been to a game at Wrigley, in fact. Lynch feigned shock, telling her she hadn't lived until she'd experienced a Cubs game there.

He handed her his extra ticket and told her their seats were in a skybox with complementary food and drinks. He promised that if she didn't have a good time, he'd make it up to her with a real date at a place of her choosing.

As it turned out, Sandy wasn't shy about trying new things. They'd had a great time together. The Cubs had won, and, after the game, they went out for another drink to celebrate. He smiled, remembering that perfect first date.

A week after their first meeting, Lynch and Sandy slept together. He'd never experienced such mutual attraction, such passion, and such tenderness in his whole life—before or since.

A year later, they'd married and through the first eight years, their love and their bond seemed unbreakable. But everything changed after he fell into depression. The memory of that time was a dark blur; he didn't like thinking about it. The last two years of their decade-long run had survived on life-support, the plug yanked out a little more each day.

In hindsight, he knew he should've danced like a happy fool; he was alive, cancer-free, and he had a supportive wife to help him through it. But he hadn't danced or shown any form of gratitude. Did he feel like half a man with the loss of his testicle? Had his brain chemistry changed with the radiation and chemo? Did the drinking make his depression worse? Maybe. Probably. But he refused to give marriage counseling a shot. He'd given up, lost interest in trying to change—even with Sandy crying and begging him to do so.

Lynch knew he wasn't that guy anymore.

These memories added to the heartbreak he was handed with Earl's death. It all made him want to just pull over and sob into oblivion.

You goddamned stupid, stubborn bastard...

Sandy had moved out and filed for divorce. The house hit the market; their belongings divided up as Lynch sat by, watching it all play out with the indifference of a man on a station platform watching his train roll out of sight.

Now Lynch's heart ached from the loss of Sandy's love. Being sober and happier made him recognize what was important and he yearned for all that basic human shit: warmth, companionship, Sandy's once-endless love and affection.

And it wasn't sobriety that had made him realize how much he missed and loved Sandy—that love had never gone away. Lynch had just let it go away in real time for some reason he could never understand.

Depression? Loss of one of my balls? Fuck me...that's all such horseshit, ya fuckhead.

Lynch sure missed Sandy's amazing laugh, the scent of her perfume and her sex. He missed the delight in her eyes when he came home and the moments in the night when they'd reach for each other, half asleep, to hold, cuddle, and whisper, "I love you..."

It was time to call her back.

No better time than now, right?

He didn't have much time, but he didn't want to keep her waiting.

Oh, boy...

He dialed Sandy as he drew closer to Melinda Hoffman's neighborhood.

"Hey there." Lynch cleared his throat as Sandy picked up.

Sandy sounded surprised. "I didn't think you'd call back."

"Yeah, I'm interested in buying some property near the lake and I hear you're a really great agent." Lynch's tension ebbed as Sandy actually laughed. "Thinking about buying a high-rise."

"Ah, I see. Well, we require fifty percent down on all high-rises. So, if you've got, like, a hundred-and-forty million dollars to start with, we can do business."

"Cool, I've actually got that on me. You take small bills?"

Sandy laughed again.

That *is the laugh I remember ...*

"Okay, what's up, Don? I've gotta do a showing soon. My client likes seeing property after dark for some reason."

Lynch paused, thinking about what he was supposed to say. "First off, I want to apologize for cutting you off on the phone earlier. You caught me at a bad time and I had to run."

"You're always running somewhere."

"You don't wanna know."

Sandy sighed. "You never kiss and tell."

Lynch struggled to respond. He didn't have time to squander. It was hard to come up with the right way to convey what he wanted to say. He looked at the street ahead and focused. "I know I wasn't the easiest man to have for a husband, but—"

"You were a drunk pillhead with heavy issues, Donnie."

No warning shot.

"We're talking past tense, here, Sandy. You know, I quit drinking and prescriptions when you divorced me. Quit smoking, too."

There was a pause. "Did it all on your own, huh?"

"Yep. No AA, no NA, no steps, nothing. I did it cold and hoped I could tell you I had my sobriety under my control once there was enough time under my belt."

"I can't deny that I'm glad you did it. And I hope telling me will make you feel better. But if that's all you have to say, I gotta get goin'."

"Wait a minute," Lynch said, desperate to maintain the connection. He fumbled, unsure where to begin. He blurted, "I love you, you know?"

As the words left Lynch's lips, two screaming Chicago PD vehicles with pissed-off red and blue lights ripped by from the opposite direction.

Sandy remained silent.

"I've been thinking of what we were, y'know? What we had and missing all of it. Missing you."

"What we had and what we were? It *was* great at one time. You let it go down the shitter, Don. Haven't we been over this enough?" Sandy paused, her tone sounding sadder. "Those last couple of years suffered a long, excruciating death. I dunno ... it all feels like a millennia ago."

Finding his rhythm, Lynch spoke his mind. "I know you wanted counseling for us. I know you were there when the cancer was found. And—"

"I was there? No shit. Please. I found the lump when I was holding your balls."

"I know. And you were always trying to get my mind clear after the orchiectomy, putting up with my bullshit. I know you wanted me to get help for my depression and drinking and I didn't give a good goddamn about any of it. My head was in a different universe, and I blew it. But I had the job, too. You knew what type of work I did. Finding the demons of the world and bringing 'em down, even if that meant not seeing you for days."

"Save the 'hard life of a detective' spiel for someone else. You've blasted that shit into my head since day one." Sandy emitted a sad laugh. "Yes, I know what being with a detective entails and I accepted it. Why? Because I loved you for *you*. Nights without you and the daily horrors you dealt with worried me, but I knew that no matter what, you were mine and you'd be home again. You always had a good head on your shoulders, but that's not the point. The job may've compounded things, but it wasn't the problem. You got cancer, lost a nut, battled depression, and you got into the pills and booze. Then ..."

"Things got to me somehow. I don't even know how I let it happen, but that's all on me."

Silence again.

"I'm sorry, Sandy. I *am* so fucking sorry for it all. Sorry to you for the heartbreak and neglect." Lynch's throat dried up. Everything was awkward...he didn't want to sound desperate or weak. "Y'see, I know the whole time I was numbing myself, I was still somehow functioning on the job. I knew you were suffering, and I just didn't do anything about it. I couldn't function in our marriage. Even though I watched our relationship crumbling, I felt helpless to do anything about it."

"I thought maybe Earl would've kicked your ass into shape. I prayed for it."

Lynch frowned and blinked a few times. "Earl died today. Cancer."

Sandy gasped. "No...oh, no, Donnie. I'm so sorry. Angela and the girls?"

"They seem to be handling it as well as can be expected, but, you know, you can't ever really prepare for that kind of thing."

Sandy whispered something he couldn't hear.

"Anyway, you should know that Earl kicked my ass in line. Told me I was fucking up all the time when it came to you. Made me look within myself, at what I was doing to myself and what I had done to *us*. Now I'm kicking my own ass. Damn, I just can't believe I let that fucking happen."

"We're divorced now. That's what happened, Donnie." Her voice trembled and then she began to cry. "I always said I'd *never* get divorced. Never. But then we did. And I wish you could've gotten your head in check and let us go through it together and continue to be what we were."

"Me too, babe." Lynch was mortified by Sandy's tears. He now felt as if he was in the bottom of a hole, hoping she'd throw him a rope. "You know, it's not too late to try giving us another run."

"What?" Sandy snorted and came back, choking up. "Damn it, Donnie. I can't have my makeup running. I've got to show a place!"

"Sorry. I wish I could make you laugh."

"You almost did with that last statement."

"What? About us getting back together?"

"Yeah." She sniffled.

"Why? Because you've got a new guy now?"

"No, I don't. But if I did, it's none of your business."

"You sure you don't?"

Sandy paused. "You trying to insinuate something?"

Lynch let a beat go by. "I literally just saw you at Irene's Bistro this week with some young stud."

Sandy laughed. Lynch loved her laugh, but this sounded sharper to him. "You were there, huh? Stalker."

"Yeah. Irene's is one of my fave places. Remember?"

Sandy sighed. "Of course, I remember, silly. Why didn't you say hi?"

"Gee, I haven't seen you in a while, figured you hated me. Last thing I'm gonna do is interrupt your date."

"Pfft, it wasn't a date, Donnie." Sandy sounded annoyed. "That was my friend Cassandra's husband. Cassandra works with me. We all went out together after work. She must've been in the bathroom when you peeked in. Some detective you are."

"Hey, it hurt. I didn't know what you were doing. So I got the hell out of there."

Sandy was silent and while Lynch's spirits lifted with this new revelation, he wondered if she was trying to discover some hidden agenda beneath his words. Then she spoke up. "How about you take me out this weekend? If things go well, we can discuss more."

A date? Lynch was already in and thinking that nothing would ruin this weekend. *Yes!*

"I want that shot."

"Donnie, I have to say, I'm fragile."

"I know, baby. I'd rather kill myself than hurt you again." Lynch's heart pounded. "I love you more than anything."

Sandy choked up again. "I love you, too. I missed you, asshole."

Lynch chuckled. "Baby, I've missed you like you wouldn't believe."

"Okay, it's way too hot out here. I gotta run, Donnie."

Lynch was falling in love all over again. "I've gotta get going, too," he said. "And Sandy? Thanks for the chance."

"I know you're a good man, Don. I love you. Always have."

Lynch longed to kiss her like the old days ... deep, the way lovers do. To smell her skin and hair again. "I'll call you again later, okay?"

“Deal. But do me a favor, okay?”

“What’s that?”

“Don’t get yourself killed before our date this weekend.”

Lynch tried to laugh, but one lingering problem remained before he could even think of going on a date. He had to bring in Derek Hoffman before he killed again.

CHAPTER 35

Derek was marinating in a world of red. He had driven his raw member into Scatt-Dogg nonstop, climaxing countless times. The constant burn of the chemicals churning inside his brain and blood had propelled him to new heights of pleasure and violence.

His murderous impulses still unsatisfied, Derek picked up the cleaver, and while ramming himself harder into Scatt-Dogg, he hacked away at his still-breathing prize, producing airborne swirls of blood, meat, and bone, until he realized that his iron-hard tool was buried in a bloody pot roast with legs.

Still, he kept at it.

The sights and smells assaulted his senses. Swamped in gore and squatting in the mess he'd made, Derek inhaled smells of semen, blood, and viscera.

I'm so high...high on fornication...high on the slaughter...on the RED.

Derek rode the chemical waves surging inside him. The blasts kept his nervous system on high-alert and his flesh prickled and burned, picking up sensations from every molecule around him, arousing him further. He loved the constant stimulation, the ever-present high. He never wanted to come down.

The sound of frantic and excited voices floated up in the dusk of the street below and then he could hear people chattering in the stairwell. He heard things like *murder* and *fucking blood, man*. Above the biting slaughterhouse aroma of the hot apartment, Derek smelled fear and detected an *urgency* in the air. He wondered if the arrivals would dare cross the threshold separating their world from his erotic, red-covered hell.

I will fuck. I will rip and tear.

I am...the god of fuck.

And then, suddenly...

Where are you, Dad Hoffman?

You need to see me here, inflicting greater pain than you ever could.

Rip the bodies with my bare hands and teeth.

Look at what I have become...father.

If only you were here to accept the same fate.

Derek, intoxicated with this newfound, unstoppable power, was falling in love with himself. Through the beatings and torture inflicted by his dad, through the humiliation and violations from the Bradley Davis School for Delinquent Boys and Young Men, through the chaotic and damaging schooling of the street, even through all his fights and problems with the law, he'd survived and finally emerged victorious. Now he was a deity whose core burned, fiery with endless lust and rage.

Derek swiped blood-covered hands through his spiked and filthy hair. The heavy air in the squalid horror-room drew sweat from his every pore, conjuring memories of the searing heat of that old horror shed of his youth. Derek longed to break, butcher, defile, and eat his father, to show him everything he'd become—and then shit him out into manure.

And what of his mother? In the last few years, she had reached out to him, apologizing for all the damage done, for asking the authorities to send him to juvie when she could no longer handle his behavior. She told him she was sorry for not being stronger, sorry for not standing up to Derek's father, explaining she'd feared her husband more than anything. Like Mr. Tobias, she had stood by and let Dad and others abuse him. She could have somehow found the strength to protect him, to rescue him, to show him someone cared for him, but she never did. So, yes, Derek and his mother had reconnected, but they struggled with awkward tension whenever they talked or met. They didn't know each other anymore: There was no love, just some sort of civil and obligatory arrangement as kin. Derek knew his mother and Sid shared a stronger bond, sustaining a real mother-child love—and that enraged him.

The sound of sirens in the distance snapped Derek out of his revenge-filled thoughts. He clambered upright, blood rushing to his legs, and admired the torsos strewn about the floor, reminding him of the limbless, headless mannequins at lingerie stores. The breasts, the bottoms, and the holes were all that his septic desires demanded.

The rest of these corporeal remains?

Slop.

The outside light had faded. Derek ran his hands over his own body, an oily mixture of blood, sweat, and semen covering him from scalp to sole. A runny paste dribbled down the shaft of his hard penis while he stood motionless, heart pounding, and took in the noises of the street.

The screams of police cars cut through the internal pounding in his ears and as they grew louder, and the sound and smell of the excited people on the sidewalk and inside the entrance of the crumbling tenement electrified his danger sensors.

Time to flee.

He took a last look at the deep red bedlam he'd created. Part of him wished he could stay here to roll around in it all, aroused and tangled in the penetralia of his playthings. But no, it was time to go. Plus, he was hungry. The onset of night and thoughts of food triggered a memory, and he realized it was...

Wednesday.

Wednesday night. His mother was expecting him for dinner.

His stomach rumbled.

His genitals spasmed.

Oh, yesssss...

He would see his mother.

Derek reflexively pulled on his sopping shorts, leaving his yellow tank top behind as he loped out of the apartment, slithered into the darkness of the hallway, and looked out for trouble before creeping to the end of the corridor. He smashed a window, looked down to an alley below. Voices carried up the rickety stairs behind him as he lowered himself out and dropped two stories to the ground, where he rolled, righted himself, and ran down the alley.

Racing into the hot night, nearly naked and covered with blood, Derek's mind flashed with images of what could be. Fucking, killing, dining on carnage—all in his mother's house.

Mother.

He wasn't far from her. As he wove in and out of the shadows, Derek thought of what his mother looked like beneath her skin. Perhaps he'd eat her for dinner after he reworked her from the inside out.

CHAPTER 36

Lynch drove fast as he focused on the job at hand; get to Melinda Hoffman, find Derek, keep Tico away.

His mission was clear, but thoughts of Sandy got in his way. Lynch imagined seeing those beautiful eyes of hers once more, of kissing her again, of seeing her in a sundress and heels, long hair down.

Sure, he figured it could all go down the shitter again, but he was excited.

Lucky me.

Ten years of marriage, then divorce. It was a miracle she'd talked to him. He knew this was his last chance as Sandy's words found their way into his thoughts...

You put me through hell.

I gave you all the chances I could and you let me go.

We're divorced now; people just don't turn that around.

You bastard.

My parents and friends will kill me if they hear I took you back.

You caused a lot of grief, asshole.

Lynch turned a corner, trying to concentrate on the positive: Sandy had agreed to see him again. Yes, that was a great thing. Yet, he couldn't shake the feeling of a certain darkness that lingered. The last few days were testing his resolve in myriad ways.

If any of the crimes Hoffman committed did somehow make the news with his name attached before he was caught, Lynch envisioned the mayor and the suits and the public pointing fingers at detectives who didn't pinch Hoffman in time, and demanding action against them. In his experience, optics were everything...the higher-ups and civilians didn't care how Lynch struggled against the CPD's lack of manpower or how hard he was trying, or the incredible odds he was up against. They only cared about results.

As for Lynch, he cared about people, period. He thought of his oath to protect and serve, a pledge that sometimes felt naïve and futile in this fucked-up world.

Getting bad guys off the street?

Lynched laughed to himself. He knew bad guys weren't just on the street. They sat in offices, delivered babies, ran the country.

Fuck it...

Lynch cleared his mind and returned to focus on what he was doing. The CPD had a full-blown description of the perp and knew his stomping grounds. Chicago was a big city, but Lynch held on to hope. Hoffman's build would make him easy to spot. There was an All Call out for the guy; patrols were keeping their eyes open.

Accentuate the positive...everything will work out.

Everything.

Lynch had less than a mile to go before reaching Melinda Hoffman's residence. The house, he hoped, had his man inside. He imagined Melinda not allowing Derek to eat until her son washed the blood off his hands.

Nearing his destination, Lynch turned on to a new street. Two blocks ahead, still a ways from the Hoffman house, he found the street clogged with dozens of police vehicles, ambulances, an ME vehicle, and many spectators. He noticed a flurry of activity centered on a depressing two-story brick building to his right. Police officers, medics, and personnel in biohazard gear coming and going like anthill employees.

"What the...?" Lynch wondered why he hadn't heard about the call to this location. "Oh, Christ." He realized that he had shut his police radio off before calling Sandy. He flipped the radio on and it buzzed with back-and-forth communications in various police codes.

Lynch heard a dispatcher call for an ambulance. There were already three on the scene from what he could see. He turned his lights on *sans* siren, still listening to his radio. A terrible, nasty feeling roiled inside him as an officer reported a definite DB—dead body. Another officer radioed in, reporting the scene as a homicide, and added, "make it a double." The codes and lingo only got worse. Was this Hoffman's work? He wouldn't be surprised if Derek got called in as a 10-91V—cop code for a vicious animal.

The street was lit up with floodlights as well as red and blues. He wove the Dodge Charger Pursuit between squad cars and ambulances. An officer in the street waved him on. Lynch stopped near the building's entrance and rolled his window down to talk to the cop.

"What happened?" Lynch showed his credentials.

The officer shot an uninterested glance at Lynch's badge then took a moment, as if considering how much info he felt like giving out. Wiping sweat from his forehead, he finally waved toward the building. "Got nothin' on the perp who made this mess. It's a whorehouse murder. Double-homicides. There's a hooker and a pimp up there in an apartment full of blood and pieces. Body parts all over." He leaned toward Lynch. "These ambulances should leave. There's no one to resuscitate. A meat wagon's what they need there. Scoop up what's left and throw 'em in a meat locker."

Lynch frowned. "Something toxic up there?" Lynch nodded toward a tech who walked out the front door of the floodlit building wearing rubber gauntlets and an orange biohazard suit.

"Got nothin' on that." The cop let out an exhausted breath. "We were told to use caution 'cause there's some weird DNA all up in there—along with all the blood and body pieces, of course. Area detectives inside are callin' it Biohazard Level 1. Just gotta have gloves 'n' shit. They're probably being extra careful. A little overdressed, though, in this goddamn heat."

"I hear ya. Perp description?"

"Got nothin'."

"Suspects?"

"Nothin'."

"Witnesses?"

"Look, we're trying to round some up." The officer's tone gave Lynch the impression his questions were bothersome. "Bystanders there came from nearby shops 'n' apartments and such, but they all got nothin'. We were told a bunch of hookers worked in that building, but they all split. I bet one or more of 'em saw the gorefest in there and screamed holy hell to the locals. A bad scene like this will make 'em all skedaddle until the CPD's gone and outta sight."

Lynch turned his gaze back toward the busy scene at the building. Cops controlling the small crowd. Cops and CPD dicks were smoking out on the sidewalk, laughing as if they were cracking jokes with medics. Officers stepping aside as techs entered the building with gurneys and reemerged holding white plastic containers. The containers looked to be sealed in clear plastic bags with orange biohazard stickers on them.

Lynch's deepest instincts told him that the massacre inside the brothel had everything to do with Derek Hoffman. But Lynch had no doubt that Hoffman was gone from the scene now and Lynch needed to find him before any more carnage continued.

Ma Hoffman's dinner bell is ringing...

"Okay, then. That's it, Officer?"

The officer shrugged. "Told ya, I got nothin'."

Lynch shook his head and put the car in drive. As he began to leave, the officer waved. "Wait a minute, man. You got a cold drink in that car?"

"Got nothin'!"

Lynch cursed to himself as he navigated through the cluster of police cars and emergency vehicles and exited the crime scene. He hit his siren and it blared as he hurriedly toward the home of Melinda Hoffman.

CHAPTER 37

Melinda Hoffman hated being put on hold. She'd needed her prescription yesterday. Unfortunately, her doctor screwed up and hadn't called it in to the pharmacy until that morning. Now the pharmacist couldn't seem to find her info. Why couldn't they get anything right? She'd grown testier in recent years. Why did it feel as if the world always turned against her?

As she aged, Melinda developed health problems, including an infection in her heart. Although she'd quit smoking ten years ago, she wondered if maybe something was waiting inside to afflict her, something nasty, left over from her days of smoking a carton of unfiltered Pall Malls every week. Or perhaps something from the air she inhaled working at Slappy's Bar and Grill was growing inside her organs.

Melinda thought everything in life was carcinogenic.

Only a matter of time until the Devil came-a-callin'...

The pharmacist returned to the phone, apologizing, telling her that her prescription was ready. Melinda sighed and hung up the phone. The Coca-Cola clock over her kitchen sink told her it was 7:30 already. Too late. The pharmacy closed soon and she knew she didn't have time to run to the drugstore and be back before supper.

Melinda had expected Derek by seven, the usual time. Tonight, she'd prepared one of his favorites—steak with baked potatoes and beer—and it was all primed and ready to cook. She had to wait until he walked in to broil the steak so she didn't have to deal with the tantrums he'd throw if she'd cooked it already before he got there and it had gotten cold.

Just like his damn father.

God help her if she ever said that to Derek, though. She didn't want to imagine the rage she'd invoke in her eldest if she ever said that.

Between her horrible marriage and the mayhem Derek had brought into her life over the years, Melinda had transformed from a beautiful young brunette with a confident, striking step to a wrinkled, gray-haired crone. Time had never been kind to her, she thought. She was only fifty-eight, but she thought she looked and felt ninety, and she walked with a stoop when her damn back gave her trouble—which was often.

Melinda initiated the Wednesday night dinner ritual in hopes of keeping Derek in her life on a regular basis. Yes, her hand on a Bible, she really did want the best for him. But he'd always been nothing but trouble and deep down in her heart, hadn't he? She often thought that Derek was going to be the real devil who'd be the end of her one of these days.

Then there was her sweet boy, Sid. She wished he'd come by for dinner...or even for a cup of coffee. He'd been the smart one who'd gone to college all on his own. He called at least once every day and always celebrated her birthday and Mother's Day with her. Yes, he was her sweet boy. They saw each other whenever he could make time—and always made it with his Gloria on big holidays. Even with his busy schedule at Peithos Labs and his fiancée, Sid remained ever-thoughtful and always in touch.

Derek, however, never remembered any special days—aside from Wednesday night dinners. He only called or visited when he wanted something. Still, she gave thanks that he kept his dinner dates with her despite being an unending source of woe in her eyes.

I could've done better for him...I could've...

Melinda thought of Derek and blamed herself for the way he had turned out. She knew how brutal and cruel her husband had been to him. Looking back, she wished she'd done something—*anything*—to prevent the physical and mental abuse he'd suffered at her husband's hands.

Stan Hoffman had disappeared years ago without a trace. Melinda thought it was the best thing that ever happened to the family. Yet, the damage Stan had already done, and the ruins he had left behind, were irrevocable. Gone but not forgotten, she figured the bastard would always haunt her.

Derek hadn't been the only target for her ex-husband. Stan had beaten her bloody plenty of times, too. God, her boys had no idea of the terrible things he'd done to her—and the terrible things he made her do *to him*. She'd never forget the times when he was drunk and got on top of her with a knife to her throat. He was just born evil. Still, he'd never laid a hand on Sid. Who knew why a father developed such a mean streak for one of his boys but not the other?

Melinda tried putting all of the bad memories and trauma out of her mind—but it would only be a brief pause before it surfaced again. She figured maybe she deserved it. Why? She didn't know...

For now, she had to get ready for Derek. With dinner prepped, Melinda waited and went to the fridge to grab a soda.

"Oh my. How could I be so stupid?"

Melinda spoke to the empty kitchen as she found a solitary bottle of beer in the fridge. Derek had killed an entire twelve-pack of Goose Island 312 at last Wednesday's dinner, and she'd never replenished it. With this realization, she dreaded his arrival more than ever. With no beer for Derek, she knew his foul attitude would become even uglier. She didn't have time to run to the store. Derek was already past due.

I wish Sid were here.

At least he could help her attempt to diffuse Derek's bad temper. Then again, Sid had never been able to calm his brother down completely.

Melinda grabbed a couple more items from a cupboard. Then it revealed itself to her: A dusty bottle of Jack Daniels tucked away behind an old set of salad bowls. She pulled it down and blew the dust off. The bottle was half full. Yes, she nodded, maybe she'd be able to tame the beast with this ... at least for a little while.

With the potatoes resting in the oven on low heat, Melinda leaned against the counter and put the cold can of soda to her forehead. Just then, the doorbell rang.

God bless it all. Was Derek here?

If he was, why would he ring the doorbell? He always entered through the back door, which was never locked when she was home. Perhaps it was a delivery or something. It sure didn't seem right to her, someone to come around at this time of night. Don't they know that most folks like her were either finishing dinner or relaxing after a day's work?

"Better not be a salesman." Melinda set her soda down and made for the front door as the doorbell rang again, over and over. "I'm comin'! Hold your horses."

She walked to the front door. Wiping her hands on her apron and smoothing out her old blue dress, she turned on the porch light and opened the front door.

"Yes?" Two large men in sharp suits and sunglasses stood in front of her. Two more stood behind them. The two in the back looked like identical twins and also wore suits and sunglasses. *Who the heck wore sunglasses at night?* Even stranger to her, the two frowning men in front spoke something that sounded foreign. Sounded Italian.

"I don't understand you." Melinda offered a tentative smile as unease began to grip her.

The first pair drew handguns from beneath their suit jackets and pushed Melinda back into the living room. She gasped as she felt her bladder suddenly threaten to empty out on her. The four men filled the room, guns out, and forced Melinda into an old brown recliner. A fifth man in a charcoal suit appeared in the doorway. Melinda thought he must be as big as a Chicago Bears defensive end. He swaggered into the living room and stared at her while one of the twins shut and locked the front door.

He flashed a lascivious smile. "Mrs. Hoffman?"

Melinda met his cold gaze. His eyes were flat and gray and icy. He smelled nice and his nails and eyebrows looked well-groomed, but his creased, pock-marked face was joyless and rough. From all her years working in a bar, she knew faces and what they said about someone—and this guy looked he'd been *around* and had done Christ-knew-what in his time.

"Yes." She hesitated, trying not to show fear. "Melinda...Hoffman."

The man's smile grew wider. Light danced in his eyes. He cracked his knuckles as he looked down at her.

"Melinda Hoffman. Glad to meet ya. I'm Tico." He put his nose in the air and closed his eyes. "*Mama-mia*. Boy, that smells yummy." He returned his frosty stare to Melinda. "I hope we're not late for dinner. Got coffee?"

CHAPTER 38

Derek weaved through alleys and backyards, slinking like a bad dream for block after block, avoiding streetlights, cars, transients, and dogs trying to bite his ass as he crept through their owners' properties.

He became one with the shadows and he found that the dark blood covering his body aided his camouflage. But Derek wasn't scared of being seen. He feared no man, but the irrepressible demands of his body and mind battled with calls for discretion. Erotic and violent desires continue to rage inside him, and he ached for new desecrations —but if people saw him streaking like a muscle-bound ghoul, they might try to stop him and interfere with his purpose. No, Derek would never allow that. The pinch of logic he still possessed inside the crimson tempest of his brain told him it was better to blend in with the night if he wanted to continue his gruesome pursuits. He thought of the bloodbath he left back at the whorehouse and he imagined that must have drawn police and many others by now.

Who might be hot on his trail now?

Let them come...let them cum.

Nearly naked, Derek burned outside and in. Sticky and coated with blood and other bodily fluids, he wore a moist membrane ... as if the placenta from his mother's womb still coated him after all these years.

He crept along, relishing his role in the new darkness as a creature of the gloom. The night air carried its own urban stench, and the nocturnal and sinister sounds lit him up.

Derek emerged from the alley into a vacant lot littered with garbage, smashed glass, abandoned furniture, and weeds. He sniffed the darkness, which smelled of so much trash, stale alcohol, and the vomit, piss and shit that numerous people had ejected as they passed through.

Crouching low, he moved across the lot with his knees bent and his head bowed, his body weight pressed down on the ground through his fingers, knuckle-walking quickly like a tanned, hairless ape. He stopped in front of the cinder-block wall of an abandoned auto garage to relieve himself and a powerful stream of urine burned through his erect penis, splattering his chest and six-pack abs as well as the pavement.

A loud clattering around the corner of the building caused Derek to whirl around. A bag lady came into view, pushing a shopping cart full of cans, junk, and bags of homeless treasure. Stooped and gray-haired, her body was clad in raggedy, soiled clothes. She mumbled to herself as she pushed the cart. He could smell a miasma of old sweat, polluted undergarments, grime, and sour wine that he inhaled deep into his nose and lungs.

Still squatting, Derek took in the bag lady with his eyes and nose as she mumbled nonsense and turned the shopping cart into the lot and toward him. He stayed motionless as the cart clattered, banged, and ran right into his immobile body.

"What the hell, Nixon?" She pushed harder, but the cart wouldn't go forward. She backed up and rammed it, and again it collided with Derek.

Derek felt nothing other than good sensations.

"Damn you, bastard-Nixon-boner." She hobbled to the front of the shopping cart and spotted Derek crouching in the dark. "What the hell're *you*?"

Derek looked up at the bag lady with his blood-covered face and bared his teeth at her. He wanted to chew her throat out and skull-fuck her. But some practical part of his brain tugged at him, telling him it was too much work to destroy this hag.

He had places to be.

Mother...hell awaits...

Rising to his full height, Derek stretched and stood over the bag lady, jaw clenched, inflexible member forever vertical and pointing directly at her face.

The bag lady stared fixedly at the throbbing cock that nearly slapped her in the face. A high scream escaped her mouth as her gaze traveled up to his glaring murder-mask.

There was a loud smack as his fist connected with the old woman's left temple, blasting her off the ground. She went down hard onto the cracked and filthy pavement. Blood ran from her ears.

Derek crept away, low and cautious, behind the garage, smashing cans and bottles beneath his bare feet, his toes striking cast-off engine parts as he went. The cinder-block wall still radiated heat from the daytime sun. Bushes and dead brush raked his skin and mosquitoes attacked him, but he remained numb to the physical discomfort. He was, however, becoming anxious, wanting to reach his destination, to get his needs sated.

Mother.

She had always been so passive. So un-nurturing. So unprotective. She had enabled all those bad things to happen to him. His rage billowed up.

The Rough Riders. Dad.

I hate you, cunt. Mother.

Her house wasn't far, maybe a block down and one street over. The familiar sights and smells of the old neighborhood provided an odd sense of comfort. He recognized the noises, too: Barking dogs in the distance. Car horns and squealing tires. The deep, thumping bass of tricked-out rides. Popping fireworks, gunfire.

The only person he could see was an old man in plaid shorts and a white wife-beater, standing on a nearby patio and cursing as he worked over a grill, lit up beneath a light bulb that was attracting hundreds of flying insects. “Only a damn madman be out on a night hot as this. Sheee-it.”

The smell of cooking meat intensified Derek’s already-stimulated stomach into a need, as greedy as his voracious cock and unquenchable homicidal yen.

Appetites need to be rewarded...

He wanted to be at his mother’s house *now*. He knew the way. Yes, he’d take the sidewalk, unnoticed, skitter down a block, then cut through a few yards to arrive at Mom’s back door.

As he moved down the sidewalk, he detected something wrong in the air. He hunched down near a row of parked cars, remaining motionless as the palms of his hands and soles of his cut-up feet absorbed the sidewalk’s lingering heat. The hum of quiet machinery approached, followed by the sounds of grit and gravel quietly squashing under rubber, then the soft squeak of brakes. A car had pulled up and stopped in the street near him.

Derek rose up from his haunches a few inches, scanning the street over the roof of a green Volvo. At the sight of the police car, every muscle in his body flexed, causing all of his joints to pop. Adrenaline blasted through his heart and veins. Why had it approached silently, slowly, like a submarine on a secret mission? Why were the headlights off? Was a cop looking for him?

A spotlight abruptly cut through the dark from the driver’s side of the car, slamming Derek’s already racing heart into overdrive. The beam of light scanned the row of cars he was hunched next to and then stopped on an old and beat-up Datsun with tickets pinned under its windshield wipers, which was parked right in front of the Volvo where Derek was hunkered down.

Colored lights began flashing from the top of the cruiser. A car door opened. Derek heard someone getting out of the vehicle and stepping into the street. He caught the sounds of a police radio and then jingling metal. His nostrils flared at the light smell of perfume and menstrual blood.

Lady cop?

Derek straightened again, just enough to see through the Volvo's dirty windows. The red and blue police lights continued to flash, but the headlights remained off and the spotlight kept its beam aimed at the car in front of him. He saw the police officer now, a tall female cop with a masculine build. She held a pad of paper in her hand, taking notes while examining the forsaken Datsun.

The muscles in Derek's legs relaxed as he realized the cop wasn't looking for him. He still considered her to be a threat, however, and remained vigilant, shifting his position next to the Volvo, preparing to retreat. His blood slam-danced in his veins and pounded into his head.

As he began slinking backwards, he lost his balance and shot his arms out to catch himself. His forearm hit the rear quarter-panel of the Volvo with a loud bang.

"Who's there?" the cop shouted in a husky, forceful voice.

Every bulging filament in his frame waited to explode as the officer hurried around the rear of the Datsun, shining a black metal flashlight.

"*Hey!*" she cried as Derek lunged and rammed into her with all his weight, wrapping his hands around her throat as he tackled her to the ground, her back smacking hard on the strip of grass between the sidewalk and the curb.

Still throttling, Derek slammed her head into the turf. She clawed for her revolver, but Derek caught her movements, seized her arm, and snapped the bone. The gun fell away.

The cop made choking and gurgling sounds as Derek crushed her windpipe. He watched her wide eyes bulge and her face turn darker. As he banged her head into the ground, her patrol hat fell off to reveal a bun of fair hair. To Derek's enhanced vision, though, the woman cop was red, as was her hair, and her face glowed crimson as he forced the life out of her.

His sweaty hands slipped and suddenly, Derek heard an audible crack, and bolts of red lightning crisscrossed behind his eyes as he felt something strike him. What had happened? His eyes had shut reflexively with the blow. Fresh, hot blood dribbled off his right brow. He looked down at the cop and saw blood from his head spattered on her distorted face. There was zero pain, only pleasure, but he knew he'd been cut open somewhere above his right eye. His vision was fucked.

What...?

Another crack sounded, accompanied by another brilliant flash of red in his mind. This time Derek saw the object that hit him, through the red filter of his left eye, as his right eye filled with blood and began swelling shut.

This persistent bitch had hit him twice with the heavy-duty Maglite clutched in her good hand. By the stream of thick blood flowing from somewhere above his right eye, Derek knew he was badly hurt, but the blows remained painless.

"Cop...you...die." Derek bellowed as he drew his right arm back and smashed the officer's face. He drew his left arm back and punched her again, leering as she exhaled a spray of bubbly blood from her razed mouth.

The cop gasped ragged breaths and muttered something incoherent as Derek wiped the blood from his forehead with the back of his right hand and grabbed the flashlight that had fallen out of the bitch-cop's spastic hand. He slammed it down like a mallet onto the remains of her face, over and over and over again until her lifeless head resembled some pulverized piece of fruit.

Derek clambered back up and looked around. All was quiet on the street. The lights on the police car hadn't drawn any attention yet. He walked over to the cruiser, and using the blood-covered flashlight, smashed all the car's lights. Nearby porch lights came on.

Maybe...no...not the best idea...

But the beating had stirred Derek's bloodlust. He was blind to anything other than fury. Control was escaping him. He was losing it more than at any other time this day. He pulled the waistband of his shorts out and gripped his hardness to steady his tremoring body and mind. He came immediately.

He looked down and in the faint light, his penis appeared to be missing a layer of flesh, its thick and swollen veins sticking out like three-dimensional ridges on a grotesque relief map. The semen pumping out was a bright, dark red, possessing a cherry glow. Maybe he'd taste it. The thought triggered a hunger again.

Derek snapped the waistband of his shorts back into place and moved on.

Walking between houses and across their dry, sunburnt lawns, Derek felt charged, alive, and indestructible. He wanted to ream the world with his giant cock. If the planet didn't have a warm, wet, and giant slit, he'd tear the world a new hole and fuck that.

Derek stopped, listening to the night and testing the air. He heard cats fighting and fireworks detonating in the distance. He knew he was home now. He *smelled* his mother's place, and with only a few more steps to go, he was poised to arrive on her doorstep in all his blood-soaked glory.

CHAPTER 39

I *just gotta make it past this week and everything will be fine.*

Lynch replayed the tragedies and near misses of the last three days, but also the good things. He'd said goodbye to Earl *just in time* and spoken to Sandy *just in time* to tell her he loved her.

And how about that testicular cancer? Yep ... he was certainly thankful to catch it *just in time,* though it cost him a testicle.

But the reality of the task at hand stopped his retrospection cold.

Would he catch Hoffman in time?

In time for what? To save others? To curtail his spree?

Of course. He'd started out trying to solve one murder that had led to chasing a psychopath on a downward spiral. Apprehending Hoffman would stop the madness, but so much damage had already been done...

Annabella Tortellio's rape.

Astroglide's murder.

And whatever the hell had happened at the crime scene he'd just left.

What the fuck else had Hoffman done...?

Lynch had kept his siren on and stomped on the accelerator and yelled at his Dodge Charger Pursuit to move faster. He sped down side streets at seventy miles per hour even though he knew it was unsafe, then cranked the wheel hard at a stop sign to get him back on a main drag.

Racing on, his eyes flicked up to the sign hanging over the entrance of a hardware store.

IF YOU DON'T PAY YOUR EXORCIST, DO YOU GET REPOSSESSED?

Humor seemed like a far-off, alien thing to him right now.

The radio blared urgent sounds of dispatchers directing units to the apartment building he'd seen already swarming with CPD. Reports rattled off a double-murder, the address, a suspect on the loose, and now an actual perp description identical to that of Derek Hoffman.

Called it.

Lynch killed his siren and was about to phone McRains, but John beat him to it.

"What's up?" Lynch spoke aloud via Bluetooth.

"Hey, D. You hear about the deal at the whorehouse?"

"Yeah, I just drove by there. It's all over the radio. Our boy."

"It's Hoffman all right. A couple of street urchins at the scene gave our guys a good description and it fits the bill. They saw him go inside with a hooker. What happened here...goddamn, it's the worst thing I've seen in my entire career, Donnie. *Ever.* The crime-scene cleaners may as well just level this building now because it's a massacre to the tenth power. There's a hooker and a pimp...what's left of 'em. Beyond annihilated."

"Yeah, when I drove by, I saw techs come out in biohazard gear, covered in blood. Talked to a street cop and he told me people were in pieces in that place."

"Two of 'em slaughtered ... the way they were mutilated, you'd think someone hacked 'em up for a barbecue. And Donnie, there's a *load* of DNA here—no pun intended." McRains paused. "The guy left his calling-card all over the joint. Bright-red spunk again, just like Astroglide's place. Get this, the Medical Examiner and the techs say even the pimp was raped. Man and woman—both raped and murdered and then raped again and cleaved and chopped up. What in the fuck is with this guy?"

Lynch wondered the same thing. “I don’t know, John. Ask God.”

“There is no God. Not in Chicago, anyway.”

There is no God.

Lynch paused on that, giving McRains remark a thought—unsure if he agreed or not, but he sure got *why*.

“Things are getting down to the wire, John. I’m not far from Melinda Hoffman’s place.”

“Her place is close enough. Hoffman may be on his way there, too. Donnie, whatever you do, don’t go after him alone. We already knew he’s one mean, pissed off, psycho sonofabitch and now we know he’s just getting worse.”

No shit, Sherlock McRains.

Lynch eased up on the accelerator. What the hell had he been thinking? He patted his .40, reassuring himself that this was his reliable source of backup—and it was still there.

Still...

“John, I *do* want backup—and I want it yesterday, or I’ll call it in myself. Tell ‘em it’s 29 East Coltrane Avenue.”

“Yeah, I know. I got you, D.” McRains paused again until the background noise quieted. “Can’t hear myself think over here. Damn news trucks are arriving now, and the street’s filled with crazies. I *will* get you real backup and I’ll be there myself in two shakes of a lamb’s dick—as soon as I can get outta here.”

“Bye.”

Lynch disconnected and exhaled long and hard, cutting back down side streets until he reached Melinda Hoffman’s block.

Coltrane Avenue looked innocent enough: one-way, short, with a generous number of trees and a lone streetlight. Cheap houses and low-income duplexes filled the lots. Cars were parked along one side of the street as per local ordinance. Lynch drove by them, slow and cautious, looking for suspicious vehicles. Nothing stood out.

Lynch, straining to identify house numbers in the dark, pulled up near Number 29, a small, nondescript ranch house with an overgrown lawn with no porch light. He drove to the end of the block, parked the

Dodge Charger Pursuit, and turned it off. No lights, no engine hum now. He sat in darkness and quiet.

Looking up and down the street, he caught an odd vibe. No noise, no wind, just the relentless heat of the night smothering him and everything else on this block. Checking and then pocketing his gun, he grabbed his keys and slid out of the car, slowly and deliberately, shutting the door quietly behind him.

He scanned the street as he approached Melinda's ranch house, noting the drawn shades and lights on inside. The front porch sat in darkness with only the glow of a doorbell looking like a distant star.

Hold up until that backup arrives. That's what I should do.

Lynch stood still. He waited several beats. He thought about McRains trapped at a crime scene so horrendous he'd never get cut loose; about backup and how it didn't arrive anywhere near fast enough for him earlier that day. If Melinda Hoffman was in jeopardy this very moment, and something horrible happened while he stood around with his dick in the wind waiting for CPD to join the party, Lynch would hate himself forever.

Fuck this. Just do it.

He approached the steps, triple-checking his gun. He certainly wasn't counting on any cops to show up soon, but at least the .40 would help him take care of business. At the top of the stoop, he did a quick, cautious recon, then rang the bell.

The shades over the front window moved as if someone was peeking out at him. He heard the sound of the front door lock being turned—but the porch light never came on.

Lynch suddenly realized he'd left his bulletproof vest in the car.

The front door creaked and a somewhat stooped, middle-aged lady in a blue dress opened the door. "Are you Melinda Hoffman?"

The woman stiffened and blinked rapidly "Yes? What can I do for you?"

"I'm Detective Lynch." He showed her his shield. "I'm looking for your son, Derek Hoffman. Mind if I come in?"

Her eyes darted to the right.

Was Derek here?

"If I don't find him soon, Mrs. Hoffman, there's a chance he's gonna get hurt." She glanced quickly to the right again, folded her arms and then shrugged. "Sure ..."

Lynch's skin prickled. He reached for his weapon and stepped forward through the doorway but froze as the barrels of two large handguns collided with his temples. A voice to his right spoke. "Don't move, pig-fuck."

Lynch stared straight ahead and didn't breathe. He knew, from having heard it earlier that day, that the voice belonged to Grotto "the Peeler" Graviano. The bear-like mobster stepped forward, keeping the gun at Lynch's temple while snatching the .40 out of his holster. Grotto tucked Lynch's .40 into his waistband and then motioned with an immense, hairy hand for Melinda Hoffman to step behind him into the cheaply furnished living room.

"What d'ya want us to do with 'im, Boss?" Lynch's peripheral vision identified Sammy Ruggio as the thug drilling a gun into his left temple.

"Bring 'im in here." Tico Tortellio's gravelly voice called from the kitchen, just beyond the living room.

"Move it." Sammy gave Lynch a sharp shove with a gun barrel while Grotto escorted Melinda Hoffman along.

All four entered the large, shabby kitchen filled with out-of-date appliances. Tico sat at the banged-up table, drinking coffee with his twins, who leaned back from either end of the table. He set his cup down and grinned. "Detective. Welcome to the Hoffman house. Have a seat."

Sammy pushed Lynch down into the empty chair directly across from Tico. Lynch glared at Tico and glanced at the twins, who both smirked back at him.

Good job, Donnie. Fuck me.

Lynch looked into Tico's face. "I went easy on you earlier today. But now, once again, you're interfering with police business and your men just drew guns on a cop. You're all under arrest, *now!*"

Tico and his crew erupted with laughter.

"That's a good one, Detective." Tico's grin shifted into a glower.

"You don't seem to understand that it's you who's messing with *my* business. I'm here to wait and see if that cocksucker decides to show up. Once he does, I'm gonna ruin him and be on my way."

"I won't let that happen."

"You can't do shit." Tico sneered and sipped his coffee. "I'm the boss here, *capisce?* I've got the upper hand, and this is my show. Get it through your thick head."

"Stupid pig," Vito chimed in.

"Shaddup!" Tico turned back to Lynch and gestured in frustration. "I'm in a very bad mood. I been runnin' 'round all day trying to find this Hoffman fuckin' guy and I'm tired of it. I'm gonna rip 'im, tear 'im, finish 'im, and then I'm then goin' to meet my wife at the hospital. That's all there is to it."

I want my gun back.

"Got everything thought out, huh? Too bad my CPD brothers are comin' to ruin your *show.* Any minute now."

"Not worried 'bout that." Tico shrugged and scowled. "They weren't in a hurry to come to your aid last time we met. And me and my guys parked a couple blocks away to keep you and 'em off our radar. No one knows we're in this hood. Even *you* didn't know it, or you wouldn't have walked into our trap. You didn't warn anyone about jack-shit."

"They'll be looking for Hoffman anyway, so they'll be on their guard and on the way."

Lynch tried to find comfort in his words, but he wasn't able to soothe himself. He figured he was fucked but good this time. His mind raced to devise some way to keep himself alive long enough for a miracle to arrive.

Tico's scowl fractured into a smile of contempt.

"Doesn't matter..." Tico cracked his knuckles; the sound reverberated around the kitchen like exploding acorns. "No one aside from my boys and my enforcers are leaving here alive."

CHAPTER 40

Tico really didn't want to whack Lynch.

Killing a cop?

Whoa, boy. This'll bring some major heat on my ass.

Tico knew too well that if he turned Lynch into trunk music, he'd be begging for a titanic mess that wouldn't be easy to clean up.

Sure, he'd contracted hits on a couple of cops before, but that was some thirty years ago. Those pigs had it coming far as he was concerned—but those hits weren't just knee-jerk decisions. Tico had laid out the contracts for approval first when his father, Carmine, sat at the head of the Outfit's table. Tico had never made major moves without permission, following the rules of their *thing*. When he had presented his case to take out those cops, his father's captains first discussed it, his father's *consigliere* had advised on it to Carmine, and the Tortellios had then asked for approval from other mobbed-up families who might have an interest in said cops before green-lighting any kind of hits like these.

Tico recalled how those long-dead cops had gotten pinched for doing very bad things on behalf of the Tortellio crime family—and they were going to testify. That right there guaranteed them an automatic death sentence. Tico didn't get any resistance from anyone after he laid it all out. Though he didn't like this Donnie Lynch detective at all, Tico didn't think Lynch was a bad guy or even a cop who ought to get rubbed out. Sure, he was annoying, meddling in Tico's business and facing down the whole crew—and Tico certainly wasn't going to forget that the fucker had put a gun to his forehead—but Lynch was just doing his job and seemed to understand, almost sympathize with what Tico was going through.

Tico respected that.

Of course, Tico had his own job to do now—it was one part principle, one part necessity. Protecting his family and avenging Annabella was paramount. Second, was maintaining his flex and position as boss. He made sure to show, that, despite being long in the tooth, he was far from weak.

Weak? Weak ain't part of my fuckin' vocabulary.

This detective had dropped eyelid-deep into the quagmire of Derek Hoffman's shitshow, and because of that, Lynch knew too much now. Why couldn't this dumbfuck just have turned his back and leave it alone? Tico could avenge the horrible tainting of his daughter, do what he had to for family honor, and then he could've moved on without having to make the detective disappear. But no, Lynch had to push it and forced Tico's hand...and now Tico would take care of this fucking cop. He had no choice, and this time, Tico wasn't going to ask anyone for permission.

Everyone—including his own beautiful daughter—had to die to make everything right. All because of this Hoffman fuck.

Tico figured Derek must've caused the detective some kinda grief somewhere down the line. He was a homicide detective, so he sure wasn't here because of Annabella's assault. What else was at play here? Tico guessed it didn't matter. He had complete control now and would cross off everybody, one by one.

"You gotta understand, when I see somethin' through, I see it all the way without stoppin'." Tico skewered Lynch with his eyes. "I've done stated my case here and I ain't showin' no mercy to Hoffman or any of you bystanders. You and Mrs. Hoffman here are collateral damage. I'll give ya both the dignity of dyin' quick, but that's as generous as I'm gonna get."

"You're a real saint, Tico."

"Yeah? And you're a real smart-ass, Detective." Tico stood, tugged at his cuffs, and walked around the table. He approached Melinda Hoffman where she stood near her ancient stove while the juggernaut Grotto held her shoulders from behind. "How is it that a little gray-haired woman such as yourself could birth such a huge, sick fuckin' monstrosity?"

Melinda didn't answer. She remained quiet, staring at the floor with wet eyes and a trembling lip. He glared down at her

"Do you know what your boy did to my little girl?"

Melinda shook her head.

"He raped her." Tico's words were honed with anger, but he kept his emotions in check. "He raped her, bit a chunk out of her shoulder ... did it all while she was in a coma. That's somethin', huh?"

Melinda gasped and tried to put a hand to her mouth, but Grotto forced her arms to her side.

"Gotta wonder what kind of stock that piece-a-shit comes from." Tico sized Melinda up then waved his arms in exasperation. "Lookin' at you makes me wanna hurt someone. I know you're thinkin' it's not your fault you gave birth to the world's biggest mistake, but it's fact. Ya did. In the grand scheme-a-things, *you* made it possible for that cocklicker to soil and hurt my daughter when she was already damaged and outta commission and couldn't fight back to save her own honor. *Vaffanculo, puttana!*"

"I'm sorry. Sorry about your daughter." Melinda's words sounded as brittle as her body. "I didn't know he'd done such a thing. I can't imagine ..."

"Can't imagine what?" Tico emphasized his curt question with a hard hand-slap on the kitchen table.: "That he'd do such a thing? Ha! I saw his record. He's been in all kinds of shit. Christ almighty, you see the big, ugly bastard every week. You know he'd rip off your head 'n' take a dump down your neck. Why you even have anything to do with 'im?"

"I didn't raise him to be so violent, and certainly not to become a rapist." Melinda trembled. "I try to this day to show him I care, and I pray that he does good. No one wants to see their children go down the wrong road."

Tico placed the palm of his large right hand on top of Melinda's head and petted her like a cat. He mustered up a pseudo-sympathetic tone. "Hey, I can relate, Mrs. Hoffman. No one wants to see their kids go bad, but frankly, kids end up goin' their own way whether you like it or not." He shot a cold smirk at his boys sitting at the table. "Tell me, where's your hubby, Mr. Hoffman? Where's he at right now? I'd sure like to meet him."

Melinda looked at her feet, let out a heavy sigh. "I haven't seen him in forever. You'd have to be the world's greatest P.I. to locate him. I hope he's rotting somewhere in hell."

Tico withdrew his hand and folded his arms. "Awww. Sounds like trouble with the honeymoon. What happened to the prick?"

The corner of Melinda's mouth twitched. "He left without a word and with his laundry still in the wash. I don't know if he's alive or dead. Not a word from him since my boys were kids. I filed for divorce years ago. I don't know what happened and I don't care. He was the worst thing that could've ever happened to this family."

"*Au contraire.*" Tico frowned. "I'd have to say your ex is the second-worst thing to happen to your family. Your oldest mongrel gets the gold medal for fuckin' you all up."

"Any badness in Derek is a result of the horrible ways people treated him. The abuse he took when his father was around would make anyone into a crippled and hateful creature. My husband was pure evil."

"The apple doesn't fall far from the tree, huh?" Tico stretched and gazed down at her. "You know, my old man was hard on me, but I didn't turn into some psycho-rapist. I mean, I kill people, but it's part of the biz. It ain't 'cause I'm sore at Daddy."

"I tried getting him help." Melinda's tears came on. "There's a lot I didn't do to stop his father, and there's more love I could've given him, but I didn't. I've tried to fix the things done to him. I never raised him to be a monster."

"But he *is* a monster." Tico turned to Lynch. "And that monster's gonna die tonight with the rest of ya."

Melinda closed her eyes, shook her head, and bawled. Tico nodded at Grotto, who released her arms, and she buried her face in her hands.

Vito checked his phone and drummed his fingers on the table. "Hey, Pop. It might not be good to be hangin' here all night waiting for that creep. I mean, we left Mickey and the cars two blocks from here, but someone still might notice somethin's up. This pig found the joint. You never know who else might show up knockin'."

Liuni nodded. "Yeah. We might be barkin' up the wrong tree, and what if this asshole's backup shows up before Hoffman does? We should get going and send some soldiers over to watch the doors."

Tico's face flushed. "You both shut your holes right now, or else I'm gonna take my brass knuckles to the two of yas." He turned and slammed his hands on the kitchen counter, and the twins shrank back in their chairs. "This is *my* show, and it's done my way. We're talkin' about your sister's honor here, goddammit—there is not one thing more important than this. I don't wanna hear shit from you. I'm the boss, 'n' you don't worry unless I worry."

Lynch smirked. "Might be a good idea to listen to 'em and get out while you can, Tico. What're you gonna do when police surround this place and burst into the house? You and your guys'll all get caught with hostages—including me, a Chicago Police Detective."

"Well, you can't make hostages outta dead people, can ya?" Tico stepped in front of Lynch and Sammy put his hands on the detective's shoulders to hold him down in his seat. He looked down, trying to cut Lynch into pieces with his eyes. "And you don't understand a fuckin' thing about my motivation. I'd fight through a platoon of Marines to get to Derek Hoffmann. I ain't worried about your buddies—a lot of them pigs are my associates, too, and they'll make sure everyone looks the other way. 'Sides, no one's gonna care about me doin' a rapist, a worthless old lady, and a nimrod like yourself."

"Confidence is definitely one of your strong points." Lynch shook his head. "And so is stupidity. You're in a world of hurt, Tico. You kill three people, no one's gonna let you just walk outta here."

"World of hurt, huh?" Tico fished in his pocket for his brass knuckles, pulled them out, and tossed them from one hand to another. "I was already in a world of hurt, you cocky motherfucker." He slid the knuckles on. "We all are, really. And since things are already in the shitter and we're all hurtin', let's just see how bad we can *really* make it."

When the first punch cracked Lynch's ribs, he let out a loud, painful cry. Tico suddenly became more confident about doing the detective.

Fuck it.

Tico hit Lynch again and the dumbfuck detective wailed and looked ready to cry. Yes, Tico suddenly felt this rotten day had unexpectedly begun to improve.

CHAPTER 41

A man's abrupt cry coming from his mother Melinda's house made Derek's flesh ripple. Alarm blossomed in his mind.

Derek felt like a match had been lit on him, evolving him into a walking, scorching being with unseen flames rising off his limbs. He couldn't see so well, his right eye swollen shut by the bitch-cop. The vision in his left eye was filled with crimson, highlighted by flares of electric heat.

I am burning red.

He paced back and forth in his mother's backyard with no real direction, half-walking, half-crawling like an agitated primate in a zoo paddock. The urge to batter and kill continued to fill his brain—as did an intense drive to fuck. That hadn't let up since he'd begun his long walk from Peithos Labs—*it seemed so long ago now*—to Mother's doorstep.

His excitement led to new streams of milky scarlet fluid spurting from his member as he prowled across the tall, uncut grass.

He crouched down in a cluster of weeds beneath the kitchen window and froze, motionless as a lion stalking gazelle. Heart banging, he tested the air with his flared nostrils and his sensitive ears. Through the humid odors of the city summer, he could detect the scents of food and men emanating from the kitchen. His olfactory senses heightened and he smelled his mother, too—the faint fragrance of her cheap perfume and traces of her perspiring fear aroused him, and the murmurs of strangers and sounds of physical pain lit up his ears.

It was too much. He felt every filament, every individual sinew inside his steroid-and-hormone-inculcated muscles contract until they made noise. He heard his body squeak in places where the strain from his flexing strength caused pieces of cartilage and bone to cry out.

Derek touched himself, grasping the rigid pipe of flesh between his legs. It hummed in his grip. The hot flow from his unremitting erection streamed over his knuckles and deadened all pain, reassuring him of his purpose.

He jumped to his feet to peer through a window. Looking through the grimy, smeared glass with his good eye, he could see the kitchen. Everything inside appeared to be awash in a red fog. A few large men were sitting at the table and a few more were standing, one of whom was behind his mother with his hands on her arms.

Derek clenched his teeth together with so much force that his molars cracked. The sight of his mother held captive fueled his wrath even further until the red consumed him, turning him into a full-blown berserker.

He tore off his shorts and threw them into the night, stepped away from the window, and smashed through the back door with a screeching war cry.

Derek Hoffman, the epitome of mayhem, had arrived inside his mother's kitchen.

CHAPTER 42

Lynch howled with a degree of agony he'd never experienced before as his ribs snapped from the concrete punch Tico delivered with the brass knuckles. Sammy Ruggio held Lynch's arms back, forcing him down in his seat as Tico wound up for another.

The pain choked him and, as he tried to catch a breath, he thought his left lung had certainly been punctured. His head dropped, loose and heavy as he moaned, rolling to one side as he tried to absorb and diminish the pain.

Lifting his head back up, he glimpsed a face in the window above the sink. It stared at him with a wide and bulging left eye. The right eye was bloody and swollen shut. The contorted, hate-filled expression startled Lynch into momentarily forgetting his pain. He yelped and sat upright as he took in the glaring mad eye, the razor-scars zigzagging across cheeks and lips, the maniacal grin full of huge teeth surrounded by a blood-red, V-shaped goatee.

What the fuck is THAT?

Hoffman is home...

Speechless, Lynch blinked and attempted to gesture, struggling against Sammy's grip, which caused Tico, whose back was to the window, to pause in mid-punch. As Lynch found his voice, the vicious face reappeared—along with the muscular body attached to it—as the intruder came smashing through the door, exploding into the kitchen like an enraged bull crashing out from a rodeo gate. Yes, it *was* Hoffman. Lynch recognized him immediately, and he could tell by the shouting of the Tortellio crew, everyone else in the room also knew it, too.

Derek rolled across the glass-covered floor, jumped up onto his feet, naked. He loomed over everyone in the room, huge, pumped, and smeared in seminal and sanguineous fluids. From head to toe, his scarred, red-washed face, his insistently spewing penis, and the tight mass of the bloody body that anchored it all emanated animalistic hatred.

Derek had fixed his good eye hard on Grotto, who Lynch figured Derek was gonna attack first, but Lynch was startled when Derek, with a great swipe of his right arm, backhanded Liuni in the face as he was rising up from his chair. Liuni's nose exploded in a blast of blood as the young, wannabe mobster collapsed back into his chair, before falling over and leaving him unconscious on the kitchen floor.

In one continuous motion, Derek leapt through the air, cleared the kitchen table, and landed on Grotto.

Melinda tore away from Grotto's grasp and screamed as she dove for the floor. Grotto's arms shot up in self-defense as the hulking Hoffman collided with him. One hand slid up under his jacket to reach for his gun, but he wasn't fast enough. Derek clamped his steel-belted jaws down on Grotto's nose and mouth while driving his thumbs knuckle-deep into Grotto's eyes. Grotto shrieked as loud as a siren as Derek's digits fingered Grotto's eye-sockets like a bowling ball.

Sammy pulled out a large .45 automatic and Lynch grabbed his chance to make a move, wincing as pain sliced through his ribs. Before Lynch could knock the gun out of Sammy's arm, he aimed at Derek and pulled the trigger. The barrel spewed deafening fire as Sammy pulled off round after round with surprising speed.

Lynch dove to the floor as Sammy's first few rounds hit Derek in his shoulder and ear, causing explosions of blood and flesh. Then, Derek's right ear blew off his head in a puff of scarlet. To Lynch's horror, however, the bullets seemed to have no effect on Derek, who stepped over his mother while still holding Grotto up with one huge hand.

Derek whirled around to face Sammy with a crazed, blood-soaked grin, holding the screaming Grotto out in front of him as a shield.

Lynch pushed himself back as Sammy continued to fire away, discharging every remaining bullet into Grotto's back.

Derek hurled Grotto's dead and eyeless body into Sammy, knocking him backwards into the wall.

Lynch noted that his .40 had fallen out of Grotto's waistband as Lynch scrambled away from the melee. He wanted his gun back but was too busy keeping his eyes on Derek, who was crazed, naked, and with a giant erection—looking to Lynch like some horny version of The Ultimate Warrior working the squared circle.

"Derek, no!" Lynch yelled as Derek grabbed Sammy's head, cracked it on his knee, and pounded his face with relentless blows. Nearby, Vito shrank back but Tico reached forward as Derek dropped Sammy to the ground, revealing a raw, meat-red crater where Sammy's face had once been.

Lynch, trying his best to breathe normally, edged across the linoleum floor toward the kitchen stove where Melinda Hoffman huddled.

"Stay put." Lynch found it hard to speak, his voice a whisper. He put his arm around her shoulders as she clutched his shirt in terror. "I'm not going to let you get hurt."

Tico roared and raised his .44, but Derek was faster and knocked the gun out of Tico's hand. Tico jumped back and bellowed at Vito. "Shoot him!"

"Dead motherfucker!" Vito aimed his automatic handgun with both hands and blasted away.

Flabbergasted, Lynch watched as Vito missed every single shot he fired at Derek—who was big as a barn and only a few feet away. Vito's firing stance was stiff, his arms were shaking with every pull of the trigger, his aim unbalanced and off by a dangerous margin. Lynch saw that this novice goodfella was destined to die.

Lynch watched all this and saw that Derek didn't even blink as shots blasted and bullets whizzed past his head and body. Then Derek lunged as soon as there was the loud click of an empty chamber.

Lynch took a painful breath as he watched Vito stand with his useless gun, his face an expression of terror and understanding.

Predator and prey. You can't make this up...holy fuck...

Fast, huge, and out of control, Derek grabbed Vito in a headlock with his pumped-up right arm. He clamped his left hand over Vito's face and with a hard, forceful jerk broke his neck before ripping Vito's head off of his body like a beer-tab. A high-pitched scream from Vito exploded and faded into sounds of tearing and burbling that ended in an eruption of blood.

Lynch watched Tico's face contort into a grimace as his son was decapitated before him. Tico quickly retrieved his gun and raised the .44. Lynch ducked and held Melinda tight as Tico unleashed obscenities as he fired two rounds, but Derek, fast and alert and anticipating what was coming, dropped to the floor and dodged every bullet. He crawled beneath the kitchen table, grabbing Liuni's unconscious body from the linoleum floor while the Meat Grinder desperately aimed as if to shoot a round at Derek through the table.

Suddenly, Derek flipped the kitchen table as he held the unconscious Liuni up by the back of his neck, thrusting him upward as another human shield—straight into Tico's line of fire as the Meat Grinder pulled off another round.

Lynch pushed Melinda down as a large and ugly hole gaped in Liuni's forehead. The bullet had entered like a kitten and exited like a lion as three hundred-grain lead blew out the back of his skull—along with his scrambled brains—all over Derek and the kitchen.

Releasing Melinda Hoffman, Lynch looked for an opportunity to safely get her out of the house and on her way.

More importantly, Lynch needed to find a way to end any more bloodshed madness and get Tico and Derek under control before they killed each other.

But how the fuck was he gonna do that? And how was he gonna save his own skin?

No way I'm dyin' in this house of horrors.

CHAPTER 43

Tico couldn't grasp that any of this was real. This was *his* show. He'd been in control...

How is this happening?

Tico felt himself plummeting into the abyss, that same Mariana Trench of ultimate horror he'd felt when he learned what happened to Annabella. What kind of prevarication dare violate his confident stranglehold on the world?

Hoffman.

This man-monster had *ripped* the head *off* one of his twin boys with his bare hands. How was this possible? And now, Tico's own mistimed shot had blown apart his other son's head.

I have no boys now. I HAVE NO BOYS!

Tico lowered his gun and stared at what he'd done, stared into Liuni's dead face and the bullet-hole in his forehead.

How the fuck am I gonna ever explain any of this? Valentina...?

He blinked and refocused. Tico was burning with hatred and a vow to annihilate Hoffman. The cocksucker stood right in front of him, keeping his one alert and feral eye on Tico while still holding Liuni up by the back of the neck, lifting the dead Tortellio twin with him as he rose.

Tico knew only three bullets remained in his revolver, and he had a name attached to each round: Derek, Mom Hoffman, and Lynch. Tico kept his eye on his three targets: the detective cop-fuck Lynch, Melinda, and Derek the beast.

Nobody moved except for Derek who dropped Liuni to the floor like rubbish. Before Tico could deliver his lead gifts, the blood and gore-covered Derek hunched over Liuni's corpse and began tonguing the bullet hole in Liuni's head while panting and violently dry-humping the dead body.

Tico was again losing his sense of reality. This *ghoul* and the blatant and fucked-up irreverence before him were too much—and it made Tico enraged and sickened.

Fuck this. ALL three bullets for you, cocksucker.

Tico raised his arm and pointed the .44 carefully at Derek, who looked big as a bear, and seemed oblivious to Tico and the menacing gun as he appeared spellbound, caught in the throes of some self-induced pleasure he was getting over ravishing Liuni's body.

Tico was about to pull the trigger, but he was interrupted. He jumped as something gripped his leg. At first, Tico didn't recognize the man attached to the hand squeezing his leg. Then the man looked up as he moved like a slug, spread out on his paunch.

What the fuck? That you Sammy?

Sammy Ruggio sure didn't look like the once brutal killer Tico had known for years. Ruggio looked more like something hanging in a butcher shop, and there was no way Tico was gonna be able to save him from this—plus, Sammy was getting in Tico's way.

"Gurrrsss ..." A wet glopping sound escaped from Sammy's crushed face.

With a single round from Tico's gun, Sammy Ruggio's head collapsed into itself like a stuck balloon and Tico's fancy suit, face, and hair were splattered with blood and all matter from Sammy's head.

Dapper Don be damned.

Tico's ears, deafened by all the gunfire, couldn't hear Derek so much as see that Derek was moving fast. Tico instinctively fired his last two rounds.

The rounds hit Derek in the upper torso as he leapt and charged Tico. Huge holes opened in the hulking bastard. His naked, bloody body flexed as he took the bullets...but to Tico's chagrin, Derek was indomitable and didn't pause for one lousy second.

Derek tackled Tico like a linebacker, shoving him backwards to crash into the stove. The kitchen walls shook. Pictures and a spice rack fell to the ground. Tico dropped the .44 as the impact sent a hard, sharp wave of pain up his back. He managed a weak, "Fuuuck..." as his breath was knocked out of him.

Tangling with Derek seemed futile, like battling an enraged and aroused water buffalo. Derek's strength and fury were unstoppable. If he could just get his brass knuckles on and beat Derek's head in...

Tico scrambled for his brass knuckles, but Derek pinned his arms to his sides, hugging him like a car-crusher.

"You cock ... suck ..." Tico gasped as his ribs and back cracked and snapped.

"Fuck you. Eat you." Derek spoke in a slow, robotic tone.

Tico looked into Derek's good eye—wide, wet, and red with a large pupil hideously dilated. Tico blinked, taking a mental snapshot of the scarred face, smeared with fresh blood, the spiky hair greasy and crusted from something nasty. The pores at his scalp and temples wept red sweat that looked like watery blood.

Trapped in Derek's powerful grip, Tico struggled to free himself as the man's foul halitosis hit him. A cocktail of sweat, grime, shit, and blood, and the sharp alkaline-scent of semen penetrated Tico's nostrils.

Guy smells like he fucked every hole in the city.

"Deader than dead...fuck!" Tico thrashed, kicking in the direction of Lynch, who was moving around Melinda Hoffman.

Fuckin' cop! Why wasn't he shooting down this monster? You'll all die tonight...!

Derek's angry face began to soften, and his arms loosened for a moment as he moaned and ground his erection into Tico's lower pelvis. Tico pushed his freed arms forward, forced Derek back, and punched him in the face.

"Cock. Suck. Er! Moth. Er. Fuck. Er! Die. Bitch!" With all the power he had left, Tico battered Derek's face with his huge fists as Derek stared straight into him with his one remaining good eye.

Furrowing his brow, Derek remained unfazed, his head snapping right back in place after every punch, his face frozen into a rictus grin.

Suddenly, Tico's head filled with a flash of brilliant white...then darkness. He blinked several times, and when he forced his eyes open, Derek's grinning face was wide in front of him, blurred. Again, an unexpected flash of white and the lights went out as pain blasted through his head. When he came to and opened his eyes, hot blood covered his face, and he could taste its sharp, coppery tang. He saw a fresh blotch of blood in the center of Derek's forehead.

What in the fuck?

Then he realized Derek had head-butted him twice. Seething with fury, Tico returned the favor and head-butted Derek as forcefully as possible, desperate to smash his skull...desperate to get away from him.

But the brute never fell or stopped grinning. The clobbering seemed to get him off; he kept moaning and grinding.

"You're...inhuman..." Tico's words petered out as exhaustion and dizziness overwhelmed him.

Derek threw his head back and howled. He squeezed Tico with a crushing grip. Tico shrieked with pain as he felt—and heard his bones breaking.

"No ... fucking...way." Tico gasped. Before he could inhale, he felt himself rising up off the floor as Derek lifted him above his head.

Derek lifted Tico's hefty body upward with superhuman strength, rammed him up into the ceiling. As broken pieces of the ceiling rained down, countless shocks of pain coursed through Tico as he was smashed into the kitchen ceiling. He fought as hard as he could and kicked his legs and smashed the light fixture with his head. The kitchen swam and churned beneath him as Derek bench-pressed him into the ceiling as if he was doing sets in a gym. Over and over, Tico's body took a painful beating the likes of which he never knew.

Suddenly, the most violent sensation of pain cut through it all and

Tico screamed, the agony was excruciating as Derek's teeth clamped down on Tico's crotch.

CHAPTER 44

"Melinda. Just go! Get out!" Lynch tried whispering his orders and it hurt to utter a syllable, but he'd take the pain if got Melinda and himself out of the house. He saw a window of opportunity for her to escape as Derek tore into Tico's privates like a pit bull attacking a rawhide chew-toy.

Those two can die together...I'm done.

Lynch turned back to Melinda and tried to nudge her out, but she refused to budge. She clutched Lynch's leg, trembling in terror with her eyes fixed on her madman of a son.

"Damn it!" Lynch muttered to himself, sliding around her as Derek continued his jaw-work on Tico's genitals, attempting to position her farther away from the grappling men. As he moved in front of her, he spied his .40 under the table, it lay there after falling from Grotto's pants.

Mustering all his strength against his intense pain, Lynch began to scramble across the floor toward the gun. But Derek, seeing the movement, turned and stepped into Lynch's pathway, stomping one foot onto his outstretched hand as he unclamped his jaws from Tico's bloody crotch, growling furiously as he body-slammed the Outfit boss to the floor with the ease of spiking a football.

As Derek drove him into the ground, Tico's head caught the edge of the kitchen counter and as Lynch tore his hand out from under Derek's foot, he heard a snap-crackle-pop sound. The Meat Grinder's heavy body flopped down and then lay sprawled out on the dirty linoleum floor, his head cracked open, his neck twisted and broken, his cold, steel-gray eyes glazed over. A large, dark red stain spread throughout his expensively tailored pants.

As Lynch reached over to grab the gun, Derek yanked him up by the shoulder. Lynch howled in pain and grabbed the kitchen chair, and with all his remaining power, hit Derek with it. The chair broke in half. Derek didn't seem to notice.

Derek grabbed Lynch and, leaning over, attempted to heft him up as he'd done with Tico, but Lynch, taking an agonized breath, maneuvered and swiveled onto Derek's back and closed his hands around Derek's throat from behind.

Derek threw himself around the kitchen, trying to shake Lynch off his back. Derek stepped backwards and rammed Lynch into kitchen counters, cabinets, and the refrigerator. Lynch thought his spine might break but he held on, riding Derek through the tsunami of pain. Dishes, furniture, and knick-knacks flew about, shattering and splintering as Derek worked himself into a frenzy in his attempts to dislodge Lynch. As Lynch continued to clutch tight, Derek bellowed out a long, bone-chilling yowl, throwing himself to the kitchen floor, flat on his back in an effort to smash Lynch.

Lynch hit the floor, feeling his bladder and lungs release their contents as Derek's huge body smothered and crushed him.

Then Derek vaulted upward, turned, and stood over him. Before Lynch could catch a breath, Derek growled and sprang on him, squeezing the sides of Lynch's skull like a hydraulic vise. His ears squashed shut by the palms of Derek's hands, Lynch heard only his blood-pressure and the squeak of cartilage in his head.

Derek stared straight down at Lynch with his one, drug-enhanced, bright-red eye, with unchecked libido, hate, stamina and sadistic aggression emanating from his pores.

Him or me ... him or me...god help me...

Lynch knew that the only way to exorcise Hoffman's demons would require a point-blank, high-caliber shot to the head with a gun. But even though it was right at Derek's feet, the possibility of Lynch being able to grab it felt impossible. It may as well have been miles away. He was helpless at the hands of this ogre.

Derek's lips curled back, revealing his toothy foamy maw as he squeezed Lynch's head harder. Lynch cried out in pain as Derek licked the left side of his face. His tongue was hot and wet on Lynch's face. His breath smelled like a swamp oozing with fetid meat.

Derek spoke words that Lynch couldn't make out. He thought he could read his lips, though...

I am the god of fuck.

I am ... the god ... of ... fuck.

It was then that Lynch accepted the likelihood that he would actually die here after all.

Derek began slamming Lynch's head into the kitchen linoleum. Three solid hits to the floor and Lynch no longer saw or felt a thing.

CHAPTER 45

"I am the god of fuck. I am ... the god ... of ... fuck."

Derek kept roaring his mantra as he squeezed and slammed this fool cop who'd gotten in his way.

The other men in the room had challenged him and he'd murdered them all with his bare hands. And it all had given him such divine pleasure to the point of climax.

The bullets inside him now began to hurt.

How could this be?

Derek paused as he gazed in disbelief at the nasty-looking holes in his body. He felt the lead burning into his flesh and muscle. There was no pleasure in this—and that sobered him with its reminder of his mortality.

Am I only a man? No...I'm the god of...?

The detective...this pussy cop...mumbled something that disturbed Derek's thoughts. He couldn't understand the meaningless blubbering of the cop getting his brains bashed in. His head was sopping wet, like a bloody sponge, and a terrible gash had split his scalp wide open. Derek bore down harder, eager to break the cop's skull and watch the brains spill out. Red lightning erupted across his vision and his member oozed as his bloodlust gave way to his implacable sexual needs.

He dropped the unconscious cop headfirst and looked around at the bodies sprawled across the kitchen floor. Yes...all of them could give Derek release. He imagined these dead men taking the pounding of his sex, he'd drive himself into their corpses.

Would they be enough? Since his new journey began, Derek's libido was always demanding, yearning for more. He wanted the sinews, muscles, skin, and heat of a *living* victim. He wanted to feel someone writhe and scream in his hands. He wanted someone who would lubricate and squeeze him as he penetrated, thrusted, and came—over and over again without end.

There was only one person in the house who could assuage his hunger.

Special little lamb. Mother...there she awaits...

Derek's mother cowered on the kitchen floor next to the old kitchen stove—the one she used to make his dinners every Wednesday. He recalled that he had Mother's cooking—it was so much better than the canned dog food that Dad had forced him to eat as some kind of punishment.

Derek could see and smell the fear floating from his mother's body.

"Mother. Little lamb..." Derek stood above her, fondling his dribbling erection. "I am burning red. I am the god of fuck."

Melinda closed her eyes and shook her head, holding her hands up as if she could wave Derek away.

Derek knew she wanted no part of him and the rejection turned him on. He detected the scent of the thing between her legs. Mother's *cunnus* was extra special to him as he thought of how he had *come* from this fissure. *That* was home to him, a secret garden. The thought threw Derek's desire into overdrive.

"I am the god of fuck, Mother." Derek grunted and released himself, grabbing his mother by the throat. He squeezed her with a sticky hand and lifted her body from the kitchen floor and over his head.

"Derek! No!"

Melinda choked and screamed and choked again. With his free hand, Derek punched her locked knees. He parted her legs and peeked between the white thighs hiding beneath the thin fabric of her apron and her old blue dress

"Mother ... I am the *motherfucker.*" Derek threw his head back and growled, then gazed at her as he held her. "I will fuck you, and I will eat you, and I will fuck you."

Derek released his mother, letting her drop to the ground. He backed up a few feet away from his mother, thrilled by the shudder of terror that swept through her body and vibrated through his own. The stench of fear and musky genitalia stimulated and intoxicated him. As his own need became immediate, he put his hands on his pulsing hardness and a flow of hot, red and white sap spurted out and oozed over his knuckles and fingers.

"Fuck-you-kill-you-tear-you." Derek spoke staccato words as he stroked himself into a fury of ejaculate and blood. He opened his good eye and bolts of crimson lightning exploded across his vision. The kitchen, the house, his mother on the floor below him, and the entire world beckoned him to fuck and slaughter.

Derek shook with rage and arousal, each blood-packed muscle and vein in his body bulged as he set his intent on his mother.

"Motherfuck—Mother!"

He wanted to shred her and spread her pieces across the kitchen as he fucked every scrap Dad Hoffman had once touched.

Strings of drool hung from his lips. His hands formed menacing claws.

My cock...is a weapon.

So it was. He let his erection lead him, hungry and merciless.

What's in Mother's hand?

Mother lifted something above her head and Derek leapt at her, thinking he'd stop whatever it was she thought would protect her.

Three loud explosions with three bright flashes of fire blazed from his mother's hands. Derek lurched backward, the air blown out of his lungs.

He watched with fascination at the bright blood running down his chest, over his cut abs, around the base of his erection, and down his beefy legs. It radiated so ... glowing almost, as if he'd shed neon-red fluid.

What...was this? What had happened?

His hypersensitive ears were deafened from the explosions, and he suddenly detected a sensation of pain, *real pain*, as it flared up his backside. Derek didn't have to look over his shoulder to know that his back muscles had been blown out and apart.

Holding himself up against a kitchen wall, Derek clutched his ever-hard weapon to comfort himself. He sniffed the air.

Gunsmoke.

Mother-bitch...shot me?

His mother sat weeping in a corner with her knees drawn up to her chest. Her thin arms and hands were clutching a semi-automatic handgun that was still pointed straight up at him.

Derek tried to speak but could only make gurgling sounds because there was blood geysering up into his throat.

I'll kill you and then I'll fuck you, Mother!

Derek stumbled forward on weakening legs, clutching his penis, which remained rigid and raw, ever-throbbing, even as a death-knell sounded in his heart.

Melinda Hoffman screamed as Derek lurched toward her, moaning and stroking himself. He heard his own heartbeat fading, drumming more softly in his ears, as if someone was turning down the volume. While he couldn't hear his mother's screams anymore, he could see her sweet mouth opening as he drew closer and reached for her.

I want more, and more, and more ...

Derek gazed through a red haze into his mother's eyes. He came again as his hand pumped. His arm flew out to grab her throat.

"I'm hungry ... Mother."

A sudden blast detonated through the room, and a brilliant, nuclear-red flash blocked Melinda Hoffman's face from Derek's sight, and that flash was the last thing he saw before his scarlet world became eternally black.

CHAPTER 46

Lynch was awash in nauseating pain. His skull was a ripe melon, bruised and broken. The kitchen ceiling swam and tilted in his blurred vision.

How long was I out? Am I alive?

A nasty ringing filled his ears. Melinda Hoffman's hysterical wailing filled the house.

She's alive. I hear her but not Derek. Is Derek in the house? Gotta get help...

He stumbled to his feet. His entire body screamed in agony. It hurt just to blink. Reaching a hand behind his head, he fingered the deep gash. Thick, dark blood soaked his palm. He slowly looked around the kitchen.

Derek Hoffman lay motionless, naked and face down in a puddle of vibrant blood, sandwiched between the corpses of Tico Tortellio and his crew. Above the neck, almost half of his head had vanished, courtesy of a point-blank gunshot.

Melinda Hoffman was huddled in the corner, rocking and sobbing, and holding a gun. His weapon, the .40, Lynch realized.

"Give me the gun, Mrs. Hoffman." Lynch stepped toward her with a slow, halting gait. He put his hand out.

Startled, she looked at the gun in her hand and then dropped it to the kitchen floor. She crawled over to Derek's lifeless body and collapsed on his bloody back.

"My boy. My firstborn..."

Lynch steadied himself, and then, feeling dizzy and fatigued, collapsed into a chair. As he adjusted to the room, his first thought was that he needed to call Sandy back. He'd give anything for Sandy's embrace and the smell of her body. But in this moment, he was simply thankful to be alive.

"Helluva day." He spoke to the kitchen while keeping one eye on Melinda Hoffman, lying prostrate across Derek's corpse, sobs wracking her body. As he carefully moved his neck to look around the room, the sight of each of the massacred bodies began to sicken him. The heat was still suffocating, and he couldn't move to find fresh air. The bile rose up and he couldn't help it—he vomited on his shoes. It was all he could do not to scream in pain as he retched until it was all out.

His breath caught as he steadied himself and wiped his mouth with the back of one hand and wiped the sweat off his forehead with the other.

I'm not dead.

I'm gonna keep that date, Sandy. Just gonna need more time to get ready ...

He winced as the sound of screaming police sirens filled the street outside of Melinda's house.

McRains...you're late again, dickhead.

Lynch buried his face in his hands and wished for some peace and quiet...wished for an ambulance and anesthetics in any shape or form... wished for the heat to wither and die...and wished for this fucking day to finally end.

POST PANDEMONIUM

Lynch tried hard to keep himself conscious and alert while he waited to talk to the myriad cops at Melinda Hoffman's house. Police cars and ambulances arrived by the dozen—as did a meat wagon to haul away Derek Hoffman along with the bodies of Tico and his crew.

The CPD also found the cop Derek had murdered in the street near Melinda Hoffman's house. The entire neighborhood had turned into a buzzing police state.

When the paramedics finally took him away in an ambulance, they told him they were taking him to a critical care facility out of concern over potential head trauma. Lynch didn't comment, he just passed out.

His lacerated scalp required a shaved head, fifteen staples, and fifty-three stitches. A long horizontal scar in the shape of a smiley face ran below his hairline. He also had a severe concussion, broken ribs, and a punctured lung, and the immediate diagnosis was that once he was up and about, he'd have to wear a brace for weeks to support his distressed neck and back.

When he woke up, John McRains was sitting in a chair in the corner of his room. "Where am I?" Lynch squinted and cast his eyes around.

"St. Cornelius." McRains smirked and burst out laughing. "How's that for irony?"

Lynch shook his head. "It feels like a sick joke." He tried to speak again but got choked up.

McRains looked up at him. "What?"

Lynch exhaled. "It would have been okay if Earl were still here and I were sharing a room with him. I missed his fuckin' funeral, didn't I?"

"It's okay." McRains offered a sympathetic expression. "They understood. You know Angela wanted you for a pall bearer."

"Fuck."

"No, it's okay." McRains straightened. "Your old man stood in for you. And he was proud to do it."

Lynch tried, without much luck, to stretch. "How's Melinda Hoffman?"

"She says she didn't know what Derek did outside the visits to her house." McRains shrugged. "They had dinner once a week and made small talk, nothin' too personal. She says she was closer to her youngest son, and she didn't really know the *real* Derek."

"He didn't strike me as a mama's boy."

"She acts ignorant about his capabilities. Says she knew Derek was no angel, but she never thought he'd rape and murder." McRains raised his eyebrows. "She was adamant about blaming drugs for all this shit. Says drugs were evil and made her son this way. Then she turns around and asks CPD for tranquilizers to make her forget about killin' her first-born. How 'bout that?"

Lynch did laugh at that one and a sharp pain burst through his ribs.

"Oh, and get this." McRains leaned forward. "Remember that trick who got shot in the Cadillac last Monday? George Pallis?"

Astroglide.

Lynch nodded. "We could have solved that one if the witness hadn't been brutally murdered."

"Turns out the bullet in Pallis's head came from a handgun we found on the pimp who Derek Hoffman butchered in the building you drove by on your way to Melinda Hoffman's house. I assume the pimp —Scatt something'—stuck a gun through the window while one of his whores was in the car and the john didn't want to hand over his wallet. Bam! Pallis got killed."

"One less case I have to solve when I get back." Lynch relaxed. "Thanks for closing it for me."

"Close it? You didn't think it would be that easy, did you?" McRains rolled his eyes. "There were no witnesses. And Pallis's family put a ton of pressure on the mayor to shut that investigation down. Family money and political flex there. No running anything through the databases, nothing. It's officially now one of Chicago's six-hundred-and-one unsolved murders this year."

"Pfft." Lynch shook his head. "Pallis. That jackass tried getting a Monday morning blow job and sure kicked off a helluva week for me. It nearly got me killed."

Lynch found it amusing how he almost never remembered what he'd had for breakfast the day before, but he could recall every detail at a crime scene—no matter how brief his observations. He could still picture the balding, dead man in his blood-stippled business suit; pants and boxers wrapped around ankles, his belly fat, the gray thicket of pubes...and poking out, the glans looking like...

A hairless mole-rat without the teeth.

While Lynch was out, the rest of the nation witnessed the massive funerals of Tico "The Meat Grinder" Tortellio and his twin sons—all buried next to each other, simultaneously. McRains had set some newspapers on the bedside table and Lynch snatched them right up after he left. He was surprised to find the coverage in the *Chicago Tribune* to be not quite deferential but still very courteous.

Thousands of mourners and curiosity seekers had lined up around the block to pay their respects at the funeral home in downtown Chicago. Family and close friends—as well as associates from around the country—also attended the private funeral, which *The New York Times* dubbed, "The Windy-City Apalachin." Clever as that headline was, Lynch figured the reference to a legendary 1957 gathering of the American Cosa Nostra at the home of mobster Joe "The Barber" Barbara, in Apalachin, New York, was probably lost on younger readers, or those who weren't privy to organized crime history.

Later that day, when his father Jake came to visit, Donnie told him the details of Tico's death. He asked his father what he thought about it. The elder Lynch fixed his gaze on Donnie and simply asked, "So, how d'ya think the Bears are gonna do this season?"

Even though Lynch had promised himself that nothing would ruin his reunion weekend with Sandy, he'd missed their date for obvious reasons. He made up for it when he was released from the hospital, taking her out for a world-class dinner at a Michelin-starred restaurant. Afterward, they caught up on a lot of things under the covers. Out of work for a month, he stayed home, laid up with Sandy taking care of him. Once recovered, he returned to his desk and the street without missing a thing, other than Earl. God, he missed his old partner like crazy. Lynch figured he'd never get over that.

The city cooled down as summer—the hottest on record—merged into fall. Lynch was dismayed that the Cubs once again didn't make the playoffs. He was, however, happy that his hair grew back, thick and healthy, over the scar on the back of his scalp.

He was immensely grateful for every little thing in his life.

Later that week, McRains called Lynch and brought him up to speed on Sid Hoffman. While the unholy mess was going down at Melinda Hoffman's house, CPD detectives had arrived at Sid's condo to ask him prepared questions like:

What was his connection to his brother's enrollment at Peithos Labs?

What was Derek was doing in the pharmaceutical study program?

Why were no documents on file for Derek's screening results and no viable samples of blood or urine?

Neither Sid nor Gloria responded to the knock, but detectives noticed smoke wafting out from under the door. Breaking it down, they found two chairs engulfed in flames and the affianced duo garroted, their hair and skin burned off.

It took Lynch less than two seconds to connect the dots on who the perpetrators were—and they were now as dead as their victims.

Tico "The Meatgrinder" Tortellio and company...

That case was closed in Lynch's POV.

Derek's autopsy revealed large amounts of an unknown drug in his system—the drug turned out to be an unmarketed, experimental erection and arousal drug, Libidonal. The Libidonal trail led to Peithos Labs.

Lynch read the testimony of other Peithos Labs employees and watched all the hospital and lab security camera footage that was recovered. There was video evidence of Derek walking through the Peithos floor, and then him again, walking across the first floor, and then in and out of the ICU, where Annabella Tortellio's unconscious body waited.

If Sid Hoffman were alive, Lynch figured he'd have been charged for falsifying blood and urine samples and aiding and abetting a felon for monetary compensation.

Lynch considered Sid Hoffman collateral damage of his big brother's actions. *Duh.* What a shame. Still, Lynch wondered why Sid did what he'd done for Derek...no one had an answer. Either blood was thicker than water or something more fucked-up was at hand with that deal. No matter, Lynch was too tired to care.

In October, Lynch was happy to learn that Annabella Tortellio had awoken from her coma, alert and on the way to functioning on some fucked-up level after all she'd been through. She was now living with her mother, who had never left Annabella's side since Tico and the Tortellio twin boys died.

Mercifully, Lynch also learned that Derek Hoffman's DNA would not live on. Annabella Tortellio never became impregnated. For that very reason, Lynch thought perhaps McRains was *wrong*. Maybe there *was* a God in Chicago after all.

A group of Peithos Labs researchers took great interest in Derek Hoffman's corpse and received special permission from the Medical Examiner to observe the autopsy. They took pictures, jotted notes, and discussed numerous confidential elements with the pathologist and the county coroner.

Discretion, however, only went so far with Paulie Tyre, the sixty-year-old, independent-minded coroner of Cook County. An old friend of both Lynch and the late Earl Tipton, Paulie spoke to Lynch over coffee one morning that fall and shared many of the details regarding Derek Hoffman's corpse.

"I tell ya, Donnie, I've seen some weird shit in my day, but this Hoffman fella ... Christ, what he had, some guys would love to have." Paulie chuckled.

"What's that?" Lynch chased two Advil with coffee.

Paulie looked around and lowered his voice. "An eternal hard-on."

"The hell you say?"

"Dead as a freakin' doornail, but still hard as a rock and ready to party and plow. Honest to Christ." Paulie held up a bony hand, palm out.

Lynch remembered what he saw that last night in Melinda Hoffman's kitchen; Derek wild as hell, insane on a bunch of chemicals, Hoffman's huge, vein-pulsing erection, eager to fuck anything that had a hole. The memory made Lynch's stomach twist. "You're saying, he was still hard when you cleaned him up? After the autopsy?"

"Absolutely. Damnedest thing." Paulie's eyes crinkled as he grinned. "We had 'im on the slab, drained what blood he had left in him, along with all his other fluids. We did a Y-incision, took out all the vital organs, cleaned 'im up, yadda-yadda. But that cock of his was still standing up, straight as a flagpole. I mean, most of this guy's skull was blown off. You gotta have a brain and blood and a pumpin' heart workin' and whatnot to make an erection, right? Well, maybe guys don't need a brain. My wife'll argue that one." Paulie slapped the table and laughed. "Maybe he had some kinda rigor mortis of the prick. Now that would be a first."

"Can't keep a good man down?" Donnie mustered his driest delivery, and they both laughed.

"Tell ya what, it was those drugs that pharmaceutical company made. The Peithos Labs guys came in and took pics and measured Hoffman's erection." Paulie sipped his coffee and began to whisper. "Said his post-mortem cock was hard from an erectile-dysfunction drug they called Libidonal. Totally experimental. Wannabe Viagra they say. Caused this guy's sex organs to swell and stay perpetually rigid."

"Yeah...I heard all about that Libidonal shit and what Big Pharma made it for. I got the autopsy report. What can you tell me?"

"Lotsa shit. Toxicology report was a laundry list of party favors. Guy was a walking drug store fulla Ecstasy, Oxy, coke, GHB, anabolic steroids, growth hormone. Should've had two hearts pumpin' to handle all that shit."

Un-fucking real.

"But that Libidonal shit was the most prominent thing. It made his skin, fingernails, and the whites of his eyes turn a strange shade of red. That same red saturated his brain and all the erectile tissue in his prick."

Lynch took the info in and thought about it. It sounded crazy. He paused and drained his cup. "That Libidonal was what really sent Hoffman over the edge, huh?"

Paulie Tyre gave Lynch a mischievous grin. "I'd say so. He was a lab rat and took so much of that experimental shit along with all his other drugs at once that his head and dick were bent to just keep killin' and fuckin', even after we took scalpels to it. Believe it or not, that cock was still ready to screw after we took scalpels to it. Whatever that Libidonal shit is, it makes Viagra look like Flintstone vitamins."

"No doubt. These experimental E.D. drugs ..." Lynch thought of his remaining testicle. "Well, y'know. Lotsa poor shmucks can't get it up."

"Unfortunate as that may be, and despite me sayin' some guys would love this, an eternal erection ain't good." Paulie wagged a finger. "That's called *priapism*, my friend, and it's very uncomfy and dangerous. In my forty years of working on corpses, I've never seen one with priapism until now. And I'd never even heard of anything like this. I mean, a hard-on on a cadaver with no blood in it? That's a fuckin' Frankenpenis."

"Sort of a stiff *stiff*, huh?" Lynch paused and then laughed out loud.

Paulie laughed louder. Lifting a cup to his weathered face, he caught his breath. "Oh, Donnie...you're the reason God created the middle finger."

Derek Hoffman was cremated according to his mother's instructions. There was no funeral service as both Melinda and CPD authorities knew a funeral would only draw nutbags and more ugly press. Lynch knew it, too. Hoffman's atrocious crimes became part of Chicago murder legend, up there with H.H Holmes, William Heirens, John Wayne Gacy and Richard Speck. He was the new champ of Chi-Town's blood-lore.

Aside from the unthinkable, carnage-laden crimes he'd committed, Lynch was still floored that Derek had managed to kill one of the most infamous Outfit bosses in Chicago history. In world history, really.

The world's press descended on Melinda Hoffman to get her two-cents, but as Lynch learned, she wouldn't comment on any of it. Lynch didn't blame her. He'd been there in the kitchen with her when the carnage and the unbelievable went down—and even Lynch didn't care to talk about it publicly. It was all too much, too outlandish, too traumatic to revisit.

What Melinda did with Derek's ashes remains unknown.

Lolinda Watson—unknown to Donnie Lynch, unknown to many in Chicago aside from the late Scatt-Dogg and his bevy of prostitutes—moved far away from the city as she had dreamed.

She didn't return to her original home in upstate New York or her previous situation in Brooklyn. With her scant savings and the five-plus-grand that she snatched—*thank you Scatt...may you rot in hell*—she was able to go to that big-ass Greyhound station and bought a ticket to Florida. During those brutal winters in Chicago, she'd often fantasized about warmer climates and she'd always been drawn to the magic of Walt Disney World. So off she flew to Orlando.

Thanks to that giant creep—who still came to life often in her nightmares—she had found salvation. Even though it happened in the most fucked-up way, she now had a chance at a new life. She didn't own a real driver's license or social security card or have any credit rating, and she had never finished high school or paid taxes or had any legal work history, but through some small miracles, she landed a legit job before her cash ran out, as a waitress at a restaurant in the Universal Orlando Resort. She lucked out again when she and an easy-going co-worker looking for a roommate found a small apartment to rent together.

She never spoke of where she came from or what she'd endured during her time in Chicago. Sure, Lolinda dealt with the anger and shame from the pain and degradation Scatt-Dogg and others subjected her to. But when she'd start ruminating, it would get dark really quickly and then the final hellscape in that tenement slaughterhouse would rise up—Cortnee bisected and in pieces, Scatt mangled and ravaged, that burly killer towering over everything, blissfully drenched in all the gore—and despite that terror, the underlying reality was that she *survived* it all.

I ain't gonna be a fuckin' victim no more.

Lolinda was now a survivor, she wanted to own that rather than pity. A *survivor,* and a strong one at that, something she reminded herself of every morning when she looked in the mirror while brushing her teeth or doing her hair. She had promised herself that she'd never blow this new chance and she would never look back. She would swallow her panic and try to focus on the *now.* And getting herself ready to clock into a job that offered honest pay for a day's work was a joyful way to start—and she embraced it.

As time marched on, Derek Hoffman faded into true-crime history, but Detective Donnie Lynch didn't forget him. He owned some nasty scars and rotten memories of that hot summer day when he tracked down a real-life ogre created, in part, by a man-made chemistry experiment.

But now he had better things in his life to help get him through the dark days. He had moved back in with Sandy and they were planning to buy a house together. It didn't take him long to relax into the same happiness and excitement he'd experienced throughout their early days together.

When the holidays arrived, with their colder temperatures, Lynch welcomed the chill. It helped him forget the misery of that awful summer heat and, although he doubted the memories of those terrible bloody days would ever leave him, he could begin to set them aside.

He was resting on a couch with Sandy in front of their TV. They had made love half an hour earlier. His lone testicle was doing fine and his doctor had said he could cut the Androgel since his libido had returned, stronger than ever. Now, rubbing Sandy's back, he began rising to the occasion.

She turned to him and smiled. "Seriously? Again?"

Lynch nodded. "Another round, babe?"

Sandy winked and shrugged off her robe. "I guess you just can't keep a good man down."

"Hey ..." Lynch thought of how he used that line when recently making a joke with Paulie the coroner, but it sounded a lot sweeter coming from Sandy.

Lynch smiled and moved in closer, and things got hot.

He didn't mind this kind of heat.

AFTERWORD

I finished the fourth draft of WRETCH in 2018—and the late, great Laura Caldwell gave me my first blurb for it back then. I wanted this novel out years ago, but a few things got in my way. I was pitching agents, then I got a paid gig to write and create a TV series and two documentaries—all with deadlines! Then FIREPROOF memoir I wrote for chef Curtis Duffy became a priority and took over my life.

Also, as I got back in to re-reading WRETCH before publication, I connected with a folks who provided me with information that helped me update some parts of the novel in important ways.

The wait to publish was meant to be and worth it. I'm super-happy I got back to it, overhauled it, polished it up, and now WRETCH is out in the world.

Writers have been told for millennia, "write what you know." So, with WRETCH, I certainly took that phrase/advice to heart as I went above and beyond to write what I know with this novel.

Writing this novel and the work I did out in the wild for WRETCH was a helluva ride—as you'll learn from the backstory on "where" WRETCH came from:

I got the idea for WRETCH many years ago when I actually participated in a pharmacological research program for Abbott Labs.

For those who don't know, Abbott Laboratories is a Chicago-based, multinational medical devices and health care and pharmaceutical company founded by Wallace Calvin Abbott back in 1888 to formulate known drugs. Today, Abbott Labs sells medical devices, diagnostics, branded generic medicines and nutritional products. Some of Abbott Labs products include Pedialyte, Similac, BinaxNOW, Ensure, ZonePerfect, FreeStyle Libre, and many more. Abbott Labs also created the first HIV Test in 1985.

Growing up, Abbott Labs was the biggest company in my neck of the woods in the northern burbs of Illinois—it's still one of the largest companies there, maybe one of the biggest in the world.

Joe Ptacek (RIP)—the original vocalist for my band Broken Hope—his dad worked for Abbott Labs for years. I also remember an old classmate of mine got a job for Abbott after high school...and his job was incinerating all the dead monkeys that Abbott used for testing—nasty fucking business IMO.

That said, when I was in my early 20's, I was broke AF and needed money. Somehow I found out that I could make money as a lab rat. So I got on Abbott Labs mailing list—a specific list for Abbott seeking participants for their pharmaceutical research programs. Back in the day, some of these trials paid $3,000—for me, that amount of money was like winning the Lottery.

One day I got a letter in the mail from Abbott Labs seeking participants for a new drug trial they were doing. I applied and was accepted into a week-long program to be a human guinea pig.

When I entered the program, I was told that I would either the actual "drug" they wanted tested on people, or I might get a placebo—

they wouldn't tell me what I got at any time. The trial was for a week...I couldn't wait for it to be over. When it was done, I felt fine and got my check.

This experience planted the seed for WRETCH...the whole "what if" someone participated in a program like this and something went horribly wrong? Big Pharma, man, they can't always predict what can happen while they're making the next FDA-approved miracle pill.

The character of Derek Hoffman who enters Peithos Labs to make a few bucks was inspired by both my experience with Abbott Labs, and also, by a few people I've known.

One particular source of inspiration was a guy I knew decades ago... a roommate of mine I had for a few months—and he was a complete sociopath. He was also a hulking, amateur, professional wrestler. This guy was huge, and if you saw him, you'd be instantly intimidated. He guy worked out daily, shaved all of his body hair off, and he cycled on all kinds of steroids. I literally watched needles go in ass-cheeks and the oral ingestion and saw first-hand how someone "juices up" to get the most insane physique possible. The guy had legit roid-rage...he had a short fuse and loved to fight. He looked for any excuse to beat people silly. I saw him go out of his way to pick fights in local bars and it was disturbing to say the least. He scared me and I'll never forget it.

I also did a lot of research on the biology of violence, abnormal psychology, and wanted to add legit layers to this type of hostile and berserk mentality. I'm grateful to my uncle Joe and aunt Shirley who are psychologists and they gave me an education in this area (outside of my own experience) with these types of anti-social and violent people.

With Derek Hoffman being formed, I worked out developing my other main characters.

For detective Donnie Lynch, I sought out help to learn what it means to be a cop in Chicago—because I'm no cop and I wanted to get it as accurate as possible. The amazing author and legal expert—Laura Caldwell—advised me on all kinds of police things and then she introduced me to the great Peter Koconis—a retired Chicago Police Detective who had done it all and covered it all: beat cop, detective, organized crime task force, Internal Affairs, Gang Task Force, homicides...you name it. "Seargent Pete" (as I call him) advised me on police procedures, shared his own experiences with the CPD, and really educated me on what it's like to be a cop in the city of Chicago and what they go through on every level.

While Seargent Pete consulted me, I actually hit the streets of Chicago for more research. I wound up in some very sketchy areas of the city and nearby areas where I encountered a diverse cast of characters who I spoke with; prostitutes and gang-bangers to drug-dealers and a few involved in organized crime. I'm happy to report that my "boots on the ground" approach left me unscathed because these areas I visited and some of these people I talked to weren't exactly good for my health.

I'm fascinated in organized crime. New York has some heavy hitters in mobland, but none like Chicago has had throughout history. The character of Outfit boss Tico "The Meatgrinder" Tortellio is based on some real Chicagoland wiseguys from the past or others I've actually known—and others who I met through "friends". These guys fortunately trusted me either because of my longtime friendships with a few, or because mutual sources vetted, or maybe it was my charming personality.

I don't look like a 60 Minutes journalist, so I didn't know if these crime figures would break my legs or threaten me when I wanted to interview them and talk shop. They were actually all quite nice for underworld guys and they didn't mind my questions. Up to a point, they discreetly confided in me on some of their business—like what they do with things that "fall off" of trucks, or how their loan-sharking works, and what some of their operations (aka: rackets) are all about. According to some of these real-life characters, the Outfit pulls all kinds of strings—be it white collar crimes to some serious shit—from downtown Chicago to the burbs to this very day.

So if anyone thinks that the Chicago Outfit is some archaic thing from the past, guess again—it's alive and well, I can tell you that much. My friend, Seargent Pete will tell you the same—he's still connected to the CPD and has arrested his share of mobbed-up guys during his time in homicide, organized crime, and gang task forces. The Outfit and other Chicagoland organized crime families are active and doing this thing of theirs.

Last, WRETCH deals with sexual themes in different ways, and on that subject, I respect whatever you're into as long as it doesn't hurt anyone or anything. There's a kink for everyone and everything nowadays, and my attitude is: "you do YOU, I'll do ME" (credit to Joe Lansdale for that line, I borrowed it from one of his posts awhile back) and if it makes you happy, fine. Be a good person, though. Don't be a monster.

Moreover, I'm an ally to the LGBTQ+ community (and the Trevor Project), I've seen friends and acquaintances who identify in their own ways deal with the mentalities of others who won't accept them, who diss them, and the frustration felt from those who are intolerant and can't find acceptance and love in their hearts for fellow humans whose choices are theirs and who deserve respect and understanding. I shed some light on this community in WRETCH. My LGBTQ+ friends who I spoke to for this novel are wonderful people, and they shared their strengths and their hardships, what they've been through—all of which is challenging in this climate we're in

Detective Donnie Lynch is progressive and he shows that not everyone is insensitive and that people DO care for others personal choices with how they roll in their personal lives.

However, this fiction, right? In real-life, my wish is to see love and tolerance adopted by the world we live in, to see it become a more welcoming place for everyone—no matter what gender you identify with, no matter who you love, no matter what race you are.

Let LOVE rule—the world needs THAT attitude more than ever— and we would all be better for it.

Thank you all for reading WRETCH and for reading my Afterword. Cheers!

—Jeremy Wagner, 2025

ACKNOWLEDGMENTS

I give my gratitude and high-fives to the following people involved with WRETCH for different reasons:

Kym Foglia-Wagner for always believing and pushing me, Laura Caldwell (miss you), the great art-god Roberto Ferri (thank you for everything, my friend), my amazing father-in-law Vince Foglia for educating me on his growing up in Chicago's Little Italy area, my awesome uncle Jack Jiganti for teaching me some other things about the Chicago Outfit—"Never call them the mob. They're the Outfit, damnit!"—Steve Wands, Kristy Baptist, Tyler Affinito, Megan Yundt, Dead Sky Publishing, Corey Soria, Stephanie Cabral, Joe Reser, Shirley Morrissey, Helen Rogan, Shawn Macomber, Jenn Proffitt, Julia Borcherts, Andrea DeWerd, Amanda Livingston, Sara Mehelic, Genessee Floressantos, Daniella Batsheva, Del James, Rio Youers, Regina Garza Mitchell, Edward Lee, Ryan Harding, John Boden, Peter Koconis, Joe Matthews and IPG.

I also give respectful nod to these writers and risqué publishing legends who inspired me as they were never afraid to push boundaries and take their brand of writing or publications to new levels:

Jack Ketchum, Cormac McCarthy, Nic Pizzolatto, Chandler Morrison, Peter Blauner, Colin Harrison, Hunter S. Thompson, Elmore Leonard, S.A. Cosby, Mario Puzo, Thomas Harris, Joyce Carol Oates, Edward Lee, Marquis de Sade, Bret Easton Ellis, Rex Miller, Larry Lynt, Bob Guccione, Henry Miller...

To anyone I forgot, sorry and thank you.

About the Author

Jeremy Wagner is a bestselling author, guitarist, and songwriter. His debut novel *The Armageddon Chord* is the recipient of the Hiram Award and Barnes & Noble Top 10 paperback bestseller. His novel *Rabid Heart* was nominated for a Splatterpunk Award for Best Horror Novel, received an Independent Publisher's IPPY Award for both Best Horror e-Book, and was a Next Generation Book Award Finalist for Best Horror Novel.

Wagner released his bestselling book, *Fireproof: Memoir of a Chef* with Chef Curtis Duffy in 2025.

Living between Chicago and Miami with his wife Kym, Wagner writes books and screenplays full time and writes music and lyrics for his bands, Broken Hope and Earthburner.

@jeremyxwagner www.jeremyxwagner.com